CONTENTS

Chapter One. 2

Chapter Two. 14

Chapter Three. 41

Chapter Four. 62

Chapter Five. 83

Chapter Six. 117

Chapter Seven. 123

Chapter Eight. 127

Chapter Nine. 185

Chapter Ten. 200

Chapter Eleven. 236

Chapter Twelve. 280

Chapter Thirteen. 325

Chapter Fourteen. 334

A Recap From Boyton. 339

Forward.

A brief explanation of why I have rewritten Captain Paul Boyton's books.

"The Paul Boyton Story" combined with "Roughing It In Rubber" and a brief description of how I completed a family circle, without knowing it. Moving to the USA, from Zimbabwe in 1984, with my two teenage children. Oops! I married a Hatfield out of Kentucky in the USA.

Cap as the family called him, was an amazing man and his story deserves to be brought back into the twenty first century.

Captain Paul Boyton

Captain Paul, was the younger brother of my Great Grand father Michael, mentioned in the book.

Michael moved to South Africa during the diamond rush, working for De Beers in Kimberly, where he died of a heart attack.
His wife returned to America, Brooklyn with the children. Minus my Grandmother Gertrude, who had met Joseph Sullivan. She married and remained in Kimberly, South Africa. Gertrude had thirteen children, eleven of which survived, my father Gerald being the third.

All Gertrude's children and forty six grand children, other than myself and older brother have remained in South Africa. Though I grew up in Rhodesia, now Zimbabwe. Never realizing my Father was also an exceptional man, his creativity and abilities were beyond the norm, I always figured every bodies dad did those things. We only got to see my Grandmother once a year on vacation, in those days we were sent out to play, hence I was unaware of all this family background.

On the journey over the Boyton's spent some time in Ireland, the older daughter married a butcher, Farrell, having one daughter Moyra. Farrell died of a burst appendix when Moyra was just nine months old. Again the Boyton's and Farrell's continued the journey to America. There is very little on the family, or what became of the three other children once back in the States.

I do know the youngest daughter, Marge never married and a brother Felix married later in life, but had no children.
Moyra married Robby Robinson, Moyra became my brother Ed Sullivan and my, American Mom.

I assume she was instrumental in giving Ed most of the information I started out with. Ed a bachelor passed away in June of 1988 from cancer. While clearing out his home I found a July 2nd. 1881 New York Irish Times newspaper, with Michael Boyton's picture and name on the front page, plus several articles on Paul.

My father had a brother by the name of Boyton Sullivan, so I figured this was some how connected. It was years later that I was able to start putting the puzzle together. What an interesting journey it has become with the help on many others. I have met and communicated with some great people while doing this research and was fortunate through another's research to get a name and phone number. Within hours I spoke to one of Captain Paul's granddaughters Geraldine Dudley in Brooklyn and her family.

My research has taken me to Paris France to meet Michel Lopez a Historian who shared his twenty five year collection with me. It was a great experience to stay with his family and am truly grateful for all the materials I received, that has enabled me to write this book.

<u>Geraldine Dudley:</u> *I often went to visit my grandparents in Sheepshead Bay, but my actual vivid memory of my Grandfather, Captain Paul was when I was about seven. We stopped at the corner of 24th street and Voories Ave. to call from the pharmacy. Not only to announce our arrival but to have them put the two large airedale dogs in the basement. I remember him as a very distinguished gentleman with beautiful white hair and mustache sitting up in bed. He called me over, put his arms around me and kissed me. He died shortly after this visit, but the image of that last visit is still as vivid as if it happened yesterday.*

<u>Craig Dudley:</u>*Growing up in the company of three of Caps four sons; Father Neil,Claude Paul and my Grandfather Joseph. Listening to many of their stories of their famous father. Decorated by many crown heads of Europe, gave me my first revelation into the theatrical and subsequently the professional theatre of which Captain Paul would have approved whole heartedly.*

"The RUBBER SUIT"

From the Captain:

"It was 1874 when I donned my first rubber suit. It was composed of vulcanized rubber and consists of two distinct sections, both joined at the waist. The pantaloons end in a band of steel over which the lower part of the tunic fits with a strap covering it all, thus making a perfectly water-tight joint. At the back of the head, the back, the breast and on each thigh there are five internal compartments, each have a tube for the purpose of inflating them with air from the mouth.

The face is the only part of the body exposed to the weather when completely encased in the rubber suit.
I float on my back, and propel my body feet foremost with a double-bladed paddle at the rate of a hundred strokes per minute. When ever I choose I can get into an upright position. For the purpose on conveying provisions etc., for a long trip I have a small iron boat, which I named "Baby Mine", this boat is thirty inches long, twelve inches wide and twelve inches deep. She is completely closed other than the hatch which is protected by a water tight cover.
With a line attached to my belt I carry the following items: couple of bottles of ginger ale, ten days provisions, cigars, quinine and other emergency medications such as brandy, etc., frying pan, coffee, kettle, spoon, knife and fork. A cup, a spirit stove, pen and ink, notebook, signal rockets, chronometer, barometer, thermometer, revolver,
charts, maps, hatchet, ammunition, including a patch cloth and rubber cement. Attached to the deck is a headlight and clock.

Journeys:

"I began my voyages on October 1874. sailing from New York on the Queen of the National Line, Captain Bragg in command, my object was to jump overboard when we were two hundred and fifty miles from the American shore. I wanted to use this method to show the rubber suit off as a life saving device to the world.

From my early childhood I had a fascination for water and the water seemed to call me, my parents did not relish the idea,and always feared I would be drowned."

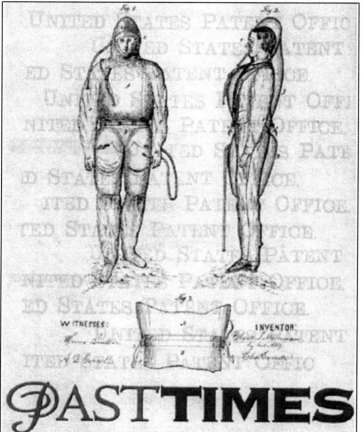

PASTTIMES

ROUGHING IT IN RUBBER

by Dave Walter

On that sunny, crisp, mid-September morning in 1881, several dozen residents of the frontier settlement of Glendive, Montana Territory, stood on the bank of the Yellowstone River in absolute disbelief. They could conceive of nothing more bizarre. Who would believe their story? No one with a firm grasp of reality!

ROUGHING IT IN RUBBER
Over 25,000 Miles in a Rubber Suit.

My various trips on the waters of the world started in October, 1874 to June, 1889.
I made my first venture in the waters of the Allegheny River at Pittsburgh, PA.

One bright morning in July, 1858, two women carrying well filled market baskets, were crossing the old Hand St bridge that spans the Allegheny River between Pittsburgh and Allegheny City.

"Oh Mrs. Boyton, do look at the child in the middle of the river, paddling around on a board." "Well", said Mrs. Boyton, "I am glad it is none of mine. My son Paul loves the water dearly, but I took the precaution to lock him up before I started for market." After watching the child who was evidently enjoying his aquatic sport, the two woman proceeded on their way home. Mrs. Boyton with a feeling of remorse for keeping her young son Paul locked up, went upstairs to release him, to her dismay he had escaped. Three minutes later a frantic Mrs. Boyton stood on the bank of the Allegheny, vigorously waving at the little figure on the board. The forward end of the one by twelve inch board reluctantly headed for shore, and slowly paddled in. As the child reached land, he was grasped by his angry mother, who beat a merry tattoo on his tender butt with a shingle.

This was not the first time that the young hero had received punishment for his love of the water. His home was just one block from the banks of the Allegheny, and whenever he could escape the vigilant eye of his mother, he was found either on the bank or in the water. One day, Mrs. Boyton, who had a fear of Paul drowning, was going visiting, determined to secure Paul against an accident.

She took him upstairs, undressed him, and removed his clothes from the room, locking the door behind her before leaving the house. The day was clear, the water blue and Paul could hear the delighted cries
of the boys as they plunged into its refreshing depths, the temptation was too great. Paul searched the room carefully

and to his delight, discovered a pair of his father's draws, he got into them and tied the waists-string around his neck. Then forcing a window, he slid down the handy lightning rod like a young monkey, and was later found in his usual haunt by his astonished mother, some hours later. From this time on, she gave him more liberty to follow his natural bent. When not in school Paul spent most of his time in the water.

In those days, driftwood, consisting of slabs, logs and boards, were continually floating down the river from the headwaters, where the great forests were being cut down. When he saw a nice piece of wood, Paul would cut through the water like a young shark, and swim with it ahead of him to the shore, where his lumber pile was a goodly size. He kept his mothers cellar full and sold the surplus to neighbors. The proceeds of which were devoted to gingerbread and even at a very early age, the abominable roll of tobacco known as the "Pittsburgh Stogies". Great rafts of lumber came down the river daily, a favorite amusement of Paul's was to run a quarter of a mile up the river bank, swim off and board it.

One day he boarded a raft, the Captain of which was evidently a stranger to the channel in the vicinity of the Pittsburgh and was unaware of the different bars formed by the bridge piers. Paul saw that it was certain to run aground. He told the captain and was so earnest in his manner, that the course was ordered changed. Less than 500 yards furthure down, the ugly bar showed up not five feet from the side of the raft, as it went gliding by. The rafts man insisted on keeping the little fellow by his side until he was safely moored to the Pittsburgh shore: then as a reward for his services, presented Paul with a little flat boat about twelve feet long by five feet wide and ordered two of the crew to tow it with a skiff to the Allegheny side. Paul's sole and only ambition for a long time had been to own a boat. As the two sturdy oarsmen with the boat in tow, neared the Allegheny shore, Paul stood erect in the stern, his eyes shining with triumph and satisfaction, loudly hailed his playmates to come and see his prize. It is safe to say that no commander of a vessel, ever viewed his craft with more pride, than Paul did his little flat-bottom boat.
He named her the "Gray Eagle."

About this time a new enterprise opened for the commander and crew of the "Gray Eagle". The city commenced to pave the streets with large round stones called "Pavers," many of which were found in pockets at the bottom of the river. One day a contractor met Paul on the bank and said: "Say, son, could you boys gather a lot of pavers? I will buy them from you and give you thirty cents per hundred." The offer was eagerly excepted. Next day the "Eagle" was anchored with a piece of railroad iron, over a pocket, and Paul began diving through the transparent water, to gather pavers from the bottom, he would retrieve one or two, return to the top, and drop them into the boat. Paul's friends all wanted a piece of this action, but he had much difficulty in teaching the other boys how to keep their eyes open under water.

This occupation was pursued with great success through summer of 1859. The boys discovered a rich pocket, right near the old Aqueduct bridge. While loathe to leave such a find, the "Eagle" was so overloaded that when the divers climbed aboard, the additional weight almost swamped her. The stronger swimmers were compelled to go overboard, and resting their hands gently on the gunwale,
they propelled her by swimming towards the shore. They had not proceeded far when the bottom, of the then well-worn "Eagle" finally fell out and the cargo disappeared back down to the bottom of the Allegheny River. Paul hung onto the frame work of his wrecked craft until the powerful current caught it, sweeping it southward. Their enemies from across the river, seeing their predicament rallied forth in a skiff to challenge them. The Allegheny boys swam for their own shore as rapidly as possible. On gaining shallow water, they faced their assailants and a battle was fought that was long remembered by the inhabitants of both sides of the river.

After the loss of the "Gray Eagle", Paul resumed his swimming and collecting driftwood. About this time, after many complaints, orders against further rows and naked bathing were strictly enforced by a constable named Sam Long.

Before the boys got thoroughly acquainted with him,
he often captured an offender's clothing, which he detained
, until the boy came ashore. Then Sam would escort him to

the Mayor's office to receive a severe reprimand, or his parents would be compelled to pay a small fine. Paul was never caught as he was always on the lookout for the watchful Sam. When the constable approached he would swim rapidly to his clothes, placed conveniently close to the water, it was neither weighty nor large, placing them on his head and tied with a string under his chin, then he would swim swiftly off to the first pier of the bridge. This was fully fifty yards out in the stream, and here Paul would sit on the abutment rocks until Sam's patience was worn out and he would depart. Then Paul would leisurely swim to the shore, dress himself and go home.

Paul's elder brother, Michael, was a studious, sedate boy who took no pleasure in the sports and adventures of his aquatic brother. But Paul's glowing descriptions of the pleasures of plunging and paddling in the cool, clear river, at last induced Michael to join in the watery gambols. One warm afternoon he accompanied his brother to the riverside. Paul slipped out of his clothes and was soon frolicking in the refreshing water, encouraging Michael to join him, Michael slowly disrobed and cautiously stepped into the water. He was no swimmer: but being surrounded by Paul and his companions, he grew bolder, waded further out from the shore and was soon enjoying himself as heartily as any of them.

Suddenly the cry of "Sam Long" was raised and most of the boys would seize their clothes and disappear in the direction of their homes. The hardier swimmers with Paul, struck out for the abutment of the pier in their usual way, and poor Michael was left alone.

Sam gently gathered up Michael's clothes, and waited for the owner to land. Michael had often heard of the terrible Sam Long so he did not go ashore, though Sam called him frequently. At last growing weary, the constable walked away with the captured wardrobe. As he disappeared, Michael started on a dead run for home. His clothes were recovered, but it was many moons before Michael was inclined to go swimming with young Paul again.

It was custom then, as is now to run enormous tows of coal barges, propelled by a powerful tug, from Pittsburgh to New Orleans. These grim and heavily loaded fleets had an intense

fascination for young Paul. Many and many a day he spent in assisting the inland sailors in lashing boat to boat and diving overboard for spars, etc., that had slipped into the river. He often dreamt of the time when he would be large enough to go down the mighty Ohio and great Mississippi. He made many friends among the coal men and eagerly devoured their stories of danger, of voyages down the river and of comical "darkies" in the far off south. Time after time he begged his mother for permission to go away on one of these barge trips, but she would never consent. One day while assisting as usual on a fleet that was about to depart, a great dark whiskered man named Tom, who was his particular friend, said: "Why don't you come with us, Paul?, we will take good care of you and bring you safe home again." The temptation was great, but the thought of his dear anxious mother deterred him. Tom still urged and the wonderful stories he told about brilliant New Orleans and the mighty "Father of Waters" rapt Paul's attention so that he at first did not notice that the tug "Red Lion" was driving the huge fleet of barges ahead of her. Would he jump into the river and swim ashore, or would he go ahead?.
"He who hesitates, is lost."
Paul remained on board, Tom took him to the lookout far ahead on the tow and Paul forgot all about home, giving himself up to the delight of watching the swiftly passing banks while he listened to the swish, swish of the water as it beat against the bows of the barges. He was seated with the men on the watch, who passed the time telling stories and laughing at rough jokes. As it was getting late Tom said, "Now Paul, its time to turn in. There's your bunk," pointing to a shelf in the dark and damp lookout house. The river men at that time were rather given to profanity, so their yarns were freely interspersed with oaths. Suddenly Tom said in a loud whisper: " Dry up! Don't you see the youngster is saying his prayers?" A hush fell on the group, all looked around. Paul kneeling on the damp dirty beam alongside his bunk, was repeating the prayers learned at his mother's knee. With the return of daylight he begged Tom to get him back or send a letter. Tom dissuaded him from returning, but helped him write a letter informing his mother that he was safe and would be taken good care of, which was posted

ROUGHING IT IN RUBBER

at Wheeling, VA. Relieved in mind Paul was soon again enjoying the beautiful scenery along the banks of the Ohio. His work was to carry coffee to the forward men on the lookout, and to help in many other ways.

Nearing Evansville, Indiana, about seven hundred miles from Pittsburgh a great shock was felt on the fleet as a great shower of coal was sent flying through the air. "Snag! Snag!" was heard from all sides: the big engines of the "Red Lion" were stopped and reversed, headway of the fleet was checked as it slowly swung to shore. It was discovered a sunken log had penetrated the bottom of the barge, leaving a gapping hole, that was taking on water. A crewman shoveled away the coal and was able to cut the snag and vain attempts were made to pass a tarpaulin under and so stop the hole. Paul stood near his friend Tom, and suggested that he dive under, take a rope with him, and so enable them to pass the canvas below.

"Do you think you can do it without drowning"? said Tom.

"I am certain," was the response. Tom handed Paul the end of the rope. Without hesitation Paul sprang into the water and dove under the then sinking barge. The rope was hauled up and another passed to him. with which he repeated the operation. The ropes were fastened to the tarpaulin, two more fastened to the other corners. The canvas was lowered into the river and the men on the other side hauled it under the rugged hole. As the canvas covered it, the inflow of water was instantly checked. With a loud cheer, the crew sprang to the pumps, as the water got low enough, planks were nailed over the hole and the "Red Lion" and its valuable cargo were saved. Paul was the hero of the hour. The Captain of the "Red Lion" transferred him from his damp and grimy quarters on the head to the comfortable cabin and pilot house. He confessed to the Captain, that he had run away from home and was anxious about his mother. That day the Captain wrote a glowing letter to his mother Mrs. Boyton and posted it at Paducah, Kentucky. From that day on he took great pleasure in teaching Paul how to steer, and many other arts in river craft.

At last the "Red Lion" and her tow were safely moored in New Orleans. The Captain found a letter waiting from Mrs. Boyton requesting that Paul be sent back by the first mail packet.

While waiting for her departure, the Captain took Paul out to see the great city. Among many places of interest they visited that day, the slave mart at the foot of the fine statue erected in Honor of Henry Clay. Paul spelled out the inscription on the monument which said "that if he (Henry Clay), could be instrumental in eradicating this deepest stain, slavery, from our country, he would be prouder than, if he enjoyed the triumphs of a great conqueror." Paul saw slaves disposed of, the auction concluded with three boys who seemed to be brother or very close friends, for the way they wept bitterly when parted. As they moved away, Paul's eyes were filled with tears at the agony of the unhappy boys, and turning to the Captain he said: "Do you think this is right?" "No" responded the Captain., "I'm darned if I do. It is an outrage and a shame that human beings should be sold like cattle." Even to his childish mind this seemed sadly inconsistent with the surroundings. The Captain secured passage for Paul on a Northern bound boat and bought him many little presents, to wishing him God speed. About five weeks from the time he so thoughtlessly embarked on board the "Red Lion", he was standing hesitantly half a block from his mother's home, holding in his hand a small cage with a little red bird, while snugly stowed away in the bosom of his shirt was his much cherished pet, the alligator.

He was not sure of the reception he would receive: but at length he steeled his nerves for whatever was in store and made a rush for the house. The delighted mother folded him in her arms and covered his face with kisses, saying "Thank God that you are safe home again." His brothers and sisters grouped around with words of welcome for the prodigal. This experience lived long in Paul's memory.

One warm day while on his way to school, he lingered so long on the bridge that the tower clock struck ten and then he argued that it would be useless to go until the afternoon session, when he could easily hoodwink his teacher with an excuse. But the afternoon came, and the wild boy was still in the water, to deeply interested in navigating his plank to realize that he was playing "hooky" and risking its shady consequences. About two o'clock, Paul heard loud cries from the St. Claire Street bridge. Looking up he saw an excited crowd gathering. The object of their excitement was a little boy who had waded out on a shallow bar above the bridge into deep water and was being carried away by the strong current. Paul caught a glimpse of him as he disappeared, springing from his plank he swam out with strong steady strokes to his assistance. The crowd on the bridge shouted loud cries of encouragement. As Paul reached the spot where the body went down, he could find no traces of him.

 A man on the bridge shouted: "A little farther down! a little farther down! I can see him at the bottom". Paul swam in the direction indicated and at the cry, "there, there," dove down to the bottom like a seal. He came up directly on the body which was doubled up against a large boulder. He grasped it by the arm and rose with it to the surface. Loud ringing cheers from the crowd above, encouraged him. He swam with one arm, supporting the body with the other. They were rapidly being carried away down stream, when a boat which had been sent out, reached the almost exhausted boy. Paul and the unconscious boy were taken ashore and conveyed to the back room of the salon, where both were revived by a doctor. As a token of recognition, Paul's hat was passed around, and soon filled to the brim with silver.

   The two boys were loaded into an express wagon and escorted by the policeman, firstly to the rescued boys home. The officer assuring the hysterical mother, assuring her, her son will be all right, they carefully carried him in, the old grandmother, who was blind, heard the story and asked that Paul be brought in. Running her trembling hands over his face and head, she blessed him fervently and to the delight of the grinning urchin, looking in at the door and to Paul's intense embarrassment, she kissed him several times. At last the policeman took Paul and his silver home. When Mrs. Boyton saw her truant son under police escort, she turned pale, but the officer called out,"You ought to be proud of this boy," and he told her the story of the rescue and handed over the silver." The mothers eye's beamed with pleasure as she listened. She praised her gallant little son and thanked the officer for his kindness. After he was gone she put the silver carefully away and interviewed the hero, as often before, with a shingle.

"Not only for playing hooky," she said " but for going in the water at all."

The little fellow that Paul rescued that day, was Thomas Mc Caffery now a member of the Allegheny City Fire Department. Many years afterwards he gave Paul a gold medal in remembrance of their first meeting.

About this time the war of the rebellion broke out and fever burned fiercely in Pittsburgh and vicinity. Paul longed to join the great bodies of troops that were being hurried to the front. He spent all his spare time hanging around the head-quarters of the forming regiments. One day he asked a recruiting officer if he needed a drummer boy.

"You are pretty small, sonny," said the soldier, "can you drum?" "No," said Paul, "but I can learn mighty quick." Pleased with the answer, the soldier took him to the head-quarters and said, "Here is a little volunteer." Paul was closely questioned and untruthfully assured the officers in charge that his mother would be glad to get rid of him. That night he was enrolled in Colonel Cases" Regiment. Next day he began his drum practice, an exercise that was rudely interrupted by the appearance of his mother, who led the "warrior bold" home by the ear.

His parents now decided to send Paul away to school. The college they selected was situated in the heart of the Allegheny Mountains, Saint Francis, Loretta PA, about four miles from Pennsylvania Railroad. It was far from any water course or river, and surrounded by dense forest's of pines. She told the faculty of his peculiar passion for the water and the dread she had of losing him. Mrs. Boyton was assured that Paul would be taken good care of. Their farewell was most affectionate. Paul cried bitterly, not only for the parting from his mother whom he loved dearly, but for the feeling that he was being exiled for all his crimes and misdemeanors.

When it came time for me to be educated, they decided it should be as far away from my beloved river, that I loved so dearly. They sent me to an educational institution that I might find it somewhat if not impossible, to indulge in my swimming proclivities. But as you will see the gentle goddess Varuna proved propitious to her child, and so I succeeded in baffling the efforts of the household authorities, else this volume would never have been written. Of all my studies that which pleased me the most was the art of navigation. This I learned at a distant college up amongst the Alleghenies.

The fall session had not yet begun, so he had time to become acquainted with the few boys who were already at the college and to explore the dark pine woods that seemed a new world to him. Paul inquired eagerly if there was any water in the vicinity. The boys told him there was a place called the "swimming hole" about two miles from the college. Next day he coaxed some of the boys to show him the way. He found a pond, little larger than a hole, surrounded by heavy vegetation and inhabited by a colony of frogs. He was soon swimming in it's depths and had induced two or three of the boys to follow his example. Day after day he visited the hole and made out to swim: but he always thought longingly of the far off, bright Allegheny.

One day a teamster who sometimes came to college, told Paul of a sheet of water that was much larger than the swimming hole. He called it "Bruce's dam." Next morning Paul and a Philadelphia boy named Stockdale, who was his particular chum, obtained permission to go out of bounds.

During breakfast they had managed to appropriate a sufficient supply of bread and butter for the day. Starting out to find Bruce's Dam, a long and weary tramp over the mountains. They stopped often to chase the gray squirrel's that abounded the forest, and wasted much time in trying to dig out a red fox, that had crossed their path and shot down a hole. They were so long in reaching the dam, they were beginning to believe that the directions were wrong. Decided that maybe they should turn back, when Paul said, "I think I hear water!" They listened intently for a few seconds. A sound again came through the woods. They struck out a little to the right and were soon at the long sought after dam. It was a body of water about one hundred yards wide and five hundred yards long. Enormous pine stumps protruded through the surface, there was a miserable looking saw-mill situated at the lower end. Two men were employed at drawing out the logs and ripping them up into boards. Paul uttered a joyful cry as he perceived that the water was both clear and deep. He hastily hastily removed his clothing and "Stockie" slowly followed his example. As they stood naked on the bank, before their plunge, a snake shot out almost from under their feet, and swam gracefully over the surface to a stump a little distance off. That was enough for "Stockie" who immediately got dressed. Paul did not really like the idea of snakes, but had hiked too far for this swim and was determined to have it, and so he plunged headlong into the water. Round and round the stumps he swam. He saw several snakes and many water lizards. After his bathe "Stockie" and Paul went down to the mill and chatted with the men engaged there. The latter assured them that the snakes and lizards were perfectly harmless. This restored Stockie's courage. He agreed to try the water before leaving, provided Paul would go in with him. The two chums had a long, delightful swim and finally as sunset approached, they suddenly thought that they might be needed at college. It was dark when they got back, they both received severe lectures for there long absence. Bruce's Dam was several times re visited and always with great enjoyment. At last the vacation was over and these pleasant pilgrimages had to come to an end.

Paul kept his promise he made to his mother. During study he applied himself with all his energies to the studies before him, and rapidly increased his store of knowledge; but he was also learning many things outside the school room. The loneliness of and surroundings of the college, increased the natural wildness of his nature.

Down in the dark pine woods Paul and Stockie, constructed a trap, consisting of: a square box placed on a piece of board and set with a little wooded trigger. When a squirrel would enter to get a walnut fastened inside, he would spring the trap, caging him there until his young captors came to retrieve him. They would slip a pillow case, furnished unconsciously by the college, under one corner of the box, turning it off the bottom board until a little opening was made in the bag. The squirrel of course would jump in, and was grabbed and secure in the pillow cover. The squirrel was a gray kitten squirrel, Paul put a collar and little chain on it, that he always had ready to train a pet. This was was so small and young that he had to feed

ROUGHING IT IN RUBBER

it with crushed walnuts and milk, and named it May. The tiny creature lived in his pocket and desk, shared his bed at night. It would sit on the off-page of his book while he studied and comb its little whiskers and brush it's tail in perfect contentment. Every one marveled at the affection of his pet and the control he had over it. Paul would let it loose in the woods, it would run up a tree and at his call, "Come May," it would return at once and with a chuckle drop into his pocket. Paul kept this squirrel until after he had left college. The crowded streets of the city seemed to bewilder it and it jumped out of his pocket to the sidewalk. A man passing struck May with a cane, killing her. Paul grieved long over his pet: but from the experience he had acquired a great control over animals and always had a supply on hand to train.

From his youth Paul showed a fondness for aquatic sports, and entered the American Navy at the age of fourteen, serving until the close of the Civil War.

   On the morning of April 15th, 1864, young Boyton presented himself at the Brooklyn Navy Yard, and was enrolled in the United States Navy as a sailor before the mast. After a few weeks of drilling he was transferred to the United States Steamer, Hydrangea, Captain W. Rogers in command, Paul was now in his fifteenth year.
He had no difficulty in passing the scrutiny of enlisting officers. He was of a powerful build and very muscular. His outdoor life in the woods and on rivers made him look older than he really was.
   The Hydrangea was ordered to Fortress Monroe, and Paul received his baptism of fire while the steamer was running up the James River past Malvern Hill, where a confederate battery was stationed. Much has been written about the war, and as this is simply a story of adventure, it will be left to better writers to record the war history many of whom have already described scenes enacted in that vicinity during the war of 1864.
   The last engagement Paul was in, was the memorable assault on Fort Fisher. When the war ended, he mustered out. At that time he held the position of yeoman.

CHAPTER TWO

Mr. Terence Boyton realized that Paul did not have much aptitude for commercial pursuits, so decided to send him to the West Indies for the purpose of collecting and shipping all kinds of marine curios, allowing him the freedom to peruse his love of the water. Paul's companion was a submarine diver whom his father had engaged. They took passage on the barge "Reindeer," bound for Barbados. They had all kinds of the latest dredging apparatus, including submarine armor and pumps in their outfit. After a tedious voyage of twenty-seven days, the "Reindeer" cast anchor in Bridgetown. Paul and the diver, who's name was Tom Scott, were kindly welcomed by the merchant, and old friend of Mr. Boyton's, to whom they carried letters of introduction. His fathers instructions were to charter a fishing boat or some suitable vessel at Bridgetown for a six month cruise among the keys and islands surrounding, for the purpose of fishing up coral, shells and other curios that he could gather. A few days after his arrival, Paul engaged a staunch little sloop, commanded by a negro, who was assisted by a crew of four strong colored sailors.

The first cruise was around the island of Barbados. Several curios were collected and purchased, shipping a goodly cargo back on the "Reindeer's" return voyage. When he received them and read Paul's accompanying letter, Mr. Boyton was satisfied that his son was now engaged in a business that thoroughly suited him. The Cayosa, for such was the name of a little sloop, was then stocked for a voyage to a group of islands that lay to the westward, where it was said that rare shells could be found. For a small fee the captain had agreed to bunk with his crew, leaving Tom Scott and Paul his little cabin all to themselves. This cabin was thoroughly scrubbed and cleaned by the pair, after which they fitted it up and placed their baggage, rifles, fishing gear, plenty of reading matter and their private stores.

While in port, Paul remained the guest of Mr. C,. the merchant, whose home was a beautiful villa situated a little way out of town. The merry, bright-eyed daughters of his host made sad havoc in the susceptible heart of young Boyton. At

ROUGHING IT IN RUBBER

last all the stores were aboard and everything was ready to set sail.

One bright morning the anchor was hoisted, and the sloop sailed away on her cruise to the island of St. Vincent, which lay about one hundred miles to the west. During this voyage a heavy tornado tested the little sloop to her utmost, throwing her up and down, and rolling her from side to side, by the end of it all she was driven far off her course. It was four days before they reached Kingston on the south of the island, instead of Richmond where they were bound. They spent a few days in the quaint, old town and picked up several curiosities. The sloop then headed for Cariacou islands, a large group which dot the ocean between St. Vincent and Granada. Many of these island are uninhabited by human beings. They are low and loaded down to the water's edge with rich, tropical vegetation. The sloop spent six weeks in this group. Every available part of the boat was packed with coral and all kinds of curios. A run was made to Charlottetown, Granada, where the collection was cleaned and waited the first ship, back to New York. The sloop was again stocked and set sail for Trinidad, and along the coast, where valuable specimens were picked up. In this same locality they struck on a reef of exquisite valuable brain coral, with which they loaded the sloop. Sail was then made for Port of Spain, the principal town of the island. In going through the Dragons Mouth, a narrow, dangerous passage between the mainland of South America and Trinidad, the Cayosa was nearly wrecked. A sudden change in the wind when they were rounding the point, drove her into the beakers. Her mast was badly sprung and only with the utmost difficulty she was saved. Limping into Port of Spain, a curiously picturesque old town. Here the collection was unloaded as before and the Cayosa beached for an overhaul.

While beached, three English sailors who were prisoners, being held for treason. The lax attitude of the prison system allowed them to work, coming down daily to lend a hand on the sloop. Being from Liverpool they were hard characters. The captain of their vessel dropped them off in Trinidad, preferring to go short handed rather than have them aboard. On the shady side of the sloop, that was high on the beach, they entertained Paul and Scott with their varied adventures. One day Paul expressed astonishment at the way they were allowed such unusual liberties. One of them, Dick Harris answered: "We are a burden to the authorities here. They would be glad to be rid of us, without the trouble and expense of sending us to England, where, no doubt, we would get the rope's end of the law."

Last night when you paid us off, we stayed out late. When we returned to the jail we had to knock again and again. The jailer called out: "Who's there?". We gave our names, he exclaimed: "Now if you blasted shell-backs can't get home at a reasonable hour, you can stay out. This is the last time I will be disturbed from my slumbers to to let you in." The three worthless implored Paul to take them away on the Cayosa. He referred them to the negro captain. The latter soon assured them that he would rather run a cargo of scorpions than risk himself and crew to to the tender care of the mild mannered Liverpool tars, When the sloop was fully repaired, she started on a trip around the islands, but the beakers were too heavy for successful work. They directed their course northward and soon reentered the Carlacou group. A couple of months were spent in these lovely islands. The great beakers that swept in along the coast of Trinidad, Tobago and Granada were missing.

In the tranquil bays and inlets, they pressed their occupation of bringing up the natural treasures of the deep with more profit and less risk. They would anchor the Cayosa as near shore as possible, in the some what well sheltered bay. Here soundings would be taken, and the vicinity thoroughly inspected. When the bay gave promise of shells and coral, a camp was made on the silver-like beach under the shade of the towering giant coconut trees. The mainsail was detached and carried ashore to serve as an awning. The large sheet-iron boilers were also landed.

While two of the crew gathered wood and decayed vegetation for fuel, the others were busy erecting a crude fire place with rocks overhead where the boilers were set. The shore camp being ready, the submarine pump would be lowered into the yawl, and with Tom Scott encased in the diving armor,

ROUGHING IT IN RUBBER

would be conveyed to the most likely place on the bay. When this was, reached a kedge anchor was dropped, the face plate of the armor screwed on, the pipes attached and Tom quietly slipped over the side and descended to the reef.

Two of the crew turned cranks to force air down to him, while Paul seated in the stern held the life line. When the diver reached bottom, he gave the signal to shift the boat wherever his explorations led him. When a lot of shells or curious objects were found, several pulls on the line were given indicating, "to anchor and send down the bucket." This bucket was a huge iron affair, holding about five bushels. It was sent to the bottom. Tom soon filled it with living and dead specimens of brilliant and beautiful shells, were hoisted and the contents transferred aboard. In the clear waters on the coral reef by Paul.

He longed for the day when he could go down and behold the strange sights below in the green, transparent water. At last, the yawl was loaded. Tom came up and the helmet of his suit was removed and he enjoyed the pure salt air once more. Then the boat was headed for shore and the treasures landed. All living shells were quickly transferred to the boilers full of hot water. They were left to simmer over the fire for a couple of hours, after which they were dumped on the sands. The thoroughly cooked inhabitants were easily removed and the shells clean and glowing with all the beautiful tints of the rose and lily, were placed in piles under the shade of the awning.

While the crew was engaged in this latter occupation, Scott and Paul, armed with rifle and shot gun, would saunter through the heavily perfumed tropical forests in search of any game they could find. In expeditions of this kind, they captured three young monkeys and a couple of parrots, who were soon trained pets on the Cayosa, furnishing all hands with much amusement. Scott and Paul shot many iguanos. These are huge lizards that abound the tropics. The captain and crew considered this meat a great delicacy, broiling and eating them with great relish. One day the black captain offered them a young lizard, daintily broiled. He assured them that it was as sweet and tender as an angles dream. They both tasted it really excellent and from that time on, both partook heartily of the dish, whenever it was on the table.

At night they frequently stretched their hammocks from tree to tree for their cabin was uncomfortably hot. After a refreshing bath in the cool phorescent water and a scampering up and down the level sands in lieu of a towel, they would turn in and enjoy a sound sleep.

They were generally awakened before daylight by the shrieking and chattering of the parrots and monkeys. Then with a spring from their hammock, they would dash merrily in to the reviving water. After the donned their white canvas suits and were ready for another day. Breakfast was taken on shore. This consisted of fresh fish, coffee, coconuts, pine apples and bread fruits. Abundance of this fruit was found on all the islands they visited. On some of the islands they
could not enjoy their nights in the cool hammocks, owing to the attacks of the malicious jigger spider and ferocious mosquitoes.

One day while at anchor over a coral reef at the southern part of Vequin, Tom Scott agreed to give Paul his first lesson in diving. Tom had been feeling sick and feverish for some days, so he was more than willing to let Paul take his place for once.

Tom gave Paul full instructions on how to act, especially warning him on not to gasp, in the compressed air, but to breathe naturally and easily. When the helmet was screwed on, Paul felt a smothering sensation but it soon passed with the excitement of his first dive. Encouraged, he stepped down on the rope ladder over the side of the sloop and slowly descended to the bottom, about five fathoms below. The decent was easy, but bewildering, when his heavily loaded feet struck the coral, it sounded to him as if the top of his head was being lifted off. For the moment he wished to regain the surface, but Scott advised him to keep cool and steady, and he quickly regained control of his nerves.

He peered through the heavy plate glass visor, curiously around at the strange sights under the green water. The bottom was as white as snow drift and the powerful sun lit up the water so that he could distinctly see all objects within twelve or fifteen feet around him. He signaled "all right' to Scott with the line and started to walk around. The signal line and hose

ROUGHING IT IN RUBBER

were played out to him, so that he could take a wide scope around and under the sloop. Not withstanding the enormous weight of lead attached to the diving dress, Paul found that he had to walk as easily and lightly as if there were egg shells under his feet, the least little pressure on the bottom had a tendency to send him up. After half an hour below, during which he thoroughly enjoyed his novel surroundings, he felt an oppression on his chest and signaled "to haul up".

The strong arms of the crew helped him up on the deck, the helmet was removed and his flushed and eager face exposed. Remarking to Tom that "diving was glorious". After a rest of two hours, the sloop having been shifted to another anchorage, Paul again descended. This time the bottom had a different aspect. It was full of dark rocks over which grew great masses of seaweed's. A few feet from where he descended, sprang up a reef of branch coral which extended as far as he could see on either side. This coral grew like shrubbery. It was hard to release that all this was the product of an invisible insect, instead of being a miniature forest turned into pure white stone. The scene was surpassing beautiful; coral branches ran up to a height of eight or ten feet from the bottom, where they looked and wove together like vines. Paul walked to the edge of this reef and gazed with delighted eyes into its liquid depths. Schools of bright colored fish were swimming gracefully in and out through the delicate coral branches. Some, more fearless than their companions, swam round and round Paul's copper helmet, and looked into the thick glass at the front.

When Paul made a sudden move of his hand, they darted away: but returned soon again to satisfy their curiosity and ascertain what strange monster had invaded their fairy land. Three sudden jerks of the life-line from the anxious Tom, recalled Paul to his work. The three pulls meant, "Where are you ?, is everything all right?" He then signaled for the bucket to be lowered. Using his pry to brake off some exquisite specimens of the undergrowth coral, which he then loaded in to the bucket and signaled for it to go up. Taking some time explore on the other side of the coral forest until he came to a small portion on the bottom that was covered with sand and surrounded with rocks. Under the growth of marine vegetation, he passed his hand, and pulled from the rocks a living shell. Paul had been fully instructed by his father in the science of cronchology, so he recognized this specimen as very rare and much sought after. It was the shell called "valuta musica." This was the first one of those shells found during this expedition. After a careful search he found about twenty-three more of the same kind, and several large shells known as "Triton's trumpet."

The bucket was filled and hoisted up, with Paul following it to the surface well satisfied with his first days work as a submarine-diver. Scott was not enthusiastic over the "valuta musica," but the captain of the Cayosa was delighted. He knew the value of the shell. He told Paul he had sold many of them to tourists in Barbados receiving from fifty cents to a dollar and a half a piece. He advised Paul not to move the sloop that night, as generally where one shell was found there would be many more in it's vicinity, and advised Paul to descend again the next day.

When the sun was sufficiently high the next morning, Paul again donned the armor and resumed his search for the valuta. Not thirty yards from where he had discovered the first one, he found a basin in the rocks filled with sand. From around this basin he took out two hundred and forty specimens of the desired shell. Afterwards it was ascertained that no greater find of this species had ever been made.

Scott was not pleased with Paul's success. He grew more sullen every day, several times he tried to resume his position as chief diver, but his strength was not equal to the strain, and Paul gladly took his place, which only made Scott furious.

The abuse and the curses he heaped on captain and crew would have resulted in something serious only for Paul. The captain wanted to maroon the growler; that is , to place him on an island with some provisions and sail away. To this Paul answered he would blow the head off any man who attempted such a thing. He then tried to restrain Scott with little success. There was no other way out of it, so Paul decided to end the cruise. The sloop had a good cargo, so he ordered the captain to sail for Bridgetown, Barbados. They arrived three months before the charter expired. Mr. C settled to the satisfaction of the Cayosa's captain and Scott was placed in the Marine Hospital. Three weeks later, after intense suffering from fever, the poor fellow died. Then Paul understood all his growls and abuse and was sincerely sorry for him. The cargo was boxed ready for shipment to New York and Paul had a pleasant time on the island, while waiting for a northern bound vessel.

One morning while sitting on the mole, fishing, he saw a staunch little schooner with dilapidated sails bear into the harbor. When her anchor was let go, a boat was lowered into which two sailors and a man evidently the captain, entered. Paul folding his fishing line, sauntered down to find out who the new arrivals were. A customs officer standing by, hailed the stranger as he came ashore with, "Why, Captain Balbo, I am delighted to see you."

"Shure it does me eyes good to see yureself," said the new arrival, in a rich Irish brogue. "Me papers air all right, so we'll have no trouble. O'ive just called in to get a bit av fresh wather, an' if the Lord's willing' something' a little stronger."

"You're always welcome," responded the officer, "even if you do neglected to get your clearances. You know there is no love lost between you and the customs house."

The schooner captain was a stout, thickset man with a face bronzed to the color of mahogany and a head of hair as red as a Pittsburgh furnace at midnight. His blue eyes sparkled with good nature and merriment, and a continual smile hovered over his massive mouth. After several hearty greetings to acquaintances on landing, the captain proceeded to the warehouses of the merchants, where Mr. C. soon afterward introduced Paul to the jolly old sea dog. When Captain Balbo learned that Paul had been down after seashells and curiosities, he was delighted and invited the boy to come aboard. Saying "om in the same line meslf. But instead of looking' afther dirty, bad-smellin' sea shells, it's afther the shells of ould vessels Oi am." Paul gladly promised to go aboard that afternoon.

The captain purchased a supply of provisions, and made arrangements for his casks of fresh water and "stronger stuff," to be loaded. Mr. C. invited him to stay over and have dinner with himself and Paul. The captain declared he could "fill himself up at the hotel with more liberty and less embarrassment." He took Paul into a roomy cabin, and introduced him to his wife, a very obese yellow woman, who was reclining on a sofa. The woman was undoubtedly of negro blood, but to Paul's profound astonishment, she had as fine a brogue as her husband. After some conversation, Paul ventured to ask the captain how this happened. The latter laughed heartily and answered, "Me wife wuz born far enough away from dear ould Ireland. "

"Oi'll tell yea how it wuz. Many years ago a parthy of immigrants left county Kerry for Nassau, New Providence oisland. Their ship wuz driven far out av her way in a storm an' wrecked on a small oisland, an' soon had foine av those thet survived from the ship an' settled on the oisland, and soon had foine homes on its fertile soil. They found only a few nager inhabitants, an'shure they tuk thim fur servants. Me parents were among the survivors from the ship an' Oi wuz born about a year after the wreck. As toime went on, the nagers gradually acquired the accent of their masters. Whin Oi grew up Oi shipped on a tradin' schooner in which we wus cast away near Nassau. There Oi joined an English ship an' fur foive years put in the loife av a sailor fornist the mast. Me heart always longed fur the sunlit, happy oisland an' me people an' at lasht Oi got back there, an' there Oi married Betsy thet yea see on her beam ends on the sofa. Soon afther, in company with others, Oi bought fur a trifle, a schooner that wuz wrecked on the Keys. Afther hard wuerk we got her afloat an' re-masted. We did good wuerk in her as a wrecker. Wan be wan Oi bought me partners out, until-today Oi am masther av the good little craft that's under yez. Me wife is always the companion av me voyages. Mr. C. told me that yea had a submarine armor an' some improved derdgin' apparatus. Me business is tradin' and wrecking.' Now Oi know where both will be useful to' yea and an' to me. There's many a wreck that Oi know' that's out av me reach wid appliances Oi have. Wid your apparatus we can get treasure in abundance."

His stories of wrecks and treasures were of deep interest to Paul. Gladly would he have joined the captain, but his father

ROUGHING IT IN RUBBER

owned the submarine armor and apparatus and he felt he ought to consult him first. But he promised to answer Captain Balbo later on. As Paul was about to leave the schooner, he remarked, "Your good lady sleeps very soundly, but she is very fat."

"That fat, me b'y," responded Balbo, "is av great variety to me. They often remark to me, that its queer how fat Betsy is whin she goes ashore an' how she much flesh she looses afther a short sojourn."

Paul agreed to meet the Captain the next morning, " Oi' hope ye'll jine me, ye'll niver regret the day yea do." "Good night, God bless yea, me son," was shouted over the dark waters as the boat shot away to the landing.

That night Paul entertained Mr. C. with an account of his visit to the "Foam" and his interview with the captain. Mr. C. assured Paul the Balbo is reliable and thoroughly honest in his dealings.

At the same time he strongly advised Paul to take passage on the brig that had just arrived in the harbor bound for New York and consult with his father before embarking on the enterprise proposed by Balbo on the wrecker.

The next day Mr. C, the captain and Paul dined together. Paul promised the captain, that if he would consent to his gathering curiosities during the voyages, they could share the profits of the treasures recovered, he would discuss the deal with his father on his arrival in New York. If Mr.Boyton consented, Paul would join him in Nassau, with all the improved apparatus he could secure while in New York. The form of an agreement was drawn up and a bargain concluded subject to the approval of Paul's father.

Three days later Paul sailed for New York on the brig Saco, and after a quick voyage arrived safely at home once more.

The collection of shells and curios he had with him and previous shipments, convinced his father that Paul had found a great career and was very profitable to his father. Paul was glad to be home with his much loved mother and had not forgotten her in all his wanderings, as he had a splendid collection of the richest, rarest and most beautiful specimens, he had gathered during his voyages as a present for her. The liberal amount of monies Paul received for his labors was recklessly divided between his sisters. A few days after reaching home, he broached the subject of Captain Balbo's proposition to his father. Mr. Boyton did not like the idea of wrecking or treasure hunting, but he was perfectly content that Paul should join the captain for the purpose of collecting curiosities and shells, and was willing to supply him with the money and all the improved apparatus required for that purpose. Paul promised his father that the outfit would be applied according to his directions; but made a firm resolve to himself that he would tackle the treasure ships mentioned to him by Balbo.

A month after he reached home young Boyton started again for Nassau where he had sent several letters to the captain of the "Foam" informing him of when he might be expected to arrive. He sailed on a trading schooner, and when they entered the harbor at Nassau, he was glad to find the "Foam" waiting there. As the schooner glided past the "Foam," Paul loudly hailed her. Captain Balbo protruded his red head through the gangway. When he recognized Paul, he greeted him with a burst of semi-nautical and semi-scriptural eloquence and shouted: "Oi'll sind a boat afther yea. Come aboard as quick as yea can."

As Paul could not leave the schooner without first having his effects passed through the Customs House, the captain himself came ashore. He nearly dislocated Paul's arm with his vigorous hand shaking and said that he had been waiting at Nassau a week for him.

The apparatus being duly passed, all embarked in the captains yawl and were speedily conveyed aboard the "Foam." There he received the same warm welcome from the captains good natured wife, who had a neat little cabin prepared for him. After supper the captain and Paul had a long talk on deck. Paul described fully his father's objection to him embarking in the wrecking business, though he is willing to enter into the arrangements, providing his share would be the shells and curiosities, that the captain regarded as trash.

"Now, Paul, me b'y," said Balbo, after listening intently to his proposition; "Oi'm an old mon an' Oi consider mesaf an honest wan. Ye can have all the shells an' other things yea consider

ROUGHING IT IN RUBBER 25

curiosities that we pick up; but yea must also have a share in anything valuable we recover, an' yea can depind on me to give you a shquare dale. A fur that paper Mr. C. drew up, there is no occasion fur it. Oi'm not fond of o'papers av ony koind fur Oi've always had more or less trouble wid'em. Oi give yea me wurrd an Oi've yure wurrd an' that is sufficient. The paper can go to the sharks where it belongs."

He then went down to the cabin and returned with the paper they had signed, which he tore in two pieces and cast into the sea.

The next morning the captain and Paul went ashore for the clearance papers and that afternoon the anchor was raised and the "Foam" sailed away to the south. Island after island was visited in the Great Bahamas group, many wrecks well known to the captain were visited and worked successfully. Anchors, chains and windleses, etc, were found in abundance until the "Foam" was well loaded and sail was made for Kingston, Jamaica. Off Morant Point, they picked up a negro pilot in his little canoe far out at sea. The pilot wore a pair of blue pants, white shirt and stove-pipe hat, given to him no doubt by some passenger or captain of the merchant man. He gravely saluted all on deck as he passed, his bare feet over the bulwarks and turning to the captain said in the peculiar dialect of the Jamaica negro;

"Does yo want er pilot, sah?"

"No." responded the captain, "Oi know this coast well enough, but Ol think yea had bether hoist that craft of yure's on boord an' come wid us into Port Royal. There is signs av a cyclone if Ol'm not mishtaken;" an invitation which the pilot gladly accepted.

His outlandish attire and quaint English greatly amused Paul, who after supper, sat beside him on the deck and piled him with questions about Jamaica. The pilot told him many interesting tales, among them one of a famous shark known as "Port Royal Tom" who was supposed to inhabit the waters of Kingston's beautiful bay.

"Tom, sah, was a pow'ful shahk, 'bout thirty feet long, but nobody know how ole he was. In de ol'en times big fleets ob English men-ob-wah use to anchor off Port Royal, an'dat shahk got fat on de refuse dat was frown ovahboahd. Sometimes de sailors would heah de yallow gals laughing' an dancin' on de shoah at night an'day longed fur to jine dem. Dey wasn't lowed to go of'en in dose days' cause de yallow fevah was dere; but when de sailor boys got a chance dey would slip softly down de side an' strike out fur de shoah. Tom he know dis custom, an' he kep sharp eye on de boys, an' I'shure yo'sah, dat dat shahk gobbled up moah seamen dan 'uld fill de bigges'ob de Queen's men-ob-wah. As lots ob de sailors went ashoah fur'sertion as well as fur 'amusement, de navy people winked dere lef' eye at de tricks ob ole Tom. I hab neber seen ole Tom myself, sah, but de say dat he is 'round heah yit. Lucinda Nelson, de great fortune tellah an' hoodoo'oman done tole me dat Tom's now livin' in a big ware-house down in ole Jamaica an'dat he sel'om comes out 'cause he's gettin'quite ole. Ole Jamaica, yo mus'remembah sah, is fifteen fathom below de ocean now. Great earthquake few yeahs ago, come up one night an'swallowed de whole town an'only a few yeahs ago, when de watah was right cleah, yo'could see de tops ob some ob de houses still standing' at de bottom. I belebe Lucinda Nelson, sah, fur she's a great'oman an'knows a heap ob tings. Folks all go to her fur hoodoos an' chahms an' I reckon she mus'be close on two hun'red yeahs ole."

Captain Balbo who was close by did not seem to pay much attention to the story of Port Royal Tom. He had heard it often before; but pricked up his ears when Lucinda was mentioned and eagerly questioned the pilot as to her present whereabouts. Turning to Paul, he said; "Oi've heard a good dale about this fortune-teller, an'Oi intind to visit her; she may be able to put us onto somethin'good," Paul laughed at the idea of her knowing anything about wrecks or sunken treasure; but the captain persisted in his determination to find her when they landed.

The wind having dropped, the schooner was becalmed and lazily pitched around on the gentle swells. The captain called loudly to his-mate Betsy to bring up some fresh cigars and a bottle of grog and settled himself more comfortably on deck to enjoy the pilot's stories.

ROUGHING IT IN RUBBER

The pilot and Paul were now all attention as the captain seemed inclined to spin a yarn.

"Whin Oi wuz a strapping young fellow about eighteen, Oi wuz sailing' aboard a trader. Wan day we were laying becalmed, as we air now, off Turk's Island. While we were quietly sitting' on the bulwarks, we saw a monstrous shark off our starboard beam. The ould mon at the toime, was snorin' away in his cabin, an' it was foine chance to have a little fun. We ooy wid the shaark hook and havin' baited it wid a temptin' piece av junk, attached it to a strong line. which we rove troo the davitts. Afther smellin' round it, the shaark turned on it's side an' swallowed it. All, hands clamped on to the rope an' we hoisted him clear out av the wather. A bowline wuz passed over his tail an' we got him on board an' few blows wid the axe along the spine quieted him down. His floppin' on the deck niver woke the skipper, so we cut him open. We slit him from close under the mouth to near the tail and overhauled everything that wuz in him. In the stomach we found a collection of soup an' boullie cans an' bottles enough to start a liquor house. As we wuz examinin' the stuff, the ould mon came on deck an' thundered out:

"Phat the blazes are yea doin' there messin' me deck up!. Get the brute overboard quick an' wash down. We hoisted the carcass av the gutted shaark an' passed it over the side. We watched the body as it struck the wather. It remained still fur a few minutes, thin, to our amazement, turned over an' began swimming'. He cast his eye inquiringly up at crew, who were all standin' along the rail lookin' at him, as though he wanted somthin'. The skipper himself was so overcome at the strange soight that he forgot, fur the toime boin', all about the disgustin' state av the deck. Quickly recovering' himself, he hoarsely ordered the crew to get the stomach and internal's av that shaark overboard and get cleaned down. Three av us grasped the shaark's insides an' liftin' thim to the rail, cast thim into the say. Whin they struck the wather they were grabbed be the shark an' swallowed. As his belly was cut wide open, they went through him an' came to the surface. Three times he done this, but didn't succeed in holdin' thim in their proper place. At this toime all hands were on the rail watchin'the sport an'ivery wan laughed loud at his maneuvering. The shaark seemed to grow more vexed at each failure an'to resint the merriment of the crew for he cast many furious and malicious glances at the vessel. Once more he backed off fur an'to a charge to swallow thim an'this toime succeeded in holdin'thim in be a nate trick. Instid av turnin' partly on his side an'showin' his dorsal fin afther he had swallowed he kept bottom up and swan slowly away, waggin'avhis tail with gratified air while a huge grin spread over his repulsive countenance."

"Great lo'd, sah!" said the pilot, "dat was wonderful, indeed!'

The captain gazed sternly into the pilot's eyes to see if there was the glimmer of doubt there'in, while Paul tumbled into the cabin to suppress his fit of convulsive laughter.

During the night the threatened cyclone made its appearance and the "Foam" let go her anchor in Kingston harbor just in time to escape the full fury of the storm. After some considerable trouble at the Custom House, the cargo of the "Foam" was landed and disposed of: except the shells and curiosities gathered in the month's run through the islands.

Those as usual were cased and left in the hands of a merchant for shipment to New York. The sale of items recovered from the wreckage amounted to three hundred and twelve dollars.

After deductions the stores consumed on the vessel, the captain insisted that Paul should at least accept one hundred dollars, Paul refused as the shells obtained were equal in value to the wreckage recovered. All business was concluded and the "Foam" stocked: but the weather was still stormy and unsettled so they decided to remain over until it cleared up.

The pilot was easily persuaded and consented to act as a guide to the cabin of the dark Seeress. A long tramp through the narrow streets and a little out in the country eventually brought them to the habitation of this famed dealer in "Black Art." The house almost buried by banana trees and heavy vines. In response to the captains impatient knocks, the door was opened by a little girl, who said: "Gran won't see anyone to-night, no use in trying."

"We must see her fur, we're goin'away to-morrow an' won't have another chance," urged the captain. A querulous voice from the inside was heard saying: "Come in, Captain, come

ROUGHING IT IN RUBBER

in if you insist," an invitation that was quickly accepted by the captain who was followed by Paul and the pilot. On entering the back room, a curious sight presented itself. The seeress looked far different from the picture Paul had formed of her in his mind. She was not over five feet high and so thin and wrinkled that she resembled a mummy rather than a human being. On her head she wore a turban formed of some bright colored cloth, while the balance of her apparel consisted of a dark robe embroidered with snakes and other reptiles. The room was adorned with skins of serpents, bunches of herbs, and many weird looking objects.

"So , Captain Balbo, you came to see me at last," exclaimed the old crone; "and who is that young stranger from the far off north that I see at your side?"

The captain was dumfounded at hearing his name announced by a person whom he had never seen before, but shrewdly remarked; "If yea know me, why is it yea don't know this young stranger?"

"Ah," responded the fortune-teller, "if he sought me I would know him. He has simply accompanied you as a sightseer. Now, Captain, what can I do for you?"

"How yea know me, Lucinda, is more than Oi can comprehend. Oi've often heard av yea. As yea know me yea must be aware av me business an' can also tell phat Oi'm here fur."

"Yes. Captain, I know both and the yellow curse you are after lays in a little bay in sufficient quantities to satisfy you, on the most southern island in a group of three that bear the same name."

The captain pondered foe awhile, then said: "It must be the Caicos, fur they're the only three islands in a group that bear the same name that Oi know of."

She then went on in her mysterious way to describe to the captain a rock-locked little bay, giving him points and descriptions by which he easily recognized the island of East Caicos. She ended the conversation abruptly and ordered them out. Before leaving the captain placed a sovereign in her hand and came away deeply impressed with what the fortune-teller had revealed to him.

For quite a distance he remained profoundly silent, then turning to Paul he said: "Oi know the exact place the old divil manes.

Though she didn't name the island she described it so closely that it is impossible to mishtake it. It is East Caicos, Oi know the bay well an'it has a great reputation of bein'a resort fur pirates in olden days, an'mark me word. b'y, the visit to that old black will be the means av making' our fortune. Instead av headin'fur Little Cayman to-morrow mornin, well pint her fur East Caicos. It is over five hundred miles north by east from here: but it will pay us to make the run."

Next morning being fair, the "Foam" left Jamaica and stood off in the direction of the island. They had good weather and fair winds. In four days they passed Cape Maysi, the most easterly point of Cuba. Here they met head winds that caused them to track four more days, then they got under the lee of Great Inagua Island. The weather was very threatening and every indication pointed to another cyclone, so they decided to run the sloop into one of the sheltered bays that abound on those coasts. Here they lay for two days while the wind whistled and shrieked through the naked rigging. As they were about to get under way the third morning after they dropped anchor, a native came off in a canoe containing pineapples and coconuts which he exchanged for a few biscuits.

The captain questioned him closely in regard to wrecks around the island and was told about a large Spanish ship that went down years ago on the southeast coast and it was a legend among the inhabitants that she contained a vast amount of treasure. Nevertheless, the captain was determined to make a try for it. The indian swore that he knew the location and for a promise of a dollar a day he agreed to pilot them to the exact place. After a cruise of about thirty miles eastward, they came to the place where the Indian said the wreck had occurred and taking soundings they found the bottom, a little over nineteen fathoms. The weather was favorable so they hoved to the yawl that contained the diving pump that was then lowered.

"This is a pretty deep dive," remarked the captain to Paul as he was equipping himself in his armor.

"It is," responded Paul, "the deepest I have ever made; but

ROUGHING IT IN RUBBER

nothing risked, nothing gained. Fasten on the face piece, and you yourself attend to the signal line."

He dropped overboard and commenced descending slowly, while the captain anxiously and watchfully played out the signal line and hose. He reached bottom which was full of rocks covered with a slimy growth of marine vegetation, the pressure on him was enormous.

It was very dark and he groped for some time without discovering anything. He signaled the boat to move with him as he pursued his explorations. At last his heart was gladdened by the sight of a wreck overgrown with a heavy mass of weeds and sea plumes. After a closer investigation he was disappointed to find that she was not nearly as large as the vessel described by the Indian, but by her appearance he judged she must have been under water many, many years, All the iron work was eaten away and the timbers badly decayed.

He gave the signal, "kedge and buoy." The answer from above was "all-right," and soon after he grabbed a kedge that slowly and silently descended near him. Having fastened it to the wreck, he signaled "haul away," and was soon at the surface and helped aboard the yawl. When the helmet was removed he was totally exhausted. The captain was enthusiastic over his discovery of the wreck.

The schooner was then hailed to come alongside and all sails were lowered. One of the largest dredges was sent down and Paul descended after it. He used the dredge to clear away the masses of vegetation which covered the wreck. He fastened the claws in the decayed wood and signaling them to haul away, an entrance was at last effected into the hull. He found nothing there to reward him for his trouble and work except long white rows, which on examination proved to be grinning skulls and bones, with traces of rusty iron chains that bound them together in life. Paul was horrified at this ghastly discovery and signaled "haul away." On reaching the deck he informed captain of his find.

"A slaver, be mizzen top av the ark," he exclaimed. 'There's no use av huntin 'through that fellow, They would have no cash aboard if the skeletons are there, they'd had to sell thim furs before they'd av anything av value."

Three days were now spent in looking for the phantom treasure-ship, but the captain lost patience finally and unceremoniously kicked the Indian overboard into his canoe and the "Foam" bore away with a fair wind to the island of East Caicos.

The schooner was anchored to the lee of a reef, while the captain, Paul and two of the crew embarked in the yawl on a tour of investigation. They pulled close under the cliff and into an inlet between two great jaws of barnacle-covered rock that towered high above them. Paul was astonished to see the exact reproduction of the word picture painted by the black fortune-teller of Jamaica, before his eyes.

They rowed through the inlet on the swell and entered a bay that was perfectly land-locked. They were surrounded by a mass of irregular rock, a couple of hundred feet high, out of which great folks of gulls and other sea birds flew angrily around the intruders. "This is the place sure enough, Paul. There's no other place loike it on the oislands, Oi couldn't be mishtaken."

At that moment one of the oarsman exclaimed: "Almighty Lord, Captain! Look over there! See the sharks!"

A short glance was sufficient to reveal the fact that the water was full of those wolves of the deep and they commenced to gather around the yawl in alarming numbers.

"Be careful there, Paul," cautioned the captain, "keep yure hands in board," as he hurriedly ordered the crew to swing around and pull out. By this time more than a hundred pairs of hungry eyes were following in the wake of the boat. As she retreated, the sharks grew bolder and approached closer. It did not require my encouragement for the black sailors to pull, as their eyes were popping out of their heads and the muscles on their arms stood out like whip cords as they sent the boat flying to the schooner. They reached the side in safety and every fire-arm and harpoon on the "Foam" was called in to play against the ferocious brutes. Many a fervent prayers that the captain sent up for the welfare of the black witch in Jamaica, whom he swore he would kill on sight.

After the adventure the schooner they headed to the northwest and for the next four months, the islands and keys were thoroughly worked.

ROUGHING IT IN RUBBER

During that time, three trips were made to Nassau and valuable cargo's of recovered articles were shipped to New York.

No great treasures of any account was found, with the exception of one enormous piece of coral, in which were embedded a number of old Spanish dollars. This was sold to a tourist at Nassau for $250's.

Experience convinced Paul that the stories of great treasures in the Indies were more fabled than real, still, strange to say, ols Balbo firmly believed in them.

In a letter Paul received from his father during his last visit to Nassau, he was informed that his share of the goods shipped, had covered the cost of the submarine armor, dredging apparatus, etc., and that he had deposited eight hundred and sixty dollars in a New York bank in Paul's name. Paul showed the letter to Balboa, who to use his own expression, was "thrown on his beam ends" with astonishment. Paul now persuaded him to give up the dredging of wreckage and treasure hunting, and devote the time to seeking shells and curiosities. The old man was loath to give up his pet ideas of treasure hunting and making long, useless voyages in quest of phantoms. He agreed to turn the schooner into a "shell hunter" as he sarcastically termed it.

Everything was ready for another cruise through the Keys and small islands, when the captain, who had secretly been consulting another fortune-teller, announced his intentions of sailing to the coast of Mexico. The first point sighted was Cape Cotoche, the northeast point of Yucatan. Along this coast they were very successful and soon filled the schooner with large valuable collection of curios with which they sailed to Campachie, where they were transferred to a vessel bound for New Orleans.

While in Campachie, news came in of the wreck of a Mexican brig that had occurred on the Alakranes Bank.

The daughter of a rich planter living near Merida, Yucatan, was one of the passengers and her father offered one thousand dollars reward for the recovery of her body. An agent was sent down from Sisal to negotiate with Captain Balbo, with the result that the "Foam" bore away to the north taking along one of the surviving sailors of the brig. They sailed to

the Alakranes Bank that lay about eight miles off
the mainland. They arrived there on Saturday night and soon found anchorage.

Sunday morning the sea was as smooth as a pond of quicksilver. When they embarked in the yawl and commenced their search, the Mexican sailor was confused owing to the different conditions of the water. When he was there last, a wild sea broke over the reefs, later in the afternoon they discovered a dark object below, which proved to be the ill-fated brig. Her bottom was almost completely torn out by her contact with the reef so that she sank instantly to the lee-ward. Through the clear water they could distinctly see her two masts standing while her shattered sails lay thick and tangled through the rigging.

Next morning the schooner was taken out and anchored close by and Paul descended to the wreck. As he struck the bottom, a few feet from her, he found her heavily canted to star-board. He walked around taking care that his hose pipe would not become entangled in the rigging and clambered over her side. Two good sized sharks shot away from the deck when they heard the hissing of the air escaping from his helmet. He could see very clearly all around, owing to the direct rays of the sun reflecting on the coral reef.

On finding the deck which lay at an angle of about thirty-five degrees he discovered the iron pumps detached from their place and pinning to the bulwark the body of a dead sailor, or rather part of his body as his legs and stomark had been eaten away. This sight rather unnerved Paul, but he worked his way aft to the cabin hatch which he found securely fastened. A few blows with his pry forced it open and descending the gangway he found himself in a cabin with four state-rooms on each side. The rooms on the lower side were rather dark but he opened each door and carefully felt the bunks and bottoms for the body he was in search of. Finding nothing in the first four state-rooms, he tried the upper ones. There was much more light in these as the sun shone down through the green, clear water and in through the glass port holes. Everything buoyant in the state-room had floated up against the deck so that he had to haul and pull them down for examination. The third door he reached he could not open. It was fastened by a bolt on the inside, but when the aid of his pry he soon shot it back. Then swinging the door impatiently toward him, the eddy brought out the upright body of a young woman in her night-dress.

Her hair floated around her head like golden sea-weed as it came forward and fell against the glass face-piece of his armor. For a moment he was paralyzed with the shock, but he quickly regained his nerves, and gently placing his arm around the dead body, he reverently carried it to the deck. Her hands were clasped as though in supplication to the great power above, while her eyes protruded with terror at the fate she had met.

Hastily signaling those above to lower a line, he laid the body carefully against the shattered rigging while he went to grasp the rope. Passing it under her arms and putting two secure half hitches on it he signaled again to haul away. As she gently ascended through the clear water, a school of fish darted playfully around her as though sorry to see her go. Paul followed after and found all on deck solemn and silent, while the captains good natured wife was wrapping the corpse in a white sheet. That night a crude coffin was made in which the remains were placed and the schooner headed for Sisal, where she sailed in with her flag at half-mast.

The father faithfully paid the promised reward and the schooner under charter, returned to resume her work at the wreck. Out of this job the captain and Paul made about nine hundred dollars each.

A cruise was then made around the Gulf of Campechie which was most successful. The catch was landed at Vera Cruz whence it was shipped to New York. Paul had informed his father of the changed condition of his contract with Captain Balbo and requested the captains half of the profits of the goods last shipped.

At Vera Cruz they found letters awaiting them, one counting a robust check for Captain Balbo, which so pleased that worthy individual, that he decided to spend at least one week ashore and enjoy the comfort of a hotel. The gamblers, who abound Vera Cruz, found a rich victim in the captain, who parted with all the money he could conceal from the watchful eyes of his wife,

Betsy, with guilelessness of a boy ten years old.

A cruise was now made along the coast of Mexico; but the collection of curiosities did not pay for the time engaged, so they decided to abandon it and go back around the islands.

At Tuxpan, where they landed for fresh water, they heard of a steamer that had been burned and sunk near Tampico, so they headed the schooner for that port.

The steamer had been burned about three weeks before and the hull lay on a bank in eight fathoms of water. The agent offered to hire them to recover the safe for which he would pay the five hundred dollars, or they could have the usual salvage of, ten percent. As the rumors claimed there was over thirty thousand dollars, besides a number of valuable packs belonging to the passengers, they decided to take the ten per cent.

For four days they worked hard on the wreck, moving the confused mass of iron, which was twisted and distorted into all kinds of shapes.

On the afternoon of the fifth day, Paul sounded something solid and heavy with his pry bar, far down through the debris near the keel, and after about an hour's hard work sent up the joyful signal,

"I've got it," which was received on deck with loud cheers. The chain hooks were now sent down and after a lashing was placed around the safe, the order to "haul away" was given. All hands manned the windlass and the safe was hauled up. Paul went up to assist in getting it on board. Sail was then made and with light hearts the headed for port. The safe was locked and seem undamaged.

"There is three thousand dollars there for us Paul me b'y," said the captain as he patted the safe affectionately.

On arrival at the dock, the safe was transferred to the warehouse, where it was forced open and to their dismay and disgust found that it contained nothing of value. It was subsequently found out that the purser, seeing the ship in danger, had quietly transferred the safes money to himself and upon landing vanished with it all.

Paul laughed at their bad luck, while the captain swore picturesquely in several languages. Preparations were again made for the voyage to the islands, which had been postponed on account of the misadventure.

Later in the evening the "Foam" stood away to the east, on smooth seas, then at three o'clock the next morning a furious gale set in and increased hourly until the vessel was under bare poles and scudding for the coast. It was impossible to attempt to beat against the storm, so they stood away helplessly before it, running on to a very dangerous coast.

At six o'clock that evening, she struck in the breakers on the beach opposite Pueblo Viego. Enormous seas poured over her and swept everything from the decks. A boat was lowered but immediately smashed to atoms. In this critical position, the coolest person aboard was Betsy. She had a life preserver strapped firmly around her and was covered with one of captains oil-skins.

"I guess it is a matter of swim for it," roared Paul to the captain, "as she won't stand this very long."

At that instant the mainmast went and as it swung clear, the stays were hastily cut clear by the captain and Paul. The captain frantically motioned Betsy to grab one of the lines attached to the mast. The next moment the sea broke over her and carried the three of them, with two of the crew hanging onto the mast, which, clear of the wreck was rapidly driven towards the shore. Once the great wave broke Paul's hold, he found himself unaided swimming in the mad surf.

He was fortunate enough to catch a hatch that was floating near by which supported him to the shore, where he was thrown with considerable force and half stunned. He managed to stagger up the beach and in a few minutes discovered Betsy dragging the insensible form of the captain out of the surf.

The captain was not dead, but very near it and one of the crew had an arm broken while the other landed without injury. The three men left on the wreck were lost. When the skipper recovered consciousness he was inconsolable at the loss of his craft. That night the party found shelter in a house about half a mile from the beach where they were hospitably entertained.

At the break of day the captain and Paul were on the beach. The sea was still breaking heavily and all that was left of the staunch little Foam were her timbers scattered far up and down the sands. Among them were found the bodies of two of the men, the other was never found.

So sudden and unexpected was the loss of the vessel that Paul never thought of his money he had safely stowed away in the cabin and he stood on the beach that morning without a cent in his pocket. The loss of his diving apparatus grieved him deeply but he felt a keen sorrow for the distress of his old friend Balbo. Yet in a way, the captain was more fortunate than himself as Betsy had safely stored all their earnings in the voluminous folds of her dress.

All day long the Captain, Betsy and Paul and the uninjured seaman, patrolled the beach in the hope that something valuable might wash ashore. But other than a few articles of clothing and some casks, nothing came ashore. The next morning after another visit to the beach a passage was obtained to Tampico, where they arrived the same evening. After some days they were at a loss as to what to do until a vessel appeared in the harbor bound for New Orleans.

On this the captain, Betsy, and the two seaman procured passage, vainly urging Paul to join them, but he had a lingering hope that he might yet recover his diving apparatus with the aid of primitive dredges of the Mexican fisherman.

He saw them on board the ship with affectionate farewell of his old friends. Before parting the Captain insisted on giving Paul a small loan which he said could be returned at any time. There was a suspicious dimness in his eyes as he crushed Paul's hands in his own, while Betsy cried as she heartily kissed him goodbye. Paul engaged a small fishing craft and went back to the wreckage in hopes of recovering his diving armor, but his efforts were in vain, abandoning the search he reluctantly returned to Tampico.

While sitting unconsolable on the pizza of the little hotel in Tampico, he was approached by an American: "Well young fellow I've heard that you have had pretty hard luck. What do you intend to do?"

"That's just about what I would like to know myself."

"Well, I think I can post you," said his new acquaintance, as he leisurely seated himself and hoisted his heels on the rail.

"There is a good chance for active young fellows just now. I preson you never did much soldiering, but I guess you can fire a gun."

"Why yes," responded Paul,"I think I could manage that."

The stranger then told Paul that he was connected with the Revolutionists, whose headquarters were then at Palmas and assured him that he would be taken good care of. Paul who was at the time open for anything that would turn up, quickly accepted the proposition.

The next morning he and fourteen others mounted on mules, and conveying a pack train were pursuing their way up the mountain road in the direction of the headquarters. His filibustering friend furnished Paul with a pretty good rifle and revolver, and informed him that they were on their way to join a party under the command of General Pedro Martinez.

He also told him that his own name was Colonel Sawyer, that he had been born in Texas, but had spent most of his life on the frontier and was involved in many of the Revolutions that disturbed the Republic of Mexico. His principal occupation was running arms and ammunition from the coast to the Revolutionists in the interior.

For three days they continued this journey, camping every night. About ten o'clock on the morning of the fourth day, they were surrounded by the cry of "Halta, halta." Looking up from where the hail came, they saw the muzzles of thirty to forty rifles pointed at them. Colonel Sawyer loudly cried in answer to their command. "Amigos." In a few moments they were surrounded by a skirmishing party of Revolutionists and escorted to the camp.

Here Paul found several Americans, all soldiers of fortune, none of whom gave him very encouraging accounts of the prospects. Two weeks were spent in the camp from which small expeditions were sent out everyday. Paul accompanied one of these to the national road running from Tampico to Monterey, and between the villages of Liera and Maleta. They had a skirmish and succeeded in capturing a carriage, hauled by four horses which contained some persons of importance as he was treated with the utmost respect by the Commander and conveyed a prisoner to the camp. The horses were unhitched from the carriage which was left on the road.

Soon after Paul and a party under the command of Sawyer, were sent to the town of Bagarono where a cargo of arms had been landed. These by the aid of pack mules were safely transferred to the camp. Soon after there was a heavy engagement in which the entire body of Revolutionists participated near Ciudad Victoria.

The revolutionists were badly repulsed and retreated to the mountains.

After this it was nothing but a series of raids which were both laborious and unsatisfactory. Paul was fast tiring of this semi-barbarous mode of warfare so that he and four of his companions decided to discharge themselves on the first favorable opportunity. It came sooner than they expected.

They were sent under the command of Sawyer and others to Metamoras for ammunition. On reaching there, they found the schooner with the promised supply had arrived. After waiting for some days news came that the Revolutionists had again been repulsed and were all in retreat.

This decided Sawyer, who said: "Boys, the jig is up and the best thing we can do is to get across the river and into the United States."

That night they crossed the Rio Grande in an old tub of a boat that they expected would go to the bottom every moment and landed safely in safety at Brownsville, on American shore.

Here Paul wrote letters home and requested his father send him money to Galveston. With the little money they had, mustangs and provisions were purchased and they started on the long ride to Corpus Christi. It was a wild journey through the chaparral, over the burnt and dried grass of the prairie, across swamps and rivers, they managed to travel the two hundred miles in eight days.

Here they separated. While his companion sought employment with the ranchers, Paul for consideration of his mustang, rifle and revolver, induced the captain of a coaster to give him passage to Galveston. He arrived in Galveston and found himself without a cent. He opportunely remembered his father had a friend there in person of ex-Governor Lubbock, whom he had found. He was cordially received by the Governor, who not only supplied him with all he wanted, but insisted upon him staying in his house until the letter arrived.

Ten days later he long awaited letter arrived with the money.

CHAPTER THREE

Paul lost no time in securing passage on the steamer Haridan bound for New Orleans and from there to New York, where he arrived on June second, 1867.

He was warmly received by his family and surprised to find that his father had a good sum of money in the bank for him. Paul was now in his nineteenth year; he was strong and so bronzed with the sun that he looked twenty-five. For sometime after his home coming and unsure of what to do, and once or twice considered investing in a new out fit and heading back out to the West Indies. But the pleadings of his mother to abandon the wandering life style that he thoroughly enjoyed, and to settle down to a steady business prevailed, and his father assisted him in opening a store in Philadelphia selling curiosities and Oriental goods.

A branch at Cape May was also opened. He was very successful and disposed of large quanties of goods to the visitors there. For two years he successfully pursued this mercantile life and was establishing a good business, while at Cape May during the summer time his old love of the water drew him constantly to the beach, where his magnificent and fearless swimming attracted the attention of all. At times he would swim so far out in the rolling waves that people could not see his head.

His extraordinary power in this line, proved of great value to many unfortunate bathers who were carried out by the under tow and were in danger of drowning. Paul was always ready to swim to their assistance, the first season he spent on the beach, he succeeded in saving fourteen lives.

Many testimonials were presented to him for his bravery. He was very popular with the visitors, but not so with the native boatman who looked upon his life saving and the perquisites attached, as their own, and wondered how a volunteer dared to do better than them.

His second season was more successful in both life-saving and business, and he made many friends with the people he had saved.

One day an excursionist swam far out over the breakers, when he turned to come back to shore, he was alarmed either at the distance or the under current, he lost his courage and cried loudly for help.

Paul was on the beach at the time, and quickly, stripping down he swam through the breakers to his assistance. The man was very difficult to handle, as he was terrified, refusing to cooperate with Paul, but he insisted on climbing on Paul's back.

After extreme difficulty Paul managed to swim to shore with the burden on his back, the man was unconscious by the time they reached the beach and Paul totally exhausted. Later that day while Paul was talking to a group of people, the excursionist pulled Paul aside, and said;

"Say, mister, I hear that you are the man that saved me this morning, I am very grateful. I am going home, and if you ever catch me in that darn water, I give you permission to drown me.. Before I go, I would like to reward you."

Paul assured him that he required nothing, and was just happy that he was alive, and that alone was sufficient reward. The persistent individual was not satisfied, he took from his pocket a dilapidated fifty-cent note, fervently pressing it into Paul's hand, he said;

"You take that and remember me."

Paul was surprised by the liberal gift, but quickly recovering, he said to the departing excursionist: "Hold on, my friend, you are forgetting something." Carefully counting forty-nine cents from a handful of change he drew out of his pocket, he handed it to the rescued man and remarked; "I could not think of taking a cent more than your life is worth."

On another occassion, Paul succeeded in rescuing a young lady who was being rapidly carried out to sea and who would certainly have been drowned but for his aid. In his struggles to get her ashore, he was compelled two or three times to grasp her roughly by the hair. When landed, she was unconscious and in that state was conveyed to her hotel. Paul met a friend of the lady on the beach and inquired, how Miss ------- was getting along. "Oh very well," was the response; but she is a very curious young lady."

"How is that?" asked Paul.

"Well, when I visited her this morning I remarked that she ought to be very grateful to you for saving her life." "I am," she

ROUGHING IT IN RUBBER   43

hesitantly answered. "But I think he might have acted a little more gentlemanly and not caught me by the hair, I have a frightful headache."

There is an old saying. "That if you wish to make an enemy of a man, just save his life or lend him money." Paul's experience convinced him that the saying was true. Many and many persons have been saved from a watery grave, who never even took the trouble to find him and say thank you.

In the fall of 1869 Paul lost everything he had in a great fire at Cape May and he left there heavy hearted and disgusted with business. Soon after his father died and home was very, very lonely. When the estate was settled up, Paul's old love for travel and adventure came strongly back to him. The Franco - Prussian war broke out.
He believed that it was the opportunity he was looking for.

He embarked from New York to Liverpool, hence to Havre, where he presented himself at the Hotel de Ville and offered his services as an American volunteer. At this time the French military authorities were not accepting volunteers as readily as they did later on, so Paul had much difficulty in getting enrolled in the service as a Franc-tircur.

A few days after he had landed in Havre, he was marching away with a chassepot rifle on his shoulder and a nap-sack and blanket on his back. His uniform consisted of a black tunic with yellow trimmings, blue pants with wide red stripes down the sides, a red sash around the waist, over which circled the belt which supported his saber, bayonet and revolver. It also held a revolver, the only one of the kind in his company, with a bowie knife, which he had carried from America, shoes, leather gaiter's and kepi or cap completed the uniform.

The company was about sixty strong, all picked men, Paul was the only foreigner in the lot. It was known as la Deuxrieme Compagnie Franc-tireurs du Havre. The only visible difference between the regular and the irregular was the lack of regulation buttons on the latter, and that they had no commissary department and had to provision themselves.

Their pay was thirty sous (cents) a day and they received their salary every morning. Out of this they were supposed to support themselves. Not withstanding this small pay it was the highest given to any of the troops in the French army, as the regulars only received six cents per day, but the Government provided them with food. Taking it in turns to cook, while the others would visit farm houses in the vicinity of the camp to purchase produce. Paul's knowledge of French was limited, but the Marchal de Logis a petty officer and a Havre pilot named Vodry could kinda speak english. They acted as interpreters for him and gave him French lessons.

In the few weeks the company was camped out near Havre, Paul acquired enough French for the necessary words and to understand the commands and terms to pass muster with any in the company. While still in camp, the news of the fall of Sedan was received and the tieures were hurried forward to the vicinity of Paris on which the Prussians were rapidly advancing.

Their first engagement was at Creteil. On the eleventh of December 1870 they were in skirmishes for General Vinoy, who had about fifteen thousand men. The engagement started early in the morning by the Franc-tireurs on the hills of Mely. They were soon dislodged by the powerful artillery fire of the enemy and retreated to Charenton.

Five of Paul's company were killed in the engagement and several wounded. After this they were engaged daily in skirmishes around Paris. Paul understood little of what was going on, through the reports from his comrades and they did not really understands half of it either. They were definitely slowly being driven back, that was very apparent to him.

In many of the skirmishes with the enemy, though several were successful, he noticed that the tireurs never pressed them in the direction in which they retired.

One day near Evereux they saw a balloon coming towards them and a cloud of dust on the road far below showed them that a party of enemy Uhlans were pursuing them.

The balloon was rapidly descending, the company was ordered into ambush on each side of the road, while the Uhlans were watching the balloon descend, they were unaware of the hidden enemy. As they rode past the ambush, the order was given to fire. Twenty riderless horses dashed madly up and down the road, while the surviving Uhlans took off on foot. The

ROUGHING IT IN RUBBER

balloon descended a short distance from the scene.

A man named Bu Norof brought them the dispatches from Paris that was then besieged, so their next engagement was Mantes, they were under command of General Mocquard, a brave soldier who was always seen out front mounted on a little wiry Arab steed.

Soon after this engagement the company, with the new men replacing the causalities, was joined to the Arme de la Loire.

On October the seventh 1871, started many skirmishes, Toureey, losing many men, then Turcos with the a French African regiment, who distinguished themselves during the fight, forty-seven prisoners were captured. October the ninth, the great battle of Orleans, which lasted for two days. The battle was a desperate one, and losses on both sides were great.

The enormous armies were engaged in this battle, the marching and counter-marching so rapid, and the deafening roar of artillery, all added to confuse Paul, and he did not realize the army was in retreat until told by one of his companions.

From then until January, the Franc-tireurs were engaged in many skirmishes and harassed the enemy whenever an opportunity arose. They were slowly and surely driven back by the great German army until they crossed the Seine. Finding themselves in the territory of Seine Inferieure, that was then invaded by advance corps of enemy.

Not withstanding all the scenes of carnage that Paul witnessed, and the dangers surrounding them. He still felt those were the happiest days of his life, free from all the business troubles and with no property on earth except that contained in his knapsack.

The old spirit of mischief in his nature was continually asserting itself, and he was always happy, no matter how somber were his surroundings. In the part of France where they were encamped the peasants were considered rich and very frugal. As before, when the Franc-tircurs camped, parties were detailed to purchase provisions for the different messes. Two would go after bread and beef, two after coffee, sugar, etc., and another two after potatoes and vegetables. The last detail was Paul and Vodry's favorite. Thus the peasants hid all the poultry in safe places, like the bedroom of the farm house, where the fowls roosted in tranquility on the head and foot of the bed, while the disappointed Franc-tircurs searched for ingredients for their soup.

The majority of peasants believed Americans were all wild indians. Paul and Vodry used this belief to their advantage. Taking a sack with them, they departed to one of the surrounding farm houses, concocting a scheme on the way that invariably met with success. Before reaching the house they would separate, Vodry going in first with the sack.

When he entered the kitchen of the spotlessly clean Normandy farm house, he would politely remove his cap and in a most courteous manner inform the peasants that he was from the Franc-tircurs camp, and came for the purpose of purchasing pommes de terre (potatoes). While the produce was being measured out, he would engage the family in some stories of the war, which would invariably end up with the question: "Bye the way, did you know that we have an American in our company?"

This information immediately aroused their curiosity, as they showered questions on him regarding the customs of the wild creatures. Vodry would then entertain them with the tale of how Paul left his distant home, thousands of miles away and crossed the ocean to fight for Le Belle France. He generally finished by saying; "Perhaps you would like to meet him. he accompanied me over here, generally he does not like to come inside the house, so he remains outside while I came in."

Then without waiting he would go to the door and beckon Paul. Paul would quickly appear from around some out-house or hay stack, looking totally different from the normal daily dress. A slouch hat filled with feathers waved around his head in a graceful confusion, a silver gray poncho blanket covered his uniform, outside was strapped his revolver and bowie knife. Several daubs of wet brick dust and blue pencil marks adorned his face. In response to Vodry's call he would bound in with a yell that made the windows in the house rattle, saluting the farmer with a vigorous shake of the hand and gracefully kissed the hands of the good dame and her daughters, if she happened to have any, then walking around the kitchen he would examine all the utensils and instruments with an absorbing interest as if he never saw such things before.

ROUGHING IT IN RUBBER

While observing him with awe and admiration for his devotion to France, they would exclaim, "What a good young man, what a brave fellow," etc., etc.

Finding that the time for action had arrived, Paul would approach the farmer and while ringing his hands, would say in broken French:

"Cognac bon, cognac bon."

The enthusiastic and sympathetic mistress of the house would immediately say: "Ah, the poor boy wants a drop of cognac! Get him some father!" The reluctant farmer procured a big bottle and a very diminutive glass known as the "petite verse," which held about a thimbleful. Paul would congratulate the good dame on her keen perception. At this period Vodry would generally object saying:

"It is not good to give him cognac as the Americans can not control themselves when they take liquor."

His objections were over ruled and the farmer presented Paul with a miserable little glass full to the brim. This Paul insisted that the matron should drink first and on its being replenished he more emphatically insisted that the farmer should drink before him.

While the farmer was drinking, Paul generally secured the bottle as if to relieve him of its charge while drinking. The moment he secured it he gave a wild whoop and placing it to his lips took a seemingly long swig, after which he executed a fantastic war dance around the kitchen to the alarm of the farmer and his worthy family who were only to glad to see him disappear through the door, Vodry remaining to remonstrate with them in regard to their folly in having given fire-water to this American. He assured them that if he could procure the liquor he would return it, then with his bag of potatoes expressed his sorrow at the occurrences.

Paul waited for him in the hedges at the dike, the two conspirators resumed their way back to camp. That evening Paul's mess enjoyed the much cherished coffee and cognac so dear to every French heart.

One day Paul was doing duty as a sentinel on an outpost, when a large fat hare appeared on a little hillock not thirty yards from where he stood. Before he remembered about the strict orders given out that there was to be no firing unless at an enemy. Paul raised his rifle and sent a bullet crashing through its body. Paul had no time to pick up the hare before he saw the relief advancing on "double quick." So he stood on his post , saluted the officer in command, and in reply to his inquiry said that his gun had gone off accidently. The officer scrutinized him closely, then looking around soon discovered the cause of the accident. He sent a soldier for the hare, examined it, and placed Paul under arrest, at the same time remarking "that for an accidental discharge of a gun it had a most remarkable effect and that only an American could cause such an accident." After a few hours detention in the guard house, Paul was allowed his liberty.

Being the only foreigner, he was a favorite in the company and many of his escapades were overlooked, if a Frenchman had been guilty of the same he would have been severely punished. The captain of Paul's company at this time was an officer whose voice was very weak, and he could never finish a command in the same pitch he had started. He invariably broke down, and the command was ended in a hoarse whisper. This peculairty often caused the Franc-tireurs to smile.

One morning as the company was ready to march, the captain, mounted on a powerful horse, was at their head. Wheeling about and drawing his sword he gave the orders: "Attencion compagnie! En evant." He then suddenly broke down and paused to recover his breath and Paul in a low undertone and in exact imitation of the captain added the word that ought to follow, "Mar-r-che!."

This drew forth a smothered laugh from the whole company. The captain turned fiercely around and demanded to know who mimicked him. Dead silence prevailed. He gave them a lecture on respect due to an officer and stated that the next offender of this kind would be severely punished: then added: " I can't find out who it was, but on my soul I believe it was that crazy American."

After this the company took part in many engagements through Normandy, principally at St. Roumain, Beuzeville, Yvetot, Rouen and Bulbec. The company suffered severely and in the last battle were a mere handful. There they lost their

ROUGHING IT IN RUBBER 49

brave lieutenant Boulonger, who was shot through the breast. Paul and a party of his companions were detailed to convey the body to Havre, his home, where he was well known and respected.

Here for the first time in his life Paul saw the French military burial mass. This was the most solemn ceremony he had ever witnessed. An officer occupied a position on the steps of the altar and with unsheathed sword faced the soldiers, then standing in the body of the church. He gave orders in a loud voice at intervals during the service and his commands sounded strangely through the echoing arches of the cathedral.

At the order "restez armes," the iron shod butts of the muskets dropped together on the stone floor, reminding those present of the stern realities of war and sweet consolations of religion.

The survives of the company to which Paul belonged were now drafted into the regular army in the section known as "Bataillon Des Tirailleurs." Paul did not relish the change from the free and easy life of the Franc-tireurs to the strict discipline of the regular army. It was drill, drill all day long and as the pay was now only six cents a day and paid only once a week, they had little chance to play their favorite game of "Petit paquet,"a game that had been more regular than prayers in the camp "Franc-tireurs." Having become thoroughly drilled in the use of the "Gatling gun" the company was ordered to the front.

One evening a comrade said to Paul: "We will have bloody work to-morrow, General Manteuffel's army is advancing." But the expected battle was never fought. That night news came that caused a heavy gloom on all in the camp. "Paris has fallen." Soon after came the news of armistice and that no more fighting will take place for thirty days, the two armies lay within plain sight of each other. Discipline was strictly enforced; several French soldiers were executed for neglect and disobedience of orders.

One cold night Paul stood guard over the Gatling gun that was kept in a shed with no sides, as the fierce cold wind whistled and penetrated his bones. He was worn out with the heavy day's drill and concluded that he could watch the gun as well above in the shelter as by standing alongside it. He climbed up on the beam and stretched himself out on a board, he knew that it was instant death to be caught causing the government a great deal of trouble, as regiment by regiment were being hurried out of town.

Paul managed to reach the capitol, and being left to his own resources he was greatly bewildered, the stirring and exciting scenes were hard to comprehend. One evening while passing along the boulevard near the Madeleine, a soldier wearing the uniform of the Foreign Legion peered into his face and eagerly inquired if he could speak United States. Paul I answered, "yes," the soldier was delighted and asked "Have you got any money? I am from Baltimore," all in the same breath. Paul told him that he had a few francs and that he was perfectly willing to share, and invited him to dinner. The two went off to the boulevard, pursued their way along the narrow streets until they struck something more in keeping with their financial standing. Here they entered a modest looking cafe and ordered a ragout.

While seated at the table they continued their conversation in English, the sour looking landlord after taking their order eyed them suspiciously for a few moments, while trying to understand their conversation. Rushing to the door of an adjoining room he loudly called:

"Corporal, come here. Prussians!"

The room was quickly invaded by a Corporal and one of his friends with drawn sabers in their hands. Paul and his companion, who saw that were about to be attacked, grabbed chairs and backed into a corner, where they defended themselves against attack. Paul asked them in his best french what they meant and assured them that they were not Prussians, but American volunteers. When they heard this information they lowered their sabers as their assailants interigated them, receiving satisfactory answers to all their questions and convinced that Paul and his companion were what they represented themselves to be. The Frenchmen gravely begged to be pardoned and warmly invited them into the adjoining room to have supper with them.

During supper Paul ascertained that their entertainers were officers in Communes that were forming groups in all parts of Paris. They were invited to join the ranks of the "liberators" as

ROUGHING IT IN RUBBER

they called themselves, after the reception they had got from the gentlemen they wisely thought they had better oblidge, and they were then enrolled.

That night they had a comfortable lodging provided for them and were told to report at ten o'clock the next morning. During the night Paul and his Baltimore friend had a long talk over the situation, they were far from satisfied. Leonard, the Baltimorean, suggested that before they took arms up against the government, they had better investigate a little further. With this intention they rose very early and started for a more respectable quarter of the city. When they turned the corner they were amazed to meet the gentlemen Corporal, who was trying the night before to slit their throats. He wanted to know where they were going.

The plausibly assured him that "as they could not sleep in their lodging on account of fleas they had decided to take a mouthful of fresh air."

"Well," responded the Corporal, "you had better take a mouthful of something else." Come with me and have a petit verrie." They accompanied him to the cafe and pretended to enjoy themselves, which however, they were far from doing. After some conversation with the Corporal said: "Mes enfants you must be around here at ten o'clock".

Assuring him that they would be on hand and to have no fear. When he had departed they quickly left the cafe and resumed their walk towards the Tuilleries. They wandered around and around through the narrow streets until they had utterly lost their bearings. Coming at last to a wide Avenue in which there seemed to be great amount of excitement. The cafe's were all full of men and woman, the sidewalks were thronged with mad crowds, while cries of "Vive la Commune" were heard on all sides. Through the crowds on the sidewalks and caf'es, observing many soldiers of the "Grand Nationals" who were under the influence of liquor. The names of "Lecompte," "Thomas" and "Darboy," were frequently mentioned by the drunken and excited crowds. A fierce cheer echoed along the street. The woman of Monmartre with long ropes attached to cannons came streaming up the boulevard. It was a wild and never to be forgotten sight. Many of the women wore army coats over which their hair floated loosely. Through such exciting scenes as these, Paul and his Baltimore friend lost all count of the hours. It was noon before they remembered their ten o'clock appointment, even if they had wanted too they could not have found the location again. Wandering around they came back to the boulevard near the Rue de la Paix. In this vicinity they saw the first engagement take place between the Communists and the body of citizens called "Les Hommes d' Ordre." While the firing was going on they stepped in a door way that sheltered them from the flying bullets. Shortly afterwards they found themselves on the Rue Rivolo.

They saw large amounts of troops marching past the building, Paul noticed an officer whom he recognized from his time in the Franc Tireurs. Calling to out his companion as he quickly entered the same building as the officer, they were instantly confronted by a sentinel asking what their business was. They informed him that they wished to see the officer who had just entered, but were told that he could not be found, they were then detained by a sentinel, who refused to allow them to leave.

He called for a Corporal du garde who placed both of them under arrest and marched them into a room where many officers were seated. Among them, Paul noticed the officer he came to see, he immediately recognized Paul and asked him why he had come to Paris. Paul told him he had come through curiosity and if necessary to take a hand in anything that was going on. Paul and his friend were then introduced to all the officers present. One of them a gray headed old fellow said,

"Well boys, I think we will find something for you to do, but as this is a quarrel among Frenchman, I don't like the idea of any foreigners being mixed up in it. However as you are here we might as well use you." Paul and his companion looked at each other with perplexity for they did not know what they were about to join. Turning to his friend the Marechal de Logis, he told him in english of their adventures the night before as asked him if this was the same army as the others. The officer laughed heartily translating the story for the benefit of the others, who all joined in his mirth. The gray haired man who had first spoken to Paul and who was evidently an officer of higher rank said in pure english:

ROUGHING IT IN RUBBER

"Sons I think you have done enough for France and it is best for you to leave Paris and go home."

Then calling an orderly he gave instructions that they should be taken to the rail road station and sent to Havre. Before leaving, he gave each of them twenty-five francs and instructed the orderly to secure them a seat on the train to the sea-coast. The orderly who accompanied them to the station was enthusiastic admirer of everything American. He had a brother in Quebec, a city he thought was about fourteen miles outside New York. So great was the hospitality that he showed Paul and his companion as they entered the station. Who then ignored his military dignity as if nothing else mattered other the comfort of his American friends.

He booked them in a first class compartment against the remonstrance of the guard, whom with drawn sabre, he defied.

As the train left the station, cries of "Vive la France," "Vive V Amerique," were exchanged.

On arriving in Havre, Paul found many volunteers placed in the same position as himself. All were awaiting a chance to return to America, most of them looking to the French government to assist them to get home. While waiting for these orders to be given, that were taking a long time in coming, Paul made the acquaintance of a Danish Count who had served all through the war. His quiet, gentle manners and evident embarrassment at being surrounded by the rough crowd of adventurers and soldiers of fortune, with whom fate had thrown him amongst, appealed to Paul's sympathy.
He said to the Count, "come with me and I will take care of you." They secured lodging together on the upper story in a house in Rue de l'Hopital for the princely consideration of a franc a week, which the landlady insisted be paid in advance.

With the air of a millionaire, Paul paid the first weeks rent and cheerfully requested they get the best room in the house. Their room turned out to be a miserable attic room, lit up with one small window. The scant bedding often compelled them to sleep in their uniforms on the chilly nights. When they reached the apartment, comparing notes and found they all money between them, amounting to eight francs and seventy five centimes, (about $1.75).

"We must sail close to the wind now, Count," said the ever cheerful Paul to the despondent Dane. "With good management we can live high on a Franc a day."

They did not live high, but they subsisted. Paul had entire charge of the budget and he drove a hard bargain with those whom he patronized. The little square two cent cakes of sausage were eagerly scrutinized while he weighed the one cent loaves of bread in his hand. Every two cent herring was examined as closely as a gourmand would a porter-house steak or some rich game. When the provisions were secured, Paul returned to the apartment " Now for the banquet," he would exclaim as he lit up a sou's worth of wood with which to fry the herring. He prevailed the Count to go down and get a pitcher of water, which made up their morning drink.

After the meals they generally went out to ascertain news from the government in regards to sending them home. This mundane routine continued for many weeks. As time advanced things were getting more and more desperate, the Count became very gloomy and despondent that Paul feared he would end his life as he had threatened to do several times, unless something turned up.

They were now indebted to the landlady for two weeks rent, she had a very sharp tongue and used to fire a broadside at them every time she would meet them. In passing her door while ascending or descending, they would remove their shoes as they did not wish to hear her tongue lashings, they had great respect for her ladyship .

Things continued to grow worse and worse until at last Paul spent the few sous they had on two small loaves and a herring. They did not have enough for wood to cook it with. Before retiring that night Paul suggested to the Count the necessity of them trying to get some work, to which the Count replied that he would prefer death any time to the idea of going to work.

Long before daylight Paul slipped quietly out of bed, dressed himself in his old uniform and headed in the direction of the docks. Near one of the bridges he saw a large group of men standing around. He joined them and learned that they were all waiting for work, and that they expected the contractor to arrive any minute. The boss soon made his appearance and started

ROUGHING IT IN RUBBER

reading from a slip of paper:

I want ten men at such a dock, five men at another place, eight men at yet another place and twenty-five men at the dry docks." The crowd separated itself into gangs, Paul joining one that was called last. As the men passed the contractor, each one was handed a slip.

When Paul's turn came to get his slip, the contractor looked at him curiously and said:

"Why you are an American volunteer, what do you want here?"

"I want work," answered Paul, "and pretty badly too."

"Well," said the contractor: "I am sorry that I don't have a better job to give you today, but by to-morrow I will have something better for you."

Paul followed the gang to the dry docks where a large steamer had been hauled up. On presenting his piece of paper to the foreman, he received a three cornered scraper, a piece of sharp steel with a handle about eighteen inches long. He was told of a certain plank suspended by ropes down the side of the vessel in company with two old dock rats who eyed him rather sullenly as though he was an intruder. Paul quickly slipped down the rope and seated himself on the plank, while the two professors climbed leisurely down and took a seat on each end, he occupying the middle. The side of the ship was thickly studded with barnacles and other shell fish.

She had just returned from a long voyage to the tropics and was very foul. The air was chilly and raw down on the dark, damp stone dock. Paul was anxious to warm himself, so made a furious onslaught on the barnacles and soon had them flying in every direction. He stopped for a breath and found that his companions, instead of following his example, were gazing at him with looks of disgust and astonishment.

One of them exclaimed:

"Regard him, look at him!"

While the other, with feigned pity, tapped his forehead with the tips of his fingers, as much as to say, "He's crazy, my brother." One of them placed his hand on Paul's arm and asked him how long he had been scraping ships bottoms.

"This is my first day," answered Paul, thinking he might have done something wrong.

"I thought so" responded his questioner. "A few more mad men like you would ruin our work in the docks. Why, at the way you are going the ship's bottom would be clean before nightfall. This is the way to do it," and he put his scraper against the side and slowly and laboriously removed a single barnacle. Then he laid the scraper down and lit his pipe. After taking a few whiffs he asked Paul where he was from and what made him seek this kind of work. Paul fully explained his position and why he needed this work. After this his two companions thawed out and gave him advice as how to waste time when the foreman was not around. At noon all hands were called up to the dock and given a card to the value of two francs, which the foreman told Paul he can have cashed at the canteen by purchasing a dish of soup or small piece of bread. Paul indulged in a five cent dinner and deeply regretted the Count was not there to share it with him. He received one franc and seventy five centimes which he carefully stowed away. After dinner the plank was again lowered and they resumed work on the barnacles. Before the six o'clock bell rang to quit working, Paul and his two companions became quite friendly. They told him that if he intended to continue this job he should remember one thing:

"Never do what you did this morning, that is slip down the ropes first, particularly when there are three men working on a plank," they gravely explained, " the two coming down last would occupy seats close to the ropes that not only act as a back brace when resting yourself, but would also be a means of saving your life in case the plank broke."

"At six o'clock Paul received another ticket for two more francs. To get it cashed he purchased a glass of wine for two sous and started on an excited run for his lodging where he fully expected to find the Count dead. He ran the blockade of the landlady's door without removing his shoes. Dashing into the room he exclaimed:

"Count! Count, where are you?"

" Here I am," exclaimed a faint voice from the bed.

" Well, I'm glad you are not dead, we dine at the window's today. Look at this."

The Count started up and gazed at the seventy-three cents Paul held out with eager eyes, then looking reproachfully at him

ROUGHING IT IN RUBBER

he said:

"Paul, I hope you have not taken to the highway."

"No," said Paul, "I worked for that and hard too, so come and we have such a dinner as we have not had in over two weeks."

That night the landlady received one week's room rent and graciously gave them three more days to settle up in full. Paul was out again before daylight and sought out the contractor. This day he got a job on the ship Fanita of San Francisco, discharging grain. It was much cleaner and easier than scraping the steamers bottom. His job was to guide the sacks of grain out of the hold while the horse on the deck attached to a long line passed over a block hoisted them up.

While working the two mates of the ship stood near the hatchway and commenced making remarks about Paul whom they thought was a Frenchman.

"There is one of those Frenchman soldiers," said one.

"Yes," added the other; he looks pretty hungary and thin, it is no wonder the Dutch licked them."

Paul smiled, but said nothing until a better opportunity presented itself, when he joined in the conversation with the mate, who was very surprised to find that he was an American.

At dinner time he was invited into the galley and served sea-pie until he was barely able to halloa "Allons," to the driver of the horse on the dock, then he resumed work for the afternoon. That evening he was asked by the caption of the vessel to keep tally on the number of sacks at five cents per diem.

A few days later an order was issued from the Hotel de Ville that all foreign volunteers should assemble there. A hundred and twenty responded to the call and a motley group they were, mustered from all quarters of the globe, representing almost every branch of the French service and wearing every conceivable kind of a uniform. Notwithstanding the fact that some of them were from Norway, Sweden, Denmark, Ireland, England, Belgium, etc., they all wanted to be sent to America.

The mayor informed them that arrangements had been made to transport them at the expense of the French government. He also said that he was authorized to give each volunteer the sum of twenty-five francs, a mattress, blanket and a supply of tin-ware.

This good news was received with loud cries of "Vive la France,"

"Vive la Republique!," and three hearty cheers very given for the mayor. As the volunteers joyously disappeared, an officer informed Paul that the mayor wished to see him in his private office.

When he entered, His Honor informed him that he would like Paul to take charge of the men on his passage back to America.

"I know they are a pretty wild lot, and no doubt will not obey orders, still I will depend on you to do your utmost to keep them quite, and not have them disgrace the uniform they wear."

He then gave Paul a strong letter of recommendation commending him for his courage and service to France, also presenting him with the arms he bore in service. To this day Paul retains (his family) his chassepot as a memento of his happy, careless days he passed, while serving under the Tricolor of France.

Two days later all foreign volunteers were mustered to embark on the steamer Stromboli, the authorities taking the precaution not to give them the twenty-five francs until they had passed up the gang plank.

As the steamer moved out of Havre the citizens turned out in large numbers to bid them God speed. And when the bows of the steamer were kissed by the waves of the channel, the boys were all pretty hoarse shouting "Vive la France" in exchange for the cries of "Vive Amerique," that was sent over the water to them from the mighty crowd on shore.

The voyage to Liverpool was an uneventful one and the volunteers behaved well with the exception of an emptying a cask of wine which the immediately filled up again with water. This was the property of two French passengers who spent most of their time playing cards on deck and whose amazement when they discovered their wine had turned into water.

On arrival in Liverpool they heard the steamer England, which was to convey them to the United States had broken down, so they were compelled to to remain in Liverpool for several days at the expense of the steamship company, until the Virginia of the same line was ready to sail.

ROUGHING IT IN RUBBER

While in Liverpool they were treated well and aroused a great deal of interest due to the varied uniforms and war-stained appearance. While Paul and three of his companions were slowly sauntering the streets early one morning, watching the sights, Paul noticed smoke coming from a basement of a rubber store, while the employees were rushing out of the building.

Paul grabbing one of them asked if there was water anywhere around, and was informed that there was both water and hose attached in the basement, but the smoke would smother him before it could be reached. Without hesitation Paul, plunged into the basement, and fortunately came right on the hose.

Turning on the water he fought his way back through the thick smoke and soon had the fire under control, It was a heap of rubbish and scrap rubber that emitted far more smoke than flame. When the fire engine arrived there was nothing left to do, the proprietor was so pleased to have had his store saved that he gave Paul five pounds.

When the Virginia was ready to sail, all the soldiers were transferred off to her lighters. On reaching the deck they were all checked for revolvers and other weapons that were turned over to the quarter-master and would be returned to them on arrival in New York.

There were a number of German emigrants and the steamship officers thought there might be some trouble. Besides the soldiers, there were eight hundred emigrants from different parts of Europe, mostly from Ireland and about fifty cabin passengers.

The voyage was very rough and took twenty-one days. Many a wild trick was played, the favorite was cutting down hammocks, dark forms could be seen on all fours making their way on the greasy slippery deck in the direction of the selected victims, causing an uproar that awakened the entire steerage. Many a skirmish was nipped in the bud through the watchful eyes of the officers, which otherwise might have led to bloodshed.

During the voyage many of the soldiers suffered from tobacco withdrawals, the ship's doctor, a little Irishmen from Dublin, often supplied them with the much need tobacco, and he had more control over them than all the officers on board. His quick wit one day prevented a fight that could have ended deadly, it was one of the fine days that the hatches could be removed for fresh air. A german immigrant drew a knife on one of the soldiers, making vicious strike at him. Sides were immediately formed between the soldiers and immigrants, as the fight went on under the main hatch. It was interrupted by a loud voice from above.

"Here you are! Here is what you want. Stop that fighting!" Looking up they perceived the little doctor seated above with a large supply of tobacco, which he was throwing among the contestants.

The fight stopped immediately, all scrambling for the much coveted weed. Before the supply was exhausted their good humor was restored and the fight forgotten.

On arrival in New York the volunteers scattered in every direction. Paul and his friend the Count started for his home. Their odd uniforms and equipment attracted much attention and many comments.

At this time Paul's mother and elder brother Michael owned a store on Broadway near thirteenth street, and when he entered in his French uniform, his mother did not know him. After awhile she reliazed it was Paul and almost fainted.

She had been told nothing of him being in the French army and believed he was off on one of his usual voyages. Paul discarded his uniform and was once again a regular citizen.

While in New York, the Count received a heavy remittance from Denmark. He insisted that Paul must share it, in remembrance of the dark days when he had stood by his friend, in Havre. He also discussed with Paul as to what enterprise or adventure they could next take on. At this time expeditions were being secretly sent out from New York to aid Cubans in their struggle for liberty. Paul thought this the most promising enterprise to get evolved in, the Count happily agreed. They secured the address of an agent in the lower part of the city with whom the had an appointment and it was agreed that they would leave on the next expedition under General Jordan; but the expedition never sailed.

The Schooner was captured off Sandy Hook, they returned as violators of neutrality law with a lot of others and spent two

ROUGHING IT IN RUBBER

days in Tombs. While there they were recipients of generous supplies of pies and other delicacies and beautiful flowers from Cuban sympathizers, and looked upon their discharge as a misfortune.

After this the Count asked Paul to go to California with him, Paul declined as he was planning another trip to the West Indies and pursue his former occupation of diving. He had sent letters to his old friend Captain Balbo with whom he often corresponded, and impressed the Count with the many stories and description of the life they can enjoy amongst the sunny islands.

The Count decided to join this venture, the continued negotiations for the purchase of the submarine armor and necessary appliances and then waited for Captain Balbo to reply before purchasing them.

A letter from Nassau arrived at last informing Paul of the death of his old friend which forced them to change their plans. While still hesitating about what to do, a letter to the Count from Denmark requesting him to return home immediately, it was so urgent and of such importance that he sailed on the next steamer.

Scanned from the Paul Boyton Story.

CHAPTER FOUR

After the Count's departure, Paul joined a submarine company in New York and pursued the occupation of diver for over six months. He was very successful and when he resigned he was the highest paid diver in the company. The cause of this resignation was the reports of diamonds in South Africa. He was determined to go and make his fortune with the diamond hunters that were going from different parts of the world to the promised "Eldorado."

Having secured a supply of implements and stores that he considered necessary, he said farewell once again to his family and took passage on the full rigged ship Albatross, commanded by a friend of his. The Albatross was bound for China by way of Cape Town, and the captain promised he could land him there.

They had a long pleasant voyage during which Paul spent his time shooting at sharks over the side and trolling for fish In passing the equator the usual tom foolery of relieving Neptune and baptizing those who had never crossed the line before, was enjoyed with one slight exception.

The imitation of God Neptune when coming out of the fore chains over the bow, missed his footing and fell into the sea. Fortunately for him the ship was becalmed at the time. With aid of a line and a boat
hook fastened to his collar, he was pulled aboard. His appearance was certainly far from god-like.
Once when Paul and Joe were talking over the bulwarks and gazing out on the glass-like surface of the equatorial waters in which they were sailing, old Joe reflectively exclaimed:

"Mister Boyton, I wish I had a hundred thousand dollars. You can be sure that I would never make another voyage and it would save me from the fate of many an old shell-back that is flying around now."

Joe's firm belief was that every old sailor who died at sea, turned into a sea-gull. Prompted by curiosity, Paul said;

"Now, Joe, what is the first thing you would purchase supposing you had one hundred thousand dollars?"

"A quart of good Scotch whisky," promptly exclaimed

ROUGHING IT IN RUBBER

Joe with a string of oaths to confirm his assertion, and he smacked his lips in satisfaction as though already enjoying it.

About two months after leaving New York, Table Mountain was sighted and the same day anchor was let go off Cape Town.

During this long voyage Paul took the opportunity to study and get more practical ideas of navigation. By the time they cast anchor in Cape Town the captain assured him that he was as competent as himself and begged him to keep on with him to China, as the first mate was very unskilled and he wished to get rid of him. Paul, however, had the diamond fever and no amount of persuasion could change his mind.

Paul on South Africa:
"1872. I turned my thoughts to the newly discovered diamond-fields in Africa, where there might possibly be less glory but far more emolument in a pecuniary sense. 1872 was the year to grace my penchant for digging diamonds."

With his usual happy-go-lucky disposition he had never inquired before leaving New York in regard to the location of the diamond fields, he presumed that they were about thirty or forty miles from Cape Town.

In Cape Town he befriended an officer of the steamer Cambrian, named John Lord, who also had the diamond fever and intended going to the fields. Their pursuits being similar they naturally became friends. Paul asked him how he was planning to go up there.

"Well," responded Lord," "I would go up in the regular wagon but my finances will not permit me. It costs twelve pounds and one is only allowed twenty pounds of baggage."

"Twelve pounds? Sixty dollars? Why, good Heavens, how far is it? I was thinking of walking up."

"A little over seven hundred miles," was Lord's reply.

Paul nearly fell over in his astonishment, but said: "We are here and will get up no matter how far it is."

On comparing notes they found that they could not afford to take the regular wagon and that it takes twelve days to reach the fields. They were told about another town named Port Elizabeth, by going there it could save three hundred miles of overland travel. Owing to the enormous fares charged in those times, they found it would be cheaper to go Port Elizabeth direct by the ox train. It takes one of these trains from fifty to sixty days to get there and was anything but a comfortable trip.

While waiting in Cape Town Paul made acquaintances with an agent from Cobb & Co., who was engaged in the transportation business from coast to the diggings. After some negotiations, Paul was hired to be an assistant to the superintendent of a heavy train that was about to start on the long tedious journey.

On their long trip, the average travel was about fifteen miles a day, when the order for outspanning was given. This order meant to dismount, unhitch, and camp for the night. As there were few restaurants or hotels on the way, a large quantity of provisions were carried, and like an army the train was made up of messes and did their own cooking. The Hottentot drivers and assistants made one mess, the passengers another, while those in command formed a third.

Lord was also fortunate in getting transportation in the same train. This was a godsend as we not only got ourselves with tools and provisions to the diggings free, and were paid for the journey.

The train consisted of fifteen immensely long covered wagons of the stoutest build. Each wagon had between seven and nine thousand pounds made up mostly of provisions and for which the moderate price of nine dollars per hundred pounds was charged for
transportation. Each wagon was hitched to a long line of oxen, harnessed to a strong chain. The Hottentot drivers were artists in handling their terribly long whips.

Beside the oxen and fifteen wagons, was a mule team with the officers in charge. Three days after leaving Cape Town, we drove the train into Wellington, fifty miles north. Soon after we entered the mountain, Brian's kloof. They had great difficulty passing over this road through the mountains. Frequently they had to double the ox teams on a single wagon in order to climb some steep ascent.

The scenery through the mountains was extremely wild and picturesque, and the Hottentot driver with whom I was talking, assured me that higher up there were leopards and fierce baboons. After a hard days travels we entered the little village of Ceres where we outspanned for the night. From Ceres we passed over a level plain occasionally passing a kraal or cottage. At some places on the road the natives sold us hot coffee and cakes.

The country over which we travelled was sparsely populated, occasionally a tramping adventurer or two would come with the wagons, all heading in the same direction.

About ten days after the train entered the Karoo, a vast dessert, horribly desolate and forbidding. It was dead level and lay like a sea asleep. The heat was over powering and water scarce as it is full of sulphur and will make both animals and man very sick. Before entering the dessert a large amount of fresh water was laid in and order of travel was changed so that they travelled by night instead of in the day.

This wilderness is about sixty miles wide and it took five days to cross. Whenever the wind rose on this dessert your mouth and eyes, ears and nose were filled with dust, making our lives miserable.

At Durands, a solitary farmhouse stood like an oasis. They got a fresh supply of water there. After leaving the Karoo they entered another desert called Kope in the Orange Free State. In crossing this wasteland, they stumbled on many and many skeletons of poor fellows, who had no doubt succumbed on account of the heat and lack of water.

The crossing of these two desserts cost them many oxen. They had to be replaced at Beaufort West by a relay that was in reserve for such an emergency.

After leaving Beaufort we were in a thickly wooded country that was a pleasant relief. Sometimes during the day, while the train was winding its way onward, the superintendent and Paul would ride ahead for a hunt. They often shot antelope and a large number of partridges, Paul was surprised to find that game was a lot scarcer than he had been lead to believe, when reading about South Africa.

Once they traveled through a part of the country where there were many ostrich farms, a business that was very remunerative. Ostrich chickens cost from twenty-five to fifty dollars apiece, in three years they will furnish plumage worth from twenty-five to thirty dollars each year.

A Hottentot told Paul that many of the ostriches that stood around had been hatched by fat old Hottentot woman who took two or three eggs away from the hens and lay them in a feather bed until they were hatched. The truthfulness of this story Paul never verified.

After passing Victoria they wended their way slowly through great plains covered with a stumpy herbage. Here they saw large numbers of secretary birds and buzzards, marmots and springbok antelope.

Every few days they met up or down carts, going or coming from the diamond region. It did not take much to recognize the successful from the disappointed, coming from the mines as they got out of the wagons to stretch themselves.

Forty days after leaving Cape Town, they outspanned on the Orange River, into which Paul, with out any ceremony, plunged with eagerness and enjoyed his first swim in Africa.

Here they had to ferry a slow and tedious occupation it was. About a week later they entered Pneil to which place the freight was consigned. The village was small one, more like a camp. Down a steep ravine tents were pitched on every available spot, where a level surface provided a floor.

Paul and his friend Lord looked around the camp and secured lodging with an old Californian who agreed to board them during their stay for ten shillings a day. After prospecting for several days and finding that they could not get a claim, unless it was for an exorbitant
price, they decided to adopt the Californian's idea and start over for the "dry digging" at Dutoitspan.

On arriving there they met a sorter who assured them that he was fully posted in regard to claims, the value of the stones found and everything else and agreed to enter partnership providing they purchased the outfit.

After some hesitation and examination, they agreed to this. They bought a sieve, sorting table, and tent with cooking apparatus, etc, and started for a claim. They were fortunate in getting one about thirty feet square. Here the erected their tent, under the supervision of the sorter who unceremoniously made himself head of the camp and who did more talking

ROUGHING IT IN RUBBER

than work. Then they began the digging of the trench around their claim, the sorting table was set up and they went to work with a will that was backed with enthusiasm and hope. The results of their diggings were turned into the sieve, which was suspended by a rope from a cross bar, with handles on one side. The digger would swing it backwards and forwards until all the loose fragments of earth were broken off and nothing remained but small stones like fine gravel. These were then carried over and dumped on the sorter's table, who examined them carefully and placed anything promising to one side.

For three weeks nothing of value was found, the small specimens that were obtained were disposed to the dealers who visited the camps and diggings daily.
The amount derived from the sales barely kept the digger's in provisions, about this time Lord became ill with dysentery, which was prevalent in all the camps in this vicinity.

Paul had to do double the work to give to the gentlemanly sorter, who refused to do any digging. Being tired and worn with two-fold labor, Paul was tempted many times to abandon the claim and take a rest, and was only prevented by the fear that jumpers would take advantage of the work already done.

The unwritten law at the time was that if a miner ceased working his claim for a time it could be "jumped" by others. About this time Paul also began to doubt the honesty of the sorter and kept a close
eye on him. These suspicions he communicated to Lord, then recovering and found that Lord had the same ideas.

So one evening after a hard day's work they grabbed the sorter and held and searched his pockets, after calmly seating themselves on his head and knees. Their suspicions were correct after discovering stones on him that were valued the next day at one hundred and ten pounds. The frightened sorter willingly surrendered all they found, and confessed under the pressure of a revolver that he had been systematically robbing them for some time.

Though pleased that they had discovered so much, Paul and his friend were both discouraged and disgusted with the diggings and they agreed that the first good strike that they made they would definitely call it quits and leave. After that they acted as their own sorters but with indifferent success, realizing this was not as easy as it sounded.

A couple of weeks later, Lord who had gone out to purchase provisions, returned with a speculator who was willing to purchase the claim. A long talk followed. At last they disposed of the claim to him with all their equipment for the sum of fifty pounds which left them not much richer than when they had started for the diamond fields.

A short time later they were back in Cape Town once more smiling and breathing fresh salt air. Here Lord secured a position on the Union Co's line of steamers, while Paul remained in the hope of finding some ship going to China or Japan. Paul remained in Cape Town for another three weeks, but no chance opened to go eastward.

He eventually decided to embark on a French vessel that came in short handed, bound for Marseilles.
Going before the mast as there was no other position on her and he had certainly had enough of South Africa and it's supposedly get rich quick on diamonds.

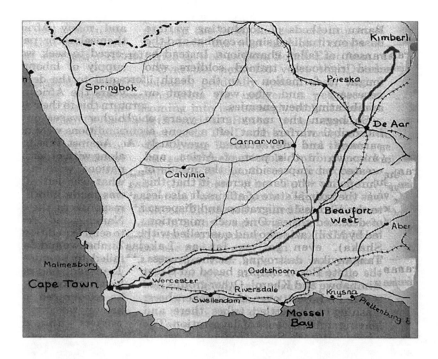

ROUGHING IT IN RUBBER

After a quick passage along the west coast of Africa they reached the straits of Gibraltar and stood across the blue Mediterranean to Marseilles.

While there, assisting to discharge the cargo, Paul fell through a hatch and badly injured his leg by coming in contact with the ragged edge of a roll of copper. At first he did not think much of the injury,
but the leg kept swelling, the captain strongly advised him to go to the marine hospital and sent him there in a taxi cab.

The ward in which Paul was placed, had about one hundred and fifty little iron beds filled with unfortunates like himself. The hospital authorities ran the instution on the principal that the less they gave the patient to eat, the sooner he would recover and get out.

Breakfast consisted of a slice of bread and a very small cup of weak wine. The supper was a repeat of the breakfast.

After a couple of day's sojourn in hospital, Paul was ravenous with hunger and would have willingly left if he had been able to do so.

In vain he assured the good sister in his best French that it was his leg and not his stomach that was ill. In response she would smile sadly as she placed the meagre allowance on his little stand at the head of the bed.

Paul was in bed number eleven, number twelve was occupied by a Frenchman, who was fast dying, and number thirteen by an English sailor with a broken arm and leg. The Frenchman was so far gone that he no longer could eat or drink. No matter his ration were still placed on the stand at the head of his bed, the rations were watched by the English sailor and Paul with keen interest, two or three times with the aid of his good leg succeeded in securing the food, before the sailor could reach them.

A couple of weeks later Paul was discharged from the hospital thoroughly cured, his ship had left port and he was eager to embark in anything that promised adventure. He was anxious, if possible to secure a ship bound for America.

Paul haunted the docks and watched every new arrival closely. While sauntering around one morning he was accosted by a rough answered "yes," but that he wanted to ship on a vessel bound for the looking man who inquired if he was a sailor and wished to ship, Paul United States. "Well," said the stranger, "I am, the captain of the bark Pilgrim and am bound for Valparaiso, why not that trip?"

Paul absolutely refused to go around the Horn. The captain then told him that they intended to start that night, but on the way out would stop at Malaga where he could land, and by going to Gibraltar get a ship much easier. He promised to pay him well for the run, so Paul agreed to go.

The Pilgrim was laying in the offing when Paul went to the landing to take the small boat to her, he found two other sailors belonging to her, who were going to Malaga on the same run as himself.

When Paul entered the forecastle he found that the crew consisted of nine men seated on their sea chests and bunks, holding a council of war. They all agreed that it was a pretty bad ship and they were determined to stand by one another. The council was broken up by a gruff voice;

"Come my hearties. Turn to with will. Get your hand spikes and man the windlass."

All hands sprang out and quickly the clanking of the windlass chain was heard coming in. " Look over the head young, fellow," said the mate to Paul, "and see how she is." Paul complied and reported, "straight up and down." Soon after a tug came alongside, the line was passed over to her, the anchor catted and the Pilgrim sailed away on her voyage.

All hands were sent aloft to shake out the sail and everything was ready to sheet home when the tug slacked up and cast off the cable. As the tug came around and returned to port she passed close alongside and the captain saluted the commander of the Pilgrim who was then showering oaths on the quarter deck and said sarcastically:

"My brave and gentle captain, the Lord have mercy on the unfortunate sea-infants who have trusted themselves in your hands."

Paul, who stood close enough to overhear the tag captain's farewell and it convinced him that the Pilgrim's commander had a bad reputation with sea-faring men. The crew except Paul, who was at the wheel, were called up and stood in a line on deck. The two "I'll take the man at the wheel." mates tossed up a coin for first choice. The first mate won the toss and said, I'll take the man at the wheel. Leaving the second mate's choice to a sailor at the right end of the line. Then they selected men alternatenately until they were divided into two equal groups, the first mate's watch being known as the starboard and the second mate's as the port watch. One watch was ordered below as the other remained on deck.

Soon after Paul was relieved from the wheel by another seaman and walking forward met the sailor who had come on board with Paul. He shared with Paul that he had a strong suspicion, which was shared by others that the captain's intention was to take them all out to Valparaiso and not allow any to land at Malaga. This suspicion was confirmed the next day when Paul was sent for by the captain to come aft.

When he entered the cabin the captain said, "young fellow, I like your attitude and wish you would change your mind and come on out to Valparaisp, I carry no boatswain. I will give you that position and a pound a month (about three dollars) extra, providing you can induce those two shell-backs who came aboard with you to do the same."

To gain time, Paul answered that he would speak to them and report back in the evening. It was at that moment the farthest thought from his mind. After a consultation with his shipmates, both of whom assured him that they would never agree to go on, it was agreed that they would all pretend that they agreed to go. They knew that the captain had the power to hold them in custody and prevent them landing, so they were determined to escape at the first opportunity at Malaga.

The captain was so delighted with Paul's report that he insisted on his having a glass of grog, and was in such a good humor that he went on the deck and amused himself by smashing the nose of an unfortunate Norwegian, who was then at the wheel. This was a favorite pastime of both captain and mate's, but it was generally practiced on those whom he knew would never resist.

The Pilgrim was a brute to steer and a very slow ship, notwithstanding they had a fair wind, it took them ten days to reach Malaga, where they anchored well off the shore.

She then commenced to receive the balance of her cargo of wine by means of lighters. The crew were closely watched during that day. At night the oars were removed from the gig, swinging at the stern and as an extra precaution a heavy chain and padlock were passed around it. For three days the lighter came alongside but no chance presented itself to Paul and his companions to get ashore. Seeing that the cargo was about completed and that it would only take a few more lighters to fill her, Paul was determined to leave that night.

A large plank that acted as a fender was stretched along the side.

This he decided to use to get his companions and bags ashore. He told them to have everything stowed away in as small a place as possible and to have a large supply of sea-biscuits and salted meat as they could acquire. It was

Paul's anchor watch that night, from one to two. When he came on deck he found it a clear, brilliant star-lit night and the sea as smooth as a cup of milk. After walking around for about a quarter of an hour he walked quietly in the direction of the after cabin and listened intently. He was satisfied that all were sound asleep. Coming forward to the forecastle he found the two sailors ready to join him.

Their clothing and provisions were firmly lashed up in a piece of tarpaulin. The three silently and cautiously crept to the side of the ship, with a sharp knife they severed the rope, that held up one end of the fender and while the other was lowered quietly until the plank was afloat on the surface. A couple of turns were taken in the rope that held it over the belaying pin, and Paul said. "Now is the time, one of you slip down the rope and deposit the bags on the planks. Then get in the water and rest your hands on the side."

The water was very phosphorescent and the fish left trails of light after them as they darted to and fro below. Just as soon as one of the sailors was about to step over and descend, either a porpoise or some large fish shot from under the vessel and left quite a trail of light in it's wake. The sailor hesitated, " that must be a shark," he said, "if we get in the water, we are bound to be eaten alive."

Time passed and Paul remonstrated with him in vain to go

ROUGHING IT IN RUBBER

down the rope, but nothing he could say, could convince the sailor. Fearing that at any moment either the captain or the mate might wake up and discover them. To show an example that there was no danger Paul grasped the rope and slipped silently into the sea. He was followed by one of the sailors, but the other could not overcome his fear and decided to remain. His decision was irrevocable for he cast off the line and said:

"Good-bye boys, I am sorry that I can't go, I dare not risk it." Paul and his companion pushed out and quietly passed under the stern and until sufficiently far away from the vessel, they were gentle in their movement.

Feeling secure they struck out with powerful strokes driving the plank that supported their bags, ahead.

The mountains that surrounded Malaga on all sides and tower far up in the starlit sky seemed only a few hundred yards away, but it was a full mile before the end of the plank grated on the shore and the sailors scrambled out on the wet slippery weed covered rocks.

They landed a little to the north of the city and grasping their bags quickly commenced their ascent of the mountain.
It was very steep and rough and exceedingly dangerous work as it was not yet daylight. Having gained good height up the side of the mountain, they decided it was now safe to take a short rest.

A faint glimmer was just then peeping through the sky and everything around them was as still as death. The gentle lapping of the waves against the rocky shore, the distant barking of the dogs in Malaga, and the occasional crow of a rooster rang out with the wonderful distinctness. The anchor light of the ship about one mile away twinkled as though only a little distance off.

Not yet feeling totally secure they began climbing higher, the progress was interrupted by hoarse sounds coming from the direction of the ship. As they sat on the rocks to listen, they heard the voice of the mate yelling out oath after oath, calling the watch and asking.

"Who was the last one on watch? Where is the watch? Turn out all hands!"

Then oaths from another voice came floating up and they

had no difficulty in recognizing the choice words of the captain as he rushed on deck to ascertain the cause of the disturbance. After this a confused murmur arose from the deck, through which they thought they could hear the blows of massive fists striking the heads and faces of the unfortunate seaman.

They distinctly heard a sharp order, "lower away the gig!" The click, click of the cleats as the rope ran through the blocks sounded alarmingly near.

Soon after when daylight broke, it revealed the boat as it was swiftly rowed to the shore. They recognized the captain seated in the stern and laughed heartily over the thought of the great rage of the commander, they knew was eating his heart out. Surmising that his mission was to go to the Consul and report them as deserters and also start the Carbineros in search of them, by means of offering a reward for their capture.

But they felt secure in the place they had selected, far up on the mountain. Quietly enjoying the scene below and watching the lighters as they carried out the last of the cargo. Laughing as they saw the captain's gig shoot fretfully from ship to shore many times during the day, while they enjoyed their pipes and ate with relish the salted beef and sea-biscuits. Late in the afternoon they observed with glee the last lighter leave the side of the Pilgrim, and the captain's gig hoisted on board, while the heavy sails loosened and dropped down. The clanking of the anchor chain was a joyful sound as it was taken on board and the Pilgrim under full sail glided away to the east.

That night they decided to camp in the mountains, but it proved to be so chilly and uncomfortable that by the time the hour of three rang out from the clock below, they decided they should move to lower ground. They carefully descended the mountain side until they found a road. This they followed until they reached the town that they passed through without any incident.

Taking the road to the south which they thought led to Gibraltar, by daylight they were well out of Malaga and walking rapidly along the road. During the day they met many pheasants and exchanged the "buenor dias" while proceeding on their way undisturbed. That night they came to a monastery,

ROUGHING IT IN RUBBER

where the pheasants assured them they could find rest and a hot supper.

They were hospitably received in the traveller's quarters. The assistant did not seem to comprehend the Mexican-Spanish that Paul brokenly spoke. He finally succeeded in making the monk understand that he could speak French and that if there was anyone around that could understand that tongue he would be more comfortable. In response to his request the assistant disappeared and soon returned with a venerable looking priest who spoke French fluently.
Paul explained to him that they were seamen en route from Malaga to Gibraltar and they wished to get some information as to the road, also hospitality for the night.

Their request was complied with and they were assured that they were perfectly welcome. Paul then questioned the priest in regards to the Carlo's revolution and said that he would just as soon join that as to join another sail ship. The priest who seemed to be an ardentadmirer to Don Carlos, assured them that it was impossible, as the seat of the revolution was away in the north and too far for them to reach it by foot. He advised them to continue on the way they were going.

Next morning after breakfast they resumed their march and two days after entered the gates of Gibraltar. Here they proceeded to a sailor's boarding house, where they were assured they would have no difficulty in getting a position on board a ship.

The George carrying cargo of coal form Newcastle England, welcomed them aboard. When the cargo of coal was discharged, they commenced taking in copper ore until she was sufficiently ballasted to proceed up the coast to Motril to finish loading her cargo hold with Spanish Grass. This is a coarse grained material something like rush, willow and bamboo combined, and used extensively in England in the manufacture of mats, chair bottoms, etc. Made up in bales that are the most disagreeable articles to stow away in the hold.
Whith the cargo now weighed and loaded, it was time to anchor away to the cheerful sound of "homeward bound" and the George started her voyage back to Newcastle, England.

Owing to the head winds the bark had to tack all the way out of Gibraltar, sometimes close under the mountain and again far out in the Mediterranean, she beat her way down the coast. The weather was clear and beautiful and the crew did not have much to do outside of cleaning her down, mending and making sails.

All who could handle the needle were engaged in sail making, they sat on the quarter deck and sewed industriously while boatswain chalked and cut the lines for them. Good natured Captain Moore spent his watch on deck, chatting away with them and listening to their yarns. He thoroughly enjoyed their jokes and superstitions with which many of their quaint stories were intermingled. While doing so he usually smoked a long clay pipe and being a very forgetful man, the moment he put it down he never remembered where he had left it. He was also very short sighted and the boys played jokes on him, by shifting the pipe from place to place while he was looked for it.

Once the boatswain, named Smith, who was as mischievous as a monkey, thought he would play a good joke on the captain. Seeing him lay his pipe on the lattice work aft of the wheel, and run down into the cabin to get his glasses, Smith jumped up and threw his pipe overboard and sketched one in chalk in the same place. Coming back up on deck, the captain took a long look at the stranger that had just come in sight over the starboard bow, then laid his glasses on the skylight and looked around for his pipe. When he saw the sketch he reached for it, but was unable to pick it up.

Being convinced by the suppressed murmur of merriment he heard among the sail-sewers that they knew of the joke, he quickly disappeared down the hatchway.

The sailors drove sail needles into each other in their hilarity. As the captain made no remark, the incident was forgotten.

The following Sunday morning the captain called Paul down and told him to order all hands on deck and get the chain hooks. This order surprised Paul as it was very unusual for any work to be done on Sunday, except to stand watch, steer and trim sail. He made no remark as to why, however, but proceeded to the deck and ordered all hands out.

The men left their washing, sewing and other domestic duties to which they generally devoted their attention to on Sunday, and came on deck more astonished than Paul was.

He then told the boatswain to get the chain hooks out. The captain then gave the order to "hoist away that starboard chain and trice it along the deck." This was a terrible job as a full sixty fathoms of the heavy anchor chain lay stowed away in the chain locker below. The men sprang to work and fathom after fathom of chain was pulled up with the aid of the hooks and triced in lengths along the deck.

When the boatswain reported "all up,sir," the order was given, "Get up the port chain." The men groaned, but complied without a murmur and link after link of the heavy chain from far below was drawn up through the iron bound hole in the deck. It was almost noon when the perspiring and worn out sailors had it all up. Again the report, "It's all up sir," was given to the captain.

"That's impossible Mr. Smith, look down and see if you can't find more."

In compliance with the order, Smith looking down and again assured the captain that it was taut.

"Look again and see if you can find it."

"Find what?" irritably enquired Smith?

"Why my pipe be sure. You can now let the crew go below."

Not withstanding their fatigue, the boys had to laugh and all agreed that that was one on the boatswain.

The crew was great on debating and many and many a foolish question came up in the forecastle. After a long argument, Paul was generally made the referee.

When they reached Gibraltar a heavy west wind was blowing in strait. Under lowered top-sails they were compelled to beat up and down under the shelter of the rocks. A large fleet of weather bound vessels passed so closely that the crews could hold conversations with each other, many a friend was recognized and hailed.

About noon the wind changed and a long eastly breeze came rippling over the waters of the Mediterranean. All sail was made and the fleet stood away through the straits. The Culpepper stood side by side for about five miles during which time the crews keenly enjoyed the broadside of compliments that was hurled from vessel to vessel by the two commanders.

The George made a fair run and in due time entered the

mouth of the Tyne and was soon after moored at the docks at Newcastle where Paul left her. He was loath to do so, as it was the pleasant'est vessel, captain and crew he had ever shipped with.

He then engaged himself as first mate on the ship Capbell, a Nova Scotia boat bound from North Shields to Philadelphia with a cargo of chemicals.

A couple of days out he discovered the second mate was more brutal than either of the worthies on the Pilgrim. He was always below during the second mate's watch on deck so he had no chance of witnessing any act's of brutality, but he was posted by the men on his own watch, whom he always treated with kindness and consideration. He informed the captain about the reports he had heard. The latter agreed that it was wrong to maltreat sailors; but Paul felt sure that he closed his eyes to many strange doings on his ship and that when a man representing himself to be a sailor came aboard and proved incompetent, there was no punishment considered severe enough for him.

Three such unfortunates were aboard this ship, one in Paul's watch and two in the second mate's watch. Paul soon discovered that the man was unskillful, he could neither steer, reef nor splice so he set him scrubbing, and by a few encouraging remarks got him to work harder than any one on the watch. While the watches were being relieved Paul and he saw their blackened eyes and swollen checks, that evidence was all too plainly the effect of the second mate's bad temper.

One night during the second mate's watch, the vessel was struck by a number of baffling squalls that seemed to come from every direction. This necessitated constant trimming of the sails and the men were kept hard at work. Every few minutes one could hear the hoarse orders given as the men scampered to and fro to man the ropes. The oaths, blows and fighting on this watch, kept both the captain and Paul awake.

Seeing the captain turn out of his bunk and light his pipe, Paul remarked:

"They are having a pretty rough time on deck."

"Yes," responded the skipper, "I presume Stanley is drilling some of those landmen."

At eight bells, when Paul's watch on deck commenced, he relieved the second mate, who was in a towering rage at the stupidity of his watch. The vessel was then under reefed topsails only and prepared for the uncertain squalls that were driving all around. At daylight Paul ordered hands aloft to shake out the reefs and set top gallants. As the top sail was raised he noticed dark blotches all across it and hailing the man aloft he asked him what had caused them.

"Blood, sir," answered the sailor.

Paul well understood the meaning of it and knew it to be the work of the second mate, who had beaten the men over the head with a belaying pin while they were reefing.

Shortly after the captain came on deck, Paul called his attention to the blood-stained sail and said: "This work has got to be stopped." The captain shrugged his shoulders.

"What can we do?"

"That's for you to say," answered Paul. "You're in command here."

"Well, I'll have to talk with Stanley when he turns out."

At seven bells the order" "Pump ship, call the watch," was given. The watch was called but failed to respond. The sailor sent to call it again reported that port watch did not intend to turn out.

It was now eight bells and time for Paul's watch to go below. The captain came on deck followed by the second mate, with whom he had been remonstrating. Paul reported that the watch had been called out but refused to come. The second mate with a terrible oath started forward saying:

"I'll have the dogs on deck mighty soon."

He reached the forecastle door and flung it back. The same moment both Paul and the captain saw him stagger and fall to the deck. He bellowed lustily for help.

The captain and Paul rushed to his assistance and found him bleeding profusely from knife wounds in the chest and abdomen, while the port watch with drawn knives stood sullen and determined looking in the forecastle. The sight staggered the captain who exclaimed:

"Mutiny by the external!" and called loudly for the steward to bring him his revolver.

Paul ordered some of his watch to carry the mate, who was groaning, aft, then advancing to the forecastle door said:

"Boys, this is not right. This must not be. Put down those knives. If you have any grievances come out like men and give them to the captain."

"Oh, we have nothing to say against you or the captain," responded the leader, "but we have decided to rather die before we turn under the man again."

Paul requested the men to keep calm and cool and he would speak to the captain who, during this interval, had slipped back to the cabin to arm himself.

Paul advised the captain, as he met him coming out of the cabin with a revolver in each hand, not to go to the men in that shape. "I am sure those men are determined. Their bloodshot eyes and frenzied manner convince me they have not slept a wink and deliberately planned this out break and mean mischief. I cannot guarantee that my watch will not join them as they are all heartily sick of the second mate's inhumanity."

The captain though it over for a few minutes and said.

"You go forward and find out what they want."

When Paul returned to the forecastle he informed that the captain, who was anxious to hear their complaint, and see that they are righted, and advised them to walk aft in a body and speak for themselves, assuring them at the same time that they would receive justice.

After some hesitation they agreed to go aft. Paul preceded and told the captain that they were coming and he could hear their complaints for himself. At first the captain seemed inclined to bully the men and assert his authority, but the determined look on their faces caused him to change his mind, and he became very diplomatic in his treatment of them.

"Boy's," he said, "I have sailed the seas for many years and always like to treat my men well. One thing I object to and that is murdering mates. Now you are all in open mutiny and I am authorized by law to shoot you."

Here the men laughed derisively.

"Now," he continued, "I am against bloodshed and I want to know just what you men want and what I can do for you."

They looked at each other and to the one whom they

regarded as the leader. He was a sturdy, powerful Scotchman who stepped forward and said:

"If you were against bloodshed, why didn't you come out last night when the second mate tried to kill some of us. We are willing to turn to again, but not under that hound. We meant to kill him, he deserved it and if he is not dead it is not our fault. We are well aware that there is no law for a sailor before the mast, so at times the sailor has to take the law in his own hands. Now me and my mates are willing to work ship under you and the first mate but you must keep that brute out of our sight, providing he recovers."

The captain made another speech to the sailors in which he promised them that they would not again be molested by the second mate. He also insisted that Paul could take the port watch and he would take the starboard watch.

The men appeared well satisfied with this arrangement and turned to with a will. The captain and Paul walked up and down the quarter deck, talking over the situation. The determined attitude of the men seemed to have caused a change in the captain's opinion, so much so that he gave Paul a long lecture on the duty of superior officers to treat their men kindly.

An examination of the second mate proved that he had been cut in five different places. All the simple remedies in the sea-chest were applied to relieve him from his suffering.

Neither the captain or Paul had enough medical knowledge to know whether he was seriously wounded or not. They had the steward clean the cuts that they then covered liberally with plasters to stop the bleeding. The captain then insisted on giving the wounded man a tumblerful of strong whisky, saying "that is was the best thing in the world to kill a fever." They came to the conclusion that there was no danger of the mate passing away quickly owing to the savage kick he made while laying in his bunk, at the head of the inoffensive steward who was doing all he could to help him. His wounds proved to be so severe that he was not able to leave his bunk until the vessel reached Philadelphia.

Owing to the new arrangement, everything went well. There was no more fighting, cursing,or driving and the work on board was done promptly and cheerfully.

In a conversation with one of the two young fellows who were the special victims of the wounded mate's ferocity, Paul ascertained that he was a delicate and well educated youth from Hartford, Connecticut, whose romantic dream for years had been to go to sea.

He ran away from home and fell into the hands of of the master of sailor's boarding house, who robbed him of all he could and put him aboard a ship bound for Hull.

From Hull he went up to Tyne on a coaster, where he joined the Campbell. He assured Paul with tears in his eyes, that several times before the outbreak in the forecastle, he had thought of jumping over board and ending his misery. He is the typical type of boy who thinks there is nothing but pleasure and romance in life on the seas.

About this time heavy westerly winds set in against the Campbell and drove her far off her course and for weeks she beat about in the most horrible weather. To add to their discomfort some of the water casks were lost, so that the crew were placed on short rations until they were relieved by a barkentine named, The Girl of the Period. She was from Palermo with fruit, sixty-three days out and bound for New York.

In exactly seventy-one days after the Campbell had set sail out of Tyne she tied up at the docks at Philadelphia.

Paul left the ship thoroughly satisfied with his experience and with the firm resolution never again to tread the plank of a ship either as sailor or officer.

CHAPTER FIVE

While in Philadelphia he met the President of Camden & Atlantic Railroad Company, who was interested in negotiating with him in regard to starting up a life saving service at Atlantic City, a great swimming place at the ocean terminus.

After a few interviews, the arrangements were made and a contract signed. Paul was installed as captain of a station built out on the beach and equipped with all kinds of life saving apparatus. During the season of 1873 and 1874 he held this position with a careful watch that he followed efficiently , it proved to be so efficient that not one life was lost, and when he left the service he had a glorious record of having saved seventy-one lives.

He also spent much of his time perfecting the life saving equipment and appliances. It was while in this service that his attention was first focused on to the life saving suit, that years after he became so famous in it's uses.

It was manufactured by C.S.Merriman of Iowa, and consists of pants and tunic made of highly vulcanized rubber. All portions are covered except the face. There are five air chambers in the costume, one at the back of the head which acts as a pillow and when fully inflated it draws the thin rubber around the face so that no water can get inside. The other chambers are situated in the back, breast, and around each leg from the hip to the knee.

The entire suit weighs about thirty pounds. When in the water, the wearer of this suit can be horizontal or perpendicular on the surface. When standing upright, the water reaches to about the breast.Then when voyaging, he propels himself by a light double bladed paddle six feet long.

He assumes the horizontal position feet foremost and sometimes uses a sail to help him along.

During the winter of 1873 and spring of 1874, Paul devoted most of his time to experimenting in the rubber suit and became an expert in it's use. His fearlessness in the water was no doubt a great aid to
him. Many a fine, warm summer night he spent far out at sea in his suit and dreamed of many voyages that he would make

in the future, but he never for a moment imagined the fame he would acquire in the later years or the extraordinary voyages he would make through it's means, but he thought of the thousands of lives that could be saved by this suit if properly introduced to the world.

With the confidence of youth and the strength of manhood he was willing to take any chances to attain this object.

At this time his passion for life saving amounted to a craze. He studied long and deeply on the best method to attract the world's attention. At last he struck upon a plan which he considered a good one, and which he was determined to put into exacutation at the close of the life saving season.

In the fall of 1874 he returned to New York.
Spending a week with his mother, to whom, however, he did not confide his intention, fearing that he might worry her.

His plan was to take passage on an outward bound vessel and when two hundred miles off the American coast to drop overboard and make his way back to land. For this voyage he obtained a rubber water tight-bag with air chambers sufficient to support about fifty pounds of provisions. It also contained a compartment for fresh water. In this bag he packed sufficient provisions in a condensed form to last him ten days, also two dozen signal lights with strikers, some rockets, compass and a knife. Besides his baggage consisted of his suit, a strong double blades axe to protect him from sharks and sword fish.

He innocently boarded several vessels and spoke of his intentions to the captain's.
They had all unanimously agreed that no attempt at suicide should be made off their vessel, for such they terminated his enterprise.

The newspapers at this time got hold of the plan and made it a subject of fun.
Tired of failure to get a captain to take him off shore, Paul decided to adopt another plan.

So Saturday, October 11th 1874, he quietly walked up the gang plank of the National Line Steamship Company's steamer "The Queen". He carried his little store of baggage as if it was the property of one of the passengers.

He walked froward and deposited his stuff, then mingled

ROUGHING IT IN RUBBER

among the crowd. It was not his intention to cross the ocean so he neglected the necessary form of purchasing a ticket.

When the Queen steamed away from her dock, Paul defended into the steerage and stowed away his outfit in an unoccupied bunk.

From that time until Sunday evening, he kept very quite and no one on board knew of his intentions.

About eight o'clock he slipped on deck and under the shelter of a life boat, and commenced to dress himself in the rubber suit. The weather had been fair and the steamer was making good headway, so he calculated at that time she was about two hundred and fifty miles out.

He was quickly dressed in his suit, and with the rubber bag in one hand and paddle in the other, as he was about to make a leap into the sea, suddenly a hand was laid roughly on his shoulder and a gruff voice said:

"Here, where are you going?"

Paul mildly explained that he was going ashore. The deck was all excitement, in that moment as the deck hand loudly reported to the officer on the bridge.

"Bring him aft," was the command.

Equipped in his strange looking suit, bag in one hand, paddle in the other and an axe strapped to his side and firmly gripped by two sailors, Paul was ushered back.

They were followed by a crowd of curious passengers. When the captain saw him he exclaimed:

"Ah Boyton you are aboard of me. Take off that suit and pass it over to the steward."

Paul remonstrated and told the captain that he did not have a ticket to Liverpool. He thought this confession would excuse him and cause the captain to assist in his return to America, but the captain would not let him jump off the vessel.

Paul was compelled to undress and his entire outfit was turned over to the steward with orders to place it in the captains cabin. The latter then took Paul into the chart room, where he had a long conversation with him.

All Paul's pleading and excuses that he was not prepared, and that he would get safely back on shore were made in vain. The captain told him not to worry about his ticket, and requested the steward to give him an unoccupied bunk in the officer's quarters.

Paul's disappointment could not be described in words. He was in no way prepared for an enforced voyage to Europe having but one suit of clothing and only fifty dollars in cash. The quarters given to him by Captain Braag were very comfortable and his treatment was of the kindest.

The next day the captain sent for Paul and they had a long talk while drawing from him many of his former experiences and adventures and was favorably impressed by the frank, open nature of the young fellow.

He sympathized with him in his apparent disappointment and shared his earnest desire to introduce the apparatus and to prove it's worth as a life saving device. The captain promised that should they
reach the Irish coast in fair weather, he would consider allowing Paul to go over board.

During the journey across the Atlantic, I spent much of my time in the chart room with Captain Braag gaining his confidence by explaining the nature of my attempted experiment, so thoroughly, that he finally agreed to let me go ahead and jump overboard in the rubber suit, much to the admiration of the crew.

The place selected by Paul was off the coast of Ireland in the vicinity of Cape Clear, as he was sure he could get under the lee of the island in case of a high wind from any direction.

With the Captain's permission on the evening of Tuesday the 21st, at nine o' clock I made the premeditated plunge into the tumbling waters off the coast of Ireland. It was night, and you may imagine how I astonished the natives of the sea. I looked beyond, and could hardly see for the surf-crested waves in the distance. A loud cheer of farewell echoed over the water. The vessel driving rapidly froward soon left Paul behind, while he stood upright in the water and saluted captain Braag farewell. I knew the direction of the wind, that was then south west and guided my course accordingly.

On every mighty swell that lifted him high up, he looked eagerly in the direction of the light and soon discovered it ahead. Perfectly content and without a fear of danger he kept paddling along occasionally cheering himself with a few snatches of sea songs, as he drove his paddle strongly in the water, propelling himself froward.

About two hours after leaving the Queen the gale was on him, the wind steadily increasing and soon burst into terrible gusts with the seas fierceness, he fought to keep his head above the overpowering waves that then drove down on him. At times a great wave would completely submerge him, then he would shoot to the crest where he would have time to breath again before he was again hurled down a sloping mass of water.

During this terrible ordeal he confessed that he firmly believed that his final hour had come and thought of all his transgressions, to use his own words;

"I recalled every mean trick I had committed against God and man in my reckless life and did my utmost to remember the best and most effective prayer that I was taught as a boy."

For hours, that seemed like weeks, he was driven along before the mighty seas. About three o'clock in the morning the water became more agitated and a booming sound, struck Paul's ears. Coming to an upright position, he peered eagerly to leeward thinking he maybe be close to Cape Clear. He saw what seemed to be a dark mass of clouds banked up against the morning sky along which ran flashes of white.

He quickly realized that he was nearing the cliffs and the flashes were the mighty waves that broke in fury against them. Knowing that to approach them would be certain death, he unlashed his paddle and made a frantic endeavor to back off through the enormous waves that were driving him slowly but surely to destruction.

Notwithstanding his almost superhuman efforts he was carried in by an irresistible force closer and closer to the death dealing cliffs.

At the same time he noticed the changing head lands, the currents were driving him southward, and hoping for an opening in the threatening wall of rocks, he redoubled his efforts to gain more sea room. I was nearing Skibbereen's rock-ribbed coast, riding on an ocean swell, dumb luck and a stiff breeze drove me headlong into a safe place of refuge. While hesitating and reversing his paddle he propelled himself cautiously towards it. The waves struck him, again and again in quick succession and nearly beat him senseless, he was hurled into a little ravine. To save himself from the retreating waves he grasped a piece of rock. Dazed and dizzy I crept rather nervously out of the water, when suddenly, as I was examining the surroundings, I was struck from behind and landed high and dry on the beach. At first I thought it was a tail of some form of sea-serpent, it was only an ocean swell.

Recovering from my ordeal I stood up, it was four o'clock in the morning, standing there dripping wet I tried to take in my surroundings in this big wide, wide world. When I discovered that the cleft that I was washed up in was a fresh water creek that flowed into the sea. He lit a signal light in hopes of attracting some ones attention, while gazing down on the mad waters realizing the danger he had been in.

The coast he intended to land on acts as a breakwater for all of northern Europe and the waves that pile up on it in a storm are enormous and can be deadly. The cliffs that resist them are from one hundred and eighty to three hundred feet high, and they are straight up and down like a main mast on a calm day.

Presently I had to do some climbing, it was not one but a thousand mountains I had to ascend, the waves were rising literally as high as mountains. The gale was furious, and I was almost blown off the cliff.

In that same storm, fifty-six vessels were lost off the southern coast of Great Britain that same night.

Fate and I are fast friends, my rubber suit proved to be a life saving device. I contemplated what next move I should make, unconsciously soliloquized Dear, O dear if my mother saw me now!".

Seeing a Guardsman in the far off dim distance , he gradually drew near, and then suddenly stood stark still, evidently taking me for the Gentleman in black or some other preternatural being from the realms below.

Seeing that the guardsman, sure enough, took me for the devil , I though I would leave him under the delusion. So accordingly, in order to make the delusion all the more effective, I pulled up my bag, and set off a signal rocket. My phosphorescent watch I placed on my forehead. "Great God!" cried the guardsman, there's "Antichrist!. And it isn't the devil, at all, at all!".

You see in the Apocalypse Antichrist is respected as an individual who is to appear at the world with an fiery eye, he naturally took me for the desperate personage.

I set off another one of my signal-rockets. Up flew the red meteor-like flame into the sky, and down went the guardsman on his knees. Fearing that the joke might become too practical, I approached the prayerful guardsman, and knelt beside him in his devotion. He thought now for sure that I was the illustrious Prince of Darkness, he literally ran away from me. A bright thought struck me, and I whistled up "The Wearin'O' the Green!", eill I heard him remark, the devil for sure doesn't know "The Wearin'O' the Green!".

I assured him that I am an American citizen, as I told him, he responded with: "and is that the way you all dress in America?" he asked.

Then I told him the whole story from the beginning -and it took me just two minutes, New York time.

He gave me a shake of the hand, and it wasn't the cold shake either, as I have good reason to know.

He took me to the coast-guard station, the furious gale tore along the street carrying slates from off the roofs of low houses, these crashed around them in an uncomfortable and dangerous manner. Rounding the bend to the village street they could see a light burning brightly in a window. In answer to their repeated knocking a man appeared and cautiously opened the door, at this moment the force of the wind pushed Paul and the guard suddenly froward and forced the man holding it over backwards, the affrighted expression of the man as he gazed on the strangely clad figure in his doorway was ludicrous. While now braced against the door, he hesitated whether to close it or let it go and expel the intruder.

The man recovering himself, inquired:

"Phere air ye frum?"

"New York," replied Paul.

"Phat air ye doin' here? How did ye come?"

Paul explained to him that he had left a ship that night when off Cape Clear.

"Phat did ye lave fur?" questioned the perplexed life-guard for Paul had not noticed that he was in a life-guard saving station.

"Well, just come ashore." said Paul.

"How maby came ashure wid ye?"

"No one."

"Phere's ye're ship now?", 'God knows, I don't.'

Question after question followed, but Paul was unable to convince the coast-guard that he had left the ship voluntarily and had landed in safety. The guard could not understand why any man would leave a vessel and come ashore on the coast of Ireland in such a gale unless he was shipwrecked. He thought Paul's brain had been injured by concussion with the rocks and a pitying expression came over his face as he said; "Well, me poor fellow, ti's no matter where ye're frum. It's me duty to help ye and yure mates an' if ye'll only tell."

phere they air Oi'll collect the b'ys an' have thim out. Now tell me as calmly as ye can, how many is drohwned besides yureself?"

Paul saw his mistake and positively assured the guard that he was the only person to land, and that there had not been a wreck and that the steamer had proceeded on her way to Queenstown.

Not understanding all this protestations the coast guard could not figure Paul out and assumed the man before him was, however shipwrecked and in distress, so with the proverbial hospitality for which the Irish are famous, the guard said:

"Niver moind me lad how ye came ashure. Ye look tired enough. Come in here an' lay near the fire."

When Paul entered the warm room he removed his uncouth suit. He was thoroughly worn out buffeting the waves and the long tramp down the road, so he gladly accepted the preferred bunk close to the fire and was soon in a sound sleep.

He was awakened by a kindly voice saying;

"Here me poor fellow, take this, 't will do ye good."

Before Paul realized it, he had poured a glass of Irish whiskey down his throat, the strength of which raised every individual hair on his head. It was then about eight o'clock in the morn-

ROUGHING IT IN RUBBER 91

ing and the coast guard's house was full of villagers, who curiously crowded around his bunk.

He informed that Trefask Blight was the name of the place where Old Neptune flung me ashore that dark and dismal morning. The landing place I just alluded to is some miles east and south of Baltimore. This rather risky performance has amazed most people and bewildered my good-natured guardsman. As a consequence I was looked upon as a curiosity and being of a retiring temperament.

I recall on two occasions to have blushed. One of the occasions was when an ancient maiden flirted with me to the extent of annoyance, the other was a more modern maiden who didn't enthuse me to any extent, but simply smiled things unutterable, I smiled too.
I was elevated, who wouldn't be in a life preserver after that?.

To renew the thread of my discourse and my rubber suit, of course, I paraded it in front of the crowds of genteel people gathered out of curiosity.

The coast guard man had drawn on his imagination, and approached Paul asking him.

"Did ye really swim from New Yark ?" "Oh thin he's not human if you can do that."

The entire village was out and crowds blocked their way, Paul found out that most of the excitement was caused by a story that he had swam all the way from New York. He assured the guard that he chose to swim ashore from the Queen to test his new rubber suit as a life saving device, this story the guard finally accepted from Paul.

In conversation with the guard he found out he was actually in Baltimore, a little coast town about thirty miles from where he had left the steamer, and also that there was no telegraph office nearer than Skibbereen, a distance of nine miles. There was but one conveyance in the village and as the driver was a very eccentric character, it was doubtful if he could be induced to go out on such a stormy morning.

Paul requested that this man be sent for, soon afterwards he appeared pushing his way through the villagers. He was a strange looking man, the coast guard introduced him:

"Here is Andy," said he. The latter acknowledged his introduction by saying.

"Did ye railly swim from New Yark?"

Paul laughed, saying; I hear you have a horse and I am anxious to get over to Skibbereen and send off a telegraph. I would like to have you take me there.

"It's no horse Oi have," he solemnly responded, "but Oi've wan av the finest mares in the av Ireland an' Oi'll drive ye over for six shillin'. But did ye really swim from New Yark?, sure it's not natural."

Soon after Andy re-appeared coming down the village street driving a sorry looking nag, he approached the tavern, he saw Paul and the guard at the door, he shouted loudly to the crowd to separate and let him through as wishing to show Paul the blood in his favorite mare.

"Phat de ye think o' that, sur? There's blood fur ye."

"But where is your cart? Hurry up and get her hitched," urged Paul. As nearly everyone knows, a jaunting cart is a two-wheeled affair. Over each wheel runs a seat, fore and aft, and in the center is a little receptacle for small baggage, called the well.

After Paul bid good-bye to the coast guard and thanked him for his kindness and hospitality, he placed his rubber suit on the froward part of the seat and sprung up behind Andy. Andy seemed in no hurry to get underway. A multitude of knots in the harness required attention and he carefully scrutinized every part of the cart while the villagers kept up a volley of comments:

"Sure it's a queer customer ye have this mornin', Andy my b'y."

"Come, come," exclaimed Paul impatiently, "let us get off." He seemed ill at ease and loath to leave, driving so slowly that Paul had to urge him on many times. Their way lay along the cliff -road and squall after squall came bearing down on them from the roaring seas. At times Andy would reach across when the booming of the breaker could be heard coming up from the ravine on the cliffs and say:

"Sure no human bein' could live in that sea, sur. Did ye come on top of the wather er under?"

"Oh, drive on, drive on," was the impatient response, "never mind." Paul who was facing windward, thought he would be more comfortable if he were to put the top half of the suit on to protect himself from the wind and rapidly advancing cold squalls, the head piece was was not fully inflated so it hung down like a great mouth.

The cart suddenly stopped and Paul felt his side sink, turning around to find the cause, and pulling the head piece from over his eyes, he saw the affrighted Andy about twelve yards away in a ditch.

His eyes filled with terror, seemed to protrude from his head while rapidly making the sign of the cross over his face and breast.

"What's the matter? What are you doing there?" thundered Paul.

"Come on, get up, what's the matter with you?"

"Och, shure, it's well Oi knew that it was no christian, that Oi had with me this mornin."

"Come on now, or I'll drive on without you," angrily exclaimed Paul, "don't you see it's only a rubber suit that I put on to protect me from the rain."

After considerable persuasion, Andy agreed to get back up and continue the journey.

Shortly after the houses along the outskirts of Skibbereen began to appear, Andy brightened up and became quite communicative, informing Paul that a friend of his had a hotel there and that it was a good one at that, so he would drive directly to it.

"Con Sullivan keepss the foinest hotel that mon er beast ever shoped at," he concluded.

There were few people on the streets as they drove up to the hotel. Paul dismounted and took his suit with him into the hotel and asked for a private room. He then inquired as to where the telegraph office was and headed straight to it.

He wrote out the telegrams, one to the Captain of the Queen, another to the "New York Herald," and Fleet Street, London. The lady operator scanned over the dispatch to London, then closely scrutinized Paul, seeing her hesitation about accepting the telegrams, Paul demanded to know what was the reason for it.

"Excuse me, sir," she said, "but we have to be very careful

about the nature of the telegrams we send out from here. I must first call the superintendent, before I can accept this."

When that individual appeared he looked it over and asked Paul if the contents were all true and correct.

"They assuredly are," impatiently exclaimed Paul, "I want you to get it off as quickly as you can," and he followed this up by several remarks not over complimentary to their method of business.

When he returned to the hotel, Paul found a large crowd had gathered as Andy had been informing them of his adventures, and the wild curiosity had spread like a raging fire through the town.

Paul apologized to the landlord who was busy unceremoniously shouldering them out of his diningroom. One of the gentleman who insisted on coming in was the superentendant of the telegraph, Mr. Joll, he apologized for his seeming discourtesy at the office and gave Paul all the assistance and information he asked for.

Informing him of the Stage that will depart in a couple of hours, that will convey him to the first railway station, some ten or twelve miles away.

He invited Paul stay to over for a few days and enjoy the hospitality of Skibbereen. Paul declined as he was anxious to reach Cork, he settled up the six shilling fare with Andy.

When the stage coach drove up to the door, almost the entire population of Skibbereen was out. Lusty cheers were given for Paul as he mounted the outside of the coach, in answer to which he the cheers he fastened the American flag to his paddle and waved it from of the coach at the cheering populace as they drove out of town. When they reached Dunmanway Paul immediately boarded the train for Cork.

Soon after Paul had left the Queen, the gale broke on the gallant vessel, the captain put her nose to it and headed right into it.

All night she ploughed against huge seas that burst over her and whitened her smoke stacks with salt. The steamer did succeed in reaching Queenstown harbor until noon the next day.

Not a soul on board believed that Paul would last in the gale

ROUGHING IT IN RUBBER

half an hour after it broke out, and the captain blamed himself keenly for letting him go overboard.

When the lighter came alongside with mail, a man passed a telegram to the captain. He feverishly tore it open and found with great relief that it was from Paul.

"Thank God that he is safe," he exclaimed, and then read it aloud to the crew and passengers. Cheer after cheer went up at the news as it spread along the decks.

When the Queen steamed into Queenstown the passengers, still full of excitement about Paul's wonderful feat that they spread the story in both Queenstown and Cork.

To their disgust, they found that the people did not believe them. Laughing at them, saying it was just another, "Yankee yarn that you are trying to spring on us."

To convince the skeptical people of Cork, a party of passengers telegraphed all over the coast to see if they could find Paul and verify the story. Skibbereen informed them that a man fitting his description had passed through and was on his way to Cork.

When Paul arrived at the station he found himself surrounded by many of his fellow passengers from the Queen, who enthusiastically received him and escorted him to the hotel.

The news of his remarkable adventure spread over Cork as rapidly as it had over Skibbereen,

CAPTAIN BOYTON'S LIFE DRESS.

so that the hotel was thronged with eager people, even the newspaper fraternity was well represented. As the story of his extraordinary daring adventure was reported all over Europe and America.

Before he could even dress himself the next morning, cards were being delivered to his room and when he went down he found the hotel packed with people, waiting to meet him. The Cork papers contained columns, describing his struggle with the ocean.

For the next few days Paul enjoyed the extravagantly warm hospitality of Cork as he was taken every where worth visiting and entertained with dinners, parties and receptions until his head swam with the whirl of attention that he was so unaccustomed to.

With sailor- like recklessness, Boyton never thought of how all this would end as he spent what money he had freely. One morning before rising from his bed, he began thinking the situation over, examining it closely and counted what money he had, the outlook took on a most gloomy hue. He was confident that he did not even have enough money to cover half of his hotel bill, without thinking of how he was going get home.

After considering the situation for awhile, he decided he could go to the landlord and offer to leave his rubber suit until he could return home and send for it and payment for the hotel bill, then he would go to Queenstown and see if he could secure a position on a ship bound for America.

Just as he came to this conclusion he was suddenly interrupted by a knock at the door. Sure this was the landlord with his bill, as he opened the door he was confronted by an energetic little man who talked with great rapidity.

"Captain Paul Boyton, I believe, sir, here is my card, I thought I would bring it up myself to save time. I have a great scheme for you."

Go on, proceed with your dressing while I tell you about it. I am the manager of the Opera Company now playing at Munster Hall and I have an idea for both you and I to make a great amount of money. I presume you are not adverse to making money?" looking inquiringly at Paul.

"What is it?" inquired Paul.

"You know all of Cork is eager to see you, and my idea is that you shall give a lecture, we can fill the Munster Hall from pit to dome."

Paul looked at the man curiously for a few moments and decided that this little man was crazy.

"Why my dear sir, I am not a lecturer, I've never even made a speech in my life."

"That's nothing," assured the little man. "I will do the lecture and all you need to do is stand there and exhibit your rubber suit."

"Well, under those circumstances" responded Paul, who considered this a means of paying his hotel bill.

"What terms will you give me if I consent?"

"One half of the house and I will do the advertising."

"And the lecturing too, remember," said Paul. "How much do you suppose my share will be?"

"Between thirty and forty pounds. I am almost certain."

"Then," said Paul "I will sign the contract on condition that you will pay me five pounds in advance?" Thinking this would end the interview and rid him of his visitor. To his intent surprise, the five pound note was laid on the table without any hesitation.

"Now make out your contract and I will sign it."

"Have already done so, did it last night when I thought of the scheme. Have it all made out. Just sign here."

Paul carelessly glanced over the contract and signed his name, after which the little man shook his hand warmly and congratulated him on having entered into a brilliant enterprise, excusing himself to go and attend to the arrangements.

"We will dine together," he added as passing through the door.

"And remember you do the lecturing," Paul called after him as he rushed down the stairs.

Next day Cork was covered with great bills announcing the lecture for the following evening and a feeling of nervousness overcame Paul as he beheld his name in such enormous letters.

The nervous feeling was in no way allayed when he pursued one of the bills and found that the enterprising manager, had not only promised that he would give the description of his landing on the Irish coast but that he would tell of many thrilling adventures he had experienced during the American, French, Mexican wars and would describe the methods of life saving devices used in America and comparing them with the British methods.

Paul immediately sought out the plausible Mr. Murphy and vehemently went for him for deceiving the public.

"Never mind, my boy, the people all understand how it is." Manager Murphy took him to the Hall where great crowds were gathering, the building was surrounded, while Murphy assured him that it was already full inside.

The arrangements were that Paul was to appear between the acts of the opera, which that night was "Madame Angot." Murphy took Paul to his own private office on the second floor and encouraged him in every way he could.

Paul listened to the music of the first act as it rolled by with fearful swiftness. Never before in his life did he experience the feelings of nervousness which now seemed to overwhelm him. Once during Murphys absence from the office he raised the window and looked down into the river Lee that ran alongside the building and wondered if he could drop into the river without breaking a leg. All that deterred him was the five pounds that had been advanced, and the hotel bill.

The fated moment arrived too quickly as manager Murphy began saying, "your suit, paddle and appliances are out on a table on the stage. The curtain is down and the moment it rises you will walk boldly out to the side of the table and I will follow you. Don't be afraid, the audience is most kindly disposed towards you and will give you a warm welcome." assured Murphy.

Up went the curtain and Murphy laid his hand on Paul's shoulder as he said: "Now, my boy step right out."
Paul braced himself and with his heart as near his mouth as it had ever had been before, walked over to the table on which lay his suit, paddle, etc, etc.

The deafening roar of applause that greeted him instantly set him at ease. Looking around for Mr. Murphy, but he was no where in sight, so making a few quick steps towards the foot-

ROUGHING IT IN RUBBER

lights, as he thanked the audience, in a trembling voice for their kindness. He told them he was no speaker and that Mr. Murphy had promised to do the lecture. At this moment cries broke out all over the house;

"Brace up, Captain, never mind Murphy, it's you we want to hear," came from the audience and many other good nature remarks. With this encouragement he calmly proceeded to give a vived account of that terrible adventure.

He grew more confident as he proceeded and the applauses that broke out gave him more time to collect his thoughts and express himself with ease. Next morning Paul read his speech in the papers and to his intent surprise and manager Murphy's, Paul had spoken for over an hour and proved that he handled it as if he was an old hand at the business. His share of the proceeds amounted to thirty-two pounds, after the five pound advance was deducted.

Paul felt more like a gentleman travelling in Europe for his health. On the same day he received three telegrams from Dublin all offering engagements to lecture, also an offer from the Cork Steamboat Company to appear in Queenstown harbor in his rubber suit, where they would run excursions. The Dublin offers he left in the hands of Manager Murphy while he accepted the offer of the Steam Boat Company. A couple of days after he appeared in Queenstown harbor and every steamer in Cork was loaded for the occasion.

From these appearances he made a little over ten pounds. In the meantime the story of his remarkable adventure on the Irish Coast had been published by the English press and so many doubts cast on it, that the prominent English papers sent their correspondents to Cork to investigate the matter thoroughly.

They learned that the place he came ashore was the only available landing for miles, the coast being formed by precipitous rocks and that if he had drifted one mile to the south he would have been cut to atoms on the sharp and dangerous reef known as "Whale Rocks."
Thoroughly satisfied with the investigation they returned to London and confirmed the story in every particular.

Paul next went to Dublin where he had a week's engage-

ment to lecture at the Queen's Theatre. His reception was, if possible more enthusiastic than Cork. He cut his lecture out of one of the newspapers and studied it, so on that point he felt more confident. He appeared every night at the theatre, which was filled to it's utmost capacity. At the conclusion of his lecture he would bow his acknowledgement to the audience and retire behind the curtains, where a tableau was arranged. It represented the scene of the landing, and him standing with uplifted paddle and the American flag attached,
a stagehand would throw a bucket of water over him, before he mounted the imitation cliffs, the curtain would open and behold the hero looking like he had just merged from the sea.

   On the last night, after everyone was paid off and feeling good, Paul in his rubber suit, stepped up to the curtain for the customary wetting down, the stage hand could not find the bucket of water for the ducking. "I had it here a moment ago, " he was heard to say, "here it is," raising the bucket he threw the water over Paul.

   Up went the curtain, the audience screamed, Paul looked down at his suit in dismay, instead of water he was covered with a white film of calsomine, when a voice from the gallery roared.

   "That's the first white-washed Yankee I've ever seen."
A white washed Yankee is an Irishman who has spent about two years in America and returns to his own country imitating the eccentricity of the accents of the down east Yankee's.

   Before leaving Dublin Paul gave an exhibition in the lake at the Zoological Gardens and Phenix Park, the people were so determined to see him in the water that the admissions raised seventy pounds.

   He also made a run down the Liffy through the heart of the city, it was estimated that over a hundred thousand people turned out to see him.

He then swam from Howth Head to the historic Island of Dalkey, a distance of about ten miles.

   The following day he was presented with an plaque, signed by most of the most prominent people of Dublin, with the most elaborately worked American flag and gold medal.
The following words inscribed:

ROUGHING IT IN RUBBER

"The scribers desire that Captain Boyton will regard this presentation as a reminiscence of his visit to Ireland and as a token of the high estimation in which they hold him as a most valuable life saving apparatus that has yet appeared."

Paul made many good friends during his stay in Dublin and visited almost every point of interest in that historic city. He found quite a character in the car-driver, who conveyed him to the theater every evening and around the quant city, entertaining him with tales of witchery.

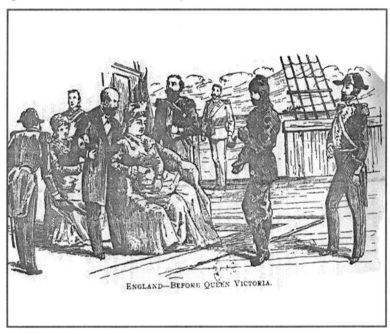

Scanned From the Paul Boyton Story.

When his engagements in Dublin were over, Paul went to London, where he found that interest in his exploit on the Irish coast was still manifested. He began a series of experiments down the Tames and in the waters around London. The papers were teaming with reports of his adventures.

About this time he made the decision to cross the channel

from England to France and was busying himself in preparation for this voyage when he received an order from Osborne to appear before Queen Victoria. Paul's friends assured him this was a great honor and one that would be a great advantage to him in England.

The order was for him to appear before Her Majesty. Queen Victoria on the river Modena, East Cowes, Isle of Wight.

He left London after making his preparations on Saturday morning he went to Portsmouth, where he was entertained by the mayor, American Consul and members of the Yacht Club. The same night he crossed over to Modena on the Isle of Wight and booked into a hotel. Sunday morning he went aboard the royal Yacht Alberta, and introduced himself to the captain, whom he found to be a jolly old sea dog.

From the letter written home by Paul about this date, the following is his descriptions:

" The Yacht I boarded seemed as big as a man-o-war. A marine stopped me on the gang plank with a question, "whom do you wish to see?" "Why the captain of course.
The sentry called to a petty officer, who escorted me to the captain, he then led me to a gorgeously furnished cabin. When I introduced myself, the weather beaten tar grasped me warmly by the hand and invited me to be seated and accept a refreshment. While discussing the plans, we also talked over my exhibition before the Queen the next day. I was anxious to present myself in the presence of royalty in a creditable manner, so I questioned the captain on all the aspects possible. He told me that to please the Queen, anything I do will have to be done quickly. In answer to my question, how will I greet her, he said: "In addressing Her Majesty. After that you may continue the conversation with the word madame."

"Well that won't be difficult, I thought, and I can get through with it alright." Before leaving the captain, I asked him to send down a few men in the morning to help me get my equipment aboard. Returning to my hotel I spent most of the afternoon writing. I was interrupted by a waiter, who informed me that General Ponson, Private Secretary to the Queen, and two ladies wished to see me.

I invited them in, the General a fine dignified old gentleman came in followed by two very handsome ladies. He introduced himself and the ladies saying. "Captain, this is the Honorable Lady Churchill and the Honorable Lady Plunkett. The ladies curiosity was so great to see you that we came down from the Castle to have a little talk. I invited them to sit down and make themselves comfortable. The General then asked me a number of questions in regard to my life and the heartily. As they were about to leave, I realized I had not been very hospitable

and excused myself, then offering them a drink, suspected that I had made some mistake, so I quickly added. At this both the ladies laughed merrily and the General said,

"No thank you Captain, they ladies and my self are grateful for the entertainment you have provided." By the twinkle in the ladies eyes, I think they would have accepted a drink if it were not for the presence of the austere General. After a warm hand shaking, they said their good-byes and look forward to seeing me tomorrow.

"After their departure I resumed my writing when I was again interrupted by the re-appearance of the General, who explained to me on behalf of the ladies that as much as they would have liked to accept my hospitality, I must not be offended at their refusal. They were ladies of Honor to Her Majesty and it would have been a terrible scandal if they had accepted any hospitality from me in the hotel.

"But that will not effect you and I Captain from drinking to the ladies good health."

The General and I passed some time together and he gave me many useful hints as to court etiquette and assured me that Her Majesty was a very kind lady and that I need have no fear.

The next morning about twenty able bodied British tars presented themselves at the hotel to transfer my effects on board the royal Yacht. By their united efforts they succeeded in getting it all aboard, actually I could have easily carried the whole outfit myself.

On arrival at the Yacht, I went down to the Captain's cabin and dressed in my rubber suit, putting the appliances in the rubber bag.

All this time carriages were rapidly driving up to the side and depositing courtiers, who came aboard and paraded up and down the decks. Standing forward with the Captain, he gave me many of names of high officers, one venerable looking gentleman attracted my attention. Startled I said: "Holy blue, Captain, look at that man coming aboard now, without any pants on."

"That gentleman," said the Captain, "that is John Brown, Her Majesty's most faithful servant and that is the National

ROUGHING IT IN RUBBER

Scottish dress he wears, known as a kilt."

Irish coast adventure, in brief I gave them the story the best way I could. They seemed thoroughly entertained as the ladies laughed.

Dressed in my suit I walked aft, paddle in one hand, rubber bag in the other. I came to a group of ladies a little separate from the crowd, around whom bare headed courtiers stood and was about to pay homage to a fine grandly dressed maid of honor, then turning the crowd on board obstructed my view so that I could not see the Queen come aboard. The Captain returning from the gang-way where he had to received her, said.

"Stand-bye now. Her Majesty is coming aboard, when I tell you, walk aft and bow to her, move to the side and do your demonstration." As I was gazing at John Brown in utter disbelief the Captain said, "Walk right aft. Her Majesty is waiting for you."

I might as well confess to you that my idea of a Queen had been formed by seeing the play Hamlet, where the Queen was this most elegant lady all dressed in white fur and a crown on her head.

I certainly did not think that the Queen of England would dress in this dull way, as I thought she would have something to distinguish her from the coterie of ladies that surrounded her on deck.

Then I saw the face of the Queen which I had seen in photographs in London stores. She was a stout, motherly woman, more plainly dressed than any one around her.
I looked at her for a second and said,

"Your Majesty I believe." With a kindly smile she answered, "Yes."

"Will I take the water, Your Majesty?"
I was confused by the mistake I nearly made, in mistaking the maid of Honor for the Queen.

"If you please," she responded with a kindly smile.
It didn't take me long to get over the the side of that vessel, as you can imagine.

Remembering the Captain's warning not to keep her waiting for to long, I dove through the exhibition as fast as I could give it and clambered aboard again, the perspiration was running over my forehead.

Once back on deck, I bowed to the Queen again and was about to go forward when she stopped me and said,

"Captain Boyton, I am both delighted and astonished at your wonderful skills in the water, I believe that the rubber suit will be the means of saving many valuable lives." She asked me how old I was and many other questions. A elegant young lady who stood at her side asked, "Don't you feel very tired after such exertion and do your clothes get wet under the suit?"

"Oh, no Miss, not the least."

After my answer a laugh went up from the royal group and I said,

"to prove to your Majesty that I am perfectly dry underneath, I am with your permission going to take off the rubber suit. I assure you I am fully dressed underneath it."

Seeing that she did not object, I quickly unbuckled the tunic and pulled it over my head, dropping it on the deck I then kicked off the pants. Standing there in my stocking feet before the Queen of England. The Queen examined the mechanism of the suit, she said.

"I would like to have a suit made for the use on this Yacht, and I wish you a safe journey across the channel."
Seeing the interview was about over I took the opportunity to say,

"Your Majesty, I hope you will excuse any errors I have made, as I am not familiar with court etiquette, as you are aware we don't have Royalty in the USA."

"You did very well, Captain."
When she left I again joined Captain Welch of the Yacht, who told me Her Majesty was impressed. "You may be sure of receiving a good reward for your performance."
Soon after Paul received an elegant chronometer gold watch with the Royal Crest and a heavy chain by General Ponsonby, from the Queen and with a request that he would send her a photography of himself in the rubber suit.

Paul continued with his plans to swim the English Channel. He visited Boulogne, Calais, Folkestone and Dover, deciding to take the course from Folkestone to Boulogne.

ROUGHING IT IN RUBBER 107

M, I'on-guety, the President of Boulogne Human Society, offered to give him the best French pilot on the channel and his lugger to steer him across. The steamer Rambler was engaged to accomodate the press representatives and invited guests. The most intense interest came in a form of request for reservations on the Rambler for special correspondents of the most noted newspapers in the world.

Europe to America. Letters and telegrams poured in from the most notables and royalty as Paul prepared for this daring challenge.

The morning was cold and raw and when the sound of the bugle alerted the crowd that it was time to start, there was a hustling of warm wraps. At the quay from where the start

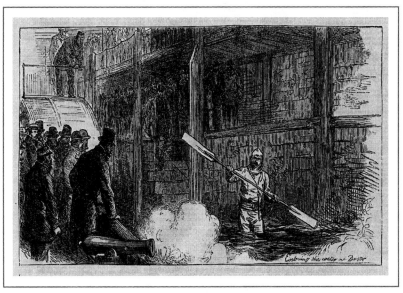

From: A Supplement, "THE ILLUSTRATED LONDON NEWS." April 17th. 1875.-373
Scanned from the writers collection.

Channel Crossing: New York's Herald requested space for their most noted correspondent. Mr. Mc Graham, who wrote the following account of this memorable trip.

"The start was to be made at three o'clock on the morning of April the tenth., 1875, from Dover, the hour being chosen was on the account of the tide. In order to be up on time the correspondents and invited guest decided not to go to bed at all, that historic night."

was to be made, great crowds had gathered, bracing the cold nights air.

There was a most horrible din and confusion, caused by shouting and the rush of people, the whiz of rockets, the puffing of steamboats and the hoarse sound of trumpets, all amid the glare of Bengal lights. The firing of the tugs gun announced the start.

A black shining figure, like a huge porpoise could be seen in the cold grey water as he disappeared into the darkness.

Those in the tug thought they would loose him, but his horn could be heard far out on the water and the tug immediately headed in that direction, in order to take the lead and show him the way.

Pushing slowly forward as they kept within his sight, the lights of Dover gradually grew dim in the distance and the lighthouse on Goodwin Sands shone clear and bright, like a morning star.

At five o'clock in the morning, when daylight broke, everything was going to plan, the course set by the pilot as Paul was being followed. Even though the start had been twenty minutes late, Boyton now paddled alongside and called for his sail, which he attached to his foot by an iron socket, without getting out of the water, he then lit a cigar and struck out again. The little sail instantly filled and helped pull him along in grand style, making a very marked difference to his speed.

Six o'clock they were just off Goodwin Sands, a little short of the point that they had planned to reach, the tide now turnin as they were running down the channel on a very comfortable breeze.

Almost in the middle of the channel there is a sand bank called the Ridge or, by the French, the Colbart. This sand bank splits the current in two directions, one along the French coast and the other the English coast. Missing his direction as they were swept down the English Ridge, he realized that all chances of reaching the French coast before night fall was lost.

Paul resolutely attacked this ridge, hoping to get over it and reach the French current in time, it proved to be a terrible struggle as the sea was foaming and tumbling him about, while he fought to cross the turbulent currents. For two hours the struggle continued as we watched him in his hand to hand

ROUGHING IT IN RUBBER

fight with the ocean, the waves seemed to become living things animated by a terrible resentment for the strange being battling to cross them. At times they seemed to withdrawn, then again come pounding down on him with greater fury from all sides. But at last he came off victorious and reached the current running along the French coast, where the sea although nasty was not so unfavorable.

It was now one o'clock and instead of being several miles south of Boulogne, as he had hoped, he was almost opposite as the current had again turned to the north thus carrying him too far. Determined to push on as he was not yet tired, though he had barely eaten since entering the water. The weather grew rainy, foggy, cold and miserable, it was becoming obvious that he would not make the French coast by dark, but was determined to kepp on regardless even if it meant all night. The sea and wind were rising fast and it looked like it was going to be a bad night.

The pilot was growing anxious and the captain unwilling to risk his ship and the lives of the passengers, in this storm while trying to continue following Paul.With the risk of loosing sight of him in the dark and foggy conditions, adding to the risk of him being swept into the North sea.
He would inevitably be lost and miss Cape Grisnez, that would definitely end up washing him up on to the rocks of a very dangerous coast line.

At six o'clock the captain made the decision to abandon this attempt at the channel crossing for the safety of all.
Paul and his brother Michael who was on board the tug boat at the time, both protesting adamantly against the decision. Paul insisted that he was still able to finish the voyage, proving he was not too tired by swimming rapidly around the ship. It was then agreed that it was not worth the risking the ship and it's passengers.

A little after six thirty Paul set foot on deck, after being a little more than fifteen hours in the water. He was very disappointed at the failure of his first attempt to cross the channel, especially after coming on to land and discovering he was only about six miles from shore. While receiving many telegrams from the Queen, Prince of Wales and many high per-

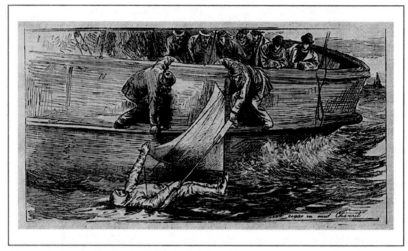

From: A Supplement of, "THE ILLUSTRATED LONDON NEWS." April 17th. 1875.-373
Scanned from the writers collection.

sonage on both sides of the Atlantic.
He was determined to try it again, as he was only twenty seven years old and did not know what fear or fatigue was.

When he returned to London, he received many offers to have exhibitions in his rubber suit, he signed a contract with a well known manager for the sum of fifty guinea's a day, about $2.50. At this time the did little more than paddle around in the water, fire off a few rockets and his exhibition would last about forty minutes, he has often laughed heartily thinking of the miserable exhibitions he gave in those early years. Not knowing a lot about show business then, Paul marvels at how the crowds gathered and cheered him while his manager made large amounts of money. Birmingham alone brought in over six hundred pounds, for three days.

Invitations continued to pour in inviting him to dinners, banquets and parties, many of which he had to decline due to the press, all this flattering attention and flood of prosperity he never lost his head, or changed in either action or speech. He looked upon it as a matter of course and felt just the same as he did diving for Captain Balbo, or bush-whacking under Colonel Sawyer.

Towards the end of May he had all his arrangements made

ROUGHING IT IN RUBBER

for his second attempt at crossing the English Channel, this time determined to reverse the course by leaving from the Cape Grisnez, France and land on any part of the English coast he could.

A couple of days before the attempt, he went to Boulogne. It was arranged that should leave three o'clock in the morning, when the steamer containing the English correspondents would arrive.

Eight o'clock in the evening, now only four miles from Dover Castle, according to encouraging news from Captain Dane. So clear is the air that Cape Grisnez and Varne are still in sight as the last of the pigeons are now dispatched, twenty-nine in all have been released during the day carrying messages ashore. The longest three miles ever now lays ahead of Paul, at a quarter to eight he called for his sail. The staunch little lath of the sail mast is fixed into a socket attached to one of his feet. The tiny sail fills, but sends him on the wrong tack, the wind still blowing west, south west.

Nothing daunted Boyton as he paddles on for another hour, he then sends the laconic message,

"All right!" by the first pigeon post of Folkestone Pigeon Club."

From: A Supplement, "THE ILLUSTRATED LONDON NEWS." April 17th. 1875.
Scanned from the writers collection.

Captain Boyton hoists his sail again at twenty five minutes to ten and takes off like some great sea-bird skimming over the blue waves.

Later paddling mechanically, he became very drowsy. Captain Dane's quite calm encouragement revives the failing Boyton while recommending food. He was greatly invigorated after the plain breakfast taken out to him by his brother Michael. No Liebig mess this time, from Dr. Howard. The morning meal and two others frugal meals consisted of half a pint of good strong tea, green with a dash of black, that wakes him up instantly, and a couple of beef sandwiches, in between meals were raw egg whipped with Cognac.

Quarter to twelve, Captain Dane lets Boyton know that he is now in mid-channel, the tide has swept him north-easterly. The French cliffs are dim, the White Cliffs of Dover are not yet visible to the naked eye. In half an hour the coast line of England looms into sight, clearer and clearer the cliffs grow out of the haze as the afternoon wears away.

At twenty minutes to two a steam boat full of tourists from Folkestone, decked with flags from stem to stern, sends a volley of rattling cheers across the water, the fair hands flutter handkerchiefs in honor of Captain Boyton, who raises up the stars and stripes in acknowledgement of their hearty encouragement. Another steamer heading across the channel joined in the cheering of Boyton by dipping her ensign in his honor. The outline of the Castle can now be seen, as Captain Boyton paddles faster and he was heard to say,

"Thou art so near and yet so far," his voice was strong and clear as he exchanged shouts with us.

Six thirty pm, a calm and beautiful evening as Paul was sailing with a faint wind and in calm water. He had already crossed two tides and was now in the flood channel. The hours passed and now there is only three miles left to reach the shore, so says Captain Dane.

The south foreland lights flash in our faces, Dover lights shine brightly a little distance to the left while the interminable three miles, felt more like thirty as he paddled on.

The crew of the Royal Wiltshire Life Boat, were sent out by the National Life Boat Association to cheer the plucky Boyton on.

ROUGHING IT IN RUBBER 113

He again asks the distance, "three miles," shouts back Captain Dane.

"Ah." grimly answers Boyton, with a spice of Mark Twaineish humor peculiar to him," "that's about it."

"They've just told me from the steam boat, it's five miles, and, as your steamer is two miles long, we're right in our reckoning all round.

Quarter to nine. Boyton gets his supper, lights a cigar and paddles perseveringly along. Although he had now been almost eighteen hours in the water he continued paddling stronger than he had in the morning, the three miles shrank to two and about this time the one
sensational incident of his voyage happened.

Captain Boyton's own words best describe it!.

"About an hour before I reached land, I heard a tremendous blowing sound behind me. Startled for a moment, I thought it was a shark, instantly drawing out my knife and coming to an upright position in the water, as I was about to attack a second snort sounded, simultaneously with the sudden movement I made, a tremendous black thing rose out of the water leaping right over me and darted away like lightening.

"It was only a porpoise."

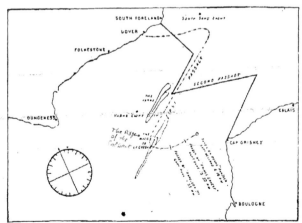

DIAGRAM OF BOYTON'S CHANNEL TRIPS. THE DOTTED LINES SHOW THE ROUTE OF THE FIRST TRIP THAT WAS UNSUCCESSFUL. THE STRAIGHT LINES REPRESENT THE SECOND AND COMPLETED VOYAGE.

Map of the English Channel Crossing.
Scanned from: "The Paul Boyton Story"

The Earnest slowly steamed along as Captain Dane lead the way, creeping so near to the towering South Foreland that by two o'clock that morning he could almost throw a stone ashore.

I could hear the intense excitement of the passengers on the bridge of the Earnest. Though the day was just breaking the sea was still dark and the curlews on the cliffs were shrilly as they heralded in the dawn, or Boyton?. A fisherman's skiff came out to show us the safest place to land.

Two thirty, loud cheers come over the water as the crowds on shore were able to see the boats. Our hearts were pounding as the rockets started rising high in the sky acknowledging that the young hero had accomplished his challenge. While we sent back our heartiest cheers back to them. The last rocket rushed up and curled in triumph over the cliffs.

No one on board was more exultant than Michael Boyton, Paul's older brother as he coolly calls to Captain Boyton through the megaphone.

"Come back in now, that will do for tonight !."

The rocky strip of beach on which the Captain landed is in Fan Bay, a hundred yards or so west of the South Foreland Lights.

From there he is speedily rowed to the steamer. Receiving a fresh round of British hurrahs, and congratulated with warm hand shakes by all, his bronzed face lite up with a modest smile, though his eyes and skin were smarting with the continuos wash of the salty sea water.

Captain Boyton is sufficiently recuperated before reaching Folkestone, to receive a new homage that the Englishmen are always ready to give the hero for his pluck and endurance.

Dover honored him with a salute of eleven guns as the Earnest glides by, on her way to Folkestone harbor. Crowds again gather to honor him by cheering the hero as he landed.

Paul received congratulatory telegrams from Queen Victoria, the Prince of Wales and President Grant.

Dover gave the Captain a dejeuner, Folkestone, or rather the South Eastern directors, a banquet in his honor on

ROUGHING IT IN RUBBER

Saturday evening. He felicitously thanked Captain Dane and others for their generous support and assistance during his successful voyage across the English channel.

After his successful attempt, which caused the wildest excitement all over the world, he rested for a few days before resuming his regular work of exhibitions and lectures, while medals, flags, jewelry, addresses and presents of all kinds poured in.

The Human Society of Boulogne honored him with their

CAPT. PAUL BOYTON.

Allen & Ginter Cigarette Card - From a Pack of 10 Cigarettes

massive gold medal representing the First Order of French Life Saving.

All during the summer, Paul appeared in different towns and water parks in England.

Getting his regular pay of fifty guinea's a day, equal to $1.750 per week.

In September his agent accepted a two week engagement in Berlin at Lake Weissensee, a very successful business adventure with tremendous amount of money made, while Paul was treated like royally by the residents, he vowed that he would never forget the generous people of Berlin.

For the first time in his life, Paul fell in love with a blue-eyed young German lady, the sweetest and loveliest girl in Berlin, he carried her colors on many a lonely voyage for many years after. His love for adventure and freedom was much stronger than anything cupid could weave, thus it resulted in nothing more than a very warm friendship.

The close of the Berlin shows, October 1875, Paul decided to make a voyage down the Rhine, this being the beginning of his daring life style in the indian- rubber suit, as he refers to it as:

"Roughing it in Rubber ."

The original Roughing it in Rubber was published and originally printed 1892 and is available on micro film in the New York Library, combined with an earlier book, The Art of Swimming.

It mainly cover the dates and places of his adventure.

Cpt. Paul Boyton.
ROUGHING IT IN RUBBER
A short story of my many voyages on the waters of the world!.
As my readers may wish to know something concerning myself while roughing it in rubber, I take this occasion to give them details of my many journeys on the waters of the world.

CHAPTER SIX

Starting from Basle, Switzerland and paddling on the very rough, swift and dangerous waters to Strassburg, with several correspondents from France, Germany and England, that were very determined to witness this trip, though they decided to join him in Strassburg when he arrived there. Paul started on this his first long river voyage, with four hundred miles to Cologne Germany.

At five o'clock in the morning he stepped into the rapid Rhine, with nothing but his bugle and paddle, his first run was Strausburg, seventy miles below.

As news did not travel very fast in those days and the peasants had no fore warning of Paul in his rubber suit, his unexpected and strange appearance caused a fair amount of panic among the people along the banks. At one point he came on three men repairing the embankment, on approaching them on a swift current he raised himself up and greeted them with a blast of his bugle. The workman looked around and seeing a strange figure standing in the water blowing a bugle, may be thought they saw Old Father Rhine, fled up the banks in sheer panic.

About noon Paul arrived at Breisgann, and then on down along the Black Forrest. The scenery is weird and somber and though the region is interesting, it is somewhat monotonous. People of the Black Forrest are a dreamy superstitious race, they would stand and look for a moment at the uncouth figure in the water, then turn and run. An old man who was gathering driftwood was so surprised and frightened that he sprang from his boat and ran up the bank without waiting to even tie it up.

Hearing a peasant whistling in the distance as he approached, asking the man, "how far it was to Strassburg?" in his best German.

"Eine Stunde, (one hour) was the reply, while fleeing for his life. Later finding out that in that part of the country, it was customary to give distance by time.

Half an hour after, the lights of the bridge of Kohl were visible, there was actually two bridges there and Paul focusing on the high railroad bridge did not notice the low pontoon bridge.

Suddenly striking one of the pontoons, that whirled him around under the water. Coming to the surface dazed and cold, he headed for shore as could not see anything ahead. Venturing out of the water he noticed a house and knocked on the door. As the woman opened the door and saw the dark figure all glistening wet, she let out screams that would have woken the dead.

The entire neighborhood was awakened by her screams.

A German policeman approaching Paul, and said,

"I recognize you, Captain, your friends are in Strassburg expecting your arrival tomorrow." Taking charge of the situation he told Paul the city was about three miles from the river and he would send for a carriage to transport him to the hotel. On arrival, Paul found three of his friends were already waiting there for him and they were surprised at his early arrival.

The next day was spent looking for a flat bottomed boat that they could purchase for the reporters to follow him down the river.

The Berlin press was represented by Count Von Sierasowsie, an invalid officer who was missing both legs. He was carried around in a perambulator (form of stroller), he had a private soldier named Simnic, who was provided by the German government to take care of him. The other reporters were from France and England.

A forty by eight foot boat was purchased and two men who professed to know the channels of the Rhine, hired to navigate. It was nothing more than an open roofless craft, so the reporters put in straw and chairs to make themselves comfortable. A place was reserved in the bow for the Counts perambulator, the following day all the baggage was loaded aboard.

Paul had three trunks forwarded from Berlin, Dr. Willi's, the English reporter noticed Paul threading a strong cord through the handles of each trunk, then tying them all together, finally securing a buoy to the end of the line. Fascinated by this, he inquired: "why are you doing that?"

"Oh," answered Paul, "I always like to be prepared. Incase the boat sinks I can easily find my baggage by this buoy that will float on the surface."

ROUGHING IT IN RUBBER

That remark did not encourage the doctor, that afternoon and night the voyage continued on a swift current. Great danger and difficulties were encountered with the floating mills as they continued down the Rhine. Keeping the crew very busy guiding the unwielding boat out of danger, the reporters did not rest much that night.

The only one on board who slept was Simnick, the Counts servant, who took to sleep like a duck to the water.
Paul kept well ahead of the boat, warning of any danger ahead.

Next day was clear and warm as they approached Worms. They were met by a brightly decorated steamers with large parties of ladies and gentleman. The Burgomaster (Mayor) was rowed to Paul's side, his boat contained a liberal supply of the famous Liebfrauenmilch. He presented Paul with an magnificently chased goblet saying, "Captain," you must accept the hospitality of Worms even if you do not stop," and filling the glass to the brim, also his and companions glasses, gave a toast "Lebenhoch!"

The most interesting part of the Rhine was now approaching, that which teems with the historic and legendary tales. The population is known by the Fatherland for it's generosity and hospitality, the rest of the voyage was nothing short of a fete. Almost every place they passed the Burgomaster with his friends would come out and invite them to drink a cup of wine, that every part of the Rhine is famous for. All day they continued down the blue and rapid waters and at three o'clock the next morning landed at Mayence, where they woke the sleeping inhabitants with rockets and bugle blasts.

The run from Strassburg had been thirty six hours, they were grateful for the warm bed and hot meal, deciding to rest until Monday. Before leaving Mayence, on Monday telegrams poured in from every point on the river below, one signed by Elizabeth, Princess of Schaumburg-Lippe, congratulating Paul and inviting him to stop at Wiesbaden. Monday they continued down the river, the banks lined with very lively crowds, perhaps no other river in the world could equal that from Mayence to Cologne in the variety of it's life and multiplicity of it's reception after reception for the heroic voyager and his party. Every community seemed to compete with the other in the warmth and goodwill of their welcome.

At Geisenheim, the committee that met Paul out on the river, insisted they land, as a reception had been prepared. He found a number of Americans waiting for him, including the Consul General Webster and about twenty young girls dressed in white, carrying baskets of flowers. They implored Paul to join in the parade, he was anxious to continue his journey, but the sweet soft tones and bright smiling eyes of the pretty young daughters of the Rhine made him an easy victim.

When they left Geisenheim, that evening the press boat was literally loaded down with hampers of food and delicious wines. That same evening they reached Bingen, here the Captain was warned to beware of Bingen Loch and the Lurlei, he took very little notice of their stories about the dangers ahead, and was secretly determined to dash right into the legendary whirlpool. The whirlpool has been the theme of many songs and tales, and the dread of Rhine boatman from the beginning of time.

Legend has it, that it's watched over by a fairy maid who lures helpless fisherman to the spot by her sweet pitched voice, then enjoys seeing them destroyed. The beauty in this part of the Rhine are the indescribable beauty of mountains towering above the water and dotted with historic castles. Time after time Paul's bugle salute was answered on the ramparts far above by fair handed maidens waving their handkerchiefs at him.

When they approached the Lurlei, the boatman used superhuman efforts to pull away from the dreaded whirlpool and hugging the opposite shore. Their cries of, "this way Captain, the Lurlei," were unheeded by Paul who kept heading directly for the jutting rocks that cause a eddy known as the whirlpool.

"Where are you going?," thundered one of the crew members.

"Oh, I am going to visit the mermaid," responded Paul and a few minutes afterwards he was in her embrace, or rather the embrace of the noted Lurlei.

Instead of swallowing him up, as had been anticipated. She only whirled him around a few times, then with a few strokes of his paddle and she sent him on his way, that little game rapidly overhauled the terror- stricken occupants of the press boat.

Paul dashing alongside with a dexterous twist of his paddle, sent a shower of water over the astounded and horror-stricken, Simnick, who was sure the voyager had to be crazy to have taken such a risk.

From then on they insisted Paul remain closer to the boat to prevent him from any further escapades of this sort, remembering his baggage was aboard, he did not require a second invtation and obliged the pressmen.

"Why," said Paul, "there are a thousand more dangerous eddies in the Mississippi that have never been heard of," and he laughed heartily, at the danger he had just passed through.

At Coblentz the Strassburg the boatman refused to go any further down with Paul, so they were sent home. The guiding of the press boat was now left to the tender mercy of Simnick, occassionally the pressmen would help him with his erratic steering that brought him showers of abuse, Simnick landed the boat on a sandbar, the pressmen minus the Count were forced to remove their shoes and help shove her off. The pressman have become so nervous that it forced Paul to swim closer to reassure them that he was able to rescue them if the need arose.

Shooting pontoon bridges was the greatest danger, so when they approached one, the pressmen's hearts were kept pounding and close to their mouths. The Count seated forward in his perambulators was almost knocked overboard while the boat grazed some bridge, on each of these occasions the imprecations of the Count, both loud and deep fell harmlessly on Simnick.

The Count adopted a new tactic when approaching a section where bad steering could cause serious trouble, he would by the aid of his hands get down on the bottom of the boat saying, "If I am going to die, I will not have my brains knocked out first."

The fifth day the party reached Cologne, where they were received by the booming of cannons and ringing of bells. The excitement prevailed in the quite old town and Paul was the recipient of many honors and presents.
One very persistent old poet, whose knowledge of the English language was extremely limited, he bored Paul considerably.

He became so inflated at Paul's praise, who had actually tried all evening to get rid of him, that he had his poem printed in a German paper in English at his own expense.

The trip on the Rhine now completed, Paul in the company old Dr. Willi's visited several cities in Germany,
Holland and Belgium, where he gave many exhibitions.

He then crossed back to England and took a steamer back to New York on a flying trip home. Arriving December the twenty eighth 1878, it's almost six months since the fateful day that he stepped foot on the gang plank of the Queen in New York harbor.

After spending a few weeks with his family, he received an invitation to visit his friends in St. Louis. While there the swift current of the Mississippi, although it still had ice floating on it, tempted him to yet another challenge.
From Alton to St. Louis, after all only twenty five miles. A boat was to follow him, as before in Germany, with the pressmen aboard, but the weather proved to cold for them, so they gave up after a couple of miles. Undaunted by this Paul continued although the thermometer was below zero and a man in a wagon had frozen to death earlier that morning in Alton.

The reception in St. Louis on his arrival was extraordinary, the deafening noise made by the steamboats and tugboats as they passed the bridge was heard far beyond the city limits. Before leaving St. Louis he gave a lecture for the benefit of St. Luke's Hospital and on that occasion was presented with a massive silver service set, by General Sherman.

From St. Louis he travelled to New Orleans where he decided to try out the stronger currents of the lower Mississippi river. He decided to make a run of one hundred miles and gave himself twenty four hours to complete it. Several members of the press decided to follow him in a rowing boat, this boat was placed on board the steamer Bismarch that was bound for St. Louis. It was arranged with the Captain to drop them off at Bayou Goula exactly one hundred miles above, to get ahead of an another boat, the steamer had to leave one hour before the official advertised time. To Paul's annoyance all the newspaper reporters, except one were left behind.

CHAPTER SEVEN

At six o'clock the next morning Paul and the reporter were landed on the levee at a miserable looking little Louisiana village. While having breakfast at the solitary hotel. Here they enquired about a pilot, and all agreed that a colored man named Gabriel was the best. Sauntering up on the levee to hunt up Gabriel, followed by a large crowd of negro's, young and old who had heard about the fearless manfish. Paul was told that Gabe was out on the river collecting driftwood, the entire colored population appeared to join in yelling for 'Gabe," to come ashore. Gabriel who was a tall sad looking negro appeared, Paul explained what he needed, Gabe retired to a log to consider this offer, joining his negro friends. After a few moments of bargaining he agreed to three dollars for the days work.

Soon after, Paul and the newspaper man were approached by a negro, who introduced himself as Mr. Brown.
He said, "I heah dat yo' hab engage Gabe fur pilot yo' down to New Yorleans. Dat niggah don't know nofing' bout de riber sah, no sah, me do, an' me'll go down fur nothin' sah."

"Are you sure you understand the channel down the river?" asked Paul.

"Deed I do, sah, I knows mo's ob the cat-fish tween heah an'dere."

"Consider yourself engaged, providing you can get the boat away from Gabriel."

"Dats all right sah, lebe dat to me," Mr. Brown answered.
A liberal supply of hay for the comfort of the reporter was placed in the row boat. Half an hour before they were due to depart the levee, was thronged with negro's of all ages and sizes, who gazed with open mouthed astonishment when they saw the dark form appear in the rubber suit and step into the Mississippi. Somehow Mr. Brown had managed to get charge of the boat, and shoved her off much to the aggravation of Gabriel, he returned Gabriel's malediction with bows and smiles.

They shot rapidly away on the yellow flood of water and were soon far below Bayou Goula, as night came, Paul requested Brown to light his lantern. He insisted on staying behind instead of taking the lead. Paul soon discovered that the negro knew far less than he did and threatened that if, Mr. Brown did not keep up, he would dump him over board, where he could renew his acquaintances with his old friends, the catfish. To this Mr, Brown responded,

"Yo' doin' all right Capen, jus' go right' long, sah."

All night they glided between the dark forests on either side, Paul often amused himself, while waiting for Mr. Brown to catch up to him by startling the negro fisherman camped alongside the river.

The negro's spearfish by the light of the fire, as he floatied along he would then stand up, the nego's would literally turn white and flee. Having to keep blowing the bugle that would make the the forest ring with the echo's of his bugle to keep Mr. Brown awake.

Paul decided there was no point in waiting on Mr. Brown any longer or he would not make the voyage in the twenty four hours, so he shot ahead and let the boat take care of itself.

Before dawn he heard the roar of a great crevasse that had been formed near Bonnet Carre, four to five hundred yards of the river bank had been washed away as great volumes of water were flooding the forest and swamps below. Without much difficulty he passed this dangerous area and at daylight his bugle call attracted early risers in the village along the river bank, here he was given a hot cup of coffee without leaving the water, while drinking it, the row boat came around the bend.

Soon after as Mr. Brown pulled lazily along, Paul, rated him soundly for his tardiness, as the reporter was sound asleep, doubled in a pile of hay.

At five o'clock that evening, exactly twenty four hours after they had started, they tied up at the levee in New Orleans where they were greeted by about ten thousand people, who covered the levee and decks of steamboats. Bands were playing and steamboats whistling creating a deafening sound. While resting in New Orleans after his voyage, Paul was introduced to a group of gentleman who said they were the committee appointed to call on him and see if he would give an exhibition in ----------, an interesting little town up the river. "Have you got any water that can be enclosed?" asked Paul.

ROUGHING IT IN RUBBER

Assuring him they have an area that would work well and could be properly fenced, he was also assured of a very warm welcome should he accept this offer. After breakfast he was escorted to the little lake, and saw to his annoyance that it was not enclosed, he remonstrated with the committee that they could not get a fence up in time. The answer was, "never mind Captain, never mind. We'll guarantee that no one stands around that lake without paying."

   All night they glided between the dark forests on either side. Paul often amused himself, while waiting for Mr. Brown to catch up to him by startling the negro fisherman camped alongside the river. They spearfish by the light of the fire, floating along, then he would stand up in the fire light, and utter a few howls, the sight of the hideous figure in the rubber suit appearing out of the dark would send them running with loud cries of terror.

   The crowds were pouring in to town and the main streets were filling up with wagons, ox teams and vehicles of all kinds carrying negro's and whites of all sizes.The Mayor informed him there would be a parade first, with Paul dressed in his indian rubber suit. At the hotel door he was mounted on a cart that had two white mules hitched to it. The Mayor mounted with Paul, behind their cart was a formation of fifty military men armed with shot guns, in front rode the Grand Marshal of the occasion followed by the band, which consisted of a solitary hand-organ. The parade, arriving at the lake, Paul was asked to sit in a little tent until the fence was made. Flustered, he tried to get an answer from the Mayor. The Grand Marshall then ordered all the people back, while he stationed the guards with loaded shotguns at intervals around the lake. Then riding his horse wildly around, informed the crowds that: " anybody coming within one hundred yards of this fence would be shot!" Two committed men stationed at the entrance with loaded shot guns standing next to a soap box with a slit in it for the money. This being the entrance, they allowed the crowds in, the exhibition was unexpectedly successful, there was not a dead-head around the lake and Paul said, "this was one of the most pleasant days that he can remember," he received two hundred and thirty dollars for his share of the gate. Soon after Paul went to Louisville Kentucky, where he made a run over the Ohio Falls, this caused the most excitement Louisville had ever known.

CHAPTER EIGHT

Returning to Europe in 1876 to continue his exhibition tours, starting in Amsterdam, Holland and then Germany. By August he was in the little city of Linz, Austria. Here he met with an accident, a
premature explosion of a Torpedo that almost cost him his right eye.

Being laid up for over two weeks in a hotel on the banks of the Danube, was the most frustrating experience and pushed his restraints to the breaking point. The constant sight of the inviting waters of the Danube drove Paul to make a rash decision of making the run to Buda Pesth, about four hundred and fifty miles below.

When Paul announced his decision, his doctors and friends were
horrified and advised him against any such voyage at this time, this never phased him and the plans were made.

The press was ecstatic and started sending telegrams around the world causing yet another frenzy of media hysteria, about Captain Boyton, who has now become a world wide celebrity.

Almost the entire city of Linz turned out to bid him goodbye, as he stepped into the Danube in the now famous rubber suit. The current was very swift, though the river was cut up by islands and sand bars, he could see nothing "Blue" about the Danube, it's about as yellow as the Mississippi, like all rivers it has it's "bug-to-bear."

The Struden is the terror of the Upper Danube. It consists of sharp and dangerous rapids, picturesquely surrounded by high wood covered hills. Great crowds were gathered here to see Paul make his plunge, he passed under two or three heavy waves that completely submerged him, he was swept away on a wild current, holding his paddle high up to acknowledge the cheering crowds wishing him well on this historic voyage.

His reception on arrival in Vienna was very enthusiastic as he was accompanied for the last two miles by swimmers from the swimming club, he was made an honorary member by a vote taken on the water, while Paul was paddling, surrounded by his swimming friends.

He was then left alone and all that day he travelled through some very barren and desolate country. Ocassionally coming across parties of gold dust hunters on the sand banks, they were a wild looking lot of people all wearing white shirts and baggy trousers, his appearance as he skimmed along the current, he never failed to produce the utmost consternation among the groups who had probably never heard of him.

It was a very warm day and the sun burned his face cruelly, in the evening the mosquitoes hovered around him in clouds making his life miserable, that night he was drowsy and exhausted after the long hard day. About eleven o'clock in spite of his considerable discomfort and being aware of the danger of the mills on the river, he dozed off.

The Danubian mills consist of two great barges fastened together with beams and decked over, with a large wheel between them, they are anchored in the swiftest part of the current that drives the mill.

He was awakened from his nap by a very loud crashing noise and found himself, just passing in between two barges. Seeing the rapidly revolving wheel about to devour him, with just a second or two to dodge it, Paul's swung his paddle into action, as the current hurled him against it, a plank hit him across the forehead as another got the back of his head. The paddle shattered in to two pieces as he was submerged into the churning waters. Feeling the warm blood running down his face, with a broken pieces of paddle he managed to gain enough space on the eddy to get to the back of the barge.

The miller was awakened by his cries for assistance and the stalwart Hungarian appeared on the deck with a lantern and threw a rope to the almost drowning faint man. Paul got a firm grip on the rope as the miller hauled him up, then the light of the lantern revealed his blooded face and glinting rubber head piece.

The miller uttered a cry of terror, let go the rope and ran into the mill, securely fastening the door behind him.

Paul now entirely exhausted dropped back into the current and floated away in a semi-conscious condition, with his half

ROUGHING IT IN RUBBER

paddle he managed to keep clear of the mills, and floated till day light.

His eyes almost closed by the swelling of his forehead, he noticed a castle on the side of the hill, arousing the inhabitants with blasts from his bugle as he was drifting helplessly along, a boat shot away from shore that boat contained an Austrian officer and two soldiers. While the officer was conveying him to the castle, he informed him that the castle was the fortress Komorm, his wounds were quickly dressed by the surgeon and two days later he had recovered enough to resume his lone voyage.

From Komorn he swam all day and the following night to make up for lost time. About daylight the next day, great mountains towered up each side of the river that was very rapid and narrow, about eight o'clock he arrived at a little village and was told he was at Nagy, here he received some refreshments and was told that it's about forty miles above Buda Pesth. As he passed the mountains he saluted a party of ladies and gentleman standing on the shore, one gentleman hailed him in German to slack up a little as they wished to come out in their boat, he obliged and stood upright in the water as he drifted quietly along. The boat slowly came along side Paul.

The boat had two ladies and a gentleman, evidently mother and daughter, the daughter about eighteen years of age, was in Paul's estimation, the loveliest girl he had ever seen. He gazed with a look of admiration on her wondrous beauty and paid little attention to the shower of questions that were put to him in Hungarian or German, he was unsure. In his best German he asked her what he already knew, "how far is it to Buda Pesth?

She smiled and answered in French, "about thirty-five miles. I presume you can speak French better than German?"

This was just what Paul wanted, she now acted as the interpreter for the whole party and her sweet voice drove away all feelings of fatigue. As the current was fast moving the party down river, the mother suggested they should say good-bye. Before going the gentleman asked through the young lady: "If M Le Capitaine would take a glass of wine?" Paul responded "that it was pretty early in the morning for a toast, but if he was permitted to drink to the health of Hungary's fairest daughter, he would sacrifice himself."

With a musical laugh she handed him a glass filled with sparkling Tokay. General hand shakes around followed and as Paul's rubber covered wet hand grasped that of the young lady, he begged her to present him with the bunch of violets pinned to her breast as a reminder of the pleasant moments he spent in her company.

She obliged and he gallantly kissed her hand, and pushed the violets under the rubber opening and down to his breast.

As he resumed paddling, he found himself humming: "Her bright smile will always be with me," he noticed a large cross on the side of the mountain, up which runs a zig-zag road. At each bend of this road a Grotto containing some scene from the Passion of Our Lord, the Cross is a celebrated place of devotion to the pious people of Buda Pesth. Paul making the sign of the cross and thanks for the blessing. Continuing to paddle his way down river with a strong steady pull as he hummed, "Her bright smile haunts me still."

The news of his approach had been telegraphed to Buda Pesth, so when he arrived at the Hungarian Capitol both banks and bridges were black with people and the cry of, *"eljen Boyton, eljen America,"* echoed from every side.

The warmth of his reception in Buda Pesth was simply undiscribable, later narrating his story of his voyage down the Danube, he mention the fair young lady he had encountered at Visegrad with: "Her bright smile haunts me still." This was later published with his other adventures, from Buda Pesth.

He returned by railroad to Vienna, where he had a scheduled exhibition at the Boat Club, with no other scheduled exhibitions, Paul was free to go where ever he wished. He followed his heart and took the first train to Buda Pesth, with his heart on his sleeve, Paul started the quest to find out who the beautiful young lady was.

Paul was requested to give another exhibition for the benefit of a girl's home that was a favorite charity in Buda Pesth. He was honored to oblige and at the end of this exhibition was bewildered by the shower of flowers and bouquet's thrown on him in the water.

ROUGHING IT IN RUBBER

Next morning he received a hand delivered letter of the most gracious thanks: *"We assure, that your name and noble action will never leave the hearts of those young girls whom we can help through your kind and generous compliance in a foreign land. Let me render with our thanks, that we will never forget your gentlemanly conduct."* signed Elma Hentallerf and Mrs. Anna A Kuhnel.

During this time Paul kept his eyes wide open in the hopes of meeting the beautiful young lady, who had left such a strong impression on his heart. While walking early one morning a Hungarian officer approach him on the street, asking,

"Captain would you like to be presented to the young lady you met on the river at Visegrad?,"

"Would a duck like to swim?" Paul replied.

The officer told him to be ready that evening and he would take him to their private box in the National Theatre. Paul was ready a couple of hours earlier than necessary...

As they entered the box, the object of Paul's dreams rose and advancing with that "bright smile," said in English,

"I am so delighted to see you Captain."

"Not anymore than I am to see you, why didn't you speak English to me on the river?"

"Well," she exclaimed, "I was a little confused and did not remember that Americans spoke english, but let me present you to my mother and the gentleman." he was introduced, to an Austrian officer and a Count.

Little attention was given to the play going on, as Paul kept up a running conversation in English mixed with French, with the beautiful young lady at his side, being the gentleman he was Paul would occasionally pass a remark to her mother in German. At the end of the play Paul offered his arm to the young lady, while the Austrian Officer took the mother in tow. They walked leisurely home through the narrow cobble stoned streets, the Austrian officer, clinking the scabbard of his long sword in a threatening manner on the cobble stones. Before they parted at her door, Paul asked for and obtained permission to visit her the following day.

He then turned away accompanied by the officer, and walked in the direction of the hotel. The officer asked him how long he intended to remain in Buda Pesth. Paul did not have a direct answer, with his heart still pounding he had no plans made for his immediate future.

Arriving at the hotel he Invited the officer in for a drink, while seated at the table the officer questioned Paul about duelling and the customs in America. Paul easily seeing the drift of his thoughts entertained him with accounts of hair raising combats with bowie knives, revolvers, shotguns and cannons, assuring him they were a frequent occourances in the part of the States he came from. He told the officer: "I don't know of one of my friends who would not participate in a dual than attend a banquet."

When the officer left Paul he was stuffed full of harrowing yarns, all of which he seemed to believe, at least his demeanor was far more gentler than when he had entered the hotel.

Paul remained in Buda Pesth for two more weeks, during which time he was a frequent visitor at the home of the fair Irene, where he was always welcomed by herself and parents. While he was planning to do a trip through the principal cities of Hungary, this being extremely successful, and not forgetting the fair Irene, with the bright smile he went to Italy, arriving on the fourth of November 1876.

Paul's Italian was very limited as was his knowledge of the river he was about to embark on, even less, so careful planning would be needed. While planning this trip down the Po from Turin to Adriatic, a total of six hundred and seventy two miles, deciding that this voyage could be used as a feat to test his endurance, making it in one straight run in the water until stepping on the banks at Adriatic.

As this would require him to carryi more supplies than on any other voyage, he decided to tow a very small flat bottomed boat to accommodate the necessary provisions, map, etc.

He was fortunate enough to find a person to make the boat in Turin, it was a little tin boat, about two foot six inches long and eight inches wide, this little craft bore the name "Irene D'Ungeria." Belle of Hungary, and very dear to his heart. This boat was the model for his later famous little boat, "Baby Mine."

ROUGHING IT IN RUBBER

All the inhabitants of Turin seemed to have turned out on that cold morning to see him start the voyage. The water was intensely cold, it's source was the run off from the Alps, that were in plain view covered with snow.

He started on Saturday morning at nine o'clock, the current was exceedingly strong, rushing over gravel beds on which he frequently grounded. The country in this area is exceptionally beautiful with high ground on each side. At every little village and hamlet, he was received with enthusiastic "vivas" and many were the kind invitations he was offered to stop and take refreshments.

All these he declined, as he had ample provisions for a four day run,in his little boat that was attached by a three yard line to his belt. She behaved very well, when challenging the violent rapids he found he would have to pick her up and balance her across his legs.

As the sun went down a lady and gentleman came over in a small boat suggesting he come ashore for the night, warning him that the dangers below were great as there are mills that could sweep him under. But his mind was made up and he went steadily along on his perilous way. It was very cold and the struggling moon, occasionally lit up the valley. He hit many rocks and found many false channels.

Three o'clock Sunday morning, he heard a loud roaring noise and presumed it was a freight train passing over the bridge at Castle.

About the same time a thick white fog peculiar to the Po, settled over the river, through this he picked his way cautiously and as the current swept in around the bend of the river, the noise seemed to become louder and possibly closer. The speed of the current was increasing rapidly and a few minutes after he was shot over the dam and submerged in the tumbling water below, fighting the currents with his paddle, he saw the little boat had been upset and was about to sink. Before he could extricate himself, he scrambled to save the boat and provisions, the current soon drove him below the dam, he managed to land on a sand bar where he was able to empty the water from his tender. Knowing the contents would be ruined, Paul tried to sorted through the soggy mess, it was still too dark to see the extent of the damage, heading on down river until sunrise would allow him to examine the provisions.

When he landed he found that all his provisions were converted into a kind of pudding, dotted with cigars instead of fruit.

The small flask of Cognac and a bottle of oil were the only things undamaged, a swig at the Cognac bottle served him for breakfast and he paddled away on his voyage with vigorous strokes.

The sun rose that morning in a deep red color and as the rays illuminated the snow clad Alps, the valley of Po and the remnants of the fog were bathed in soft red light. A sight that was indescribable to Paul as the river seemed to shoot from the hills into the lowland, on each side was a heavy growth of willows swaying in the gentle breeze.

Paul thanked him and explained he could not return or leave the water, the officer then asked if Paul needed anything?.

He never saw anybody until about nine that morning, when sweeping around a bend he came on two men in a boat duck hunting with a swivel gun, startled the men turned the gun on him. Paul shouted loudly at them not to fire, fortunately for him they obliged instantly.

He swam alongside and held a conversation with them in the best Italian he could muster. They told him he was very close to the bridge at Frassinetto and offered him fresh food, he gratefully accepted a piece of bread, which he ate and then paddled on down the river.

A couple of hours later he came to the flying bridge, a common sight on European rivers. It consists of a long line of small boats strung together on a heavy cable and anchored in the centre of the river.

The boats supported the cable, the last boat on the line is the ferry or bridge, this is much larger than any of the others and has a steering oar, when cast away from one shore, the ferry is steered diagonally against the current to the opposite side, while the line of smaller boats support the cable and swing with it.

Paul found these bridges to be exceedingly dangerous particularly at night, the ferry is always tied and the line of small

ROUGHING IT IN RUBBER 135

boats lead from the center to the sides for about one hundred yards below.

The bridge men at Frassinett were warned of Paul approach by the sound of his bugle, never having heard of him before, they rowed out in a skiff to preform a rescue and were very indignant, when finding out that he did not require rescuing.

All day Sunday he paddled ahead on the rapid current, looking at his map, that he had managed to save, though a bit worse for wear, he realized he was not going to make it in the four days, a little disappointed but not deterred. Sunday night he managed to get food from a miller down river and now was really feeling the strain and intermitedly, dozing off here and there.

The roar of the waters around the mills kept him pretty alert as he kept going all night, by Monday morning Paul was exhausted and feeling rather faint, but was encouraged by thought of reaching Piacenza.

He had arranged to meet his agent there and would definitely need a fresh supply of provisions and lots of rest. His agent was a Scotsman, he had met in Milan, before going to Turin. He had tried to become a tenor singer without success and was looking for another occupation, as he was fluent in Italian and a good businessman. Paul hired him, learning afterwards that instead of him waiting until Saturday his agent full of self importance left the same day as he did.

Contacting the newspapers and making many announcements that Paul would arrive on Sunday evening, the entire town, men, woman and children lined the banks for about three miles out of town. He kept assuring the agitated crowds that Paul would be there, as the night grew darker, he boarded a train and slipped out of town, when he could not be found the angry crowds resorted to satisfying their anger by burning an effigy of him in the town square.

Monday morning broke chilly and uncomfortable with a fast current, once in awhile a faint gleam of sunshine would light up the river and taking advantage of long runs ahead of him, free of mills to take naps. He woke from one of these naps at the sound of a fisherman yelling as he saw the lifeless object floating down river, Paul half opened his eyes and saw the intense gaze of disbelief on his face, though tempted to see the effect it would have, should he become upright, he decided to rather let the current run him to shore, the fisherman was running down the bank with a pole in his hand, waiting to capture what he may have thought was a dead body or ?, as he thrust the pole out, Paul rose up and saluted him with the words,

"Buou giorno."

The pole dropped from his hand and with a very frightened shriek, the fisherman rushed up the bank and disappeared.

About one o'clock the bridge at Piacenza came into sight, but instead of being full of people, as he expected, Paul only saw a few workmen and some soldiers, no sign of his agent either. Paul decided to go on down, about another twenty five miles to Cremona.

The day was becoming very dreary and cold, feeling like it was about to snow, undaunted he continued paddling steadily down the river when he was suddenly startled by a voice behind him, coming upright and wheeling around, he saw a young officer standing in a boat pulled by about twenty pontoneers. As he shot alongside, the officer stretched out his hand to shake Paul's, and said in French,

"You must come on board and go back to Piacenza. The people were greatly disappointed, your agent said that you would be here on yesterday and a great reception was prepared for you."

Paul thanked him and explained he could not return or leave the water, the officer then asked if Paul needed anything?. Paul explained about his provisions and asked for some oil for his lamp. He had missed the little light on the head of the Irene during the long lonely nights on the river.

"There is a village a couple of miles below," said the officer, "and if you will slow down a little, I will run ahead and have all you need by the time you come up opposite." The pontoneer's boat shot away and Paul followed quietly after them.

The boat came out with not only the provisions but a meal consisting of hardboiled eggs and other nutritious edible's, with a bottle of fine old Barolo, the sparkling red wine of that country.

While eating the food alongside the boat, he drifted slowly with the current, during this time found out the young officer was indeed the son of General Pescetta, MInister of Marine.

Shortly before being overtaken by the friendly Italian, Paul was beginning to feel extremely tired and had serious thoughts of abandoning the voyage. With the effects of this hearty meal and the invigorating wine, his energy was renewed and he was confident he could easily complete this voyage.

All that day he passed through lonely and miserable looking country, swampy lands and rice fields bordering both sides of the river. About five o'clock he saw two men on the river bank and called out to them, asking how far it was to Cremona. "Molto, Signor, mollo," was the answer, which means, "very much, very much, very much."

It is the usual reply of all Italian pheasants when asked regarding distance. Paul was so refreshed that he did not mind the discouraging answer, he was in buoyant spirits and felt like he could dash along forever with out tiring.
This unusual animation and feeling of wondrous power, he could only attribute to the effects of the good food and wine.

Paddling along steadily he suddenly felt a tremendous pressure building in his head and with out the slightest reason, blood spurted from his mouth and nostril's, assuming he had broken a blood vessel.

Burning lights seemed to be all around him, with intensity of electric search lights. He noticed a village on the bank and decided he had better go over, he was bewildered to find it was only a mud bank with nothing there.

Paul was now becoming startled and wondering if something was wrong with his brain, his mind was wandering between the hallucinations of fever, and lucidity. Feelings of a high temperature, would suddenly vanish as the struggling mind briefly restored itself.

He began frantically paddling, as some swaying willows became three ladies in dressed in Grecian costumes.

Smiling and bowing to him, his mind told him they were only willows, but his eyes could not be convinced.

Darkness fell around him, he had no idea of where he

was going, then suddenly the lights burst on him again with increased brilliancy. No matter where his eyes turned, the intense rays were shine in his eyes. Believing that he had arrived at Cremona, and that some men were turning the reflector on to annoy him.

"Keep those lights off." he shouted, "don't you see they are blinding me?"

Reasoning came back for and instant and told him there was no town or lights, he then knew he must call for help. Several minutes elapsed before he could remember the proper Italian word.

Then he cried out: "Soccorso, soccorso!"

But only the echo responded from the lonely shore, again reaching the bank and landing on the dyke, which protects the lowlands from the floods. He climbed to the top, carrying the little "Irene" in his arms, then hearing a tack, tack, tack, like someone pounding, and through an open door he saw a shoemaker hammering away at the sole of a boot on his knee. Attempting to enter, he staggered against a tree. The shoemaker appeared in another direction and the sound of the hammer was constantly with him.

Almost over come with fatigue he decided to sit down, then his paddle assumed the character of his companion, remonstrating with him and advising him to move on.

"I think I will sit down here," Boyton would say.

"Indeed you won't," answered the paddle.

"But I must." "If you do, you will die, Come on." the paddle insisted.

Endeavoring to obey the commands of the paddle he continued to stagger on, falling at every few steps, then regaining his footing, pressed forward. Intense thirst came over him, he returned again to the brink and drank large quantities of water, burying his face in the muddy stream, the paddle continuing to telling him to move on. Along the top of the dyke were three posts to prevent cattle leaving the road, these posts became sneering laughing men, wearing cloaks over their shoulders, Italian style, they were insolent and he challenged them to a fight, but they only ridiculed him. "You are the fellows that have bothered me all night," he shouted.

ROUGHING IT IN RUBBER

Dropping to one knee, he took his knife from it's sheath and plunged it into the chest of one of the men. In a flash of reason he saw the knife quivering in a post. Again the fevered voyager started to walk, the paddle assuring him all the way that he would find a small town or village really soon. Two or three times the overwhelming thirst drove him back down to the brink, drinking vast amounts of water, climbing back up the dyke was draining his strength rapidly, attempting to lie down again, the paddle earnestly remonstrated,

"It's death, death if you lie down, keep on," it kept saying. Exhaustion finally took over, and he lay down, barely stretching his legs on the muddy dyke, when he heard "dong, dong, dong," of a great bell clanging, he counted twelve strokes.

"Ah," that's another illusion," he thought, as it brought him to a sitting position, just as the bell sounded with a different tone, "ding, ding, ding," and again he counted twelve strokes again.

The second sound convinced him that he was near a village, and obeying the commands of the paddle, he struggled to his feet and followed the road, passing under an old arch that spanned the road. He was afraid to touch it as he was sure it would also disappear, shortly he was on a cobbled stone street, he saw houses on either side but under the delusion that they would also disappear if he approached them, as he advanced on the cobble stones, treading lightly for fear of scaring them away.

Advancing down the street while still arguing with the paddle, that it really isn't a village, a light shinning through a transom over the door of some out building, attracted his attention. Hearing the sound of voices he approached the door, listening to men laughing.

A mad thought came to him, that he must make a desperate dash at the door before it vanished, he did so, and the frail barrier gave way under the pressure of his shoulders, stumbling headlong inside a room. He disturbed several men who were drinking and playing some game, as he regained his balance he saw two men trying to escape through a window, while the others seized chairs and benches to ward off an attack of what they imagined to be the Evil one.

"Mollo malado!" cried Boyton.

At hearing this, they gained confidence and put down their weapons.

"Nedico Albergo," inquired the voyager.
One of the more intelligent in the room said, "Ah, he want's a doctor and a hotel, he is sick." They escorted him down the street, the men advanced in a group as Paul stumbled on behind until, they reached the hotel, some of the party started throwing pebbles at the upper window and shouting to awaken the landlord. While they were doing that Paul counted them and there was twelve, he decided that they had to be the twelve apostles.

"Pedro, Pedro, come down, shouted one of the apostles, "a Frenchman want's to get in." Pedro opening the door and seeing Paul in the rubber suit and covered in mud, said, "No room, no room."

Boyton said, "Vino," a touch of reason coming to his aid.

"Yes," replied the landlord, "you can have wine."

He opened the door and the group all entered a large room with an earthen floor with common tables polished to a snowy white.

The landlord eyeing Paul with suspicion, as he took out the map book from the little boat he was still carrying, in the pages was ten lire, Italian paper money ($2) and putting it down said, "wine for all."

The apostles were excited and becoming rowdy, while Paul trying to drink a glass of wine, while listening to the conversations of his strange comrades dozed off. Leaving the twelve apostles to finish up the ten lire of vino as if they have never had such a windfall.

The noise had woken the landlords wife, she entered the room looking for the cause of all the excitement, noticing Paul slumped over, she stepped over, and lifting the rubber head piece, exclaimed angrily to the men,

"Can't you understand?, this man has: feber del fuoco," high fever.

Taking away the glass she order her husband to build a fire and began taking off his rubber suit, the apostles offered to help, removing the tunic as steam rose from his body like a boiler, when the pantaloons were removed, the good hostess while thanking them, unceremoniously ordered the twelve into the street.

She procured a chicken, which was soon boiling and with some kind of tea, insisting Paul consume it after which he was escorted to a room and snugly covered up in a big canopied bed. He was no sooner stretched on the mattress than he was sound asleep, not waking until the sun shone through the window the next day.

Hearing the murmur of voices in the street, jumping up, his feet struck the cold tiled floor sending a shudder through his body. Peering through the curtains he saw a crowd of people looking up at his room and a buzz of voices could be heard all around the house. Not knowing where he was or how he got here, he pulled the bell cord and the summons was answered by the land lady.

Greeting Paul kindly and hoped he was feeling better, she informed him, that two gentleman were below who wished to see him.

"Let no one up, but a doctor," answered Paul, but within a few moments three men entered. He was unreasonably suspicious and testily told the men that he only wanted to see a doctor.

One of the men explain that he was the Mayor of Meletti, that one of his companions was a doctor and they had come to take care of him, such gracious answers to the roughly suspicious Paul, disarmed him and they were soon on friendly terms.

The mayor informed him that a carriage was at the door to take him to his home where better care can be given to him, Paul explained that he had nothing to wear other than the under wear he was wearing, the mayor immediately arranged for clothing to be delivered and escorting him to the waiting carriage, through crowds of gapping people cheering at the sight of him, as rumors of the great man in a rubber suit had been spread in the village, that he had come down with the dreaded fever.

The journey was an hour long, but comfortable and arriving at the mayor's mansion Paul was installed in a room under the care of a distinguished physician, no one could have had better care than this.

He later learned that his host, beside his official position was a large proprietor, owning most of the village and was a member of the Gattoni de Meletti family.

Reports of Paul's, 'Man in the Rubber Suit," having come down with the dreaded fever, spread all over Italy.

Great numbers of people came from surrounding towns and villages to see him and inquire as to his condition. "Febbre del fuoco" known as " The Fire Fever," that Paul had got is peculiar to the district along the Po, and he had been eighty-three consecutive hours in the water when it overcame him, normally this severe fever would cause the death of many a healthy man along the river.

For more than a week the doctor kept a very close watch on Paul, until he was sure that Paul was strong enough to get around, without a risk of relapse. The mayor took time to show him everything of interest, among his other properties he owned were, many farms with great droves of cattle, the cows in this vicinity are well known all over the world for suppling the milk for the famous Parmesan cheese. The mayor's herds wintered in long sheds and looking across the stalls the cow's all seemed the exactly same height, they seemed as level as the floor. Paul remarked to the mayor at,

"how clean and sweet smelling his stalls and sheds were kept." The mayor shrugging with pride as they continued their tour.

The notoriety given to the town of Meletti by Paul Boyton's presence caused quite a lot of envy in the villages and surrounding town's.

Castlenuovo Bocco d'Adda, the town in which he first appeared, they were convinced they had been cheated out of the fame by mayor of Meletti taking charge of Paul. In order to even things up and honor the distinguished guest they formed a Paul Boyton Club and held a banquet in his honor, this was then followed by a more stupendous evening of entertainment by the people of Meletti and thus created great rivalry between the two towns. At the Meletti evening people came from Cremona to see Paul give an exhibition in aid of a benefit to raise funds for the poor.

ROUGHING IT IN RUBBER

Paul now fully recovered from the fever, continued his voyage on the Po, starting at Meletti as crowds cheered him all the way down the river, on the fourth day after no more delusions or incidents, ended his journey at Ferrara.

When he landed he found his enterprising agent had again used the same tactic's here as he had done in Piacenza, with large crowds lining the banks and bridges for Paul's promised arrival.

On the day set by Paul' agent for Boyton's arrival, as great crowds has gathered for hours to welcome the hero, they becoming impatient with the agent, as he noticed a log floating down the river and alarming the crowds with, "there he is." As the excited people squinted in the fading light for a glimpse of Paul the scoundrel made his get away. The agent having reached the limit of his credit in Ferrara disappeared to the shades of Milan, where we suspect he resumed his operatic career.

Paul was treated like royalty by the people of Ferrara, and to show his appreciation for all they had gone through, and the hospitality they now showered on him he gave an exhibition for the benefit of the poor in the moat of the Castle in which Luczreta Borgia was born. He was then presented with a silk flag and many great references.

After leaving Ferrara, he gave many exhibitions through the interior towns of Italy, and being persuaded he finally made arrangements for a voyage down the Arno from Florence to Pisa. This would mean a days run of about one hundred kilometers.

Florence became another frenzied of media from all over the world, with people of all nationalities flooding the city to witness the "Intrepid American," as he was now being called. Paul enjoyed the new title as prior to this he had been called a "Man Fish", the new title carried a little more dignity with it.

The city of Florence was so excited with this news, people started gathering from all over Italy and lining the banks of the Arno for days before the scheduled start, before two o'clock on the following afternoon.

 The river which is fed by mountain streams, was rising rapidly, owing to the recent heavy rains up in the mountains and many people voiced their doubts as to his ability of Paul to accomplish this undertaking.

A dam called the Pescaia, spans the river diagonally, in the midst of the city and it is considered an extremely dangerous obstacle. At nine o'clock in the morning of the scheduled start day, Paul arrived to large cheering crowds and well wishers as he was preparing and checking the currents for his two o'clock start.

A successful start was made just before two o'clock in the afternoon, as the rapid current assisted by the powerful strokes of his paddle soon carried Paul beyond the sight of the crowds, he as went over the dam safely.

At twenty minutes to nine in the evening he arrived at San Romano where an immense crowd of people, including the notables of the district, with the municipal junta of Montopoli, awaited patiently for his arrival. Torches blazed along the bank to show him where to land as loud cheers roared from multitudes of people along the banks when he came out of the water.

Paul was escorted to a small Inn where his only refreshment was two cups of tea, the crowds calling for a speech, to quieten the yelling, he stepped out on the porch and delivered the speech in the only Italian words he knew, "Signori, Taute grazie di vostra accoglienza, arrive derie, ciao!"

The speech was received with great applause and the crowd dispersed with satisfaction. He remained at San Ramono for a short while, though the people advised him to stay over night as a little below the village there is a weir that is considered a most formidable spot by the inhabitants, proved to be a mere toy for Paul to frolic in.

Laughing at their fears as he entered the water, paddling away on the rapid current, the water was now much higher than when he first started, regardless of the late hour the banks were lined with people and torches for miles, cheering him on.

The whole population seemed to have again turned out, as Paul came opposite he stood up in the water saluting the cheering masses along both banks.

Resuming his recumbent position, and began to paddle as

ROUGHING IT IN RUBBER

his hand came in contact with the upturned face of a dead woman, for a moment he was horrified. Fastening the body to a line, he carried her to shore, while the band played and people cheered, not realizing the voyager had such a ghastly object in tow. He called out that he had the corpse of a woman with him, some of the authorities took charge, but the crowds seemed unaware of it as they followed him up the street, cheering and tripping over each other, scrambling to get close enough to see him.

One enthusiast, who thought he was being unduly crowded out, pushed his torch down another mans throat.

To calm and quieten down this crazy crowd Paul was forced to repeat his Italian speech that he had made at San Ramono, "Signori, Taute grazie di vostra accoglienza, arrive derie, ciao!" An impronto banquet was set up, that proved to be a noble success, but very tiring to the aggravated landlord, who seemed to be completely overwhelmed at having such unusual trade. Instead of forfilling more orders for edible's, he would rush into the banquet hall every few moments and nervously count the empty wine bottles.

The guests yelling at him to hurry up with their food, but those bottles were counted several times before any food was placed on the tables. Paul remained in Pontedera until morning, simply because he did not want to reach Pisa, until around noon the following day his, scheduled arrival time.

It was eight o'clock in the morning when he entered the river, after being escorted by the same enthusiastic crowds, as he again paddled away, arriving at Piza at noon.

A unique reception had been arranged by the mayor and all the authorities were out to meet him in those peculiar looking boats "Lancia Pisana," unknown or seen anywhere else in the world.

About thirty feet long and richly carved, then gaudily painted in bright colors, this type of boat is of some historic origin in Italy.

Under the escort of these gayly colored boats containing the notable people of the city, Paul landed to huge cheering crowds, Assuming that Paul could not speak or understand Italian, they hired an interpreter for the occasion, who was supposedly a great English scholar, this Paul doubted, as the evening banquet progressed Paul's suspicions proved to be correct.

The fellow was a burr, sticking to the outer shirts of respectable society, and when engaged to act as interpreter he was so over weighted with self importance, seated at Paul's right arm, when ever a toast was to be made he would stand up and bow in the most gracious manner, he became an embarrassment to Paul.

He had been honoring every toast with large quantities of wine and became highly intoxicated.

The fellow was having way too much fun to be easily disposed off, as he mentioned this fact to one of his entertainers and it was not until some harsh words were expressed to the interpreter that he agreed to leave the scene. In the meantime he had been wandering the streets and the more he thought of his dismissal, the deeper became his anger and feeling that he had been insulted. After a few more glasses of wine at the cafe the interpreter decide to write a challenge to Paul, entering the lobby of the hotel with an air of great impor
tance, and calling to the waiter in a tone that could be heard through the hotel, "Waiter a, pen, ink and paper, I wish to write to Captain Boyton." The stationery was provided and the English scholars challenge, was no more than a couple of uneligible scribbles.

Next morning Paul returned to Florence and that evening while entertaining some friends at the hotel, one of the guests looking out of the window remarked how much higher the river was than when he started for Pisa, other guest adding, that it would be impossible for him to go into the river as it's flooding. Paul overhearing them said, "Ladies and Gentleman, if you will step out on the porch , and waite a few moments, I will go into the river and paddle through the city, to show you that I am as safe in this flood water as I would be if it were as smooth as glass. While he was preparing for this short trip, the news spread over the city like a wild fire, people flocked to line the shores.

Paul had forgotten about the dam below, the water was pouring over it in great torrents, it was extremely dangerous.

ROUGHING IT IN RUBBER

He entered the raging current and was rapidly carried towards the dam, realizing the danger he was approaching, it was too late to stop now as the power of the raging current was carrying him directly to the falls.

As he went over the sloping volumes of water, he was met at the bottom by an immense back wash which drove him under.

Where the crashing waves met each other that rolled him over and over like a great log, he was caught between a back and a undertow. Thousands of people were gathering at Piscaia, believing Paul was lost.

Men turned pale and women fainted as they occassionally caught a glimpse of an arm protruding from the dark angry waters.

"Only God can save him now," yelled an old Italian man in the crowd.

The multitude of people felt that there was nothing to be done, but stand by and watch him drown. As this all transpired, Paul thought, if I don't get out of this fast, they will be giving my mother the news of my death on Christmas eve. What a sad Christmas that would be for her, I cannot let it happen.

With that thought he struggled with all the strength he had against the awful power of the contending waters, and fortunately with his paddle, succeed in throwing himself out on a large wave as he was carried down stream. A great sigh of relief coming from the crowds sounded like the rush of distant wind.

Soon after Paul was pulled from the river insensible, once he recovered from this ordeal King Victor Emanuel gave permission for him to appear in Jardin Bobili. The crowds were so great and the excitement was at fever pitch during Paul's appearance in Jardin Bobili, that the ticket takers at the gates, were carried away by the crowds, as many entered free, several thousand francs were raised, as several more were surely lost.

Paul was now the fashion in Italy, songs were composed and sung in his honor at the theatres, brands of cigars and other items were given his name. Business's had their calendars for the new year printed with his story and pictures and the citizens of Meletti named a lake after him. Managers of amusements, advertised that he would make an appearance for their entertainment, drawing hundreds more people to their gates, and every where the praises of the 'Intrepid American" could be heard.

From Florence Paul went to Rome, where he visited General Pescetto, Italian Minister of Marine (Navy), with whom he had a pleasant conversation, during which Paul's meeting with his son on the Po was mentioned.

"What can I do for you?" cordially asked the General.

"Well," answered Paul, "my business is introducing my Life Saving Suit, which will help you save many lives on the coast, as well as on the Men-of-War that you are now building."

"Ah," you have proved the value of your rubber suit, I have no doubt of it's efficiency, but our government has spent vast sums of money for the benefit of shipwrecked sailors," answered the General.

"In regards, to using your suit on our Men-of-War, I fear you don't understand the Italian sailor, should we furnish your life saving suits, our sailors would suspect that the Man-of-War, were not sea worthy, we already have enough trouble getting the young men to enlist." responded the General.

"Suppose I could prove to you that it would be possible to slip under one of your Men-of-War on a dark night, and blow her to atoms. How would that be?" Paul replied.

"Ah," responded the General earnestly, "that is a different question. If you can prove that to me, I will call a commission to investigate this possibility." Ample proof was given to the effiency of the rubber suit.

Arrangements were later made for an exhibition in the Bano del Poplo. While making preparations, Paul first experienced the manner in which European artisans have, of doing business and their original manner of billing for services rendered.

He needed to hire a carpenter to build several small boats to use in this exhibition. The landlord recommending a carpenter, Paul negioated a price of five lire each, and supplied the specks. The carpenter had the little boats ready on time, and during the exhibition, appointed himself as the major demo man, always being in the way and annoying Paul. At the close of the exhibition he presented a bill for seventy five lire, according to his contract it should have been thirty five lire, Paul demanded an itemized bill from the carpenter.

This is a copy of the billing submitted by the carpenter, which should be of interest to any businessman:

To six boats, per agreement............................ 30 lire.
Wood for building same...................................11 "
Nails.. 2 "
Labor and making..14 "
Pieces broken in bending................................. 5 "
Carry boats to Bano.. 2 "
Time lost while at exhibition.............................10 "
Wine for poor boy who fell overboard.............. 1 "
Total .....75 lire.

Paul paid the carpenter the thirty lire owed to him, receiving the profane blessings of the irate contractor.

Boyton was just in time for the great Roman Carnival and had the pleasure, if such it may be called, of witnessing the spectacle of barbaric behavior. This was a cruel and dangerous sport, a horse race along the Corso, the principal thoroughfare in Rome, which is a narrow winding street. The race is between five or six thoroughbred horses, almost wild and very vicious. They are turned loose in the street without bridles or any other harness, only a surcingle, from the sides of which hung like tassels, steel balls with sharp needle like points protruding from them, that serves to prick the animals to a frenzy of speed. The streets were lined with people and it took the guards all they have, to keep them back and out of danger. As the canon is fired, the terrified animals dash madly down the street with the wicked steel balls swinging in the air. People and horses are always killed at this barbaric Roman Carnival, the carnage and cruelty of horses has since been outlawed, in Italy and I believe all of Europe.

While in the ancient city Paul was determined to make a voyage down the Tiber. Going up the river as far as he possibly could get, to Orte, measuring the distance from Rome to Orte, about ninety miles by river. The news of him travelling up the river reached Orte before he did, and another reception awaited his arrival, he was royally received by the authorities and towns people.

When the start was made, Paul was escorted to the river by the mayor, lustily blowing a horn all the way, like a fish peddler trying to attract attention. The Tiber is an uninteresting stream, running through the Roman Campagna, and is made up of great bends.

Leaving Orte in the afternoon the night came in quickly as the night became terribly cold and now and then he would get a cheer from people along the banks.

He paddled rapidly along all night without any adventures worth mentioning. About six o'clock the next morning he was caught in an awkward manner in the branches of a tree that had been washed into the stream, having to use his knife to carefully extricate himself from the limbs without damage to the crutch, or of course the rubber suit. All day he day he paddled energetically along, the stream turned, and twisted, so much that he frequently passed the same village twice as he swung around the great bends.

That night Paul came near to frightening the life out of a shepherd, not knowing where he was on this long winding river, and hearing a dog barking, he climbed up the bank to ask his location, at the top of the bank, meeting a shepherd face to face. Before he could even ask the a question, a look of disbelief on the shepherds face, startled and yelling something unbeknown to Paul, ran across the plains as fast as his legs could carry him.

Paul was met by the Commodore and members of the main boat club of Rome, The Canottiere del Tevere, and was accompanied by them for the rest of the journey down river. Next morning, just outside Rome they hauled up at the club house for breakfast. Miles before reaching the city people on foot and horse back came out, lining the banks to cheer him on with "viva's, viva Boyton."

At three o'clock as Paul stepped out of the water in Rome, he was welcomed by thousands of people, Paul was astonished as a band was playing "Yankee Doodle" in his honor. People were cheering and every available space, balconies

ROUGHING IT IN RUBBER

and windows were jam packed with people trying to get a glimpse of him.

The elaborate reception was in a house just off the banks of Ripetta Grande, and to his intense amazement an undescribable sight, the house was all decorated with American flags, flying proudly in the breeze.

While a large barge on the river was packed beyond it's capacity with well wishers, in the frenzy of excitement of the passengers, it capsized, spilling them all into the water, fortunately close enough to the bank for the occupants to survive. So great were the crowds around him that the pressure crushed the iron band around his waist as if it was no more than an egg shell. No end of fetes and invitations followed, the citizens seemed to compete as to who could give the most splendid and extravagant receptions and banquets to the Intrepid American.

Naples was to be the next stop, with the intention of crossing the famous bay, arriving in the city, in time for their carnivals.

Paul arriving in Naples, attended the carnival and was thrilled to see Victor Emanuel, that grim but kind natured old king, opening the carnival by driving through the streets and submitting to the bombardment of confetti. His majestic smile and bow as he passed along throwing some of it back at those who were standing close by. The confetti was made of plaster of paris and easily crumbles to powder, as it is thrown everywhere, at everybody by the gay, laughing crowds of people.

On the afternoon of February the sixteenth, 1877, Boyton crossed on the steamer to Capri, having decided to start from that point. While on the island that afternoon, he visited the Blue Grotto. an opening in the island leading to an amazingly beautiful cave, which is a great tourist attraction, attracting people from all over Europe. On a boat passing through the entrance, you are shrouded in intense darkness, but the moment anything touches the water, phosphorus causes it to light up a vivid silver like color. The overwhelming urge to try out this water, had Paul in no time putting on his rubber suit. He paddled through the wondrous grotto, the wet rubber, lighting him up like in a bright silver armor, as his paddle disturbed the surface of the water.

At three o'clock the next morning he started on his trip across the bay from the steamboat landing. Not minding the very early hour of the morning the inhabitants of the island were on hand to witness the start, with the usual cheers of encouragement.

He was supervised to find that in the dark the water had the same effect on his suit as it did, in the Blue Grotto, even the fish were leaving phosphorescent trails as they darted about.

Mt. Vesuviuslooming up above seemed very close to Paul as the sun rose. He became concerned that he would reach Naples too early for the scheduled arrival.

About nine in the morning the bay became very rough, soon the blue waves were washing over him, he kept paddling with all he had and yet the grim smoke-covered mountain seemed no closer. At three in the afternoon he saw a felucca bearing down on him, as it approached close enough, he rose up in the water and hailed at her. The occupants came to the railing, pointing at the unusual object in the water, then the great sail was veered around as they scudded swiftly away.

Sailors on the bay are superstitious about picking up a dead body, possibly they thought he was dead or some mysterious denizen of the deep. Either way, they were obviously too terrified to investigate what they had seen in the water, any further.

At five o'clock he was now close to Naples in very rough seas, the excursion boats were out to meet him, almost missing him in the rough rolling waves, Paul had to sound the bugle several times to attract their attention.

Seven o'clock. Paul landed at the city to enormous crowds of people, among whom was King Victor Emmanuel, the *sindaco* with other noted authorities of Naples. The banquet was prepared in honor of him being presented to the King, making it very late before all the ceremonies were over. The fishermen's organization presented Paul with a chart signed by over four thousand people connected with the water, and Marianne Aguglia, Comtesse Desmouceaux, published a poem commemorating the event.

ROUGHING IT IN RUBBER

King Victor Emmanuel invited Paul to give an exhibition before him at the arsenal, or military port. The King was accompanied by his morganatic wife, the Countess of Miraflores. He was delighted with the performance, particularly with the torpedo. One of the pieces of timber from the explosion, fell near his feet. He laughed loudly, as the Countess withdrew in alarm. After the exhibition, Boyton removed his suit and standing clad in a well worn American Navy uniform, he was escorted to join the royal pair by Admiral del Carette.

The King asked Paul many questions in his quaint, Piedmontese French, and then realizing that the Intrepid American was looking rather tired, he ordered two goblet's of wine to be brought in; with these good health and fortunes were pledged.

An officer was ordered to bring the cross, which the King himself pinned on Paul' blue shirt. Knighting him with "The Cross of the Order of the Crown of Italy." saying,

"You are a brave man and deserve this token of our appreciation."

Paul did many exhibitions in and around Naples. This tremendous success brought in large sums of money. While in Naples he had decided to attempt the dreaded straits, and risk the dangers of the noted whirlpools of Scylla and Charybdis, he was warned in Naples, that should he attempt these whirlpools. He would be committing suicide, as not only were the straits deadly, but were infested with sharks. From Naples he moved on to Messina, determined to check out the stories of the sharks.

Early the next morning he went down to the market place and purchased a very large piece of meat that he took out to the Fort where the sharks were supposed to be numerous. Throwing a piece of the meat into the water and watching it sink, believing that the stories of the sharks were highly exaggerated, then suddenly the meat was gone, throwing another piece in, it barely touched the surface before a rush and a swirl, as the meat was snapped up. An old hat was thrown in next and it was torn to shreds in seconds, this was undeniable proof that sharks were more than plentiful in the straits.

Paul was somewhat disappointed as he had made his mind

up to do this voyage, and never backed down on his decisions. People were already talking about Paul going to attempt to swim the straits and bets had been placed from the country and city people, to his chance of survival in these waters. The excitement was growing all around. One man was heard to say,

"If the sharks don't get him, the whirlpools sure will."
One evening sitting gloomily at a corner table in the Cafe, Paul overheard an older gentleman wager his oxen, "that the American would not attempt this voyage, and he could not cross if he did."

Though very disheartened, when he heard this, as well as many more doubts expressed as to his ability to accomplish the feat.

Made Paul all the more determined to attempt all risks and hazards.

An old legend is extant among the fishermen and peasants of the locality, that the only human who ever crossed the straits without the aide of a boat, was St. Francisco, who, was being pursued by enemies, spreading his cloak on the water and stepping on it, was wafted across without harm safely escaping the enemies.
So Boyton's attempt was sure to result in his death.

After deciding he would try the crossing, Paul hired a Felucca,
owned by the most expert spearsman in those waters, to accompany him, and another for the invited guests and newspaper men. These boats were ready on the morning of March the sixteenth 1877.

They sailed from Messina for the coast of Calabri where the start was to be begin, arriving at seven o'clock that morning. To a small scattered village on the Calabrian side, the Felucca transported Paul and his guests. After being put ashore the preparations were made for the start.

The party consisted of several prominent men from Messina, among them the editor of the Gazelle. Everybody was well armed for the wolves of the deep as called in this area. The editor was very bold in his assertions of how he would protect Boyton from their attacks. As Boyton was putting on his suit, a sirrocco was blowing, sending a heavy tide in the direction of the whirlpool of Scylla, or the Faro, as they called it. The sea grew rougher as the little party stood on the beach, the most anxious one, was the enthusiastic editor who was pacing back and forth.

Inhabitants from the little village began crowding down to the shore, and learning what was going on. An old white haired man, approached Paul, and in the most earnest manner, addressed him in the Calabrian dialect pleading, "don't go, don't go," he cried.

"I had a boy such as you, who was lost out there, the devil of the straits will get you."

The appeal of the old man was interpreted to Paul and was the only occourance of the day that had a tendency to upset his nerves.

The expert spearsman had arranged a place on his boat where he could stand and harpoon any sharks that might attack the swimmer, while the guests on the other boat were pretty well equipped to keep the monsters at bay.

Everything was now ready and the Felucca backed in from her cable to load the guests on board. All were safely on except the bold editor, he was pale and his knees were knocking together. His courage was gone and he insisted on staying on shore, until one of the sailors lifted him bodily aboard. The sea was now very rough as the crafts moved away from the beach, the waves splashing over them..

Paul going overboard, struck away as fast as he could as both Feluccas kept a sharp lookout He reached mid channel without encountering any danger, stopping to look around and get his bearings, he presumed he was close to Charybdis. As the foremost boat rose on a huge wave he saw a shark right under it, removing his knife from it's sheath, Paul was ready to defend himself. As the Felucca's seemed too far away for his comfort, he started to become rather nervous, he called out that a shark was insight, and was told afterwards that the brave editor dropped to his knees and prayed that
they would not all be swallowed up.

The shark was darting from side to side of the boat, then spotting Boyton's black figure, instantly turning on it's side and heading straight for him. Paul braced for the attack, as the monster was close enough. He ripped at it, getting it right under the mouth, as the tail swung around, swiping Paul, with a severe blow to his side, the shark disappeared in a trail of blood as it went under. Paul swam away as fast as he could, grateful to have escaped the great monster.

The challenge continued as the tide was carrying him directly into the spot he had first discovered sharks, rather hesitantly he continued paddling along as a number of boats came out from the Messina shore, people yelling and splashing in the water as this helped keep the great brutes away.

On the outer edge of the whirlpool of Charybdis, which is a great eddy caused by a jutting point of land on which a fort is built, and on it's ebb tide, strong enough to swamp a boat. Paul worked for an hour without advancing a single yard, the people meanwhile expecting to see him get swallowed up by a shark, were yelling many encouraging words and blessing. He held out however, and at lastmoved through the waters to landing safely at Messina.

The American ships in port, dipped their flags to salute him, while the astonished population, congratulated him on his

ROUGHING IT IN RUBBER

unbelievable success. The valiant editor of the Gazette, now safely landed became the lion, graphically telling story to the admiring crowds surrounding them.

From the warf to a reception at City Hall, streets were lined with thousands of cheering people, soldiers were brought in to protect him.

On arrival at the hall, he fainted. An examination showed that three of his ribs were broken, and the steel band around his waist bent and pushed in too close to his body by the great force of the blow from the sharks tail. Paul was taken to the hotel, where he remained for two weeks recovering from that blow. Then taking life easy, he visited Mr. Etna, Catalana, Syracuse and other places of interest in Sicily. At Syracuse, he spent a lazy week, it is one of the dirtiest towns in the Paul enjoying every thing he saw, walking down the streets, he was always followed by groups of little boys trying to sell him all sorts of little trinkets. One boy was especially persistent in trying to dispose of an ancient coin of the Ceasar's. That he claimed it was very valuable, and will sell it for the paltry sum of only ten lire. Boyton told him he knew all about the coin, and he would give him two lire to find the man who made it. The young villain mysteriously whispered the information, which surprisedly was later found to be correct.

Some of the boys would get him, ten good oranges for one cent, with an extra penny for going on the errand.

The favorite amusement of Paul and his agent, was to go out on the road in hopes of encountering brigand's(bandits). They would enter some low Cabriolet that was suspected of harboring these knights of the mountains. With carbines concealed under their coats, they would make an ostentatious display of rolls of Italian paper money, hoping that some of the robbers would follow them out to the streets, and stir up a little bit of excitement.The brigand's were either to busy or assumed the American was not the one to attack, for they never showed up, much to Paul and his agents disappointment.

Before leaving the old town, Paul was asked to give an exhibition. Before the start Paul hung his rubber suit over a stone wall, as the crowds gathered, he hurriedly got dressed. He flung it off with greater rapidity, when he found it was full of little green lizards, which are abundant on the island. The exhibition was delayed while the vermin were removed, much to the amusement of the of the islanders.

When the P&Q Steamer arrived the next morning, Paul and his agent embarked for Malta. This is where they had their first clash with authorities.

There is a peculiar law in that sleepy old town, which prohibits the posting of any posters larger than a small sheet of note paper.

The night after their arrival, they plastered the town with regular size page posters, which looked to the natives, bigger than they were. Next morning the inhabitants were aghast at the audacity of the Americans in doing such an unheard of thing.

They were called up before the Governor and the enormity of their offense solemnly revealed to them, but owing to the plea of ignorance of the law, they were discharged and ordered to take down the posters as quickly as possible. In obedience of the Governor, they employed a sleepy eyed native to do the work, with the instructions to take his time. It took two days to undo one nights work and the authorities were more than satisfied, and the exhibition was the best advertised than any other had been, in Malta.

Paul became a great favorite with the boatmen and fishermen of Malta, and spent all of his leisure time with his new friends, going out fishing with them often. The boatmen are peculiar and their boats are queer affairs, every one has a large eye painted on each side of the bow. Paul asked a fisherman, "why are eyes painted on the boats?" and he gravely replied,

"How could the poor things see without eyes."
Not one of these men could be enticed to go out in a boat, that had no eyes painted on her.

From Malta, Paul went to Tunis, and landing there was genuinely surprised. The passengers and their luggage were loaded into boats, to transfer them to shore, where they were met by crowds of bare legged natives who waded out as far as they could, and when a boat was close enough they scram-

ROUGHING IT IN RUBBER

bled to grab the luggage and taking off with it, regardless of the objections, from the owners. At the customs house, the luggage was found, each native sitting stoically on whatever he had chanced to capture, with an air of absolute proprietorship. After it was cleared by the agents, it was carried to the hotel by the howling mobs, where, with many kicks and cuffs administered by the landlord, it was reclaimed by it's rightful owner. For of course the much sought after tip, for services rendered, when it was forcefully obtained.

Paul gave an exhibition at this place at which the awe stricken exhibitions all over the country, with tremendous success. While working north he received an invitation to visit Lake Trasmene, where they hold a historic Roman celebration. The villages around the lake join in a the celebrations at Pastgnano.

Boyton's goal was to cross from the old town of Castiglioni de Lago to Pastgnano, the mountaineers living near the lake came out in queer boats loaded to the waters edge as they followed him across.

The wind was blowing and Paul was concerned for the heavily laden little boats, they did not look as if they could stand any form of rough weather. He warned them and he then began begging them to go ashore, but very few heeded his warnings.

Scarcely had he landed when an Italian officer rushed in to where he was undressing, excitedly shouting.

"Oh, go back, go back. They are drowning out there."
As quickly as was possible, Paul returned to the lake and saw that one of the boats had swamped. The three occupants could not be found and were assumed drowned, the effects of this accident put a damper on the festivities for the day, the music was hushed as much sorrow was expressed for the unfortunates.

The Syndaco, however invited Paul to dinner. They were just beginning to relax and enjoy themselves under the sad circumstances.

A delegation of people arrived to inform them, that the majority of the crowd was dissatisfied, many had come a great distance and demanded to see L'Uomo Pesce, IMan Fish a name they had given Boyton." Some of the leading men advised Paul that it would be better for him to give some form of exhibition to prevent a riot. Much against his will, Paul went out and gave a very successful exhibition, before the bodies of the unfortunates were recovered. The mountaineers were satisfied, however, and returned to their homes with all sorts of opinions of "Man Fish." That night after sunset the bodies were found and brought on shore, for the families to claim. The night was dark and airy as the weird sounds and wailing from the families, echoed through the night until sun rise, this is supposedly to call spirits.

Next day Paul and his agent stayed over to pay their last respects and attend the funerals. They witnessed the peculiar ceremonies of Misericordia, a society that has a strange tradition of burying the dead. They wear long white robes, covering their entire bodies, with holes cut for eyes, nose and mouth. Forming a grim looking procession, and as they turned those grim expressionless faces towards us, it sent cold shudders down our spines. Regardless of this uncanny feeling Paul and his agent followed the procession into the church, and by doing so gained the goodwill of the villagers, who assured them that they were in no way to blame for the accident. The entire monies made from that days exhibition, with a liberal addition from him, presented, the families of the drowned men. Paul now feeling reassured, continued with his prior plans and left the next morning to return to Milan.

Exhibitions were performed in Milan, Turin, Genoa and other cities in northern Italy, with great success and admiration of the Intrepid American. Then the travellers moved on to France, to the headwaters of the Rhone. Paul intended to make this his next voyage. With the goal of going down the entire river, from it's source to the Mediterranean. He visited Geneva and Switzerland. While in Geneva, he found that it was impossible to start at the source of Rhone, as the river actually flows through a cavern and goes under the mountain, then reappears. Paul was intrigued and anxious to try the underground current, he decided to do some test runs on how long it would take to go from one end to the other before attempting it himself. Firstly having his agent watch the other end of the cavern, while Paul, miles above at the mouth of the cavern, sending two logs through. They did not go through, then a couple of floatation devices, nether of these reappeared. Not prepared to be discouraged yet, he acquired a pair of ducks and sent them into the cavern, sadly they were lost. This was the deciding factor, that he would start at the end of the cavern, selecting the little village of Seyssel as the best point to start this voyage down the river.

The Rhone when high, is one of the most rapid rivers in the world, his trip from Seyssel to the Mediterranean was the swiftest he ever made, a distance of five hundred kilometers, or three hundred miles.

Paul got an early start on this challenging river, he was able to make great time due to the speed of the current, though quite a challenge at times to stay out of danger, the perilous rapids of Saute du Rhone were an experience he never wishes on anybody, especially when the river is the high flood level. Making very good time as he neared France, Paul had a narrow escape.

The authorities on the frontier are kept busy watching for smugglers who run contraband goods from Switzerland into France.

Large quantities of goods are smuggled through, by floating them down the river at night, and in order to catch such articles the officers of Duane stretched a strong gate chain work across the river just at the border. This gate has sharp iron hooks attached at intervals, the packages become hooked up as they floated down river.

Unaware of this obstacle, as he neared the frontier village, he noticed large crowds congregating along the banks, as this was a normal thing in his travels, he rose up in the water and waved back. From their weird gestures and wild gesticulation, he could see they were shouting, but he again just thought they were cheering him on as he continued his rapid approach down the river. When closer to the crowds he saw they were shouting and making motions for him to stop, the current was too swift for him to even attempt getting to the banks, as he was being carried along by the force of the water. He suddenly noticed uniformed guards rushing out on the bridge, throwing off their coats and began quickly turning large cranks, then he saw the sheet of glistening heavy metal hooks slowly rising out of the water. He suddenly understood the warnings from shore, it was too late to change his course in the swift current, submerging himself as flat as he could, drawing near the wicked looking points and slowly, oh, so fearfully slow they rose, just above the water, then the second row of hooks started to appear. The crowds were breathless, as the guards bravely strained every muscle, but the thing was unwieldy and the work was slow, fearfully slow.

The terror of the people was depicted on their faces as they saw the row of hooks barely touching the water, was there enough for him to clear them, it would be certain death if he was thrust against the hooks at the great force of the water, he would certainly be mutilated.

The panting, perspiring guards, redoubled their efforts with a last turn of the heavy cranks, as Paul slid under those dreadful hooks with barely enough room to come out unscathed.
A great shout went up from the crowds, as Paul struggled to recompose himself and head for the shore. The water was measured at twelve miles an hour at that point, which made it extremely difficult.

He thanked the guards profusely, however they were more interested in asking him questions,
"What does it feel like, going so rapidly on the top of the water?,"
"Such a lively motion, excites me greatly, my heart beats fast and I feel as I have a great power, but have no power at all." he replied.
"Is there something in the danger that pleases you?" asked the other guard. "Yes, the challenge to concur the water." replied Paul.

After passing under the smugglers chain gate, his course ran between lines of hills which fringe the banks of the river. He kept seeing old women with a cow on the slopes, and was wandering if every cow had a woman attendant in that country, every now and then a woman would catch sight of Paul, gaze at the unusual object for a second and then left with her cow. One old dame and her cow were closer to the waters

ROUGHING IT IN RUBBER

edge, rising up and saluting her, he shouted, "Bon jour." She crossed herself and pushing the rear of her cow along, as they fled.

Next morning as he was nearing the rapids of Saute du Rhone, and asked a few of people on the bank, "How far is it Saute?"

"About two kilometers," was the answer."

"Which is the safest side?"

"The left." The next one told him to keep right, while another advised him to keep in the center, realizing he could not get any reliable information here, he rose up and looked around to see if there was anything visible to look out for.

Ahead of him he could see what looked like rapids, so running between big black rocks, with a bridge over them, that seemed to have crowds of people on it. It was too late to change course now and as Paul flew over a falls at the speed of an arrow, hitting bottom, the force of the water threw him against a rock wall, almost blinding him as he hung there for a moment trying to recover.

Again feeling the current sweeping him away, as fast as it swept him through the rapids, surviving this incredible encounter, he continued down the river as people cheered and extended many invitations to stop over. Had he accepted a third of these kind invitations, the trip would have taken at least three months to complete.

On one lonely stretch he saw a solitary old farmer standing on the bank,

"Ho, ho, my good friend," Paul shouted.

"Who is there?" asked the startled farmer.

"The devil."

"Where are you going?"

"To Lyons." responded Paul.

"Well, get along, then, you are going home." the farmer replied.

The farmer obviously did not like the city or Lyons.

Two o'clock, landing at Lyons after being on the water for twenty four hours. Paul was given a tremendous welcome and a great banquet was enjoyed by all, and before leaving he was presented with many excellent souvenirs.

Resuming the journey at about fifteen miles an hour on the flooding river, he was accompanied by several boats for a couple of miles down the river. Many of the banks had been broken with the water flooding over the lowlands, dodging through the groves of trees, using the paddle to avoid being caught up, as the current pushed him on. For the next day and two nights, Paul paddled his way down the raging river without any serious incidents.

When he reached Pont St. Esprit, with it's long stone bridge, the river rushed him through the arch, as he reappeared the crowds cheered him on. The next day Paul arrived safely at Arles after an exhausting sixty hours on these rapid flood waters.

The entire population was out to welcome him, not realizing how exhausted Paul was, a group of Gendarmes, sent by the Mayor to escort him to the hotel de Ville. Turning a deaf ear to his request for a carriage, they insisted Paul walk through the hot dusty streets, encased in his heavy rubber suit, carrying his paddle and little boat, so the people would have a good opportunity to see him. Though they meant well, their kindness coupled with ignorance, resulted in Paul almost passing out and barely able to walk by the time they reached the hotel, expressing his gratitude in rather vigorous terms.

From Arles, Boyton visited Monaco as a guest of Monsieur Blanc, who was then the head of the great gambling institutions. Paul was asked to give an exhibition for Monsieur Blanc, after a very successful exhibition, obviously thoroughly enjoyed by all, he was presented with two-thousand and five hundred francs by his host. The next evening Monsieur Banc gave him a tour of the magnificently decorated casinos, escorting Paul through the sumptuous gambling rooms.

Assuming to be polite, after the generosity of his host, Paul, placed a few francs on one of the numerous Rouge etc Noir tables and as he was about to lay down a Napoleon coin, his host noticed it.

"Don't do it," he quickly said, grasping Paul by the arm, "there are fools enough here without you becoming one." Monsieur took Paul into his private offices where rouleaux of gold were stacked up high around the walls, and pointed out what is lost.

Paul sauntered through the great halls, fascinated with the excitement He was besieged by a group of young ladies recognizing him, claiming, "why Mr. Boyton, you are lucky, place this bet for me." Paul resisted these temptations.

After leaving Monaco, Paul gave successful exhibitions in the principal cities of southern France and was honored with several rewards.

At Lyons his exhibition was for the benefit of the poor, preformed in the Golden Head Park, a record sum of fifteen thousand francs were raised. One of the most beautiful ladies Paul had ever seen, dressed in one of the rubber suits, then joining him in the water, was a great hit for the benefit. The city people were so grateful and impressed, that they presented him with a magnificent poinard , sheathed in a richly carved scabbard, with an artistily designed handle. This exquisite piece of solid silver, weighed about ten pounds, without the blade that was of fine steel.

From here exhibitions were given through out Belgium until November the fifteenth 1877. The monies raised in Belgium, amounted to, one thousand dollars a day for four days.

Arriving in Brussels, Paul was again asked to do a benefit for the poor, this being held at the lake of the Bois de Cambrai, under the patronage of King Leopold. The entire royal family was to attend this exhibition, which meant Paul needed to do extra planning for this demonstration, repeating the explosions, he demonstrated in Italy.
Huge crowds attended this exhibition, and an extremely large sum of money was again raised.

King Leopold was highly impressed and presented Paul with, the medal of The First Order of Life Savers of Belgium. November the seventeenth he began a voyage down the Somme, which took two days.

Starting at Amiens, on the evening of the first day, just before reaching Ponte Remy, where he intended to stay overnight, a couple of duck hunters hiding in the shrubbery on the river bank, mistook his his two feet, for a pair of ducks swimming down river, and started shooting at them, fortunately the heavy rubber soles repelled the bullets, and no damage was done. Rising up in the water with a torrent of forcible comments in English, the frightened sportsmen rapidly disappeared in the darkness.

Early the next morning, he continued with this trip, arriving at Abbyville that evening, where the customary generous reception awaited him, after two days on the river. The next day returning to Amiens for a scheduled exhibition, which again was most successful, and then on to Paris. Arriving in Paris, he had a new little boat built, often called tender, the first one was in disrepair after all the rough river rides it had encountered. Again naming her "Isabel Alvarez" in honor of the fair maiden in Italy, who stole his heart.

He began the voyage on the Loire, December eighth, 1877, at Orleans, to make the four hundred and nine miles to Nantes.

The weather was cold and miserable, this river has numerous dangerous shifting sand bars with quicksand, that makes it difficult to stay in the channel. The lowlands through which the river runs, are a channel for the winds, hence a great area for sail boats to navigate.

They are mostly wood or provision boats, flat bottomed and built somewhat like the canal boats, using enormous square sails on a single mast, way larger than any sailing ships.

Nine o'clock in the morning, he started from Orleans arriving at Blois that evening, as he came into shore he collided with a pylon under the pier, this was a close encounter as Paul was sure his arm was broken, fortunately it was only badly bruised so he stayed overnight to recover, to the pleasure of the inhabitants who lavished him with their hospitality. The following day he started again, for an all night run to make up for the lost time. The night grew intensely cold as ice soon formed on the exposed parts of his body. The lamp light on the bow of the tender gave him plenty of light and some entertainment. Along the frozen road that follows the bank, Paul could hear in crunching of boots and clattering of sabots as a pheasant, was happily singing his way home. Paul darkened the lamp, by placing a piece of rubber over it. As he came alongside, removing the rubber, the light shone on the man. Paul made an unearthly sound on his bugle. The startled man was speechless, but the distant sound of the clinking sabots, was enough to tell what a fright he got.

About four o'clock in the morning after dozing off, Paul woke as he felt the bottom of the river, realizing he had gone down a false channel, with much difficulty he got into an upright position, and as he did this, he felt a vice like grip on his legs.

He was caught in the quick sand, with a feeling of horror, he could feel himself, settling in the treacherous sands, until he was sucked down to almost his neck, as his face became almost even with the surface. The dark water gliding by him like some slimy serpent in the night, the tender swung around with her bow pointing towards him as the strong light from the lanterns rays, almost blinded him. The little boat tugging at the cord around his waist, seemed to realize his predicament and was trying to get free, or free him?.

All this time Paul was trying to free himself, the efforts were only sinking him deeper, with every movement. Beginning to realize that he was not going to get out, and thinking that no one would ever know what had become of him, should he die in this sand.

His nature was not one to give up, until the last gasp. A thought came to him, to try and fully inflate his suit, which should have the tendency to lighten him, giving more buoyancy, grasping the tubes he started to blow into them, as if his life depended on it.

Feeling himself becoming lighter as the chambers filled with air, the suit was inflating to almost bursting point, as he gasped for more air he felt a slight upward movement. Capping the tubes, Paul mustered up enough energy to thrust himself over backwards, landing him
on his back. Bursting with another powerful effort, he was lifted clear and moved away on the gliding water, he slowly deflated the suit and continued the journey, with a prayer of thanksgiving in his heart.

Ten o'clock, the next morning he arrived at Tours, with considerably shattered nerves, and excepted the invitation of the municipality to stop for refreshments, the hospitality of the city was overwhelming, he only remained long enough to rest and gain his strength back, and headed back to the river. At every village down the river Paul was given a very warm welcome, the weather being cold the mayors always insisted he stop and drink hot highly spiced wine, while being asked many questions about his suit and travels, the same question in every town, village and city, "Don't you get cold and wet?"

The little boat was loaded down with supplies and invitations were continuous from chateau to cottages, to partake of food and refreshment. Many times he would have to travel late into the night. to make up for the time spent excepting invitations. Usually his rest was broken by bands turning out to serenade him, at one town where there was no band, an enthusiastic admirer blew a hunting horn all night under his window, it was a frightful, but well intentioned serenade, that Paul could have done well without.

When he reached Ancenes he was met by a group, headed by the mayor with a liberal supply of hot wine. A boatman who was normally employed to place stakes to guide navigators, informed Paul that from here on there was a dramatic change in the currents, and insisted on accompanying him as his pilot. Paul assured him, that he had travelled this far, without a pilot and surely would not require one now. He could not get rid of the fellow that easily and was becoming annoyed at the man's persistence.

"I know the river well," he said, "and will pilot you down."
He could not get rid of this fellow, so considered another plan. They had only travelled a short distance, when Boyton asked the persistent boatman to join him in a drink, handing him a bottle of very strong wine that had been given to him incase he needed a stimulant. The fellow already half intoxicated, absorbed most of the contents and was soon maudlin, he ran his boat around and across Boyton, to the latter's great annoyance.

The fellow was becoming drowsy and started dozing off, this was the opportunity Paul had waited for, pushing the boat closer to the bank, he took the anchor from the bow of the fellow's boat and dropped it in the water, the boat swung around and hung there, Paul paddled away at great speed.

Paul was about one hundred yards away when he heard,
"Captain, Captain, where are you?"

ROUGHING IT IN RUBBER

The boatman thought he was drifting, Paul never saw him again.

Continuing down river, as the village people continued to come out and cheer him on, many offering refreshments and food. On several occasions Paul accepted the hot spiced wine, as this kept him warm and motivated. As he neared Ancenes he realized the four hundred and nine mile journey was about to end, and other than the quick sand it had been a very enjoyable and uneventful.

Below Ancenes Paul was met by Jules Verne, the distinguished novelist, who came up the river on a boat rowed by some of his sailors. He accompanied Boyton all the way to Nantes for the finish of his trip on the Somme.

The entire journey had taken eight days, excursion steamers met them and fired salutes, the Hospitaliers des Sauveteurs Bretons, the leading life-saving society of France, elected Paul an officer of the first rank and presented him with a diploma and medal.

The two men became great friends, and Paul thoroughly enjoyed the novelist's company on his yacht and also in his magnificent home in Nantes, Monsieur Verne used illustrations of the indian rubber, life saving suit, in scenes in his well known novel entitled, "The Tribulations of a Chinaman."

Paul remained in Nantes until January the fifteenth , enjoying the company of the novelist and many prominent people, while giving exhibitions and attending many banquets in his honor.

Deciding to next visit Spain, Paul started making the plans to move on to his next challenge.

Arriving in Madrid in mid January, the weather was bitterly cold, Paul's plans were to make a voyage on some of Spanish rivers, after looking in to the options, he decided on the Tagus. Being the least known, and promising more adventure than any of the other rivers.

Announcing that Paul was going to attempt to go down the Tagus, several prominent citizens endeavored to dissuade him against this trip, receiving many letters, pleading with him not to attempt the river, as it was not navigable. Running through a wild mountainous country, and full of very dangerous waterfalls. Paul decided to take a better look at the river, after all the warnings and concerns, he decided to form his own opinion.

Travelling to Toledo to see for himself the supposed dangers, here he found a narrow, turbulent river, rushing over great masses of rock.

He hired a mule and rode several miles down the banks, discovering no improvement. Making enquires from the natives about the condition of the river, the invariable answer was. "Mucho malo, Senor, mucho malo." Very bad, sir, very bad. Boyton was not very happy with what he found, and heard, but made up his mind to do it anyway, especially as everyone told him, he could not do it.

After deciding on a course, he returned to Madrid and attended the carnival. Paul was honored, to have been invited to King Alfonso and Queen Mercedes wedding, which turned out to be a grand affair.

The young King was extremely interested in the up coming voyage on the Tagus, making an announcement to all of Spain, that Captain Paul Boyton the Intrepid American, was a guest of all the people of Spain, and telling his people, to treat him with the utmost respect and hospitably. Before leaving Madrid to begin the perilous undertaking, the Minister of Interior gave Paul maps of the river and information about it. Amazed, at how little information was available on this river, the maps were glaringly incorrect, as was afterwards learned. Many of the towns listed along the river, were not even close to it.

Finally when all was ready, Paul's agent and baggage, were sent to Lisbon to await his arrival. While Paul returned to Toledo, to make the final preparations for the trip, which was one, that had never been attempted before.

As far as known, the river had never been navigated from source to mouth. The river is three thousand five hundred feet above sea level at Toledo, which accounts for it's rapid descent.

On his return to the famous old city Paul was met by an aid-de-camp, of the governor who provided his hospitality for the day, the day was spent visiting interesting points.

January the thirty first 1878. Paul drove to the river, through the Gate of the Sun, finding the crowds had already gathered to witness the start. Within a few moments he was in the water, and the crowds cheered lustily as he began paddling energetically away. As he turned the bend at the end of the first half mile, he took his last look at the stately Alcazar, away on the crest of the hills, and at the ruins of Moorish mills on the riverside below, as the bright, sunlit vision faded from his view.

"Now that I have started," said Paul, detailing an account, at a later date of, his wondrous journey.

"I felt easier and stopped at noon to enjoy a light dinner. I knew I was in for a tough ride and made up my mind to go through with it.

The river ran all over the country and was as changeable in temper as a novelist's heroine. Sometimes it was a mile wide, running slowly, with the calm and smooth surface of a lake, then again at the next bend it would dart towards a range of hills, and instead of going around them as it's previously erratic course, led me to expect, it would plough straight through the solid rocks, by becoming a very narrow canal. As deep and rapid as a mill race, and in some places hurried along with the speed of an express train.

The country was utterly wild, and it was not unusual to paddle from morning to night, without seeing a human being. As I knew nothing of the river, except that I was bound for Lisbon, you can imagine what was going through my mind, what may be around the next corner?. Is there an angle in the next canyon waiting to throw me over another, waterfall or into a whirlpool?

A great majority of the peasants, do not read, and were ignorant of my undertaking. They are somewhat superstitious, and my first encounter was with two of them. It was some hours after leaving Toledo, that I first saw these men, great, hulking fellows. While rolling a large stump up the steep hill, from the bank of the river. Slipping quietly along the surface, I got close behind them without them seeing me, then hailing them. After a startled look they let go of the stump which came crashing down to the river, while they ran up and disappeared in the recesses of the hill. They never even stopped to take a second look at me.

I thought I would reach Peubla the first night, but due to all the extraordinary bends in the river, nightfall came on me, in a terribly rough section of the country. I kept dashing from waterfall to waterfall and then rapid to rapid until two o'clock in the morning. Hearing a dog barking close by, it was intensely cold and I was exhausted as I hauled myself on the bank. I blew a couple of blast on my bugle, couple of very rough looking men came down to the bank. They were shepherds, who very kindly took me to a hut, not very far from the bank. These shepherds had the queerest way of making a fire, that I have ever seen. It was made of straw, the ember's banked in such a way that it only appeared to be a black mass, when they blew on the mass, a red glow blushed from it, throwing out intense heat. After having a bowl of warm soup, I stretched out and slept until sunrise, while they stood around, speaking their mountain patois, which I did not understand.

I left them early in the morning, passing through wild mountain scenery, with no signs of habitation. No railroad or telegraph lines cross the river until near Lisbon, there was no way for me to get word to my agent.

Arriving at Peubla at twelve o'clock, as I was going by, I ran onto an old, broken bridge submerged in the water, that cut my rubber suit, thus forcing me to haul up on land.
The Alcalde was out in his high picturesque cart, drawn by a team of mules, accepting his invitation, he drove me through the olive groves, to his house. That night there was a banquet in my honor, having no clothing with me, except my heavy underwear. I was forced to borrow a suit from Alcalde, to be presentable. The woman was most gracious and the children as pretty as pictures. The Alcalde's little daughter took a liking to me, she talked a great deal, and in fact I could understand her Spanish, better than that of the adults.

What a pretty little thing she was-a perfect Spanish beauty. She tried her best to deter me from continuing my voyage, however the next morning she went to the river to see me start. In fact the entire village was there, as I was about to step into the water, bidding her adieu, she pressed a religious medal into my hand saying,

" Oh, I am so afraid you will never reach Lisbon, take this, it will help you. The Blessed Madonna will protect you from danger." I kissed the little one goodbye and slipped into the water, amid the viva's of the crowd. I was extremely grieved, when reaching Lisbon, to hear the little girl died of some type of fever a few days after I left.

Nothing of great interest occurred during the next day, other than it was very cold and rough, as a snow storm was raging. On Sunday morning I arrived at Talavera, where the kindness of the people was so great, that I was compelled to leave the water and rest for awhile.

From there the river ran through the lower country, it wound around so much, that I could never see more than a quarter of a mile ahead, the constant changes in the current, now very rapid and then again sluggish, then smooth. Just below the town is a waterfall of considerable proportions, as the crowds had gathered there to see me shoot over it, in the spirit of bravado, I stood up as I got to the brink, and was hurled over head first. The crowed cheered as I realized what I had done, they believing it was the way I went over waterfalls. While I vowed never to try that again, fortunately for me I did not go head first on to a rocks.

It was not long before the land began to rise higher, and higher, or as it appeared to me the river began to sink lower, and lower, settling down among the great hills. I could not tell the distance from the maps, and was anxious to ask someone, how far I had to go.

During the day on Monday, as I was flying around a bend on a rapid current, I noticed two men on the bank, one surrounded by sheep, the other in the tree, cutting off greenery for the sheep.

I hailed them with, "Hey, brother." The man in the tree, turned around, at the sight of my black figure in the water let go and fell to the ground, while the companion startled, but recovering, ran up the bank, yelled something, that seemed to be a warning as they both disappeared, and as I passed on I saw why he had shouted.

A young gipsy-like girl standing on a rocky ledge, surrounded by long-bearded goats, as the current was taking me towards her, she gave a cry of alarm as I approached, they formed a beautiful picture, not wanting to frighten her, I called out some reassuring words in Spanish, hoping she would not be frightened as were her male companions. She seized a big stone and raising it defiantly over her head, as I passed waving an adieu, suddenly she dropped the large stone, barely missing me as she fled up the mountain, with the goats right behind her.

All day I picked my way cautiously along, using all my energy to avoid the numerous boulders that jutted out of the water. At one time it felt like I was shooting down a very steep hill, with huge boulders rising up like high walls on either side of me, there was no possible way out. For awhile I felt as if I was going into some subterranean passage, as the perpendicular walls were closing in on me, they swallowed up the entire river. Being swept down by the mighty, narrow current. I was sure that I was would be carried into some underground rapids, when suddenly I was dumped into a deep pool, where the river was running smooth and placidly along, almost at right angles with the rapids above.

At this abrupt turn it revealed evidence of former floods, immense rocks were cut and carved in spiral columns as skillfully as any sculptor could have chiseled them out. Great flocks of wild black ducks, common to the Tagus, continued to rise, as I approached.

At ten o'clock that night, hearing the heavy roar of rapids below and the river becoming wilder, I decided to stop until daylight so cautiously headed towards the shore, until I found an opening land on.

There was no wood to build a fire so I lay for several hours in my rubber suit. At daybreak I resumed the voyage, and it looked as if I was penetrating the very bowels of the mountains, whose crest loomed high above in the skies.

I soon discovered the cause of the herendious roar that had prevented me from going any further last night; an ugly violent rapid had me fighting madly to avoid the sharp broken rocks, as I was swept in amongst them. While trying to find a channel to escape, the backwash caught me, turning me so quickly that the little tender capsized.

Trying to stay upright and recover her, she was torn from my belt and thrown in to the vortex, as I was swept down the other side.

I never saw her again and what's more, I was left without my lamp and all my provisions.

That afternoon as the river increased it's speed, I dashed along at a mad rate. Once in awhile I was swept around sharp bends, and could hear a sullen roaring, that warned me there was a waterfall below. I kept driving steadily along, enjoying the exileriation of the rapid pace when I was startled by the sound of a gun shot, looking up I saw *a guarda civil*, the gendarme of Spain, who held his carbine up, and vigorously waved his hat with the other hand as I shot by.

The current increased as the roar from below became louder, going around another bend I saw a number of people on the bank waving their hats with a downward motion. That is a signal used in Spain when you are approaching. I had misunderstood them, thinking they meant me to take the other side, which I did and found myself in a current that I could not get out of, another sharp turn and the village Puente del Aracbispo came into sight, with the heavy spray from the falls rising high in the air. The roar was like a deep rumbling of thunder, as it came closer and louder, not paying attention to the people shouting, at me to stop, as I could not get out of the current anyway. I was concentrating on navigating the falls as I noticed the water was disappearing. My only chance of survival was to reach that channel, it took all the energy and strength I could muster, and in an instant I was in a series of falls, tumbling from ledge to ledge like steps on a colossal staircase.

Fortunately I landed in the deepest channel as I was covered with foam and spray and could not see anything around me. All I could do was to trust Providence and the depth of water as I found myself spinning around in the great pool below.

Half stunned and smothered by the frequent submerging of the weight of the volumes of water coming down on me, I drifted helplessly towards the bank, the next thing I remember, was a hand reaching down and grasping mine, as a voice said, "You live."

Its about all I do, "was my answer." As the strong arms hauled me onto the bank, the man who rescued me was a priest.

Through the midst of the madly excited crowds, I was escorted down the streets to the home of the archbishop, a quaint old building, almost in ruins. The kindness of every possible form of care was given to me, it's beyond what I could even describe, from the diocese, military and religious authorities.

As a banquet was arranged, I was dressed in partial clerical and military, enjoying as much as my tired bones would allow. I excused myself as early as I could, intending to continue the journey, after a good nights sleep.

When morning came, I felt so sore and bruised, that I could barelymove out of bed, deciding to stay over and rest for that day. I was then taken in hand by some of the prominent citizens, and shown the places of interest in this old town, the most interesting to me, was the olive mills, for which this town was well known.

The town is well known for it's superior olive oil, the method of producing it, is so primitive, that it was the same used by the Moors, hundreds of years ago. Firstly placing the green olives in sacks, then set in a large stone bowl, a flat cover is placed on the bowl, as an old type of screw, with a beam attached, presses the stone cover down, an ass, hitched to the end of the beam, tramps wearily round and round. The screw presses the stone down on the olives, squeezing the oil through cemented grooves in the bottom of the bowl, as it flows into casks. The pulp, or pummies, as we would call them, is fed to the hogs and cattle. It struck me at the time, that with our improved American machinery, we could extract about four times the amount of oil out of the pummies that are thrown away, as they get out of the first pressing.

Another place I visited, escorted by the good padre and an officer, was the prison. This prison contained as choice collection of murderers, who prayed on helpless traveler's. The news of my visit, was announced, ahead of me, as these free knights of the mountains stood in rows along the corridors

ROUGHING IT IN RUBBER

to receive me, backed by several well armed carbineros. The worthy padre would point out the most distinguished of these gentleman. "That one' he'd say, 'is in for killing two travelers at the saloon, that one' he'd, abducted a wealthy man, demanding money from family, that one over there, killed ten men, before he was caught," and so on down the line, as such cheerful histories were told. I politely saluted each artist of the knife and carbineros as I passed, one of them stepped forward and speaking in patois, which the padre translated. The request he made, struck me as so ridiculous, that I could scarcely refrain from laughing.

It was to this effect, that they all had heard of my voyage down the river, and were anxious to witness my departure the next day, and knew if I asked the Governor, they would be granted the pleasure.

The request was so absurd, that I had no intention of mentioning it to the Governor. We had been invited to dinner that evening at the Governors home, and while being entertained there, I jokingly told him of the queer request from the prisoner, I was more than astonished at his reply.

"Como no! Senor" - Why not, sir."

When starting the next morning, I was frequently warned that the river was very bad and dangerous, but could get no information of any value, except that it wound through many canyons.

The whole town was there to see me off, as I was heading down to the bank, astonished to see all those gentle murderers standing in a row with carbineros on either side, guarding them. One of the brigands, the spokesman from the day before, stepped froward and addressed me as thus: "Illustrious Captain. We would like to escort you down river, to protect you from the lawless characters, which we are aware infest the mountains below, but being detained here against our will, we are unable to offer you that homage.

But as a mark of our pure regard, on behalf of myself and worthy companions, I present you with this purse, of our own handicraft, and may you never lack the means to keep it full." The purse was a long knitted affair, in colored yarn, looking like an old fashioned necktie. I thanked them, and regretted the cruel circumstances which prevented them escorting me. Secretly rejoicing that such a disreputable looking group of villains was closely guarded.

Taking to the water again, the mountains still looked as if they were closing in, at times I would sink into quite pools, that would require incessant paddling to push through, and then be swept along and over the next rapids.

With the constant danger of being thrown against the rugged sharp rocks. I ran all day without seeing another human being. About ten o'clock that night, I noticed a light a little further down stream, as I was now very cold and extremely tired, sounding my bugle in the hopes of getting someone's attention.

Hearing a hail, from the bank, I landed at a sort of ferry and found a man and his wife waiting for me. They escorted me to a little cabin that was lit by a warm fire, made up of weeds and other stuff, wood is very scarce in this areas. As they conversed in their patois of the mountains, I could not understand a word they were saying. By, signs, however we understood each other very well, as I indicated that I would stretch out on the floor in front of the fire, they refused, but indicated, I think, for me to take the bed as the man was going away somewhere. This I did and was soon sound asleep, at one o'clock in the morning I was woken by the presence of a man at my bedside, I looked up through the dim light and towering above me, a tall stiff upright figure, a three cornered hat on his head with a sword at his side. In response to my startled look, he raised his right hand and saluted me, as I asked him, "Que esta, Senor?" - What is it, sir?

"His reply was, "By order of the the King, I am here to offer you protection and assistance."

"Thanking him for his courtesy," I turned over in bed and went back to sleep. After a breakfast of wild boar bacon, which was the sweetest meat I have ever tasted, the guard and my host accompanied me to the river. I carried a good supply of gold and silver with me, but all offers of money, throughout the entire eight hundred miles, of this voyage, were peremptorily refused. It was impossible to spend a cent, in fact the money wore through the little bag I carried it in, that I later found it

ROUGHING IT IN RUBBER

loose in my suit.

The only place I used a cent on the trip was in Talavera, a boy who ran an errand for me, accepted a *peseta,* but when it was found out, he was sent back to return it, and apologized for his conduct.

The river now began to get very narrow, burying itself in canyons, so that during the day the sun scarcely ever reached the water, except at noon, as it was directly overhead.

Since loosing my little tender I was no longer able to carry provisions, except in a small oil cloth strapped to my chest. The host of the cabin had insisted on me taking some wild boar bacon, but seeing how little food they had, I only accepted a very small amount, which I devoured entirely at noon the same day.

For three days I continued the voyage through the canyons, during this entire time, the only signs of human life were occasional glimpses of people far up in the mountains. My progress was slow along the stretches of dead water, it was silent and lonely. The wild ducks were the only signs of life, as they flew up when I approached. The only sleep I could get, was during daylight, by hauling up on shore to a dry rock, and within minutes, was in a deep sleep.

The nights were long, dark and cold as the fierce plentiful howling of the wolves along the Tagus, their dismal yells warned me to be aware of their danger, compelling me to remain in the water from sunset to sunrise.

On the morning of the third day in the canyons, I was stiff, sore and hungry, having eaten nothing but wild olives, gathered along the banks for the past two days. That morning I was beginning to wander, if I had gone up some false channel, or branched off the Tagus, making no headway, rising to an upright position, with every sense sharpened by hunger, listened for any ringing of a bell or barking of a dog, or signs of life, deciding I should probably leave the water and start climbing the mountain in search of a cottage or village.

Not a sound broke the death like stillness, except the distant rumbling of the rapids, I had passed over, or were still below me.

As I wearily sank back down in the water, grasping the paddle in hopes of finding an opening in the mountain down river, that would give me a chance of escaping. Something familiar struck my senses, not sure what it was, intangible and familiar, as I realized it was the smell of smoke, that the breeze was gently carrying up the river.

With all my strength, the paddle went into action, as I rounded the sharp bend. Landing a little above I saw a thin blue streak curling up from the the side of the hillside. I clambered over great detached rocks until I was level with the source of the smoke. As I paused, I heard the muffled sound of voices, coming from behind a large rock.

My soft rubber boots made no sound, as I rounded the rocks. I surprised two shepherds, one of them stooping over the fire, stirring something in a stewpan, while the other was rolling cigarettes in corn husks. Previous experiences with these simple mountain people had taught me how superstitious, and easily frightened they are, trying not to scare them,I wanted to get information from them, also desperately needed food. Saluting them with, *"buonos dias mis hermanos,"*- good day, my brothers.

The men sprang to their feet, with wild yells that echoed through the mountains. They dashed away like a pair of frightened deer.

At every call, for them to stop, it only doubled their efforts to escape, disappearing up the ravine. I sat down and had breakfast of the provender they had left behind, also absorbing a pig skin flask of Spanish wine, while removing my suit and drying myself before the fire, in hopes the shepherds would find the courage to return, but they never did. Before dressing I left a Spanish dollar, on the upturned stewpan. Returning to the river, much refreshed and exelerated from the food and wine, all traces of hunger gone, I was able to proceed at a greater speed.

I had not gone far when I noticed a man on a mule observing the river from a rocky ledge, the man seeing me, raised a bugle to his lips and sounded a merry blast, which was answered by loud cheers further down. As I arrived opposite the lookout, I was informed the Governor of Caceres and a party of ladies and gentleman, were waiting for me a short distance below. Landing a short distance below, I was warmly received by a numerous gathering. The Governor informed me that he had driven across from Caceres the day before, to intercept me and had a message from King Alphonso, *"to be sure that I wanted for nothing."*

He kindly told me in French, that it was an old Spanish custom to say, *"my house is yours,"* but for me, he would change the saying to, *"my country is your country."* The place where I had landed was a ford, or ferry, the Governor and his party were in a large tent, that had been erected for the occasion, and were attended by a troop of servants and cooks. The later had prepared an elaborate banquet in
my honor. How I wished, I was able to take some of this food aboard, to last me several more days, unfortunately the shepherds meal had replenished my appetite and I was unable to partake of the many splendid dishes, I could do scant justice to the scrumptious luxuries they spread before me. I spent a pleasant day with them, before starting the perilous journey ahead of me.

The Governor's engineer, who was one of the party, gave me all the information he had on the river, warning me of the terrible rapids, that are just down river, know as: *Salto del Gitano* - the *Gipsey's Leap*.

After leaving the delightful company, I speed away on a flying current and soon heard a roar below, warning me that I was approaching the dangerous point, preparing to do it, no matter what it had waiting for me in those waters ahead. The river closed in between two natural walls of stone, as narrow as a canal, as it danced away at a lively pace, the water dashing over the rocks that obstructed it's passage, and was churned into foam with spray that rose up high.

As the roar below became unbearably loud, loosing some of my courage, and endeavoring to grasp at the rocks, fearing another encounter with backwash. Attempting to stop myself, I was able to grasp a rock, as I was being carried by, but I did not have the strength to hold on for long, as the force dislodged me and the current hurled me along. Judging the speed of the water, I was travelling at about twenty miles an hour, the rocks were so high on either side, that only a small strip of sky was visible. The stream taking an abrupt sharp turns, about every hundred yards, the current became peculiar, as it repeatedly tossed from one side to the other, by some strange action I was bumping against the rocks. Dashing through two or three more rapids, was being rapidly swept along to the water falls, that almost deafened me with it's roar.

I saw the water in front of me rushing to create huge waves as it jumped up leaving nothing but white foam to show, where it had disappeared, as I was drawn down and whirled around, then thrown about. How I came out, I can't tell you, I do know, that I was puffing and gasping to breathe. It was quite awhile before my head cleared, after that shaking up, but I kept going right along through the night, in rapids, until about two o'clock in the morning.

I could see in the distance, by moonlight, what seemed to be a long string across the river, as I approached, it was the bridge at Alcantara. A queer stone bridge, with two abutments and one arch, stretching from one mountain to the other, high up in the air. There was no one out as I climbed up to the level of the bridge, by calling and blasting on my bugle, making enough noise, I succeeded in arousing the bridge tender, who then took me to the house of the Alcantara. Where all turned out to welcome me, I stayed over until Sunday and thoroughly enjoyed myself.

The evenings were spent at the theatre, I was asked to make a speech, responding to the best of my ability in Spanish. Being presented to many ladies, whom I thought were the most beautiful, I had yet seen in any part of Spain.

Starting early Monday morning, I shortly came to the point where the river is boarded on one side by Portugal.
As I noticed a Portuguese flag flying from a mast, hearing the loud cries of "Viva's" from the crew of a flat bottomed boat with a cabin.

As I was running alongside I was relieved to find, that a boat had been sent by the Portuguese government to meet me.Tthe Captain informed me that he had a letter from the Minister of Marine, placing the boat at my disposal.

The hard work was now over, as I simply followed the government craft for the remainder of the journey, it was quite a novelty at first to take my meals regularly, as there was an abundance of everything, I began to enjoy the trip. We would be moored every night and I would occupy the cabin, assuring me of a good nights sleep.

At Portes de Rodas, the first town we struck in Portugal, I met with a peculiar Portuguese reception, every person was supplied with detonating rockets which were fired of in showers, as a means of showing goodwill from every town in the country.

Continuing down the river, with no more rocks, the river broadened majestically as the tides from the Atlantic flowed in. At Abrantes and Santarem, the crowds were wild as they came out to greet me, with tremendous enthusiasm. This was the first time, I heard the peculiar name the Portugese had given me,

"Homem das Botas."- The man with the boots. This was an ancient name from the Tagus, legend has it that the Government wanted to, pass a law that the people objected to, while rebelling against it. A shrewd politician circulated a rumor that a man in boots, was going to walk on the Tagus. Peopled flocked to the river for days, to witness this event, while the law was passed uncontested. For years people had talked, and at last joked, about the "man with the boots," so when I came down river, there was a reason for their cries of." *"Homen das Botas."*

As Paul approached Lisbon, he had to work the tides, the river ran through a very low countryside and then stretched in to such a wide expanse, almost forming a bay. He arrived in Lisbon after eighteen days from the time of starting, which included nine nights paddling on the water. The tremendous welcome he received, as an estimated one hundred thousand people were out to see him land, just before going ashore, a steam launch was sent out to him, with telegrams of congratulations from the King of Spain and Minister of Marine.

A company of horse guards escorted him to the hotel, as thousands lined the streets to cheer him. The usual banquets and receptions followed, as he was honored, after one of the hardest rivers he ever navigated.

The imformis Tagus had never been navigated before, this created a profound sensation all through Spain and Portugal, as Boyton was kept busy acknowledging telegrams of congratulations. The Governor of Toledo sent the Spanish consul, at Lisbon a telegram, as follows:

"I beg you to heartily congratulate Captain Boyton in my behalf for the happy termination of his difficult voyage on the river Tagus, which has once more shown his intelligence and courage."

Before leaving Madrid to begin his next journey, Paul remarked to an American friend, "the foreign colony warned me, not only of the dangers of the Tagus, but also the people along the river, who were wild and ignorant and likely to kill me. On the contrary I found them kind, hospitable and generous, both in Spain and Portugal.

The Geographical Society of Lisbon requested Paul, to give a lecture. Though the members of the society lived on the banks of the river, they knew nothing of it's scientific importance. Amongst many other things he told them, he described ancient masonry he had seen, that could be remains of ancient Moorish structures. An expedition was sent out weeks after Paul's lecture, verifying Boyton's findings and opinions, regarding the Moorish masonry.

Paul remained in Lisbon during carnival week, and was entertained until he grew wary of so much pleasure. He gave an exhibition in the Arsenal de Marina before the King and Queen of Portugal, receiving numerous presents and decorations.

The Tourist news clip March 4th. 1877

"We are happy to inform our readers that His Majesty, King Victor Emanuel has been pleased to confer on the renowned Captain Boyton, the high distinction of Cavaliere the Order of the Crown of Italy. ..."

CHAPTER NINE

Moving on to Gibraltar, he was determined to cross the Straits of Gibraltar, but was given very little encouragement. He was constantly being warned about the sharks, which were supposedly numerous in these waters. An English officer took Paul to the back of the Abators, this building is on the water, so he could see the large blue sharks waiting on the offal, that's thrown from this slaughter house. Not even this was enough to make Paul change his mind, as he continued his plans for the trip.

His first plan was to paddle from Gibraltar to Ceuta, which is almost straight across the straits, as the currents would not let him do this, the plan was changed to Tarifa, the lowest land in Europe. From this point he should be able to strike the African coast. The Spanish felucca, San Augustine, was chartered for the two men from Gibraltar and the captain with a crew of five sailors.

Thursday, March the nineteenth, they sailed from Gibraltar. Nearing the Spanish side, flying the American flag, when they were pulled up by a Spanish gunboat, searching the San Augustine as they were under the impression that, they were smuggling tobacco.

It was extremely hard to get the officials to understand, what Paul was planning to do, finally allowing them to continue the voyage.They arrived off Tarifa at eleven o'clock at night, being this late, and the captain refusing to cross without clearance papers, they landed. Going into the old Moorish looking town, waking up one sleepy official after another, it was not until seven the next morning, before they could get clearance papers.

Sharks were not the only danger Paul had to deal with, the wind and currents are usually variable. In the middle the current could be
eastward, but on each side both flood and ebb tides, extend between a quarter of a mile, to two miles from the shore. This can change several times a day, according to the weather and winds.

Seven thirty am, Paul was dressed and ready to set off,

for the first time in all his voyages, he took the precaution of screwing sharp steel sword blades to each end of his double bladed paddle, with these he felt confident that he could stand up in the water and rip open any shark that approached him, also carrying a large dagger fastened to his wrist. Jumping into the sea amidst the enthusiastic cheering crowds that had assembled on the beach to see him start. Paddling out to a rock close to Tarifa lighthouse, known to be the extreme southern point of Europe, which he touched, then turned and waved an *"adieu"* to Spain. Starting his journey, paddling southward in smooth seas with calm weather, he was in excellent spirits, and fully confident of success, as he continued to paddle southward, he expected to meet the current going eastward, that would carry him towards Malabata, being directly across from Tarifa.

His calculations were off, as the current was now going in the opposite direction, westward as it was gradually taking him west.

Shortly after eight o'clock in the morning, Paul was singing as he paddled along and came very close to running into a school of porpoises, a couple of shots were fired into them from the felucca, scaring them off, it's believed that sharks follow them. A few moments later another school appeared, again shots were fired, this time it was successful. Realizing the current was taking him too far west, he turned his course due south, with the rising winds, he attached a small square sail to his boot, this did not improve his performance as he had hoped. After passing over Cabezes Shoals, the wind began picking up, he was still being carried westward, now nine thirty in the morning, Paul hauled up for a quick breakfast of bread and cheese. Paddling along, he once again became creative, by tieing a white square handkerchief, to an eighteen foot cord from his belt , allowing the handkerchief to drift astern, this was another precaution against sharks, as it's known, their malevolent impulses are more likely to be excited, as they attack white objects. This idea was that a shark attacking the handkerchief, would jerk the cord, that would then warn him of it's presence, giving Paul time to prepare for the attack.

The wind increasing from the east, Paul again tried the sail, but found it ineffectual, still steering south towards Malabata Point, about nine miles from Tarifa, though paddling all this time he was not tired. The westward current continued, the risk of being carried into the Atlantic became greater. He again turned his course southeast and fought to maintain it, as the British steamer Glenarn, eastward bound, passed him with loud cheers from the people on her deck.

Two thirty in the afternoon, a strong wind, with a rapid eastward current, caused a high sea, causing Boyton to have difficulty keeping close to the boat, as his distance increased every moment, until he disappeared from her sight. The captain's concerns grew, ordering the sailors to pull harder, about twenty minutes later he was sighted more than a half a mile ahead, as the sail was hoisted on the felucca they were able to close the gap, which was done with a lot of effort by the anxious crew.

The captain and crew of the boat, advised him to give up the attempt to cross, with their extensive experience of the straits, it is impossible, under the current conditions to complete the crossing. Boyton positively refused to give up the undertaking as he forged on ahead undeterred and in positive spirits, as the felucca soon discovered, it was impossible to keep up with him, with oars only. The boats sails were reefed and hoisted as the steering was close hauled, they were still barely able to keep him in sight.

Three o'clock in the afternoon, Paul was half way across, keeping south south east, as the wind continued to increase, as did the danger of him being carried into the ocean. With the waves constantly breaking over him, and the salt encrusting on his eyebrows, his skin smarted from the irritation. It was almost five o'clock and he was just off Boassa Point, bearing south, with only about three and a half miles from the African coast. Making another attempt to use the sail, but the wind was too strong and he had to give it up.

It began to grow darker as the wind increased with fears of a gale building up, the boisterous sea and wind in conjunction with rapid currents and heavy waves, caused the boat to loose sight of Paul.

After cruising around in all directions and yelling at the top of their voices, the captain, crew and his friends were relieved to hear his distant response. Finally catching up with him, the crew became adamant in their language, as they insisted he give it up, and come on board as they were all drifting into the Atlantic ocean.

Boyton however was firm and determined to keep going, until he reached the African coast.

Seeing no other way to stop him, three of the crew, leaned over the boat's side and tried to drag him on board forcefully, this attempt annoyed Paul, as he stood up in the water glaring at them and threatened to attack any man with the sword bladewho dareed to touch him again.The men took to their oars as Paul started singing, with the intention of calming down the situation as he paddled away. At seven thirty, the felucca St. Augustine again lost sight of Paul, the current with the heavy waves, constantly caused him to go under as it washed over him, the boats crew, were having a rough time riding over the huge waves, as they again searched for any sight of Paul. The current now going eastward to La Ballesta, he was again sighted after a lapse of twenty minutes, the increasing darkness and bad weather, was causing a lot of hard work for those on the boat, keeping up with him. Clouds gathered fast and a heavy mist partly obscured the moon, which had a large circle around it, the sailors called it " *a weather band.*"

Directly after finding Boyton, those on board the felucca, were startled by his cry of, "Watch out, Oh, watch out!" In answer to the excited inquiries from the boat, he told them to be prepared to fire, at the same time pointing to the other side of the boat, where there was a great commotion in the water causing a bright phosphorescent glow. That left no doubt of the proximity of a shark, or some other huge denzin of the deep, as fears for Paul's safety were quickly dispelled by the disappearance of the creature, what ever it may have been, as all preparations to give it a warm reception proved to be needles.

Bonfires could be seen, a distance from each other, along the African coast. It was later discovered, that they had been built by the order of Colonel Mathews, the American Consul General at Tagier, as beacons to guide Boyton and the felucca St. Augustine into shore.

It began to rain and the boat labored, rolling heavily on the waves, now eight thirty in the evening, the crew becoming despondent, though Malabata Point was only four miles off. The westward current was driving them northwesterly, as they searched for the fourth time for Boyton, who had not been seen for more than a quarter of an hour. Gale force winds and heavy seas pounded the felucca as she fought through the waves, the captain and crew, yelling repeatedly for Paul, began to wonder if he had been attacked, or injured and needed help. As their concerns grew, so did the gale, with the sea becoming angrier as the precious minute's went by.

Just after nine o'clock, with the wind blowing violently, the current carried them westward as the high seas increased every moment, the concerns grew greater as Boyton had not been seen for more than forty minutes as the repeatedly yelled for him. The thoughts of any further attempts to find Paul were becoming futile, as the exhausted boat's crew, having had nothing to eat and fatigue taking over, dropped the oars with language more forcible than elegant, as they prepared to buoy up, believing that he was lost beyond recovery.

VOYAGE ACROSS THE STRAITS OF GIBRALTAR FROM SPAIN TO AFRICA SHOWING BOYTON'S COURSE.

The joy of all can only be imagined, as they heard the echo of a distant hail from Paul, in answer to a call from the boat as to whether he needed anything?, he replied, "No, thank you, all's right."

As the strain of the voyage, was

beginning to effect Paul, he told the captain that he had fallen asleep and the pressure of a huge wave had caught him alongside his head, abruptly waking him, it took him awhile to recover, as he heard the calls from the felucca.

The crew now expressing their great admiration and appreciation of his courage. Boyton's intrepidity and power of endurance, as he had travelled three times the distance of the straits, and had persistently turned a deaf ear to their demands of giving up the voyage.

At eleven twenty, the bay of Tangier was sighted, as the wind had lightened and seas a little calmer, they were rapidly approaching the Tangier Reefs. The concerns of the crew as they feared being broken up on these reefs, put a damper on all on board, as the current carried them them closer and closer as they passed the headlands, these reefs form a natural breakwater for the bay, advising Paul to take a line, they would set sail and tow him around the point.

As the tide was low, Paul agreed to being towed, rather than risking broken bones by going over the reefs, he embarked on the towing, no longer needing to paddle, was able to get a brief rest before the anticipated excitement of his arrival.

Three quarters of a mile from the landing he let go the rope and paddled to the beach, emerging from the surf and standing on the beach, at exactly twelve fifty five. Some of the native soldiers were aware of a man crossing the straits, while others were not.

The moon was shinning brightly as a guard on the wall surrounding the city, noticed Paul coming out of the water, sending up a terrific cry in Arabic. Soon the bells began ringing from the mosques as a great commotion was evident, the gates opened as soldiers and people rushed through with torches flaring. Paul not knowing what the natives might do to him, so he walked a short distance down the beach, noticing an upturned hull of a wrecked vessel, he crawled under it. He had scarcely done so when the beach was swarming with people. A soldier noticing Paul's trail, followed it to the old hull, as the crowds surrounding it with wild discordant cries.

Paul heard a voice calling in English, stepping out to meet the son of the American Consul, Colonel Mathews, who then

explained the reason for Paul's appearance to the natives.
It was later learned that the peculiar cry from the guard on the wall was: *"Awake, awake. Ti's better to pray than to sleep, for the devil has landed in Tangier."* All the explanations, did not prevent at least one man running back in to the city with the story, as he told it: *"he had actually seen a christian walk on the sea."* As the crew on the boat, heard all the commotion, they feared for Paul's safety, they were aware of the superstition's of the native people, and that the superstitious Moorish guard got so excited at seeing the apparition of a strange object emerging from the sea, at that late hour of the night, could easily lead to violence.

Accepting Mr. Mathew's invitation to enter the city as his guest, Paul, explained that he needed to paddle back to the boat to change his clothing. While at the boat, he soon discovered that the water had seeped through the the suit along the side of his face during all the submerging, his under clothing was saturated.

Borrowing a fresh outfit of clothing, Paul accompanied Mr. Mathews into the city. Not feeling his best as the effects of the herendious crossing became evident, with acute pain in the wrists and hands that were covered with large blisters, his sight was blurred from all the salt water as Paul tried to make the best of the banquet prepared for him. Later returning to the boat, a fire was lighted in the cooking \stove as the violent shivering shook his body. In the cold and cheerless morning Colonel Mathew's son took the party to the landing, where Boyton was honored to meet many official's who were waiting to welcome him, offering their congratulations and hospitality. Accommodation was provided for the party in the Consuls house.

Taking Paul the following day to meet the old Sheriff of Tangier, as he was introduced to the old man, as Colonel Mathews interpreted,

"We are pleased the water god of America has made his appearance on these shores, as there has been a terrible drought here for sometime, and we are sadly in need of rainfall to moisten the parched lips of our soil and hope the great water god of your country will favor us."

Paul had noticed the clouds building for the past two days, his crew had warned him of a pending storm, with a sly wink at the Colonel, he answered the old Sheriff, " The request of the Sheriff is well. I promise that rain will come within a short while." Before they left the house, luckily for Paul it began to rain and the old man was absolutely bewildered and astonished, having no doubt that the rain had been called by the American. The superstitious Moors looked at Paul with great respect after learning the story of the old Sheriff, and to this day the story is still told of the wonderful American who ended the drought, when he came out of the sea that dark night.

Returning to the Colonels house, Boyton found a delegation of distinguished Moors waiting for him, old white bearded fellows, in turbans and burnous. Each of them offering presents, one a pair of Barbary pheasants, another a young wild pig in a crate, quaint arms and one a rare species, of chameleon that he carried on a twig of a tree. Paul was addressed by older one, with a request, "would he kindly walk on the water in the daylight, as the soldiers had seen him do the night he landed, so the people can see him do it?."

In response to their request, he promised to give an exhibition the next day and demonstrate what he can do in the water, much to their enjoyment and surprise. After the exhibition he was shown the sights of interest in the city, one of the most exciting was the wild boar hunt, enjoying the excitement of this sport.

Headed by Colonel Mathews, early in the morning, Paul riding a wiry little Arab horse, armed with bamboo sticks with sharp pointed spear like tips, they rode over the hills into the dessert. After some distance, when no boars had been seen, they were becoming somewhat disappointed as an they noticed a camel train from Fez approaching, "I'll ask these people if they have seen any boar along their way, said Colonel Mathews. He rode up to the leader, and this was their conversation, as translated by the Colonel's son.

"Mahomet protect my brothers. You came afar, but your journey will soon be ended and you will have blissful rest", said the Colonel.

"Allah bless you master, we are weary and glad to approach

ROUGHING IT IN RUBBER

our journey's end," replied the head of the caravan.

"Have you seen any wild boar in your last day's journey?"

"We have, my master, in great numbers not far from here."

"Good ones?"

"As large as an ass, my master.' "In which direction?"

The Moore responded by raising his hand and pointing southeast.

After riding in that direction for about an hour, they stopped on the crest of a hill, scanning the desert for any signs of game, and discovered two skinny looking little pigs running across the valley below.

"Those are not the ones the Moor saw?" asked Paul.

"Oh yes they are, it's a wonder he imagined them so small as an ass, for it is their natural characteristic to exaggerate." There was very little sport in running down and spearing the skinny little wild pigs, but after it was done the party returned to the city, as experienced hunters, they knew there would be no use looking any further that day.

One place in the queer old Moorish city, Paul enjoyed visiting was the market. The women with covered faces, squatted on the ground displaying their little bowls of beans, peas, etc., for sale.

As the tired camels from the dessert lay with their noses buried in the sand, taking much needed rest while their owners, stood around and bartered their goods. Once, while walking through the market with the Colonel, Paul saw a man sitting cross-legged on the ground in the midst of a circle of merchants, who seemed deeply involved in the discourse and gestures of the central figure.

"I bet I can guess what that fellow is, even though I don't understand Arabic," remarked Paul, " an auctioneer," said Paul proudly.

"Wrong. He is a professional story-teller, as imaginative as Scherherazade while the merchants here are so busy, they always have time and the inclination to listen to his long fairy tales," said the Colonel, "after each story the listeners drop one coin, worth one twelfth of a cent, into the story-teller's hat."

Another thing that amused Paul was the indiscriminate use

of guides made of stout sticks, whacking the natives that got in their way down the narrow streets, as mercilessly as the ass's they drove. The women were all heavily veiled, their faces jealously hidden from the eyes of men, except when some giddy girl with the intention of flirting, allowed her veil to slip down as if by accident.

Returning to Gibraltar, Boyton visited Cadiz, Seville and the principal cities of Spain, with tremendous success and constant ovations. While giving exhibitions in those cities, he decided to make the run from St. Geronime to Seville on the Guadalquivar.

It was an very pleasant uneventful trip, completing the journey in three days, March 29,30,31. His only encounter was being chased back into the water after going ashore to look at one of the famous Andalusian fighting bulls, that was grazing close by, kicking up the dust with it's hind legs and head down, charged at him.

Returning to Madrid by the invitation of the King, for the grand exhibition at Casa de Camp, the royal gardens that are built around a beautiful little lake. As a tent was erected on it's bank and every assistance was offered to Paul in the preparations for this exhibition.

Several small boats were built for him, to enable him to demonstrate how the torpedo works in naval warfare. The King was very interested in this, as he was about everything American. He treated Paul royally with tours of the Palaces and the Royal boathouse.

During the tour through the royal boathouse, Paul noticed the mahogany boats, that take four men to lift, the King was astonished when Paul explained, that boats like these were now being made of paper and were so light that one man could carry it under his arm to where ever he wished.

On the morning of the exhibition, the finest military band in Madrid was playing as the King and Queen arrived with the Royal family.

This was a private exhibition, by invitation only the audience was made up of all the noble and notables of the city. In one part of the exhibition Paul used a pair of white doves to demonstrate how the dispatches are sent out, when released, one

ROUGHING IT IN RUBBER 195

instantly flew off, while the other bewildered, circled around and landed at the Queens feet. The little Princess of Asturas captured it for the Queen who fondled it through the remainder of the exhibition. When the exhibition ended the King had requested Paul to end with his landing where the royal party was seated. He congratulated the hardy navigator, as did the Queen. Thanking him for the pleasure he had given her, Paul replied, referring to the dove, how it had landed at her feet.

"I hope it will prove a good omen, your Majesty."

Turning her wondrously beautiful, though melancholy dark eyes on him, replied, with a bright smile, "I hope so."

She then conferred on Paul the order of *"Hospitaliers of Spain,"* this was the second time he was knighted in Spain.

He is the only foreigner ever knighted by Mercedes during her short reign. The King then proceeded to present him with the *"Marine Cross of Spain"* and a photograph of himself with the King and Queen. Before he left Spain the beautiful young Queen died, as Paul hoped that the white dove was not a bad omen. Leaving Madrid, to appear in all the principle cities of the northern division of Spain, he was welcomed and treated with the greatest respect.

In Barcelona he gave an exhibition for the benefit of the families of fisherman lost at sea, The fishing folk of Barcelona are peculiar in their costumes and characteristics like no other people in the world, they are a world unto themselves. He was surprised one morning to be summoned to the court yard of the hotel, and found a large gathering of people in their peculiar form of dress. *"National Costumes."*

Paul was a little taken back with the group that had assembled to offer their thanks. A speech was made, professing their gratitude for his kind donation to the families, they wished to present him with a gift, little pear-shaped iron locket, inlaid with gold and silver, that had been made by a crippled fisherman, it was a magnificent piece of ingenious workmanship. He valued it amongst one of his most treasured possessions.

Toulouse, France was his next stop and while there, he decided to make a voyage down the Garonne from Toulouse to Bordeaux, estimating the trip to take about six days, May the nineteenth to the twenty fifth 1878. There was nothing but pure pleasure on the trip down that beautiful winding river, through the rich wine valley's of France. The peoples hospitality was astounding as they welcomed me, filling my little tender with rare French wines and luxury provisions, as the beautiful elegant daughters of the wineries, had great delight in topping the little tender with flowers, tormenting Paul's heart strings. One particular young lady caught Paul's eye, she had his head spinning, while his heart pounded at every glimpse of her.

With many thoughts of abandoning further journeys and settling down, Paul was in a dilemma, finally deciding that he must continue with the voyages. Finding a kindly soul to present him to the young lady, proved easier than he imagined, as all were keen to please him.

The beautiful young French girl was Elise Sauteyron, her father a prominent wine maker with very large vineyards, and well known for his excellent wines. Paul received permission to visit the young lady and her family, spending many very pleasant days in their company. Her father and brother were gracious enough to give him a tour of the vineyards and winery, never realizing what a complex process it was to produce such high quality wines.

After the Garonne, though reluctant to leave, he had to go to Paris for the Exposition. Before going to Tagus he had ordered a steam yacht, named, "The Paul Boyton," she was a magnificent little vessel, in which he intended to sail and steam to India, China and Japan. He remained on board the yacht, that was docked at the Paris Exposition grounds, the Expo of 1878. The little vessel was always full of distinguished visitors, and many pleasant excursions were taken up and down the Seine.

During this time Paul became acquainted with the ex-President of Peru, Don Nicholas de Pierola, then in exile. They quickly became friends. The ex-President taking a lot of interest in the torpedo work, and they frequently made quite experiments in isolated places along the river. Before they separated he assured Paul that if he ever regained his position in Peru, he would remember their pleasant times aboard "The Paul Boyton," and the many torpedo experiments.

August the twelfth, Paul began a voyage down the Seine from Nogent-sur-Seine to Paris, a distance of two hundred miles, which he accomplished in four days, landing at the Exposition building, Camps de Mars. The immense crowds that lined the banks of the Seine, were believed by *Figaro* to be around half a million. As he passed under Pont Neuf he stood up and dipped the stars and stripes in a salute, as mighty shouts went up from thousands, *"Viva l'Amerique, Viva Boyton.*

November of the same year, he went down the Orne from Lou to Caen, in two days, the trip was enjoyable though uneventful, and soon after he returned to America Pauls letter to Elise Sauteyron.

Pontavary, November 27th 1878.
My Dear Elise,

How can I expect to be excused for my long silence. Both of your most kind letters came to me. I would have answered the first one but at the time I was very busy and before I was aware the months have passed. Then I was afraid to write thinking you would not get me letter, as you informed me you would be away from Paillet. I was hoping everyday you would write again and you have been kind enough to do so, for which I am truly thankful to you. From your last kind letter came to me yesterday and it made me very happy indeed. But I will commence and answer the former one first. You seem to be angry because I expressed a doubt of sincerity, It was hard for me to understand you when you say there are things which cannot be written and it for that reason that we should see each other and have a talk. How this is to be done exists with you. I was sorry I could not forfil your last proposal to go to Paillet; at that time I was engaged in important business, could you manage to go to Bordeaux and then when we know each other better I would write to your father for permission to ... my adless to his dear daughter if I went to Paillet I would be sure to be noticed. If you can possibly come to Bordeaux it would be muuch better. I would call on you at your friends house in the presence of your friend or we could go out in a carriage to the theater or any where you would wish. Of one thing rest assured. that my intentions are honorable and your honor and name is as safe in my hands as would be that of my sister. To step over the bounds of etiquette for the circumstances of our acquaintance are of an extraordinary kind. If you can't come to Bordeaux, suggest some other way that I can see you, I must go to New York in December. I sail from England about Dec. 10th and I must see you before I go. I only go visit to transact some business and to see my mother as it may be the last time I will ever have a chance to do so. I will return to Europe in about two months. I thank you very much for the photo, as it is a good one, without the demonstrations when I have one taken. Write to me soon for I will be ancious now to hear from you. I did not know I was jealous until you mentioned otheres.

You must not allow them to steam the heart of my own dear Elise. My dear you will be tired of reading this long letter.

God Bless and love you my noble dearest girl. Have trust in me and believe in my sincerity. I love you and will ever contanue to do so, I honor and admire your fearless character. Pray don't Elise keep me long writing for a answer.

        I remian darling Elise your devoted Paul.

Address,
Consul des Etats unis. Paries.

CHAPTER TEN

For some weeks Paul remained in New York, much to the delight of his mother and family. Now being a celebrity he was constantly invited to many functions and asked to gives many demonstrations, and lectures by most of the prominent citizens of the great metropolis. During his stay at home he amused himself by paddling from the Battery around to Hunter's Point, and one night crossed down the bay through the Narrows, almost loosing his life in the ice off Staten Island.

An invitation from Congress, took Paul to Washington DC, being received by President Hayes and his Cabinet. On the afternoon of February the first 1879, at the request of the President, members of Congress and the House of Representatives, Paul gave an exhibition in the navy yard.

While in Washington DC, he received an invitation from the leading citizens of Pittsburgh, thrilled to return to his former home and beloved old river of his boyish gambols, he gladly accepted. February the fifth he arrived in Pittsburgh, and happy to see many of his playmates of former years, while being met with a great welcome.

On the evening of his arrival, while resting in his room at the hotel, he was visited by a fireman in uniform, who grasped his hand with great warmth and enthusiasm, at the same time remarking,

"I don't suppose you know me Captain Boyton?"

Paul taken by surprise, responded, "My memory certainly fails me."

"I am Thomas Mc Cafferty, who's life you saved more than twenty years ago, I have waited for many years to thank you personally."

Before Paul left Pittsburgh, Mc Cafferty presented him with a gold medal, commemorating the event from his childhood. Some time was spent around Pittsburgh, while he was making the preparations for a voyage down the Allegheny and Ohio rivers. Deciding to start on the Allegheny at Kittanning, then after examining it thoroughly, he decided to start from Oil City, a distance of one hundred and forty miles.

There was great excitement at Oil City, when they heard

ROUGHING IT IN RUBBER

Boyton had arrived and was contemplating paddling down the river, many people believing it could not be done due to the current extremely cold and icy weather.

They were amazed when Paul arrived early in the morning of February the sixth, equipped for the dreary voyage. Given an enthusiastic send off, his progress was slow on the first day, mainly due to the blocks of floating ice. At Black's Riffles he ran into a rock with the force enough to turn him completely over and almost knock him senseless, fortunately his rubber suit was not damaged and was able to continue the voyage to Emlenton, forty three miles from Oil City, where he decided to stay overnight, instead of Kittanning as planned, to recover from the accident and being almost frozen stiff, needed to thaw out.

All the towns he passed through going down river, the banks were lined with people cheering him on, a wager was building as to who could get him to stop at their town, the reasons given for getting him to stop, were becoming very funny.

A citizen of Parker came forward with, what he thought was the best yet. "Tell Boyton," he said to one of newspaper reporters who were following Paul down river by train, "that he should stop over at Parker instead of Kittanning, because Parker is an incorporated town and Kittanning is not."

Paul was well rested by the night over in Emlenton, though his hands and face were badly swollen, also suffering from a painful mild frost bite. He became somewhat depressed and despondent when he realized that he would not be able to reach Pittsburgh before Sunday. He bravely reentered the water and shot over Parker's Falls.

Before he reached Mahoning, a large crowd had gathered, in the crowd was one of those wise bodies who thought they knew everything and cannot be fooled, making himself conspicuous in the crowds by professing, that they were all being fools to believe a man was going to swim down such an icy river.

"I am on to the whole thing," he professed, "it's a block of wood covered in a rubber suit, that floats down as 'ere Boyton sneaks along the bank with the reporters."

He was one of the people at the front when Paul arrived,

as he had made up his mind to dash forward and tear the suit off the wooden block, assuring the crowds that he would expose the whole thing, as he could not be fooled, as they were being. As Paul walked up on land, the mans eyes almost came out of their sockets, as he retreated with an angry crowd pursuing him with derisive shouts.

Paul was more interested during the cold cheerless trip in the immense pillars of fire that belched from the many natural gas wells down river through the famous oil country of Pennsylvania.

A large crowd had gathered for his landing, even though the little cities misfortune of "not being incorporated," at Kittanning, as the Mayor gave a welcoming speech with a great banquet.

As he got closer to Pittsburgh's suburban places, the people lined the banks cheering him along until he reached the Point, where the Allegheny and Monongahela forms the Ohio.

Thousands of people jammed the bridges and banks to salute Boyton, as a waiting carriage whisked him away, to the hotel, to the disappointment of many who lined the streets. He was half frozen and looked very tired after an incredibly trying trip, which was accomplished in a little less than four days. After a little rest and warm food Paul was ready to resume the voyage.

Starting from the foot of the Seventh street bridge on February the twenty forth. The Ohio was so full of ice that it was extremely difficult to forge ahead, the first days run was to Rochester.

He arrived very late, due to the icy conditions of the Ohio, the band and many people who had been waiting, had gone home while the others sought refuge in a local bar.

Mr. James Creelman of the New York Herald, who had been assigned to follow Boyton and report on his voyages, and two other newspaper men, were all placed in one hotel room. Paul was totally exhausted and just wanted to get warm and go to sleep. The news spread fast of his arrival, the people started to gather at the hotel, they asked for a speech, the landlord was sent back with an apology, that Boyton was in bed and did not wish to be disturbed. Then they asked if he would just fire off one rocket, that was ialso mpossible as the little boat, now named "Baby' Mine," had sprung a leak on the sharp ice, wetting all the fireworks.

The landlord believing he could set off one of the rockets to please the people, acquiring a large detonator, and with a red hot poker attempted to light it, finding the fuse that he thought was too wet, dropped the rocket on the floor and left the room. Soon afterwards Paul heard a hissing noise, then realized that the landlord had left a lighted fuse, as he drew the bedding over himself, a dreadful explosion occurred. Shaking the whole house as it scared the occupants out of their wits, the landlord rushed into the room with a, "hip,hip, hooray." to his delight as he said, "that's it, that's good," regardless of the carpet burning and the room littered up.

Between Rochester and Wellsville, Paul had an awful time in an ice gorge, he could hear it cracking and grinding below as he realized there was danger ahead. As he managed to climb on top of a large piece, that carried him over the top, to avoid going under, he was then into the flowing waters on the other side.

Below Steubenville, a native from the West Virginia side rowed frantically out to him.

"Hold on, stranger, I'll resky yo' in a minit," he yelled. When he drew up alongside Paul and spoke to him, he was as tickled as a boy at a monkey show. 'Wal, ef, yo' aint jus' cutees' little cuss I ever did seed paddlin' aroun' out here in the ice like a beaver." He expressed much disgust, not to say contempt, when Paul refused to land and take a drink of "Virginia's own Mountain Dew."

After all the hard work through the ice gorged river, Paul reached Wheeling and rested there until morning, resuming the voyage, he would frequently ride on an ice block while looking for open water to paddle, keeping his his circulation going. Looking along the shore line on a frosty morning, Paul noticed a woodcutter as he approached about the same moment the worthy saw him, the tall lank West Virginian eyed the strange looking creature for a second, dropping his axe and loped for his cabin. Suspecting that the curious lands man was going after his rifle, as customary for them to shoot anything they don't understand, Paul blowing a couple of blasts on his bugle, in hopes of avoiding being shot. The man returned to the water's edge, loosened a flat bottomed boat from the ice and rowed out as Paul was advancing on the rapid flow. Paul thinking, here comes another lantern-jawed individual who want's to ask me if I am cold. To his surprise the man never opened his mouth, but ran his boat as close as he could get it to the object and after a long stare, turned his boat and rowed away. About twenty yards away he stopped as though he had forgotten something, and seriously inquired.

"Say mister, be yo' stuffed wuth cork or wind?"

"Wind," replied Paul, he waited for no further reply as he rowed back to shore and headed for his cabin.

Just below Pomeroy, Paul made his first all night run and was drowsily moving along mechanically as he was startled by the sounds of the paddle wheels of a steamer. The Telegraph was bearing right down on him, as he stood up in the water yelling, "Port, Port or I am a dead man." Instantly the wheel was put over as the steamer glided by, barely missing him. Six o'clock the next morning, he was nearing Gallipolis, he noticed a boat coming out from one of the floating houses, Jo-boats they are frequently known as, and frequent the Ohio and Mississippi rivers, they are river gypsies. Paying no attention as they came up close behind him, then he stood up, intending to ask the time of day. Making the movement just in time as the man was taking deliberate aim at him with a musket, Paul yelled out as the trigger was about to be squeezed. The river gypsy was profuse with his apologies.

When nearing the mouth of the Big Sandy river, which forms the boundary between West Virginia and Kentucky, Paul was met by the steamer Fashion, loaded with ladies and gentleman, who gave him a hearty welcome to the shores of old Kentucky. At Cattlettsburg, a banquet was spread on shore, of which he partook and then slipped back into the water. He arrived at Ironton at nine o'clock that night where he remained until morning.

At ast a welcome letter from Elise was waiting for him, getting off a quick reply in the midst of this long hard voyage.

> Norfolk US, 18-4-1880
>
> My dear Elise,
>
> I was surprised and pleased to hear from you, as I thought you had forgotten me. I have been in Florida all the winter and received your letter only yesterday. I wrote to you before I left France. I wonder if we will ever meet again, I cannot say when I will get to France again as I have work for full two years in this country, yet I will never forget my dear little french friend and I do wish you would write to me often. I have fully recovered from my accident which was not very severe.
>
> Not being sure you will receive this letter, I will not make it long but when I get another from you I will write a good long one.
>
> Good by sweet heart,
> With best love ever, from friend.
> Paul Boyton

From that point to Cincinnati, all the towns down along the river were lined with people and bonfires built at night so they could cheer him on. A short distance above Cincinnati he was met by an excursion steamer with notable people and newspaper reporters from the city. Madame Modjeska, who was with the party kindly presented him with a beautiful silk flag.

The river was crowded with boats and people, as a large barge loaded down with people, was driven against a pier and almost sank with all aboard, Paul made a brief stay in Cincinnati.

Continuing his voyage accompanied by a boat load of reporters, among them was the actor, Oliver Byron.

As the ice was melting it left the water extremely cold, he averaged about five miles an hour on the lower river, the oarsman on the reporters boat had a hard time keeping up with him. At Delhi the two experienced oarsman, went ashore leaving Creelman, Byron and the two Cincinnati newspaper men to manage the lumbering boat.

The enthusiastic oarsman first removed their overcoats, then undercoats followed, as collars were unbuttoned. It was fortunate for them that most of the spectators were focusing their attention on Boyton, as no such rowing was ever seen on the Ohio again, Paul constantly looking back, as his safety had a lot to do with this watchful care, they came close to running him over several times, as they working independently of each other, it was pretty hard to tell which was the bow or stern of the boat. One of them saying, "it wasn't the length of the river that bothered them, but the width." A ragged urchin rowed out from shore to see what they were doing, sarcastically asking if they were rowing over stumps.

The infuriating remark, caused them to raise the oars at him, lucky for him there was no revolver or shotgun on board, there would have been a funeral in the lad's family.

Row boats would come out from shore, the occupants wishing him well and as many asked ridiculous and painfully ignorant questions, "Do you have you springs in your arms?", "Can you blow your horn, how far can it be heard?", "Are you going to travel all night?", "Are you going back to Cincinnati to-night?", "Let me sit on you.", "Do you get tired?", and the favorite "Are you cold." When the press boat was not trying to climb the Kentucky hills, Paul would cheer himself by going alongside and conversing with the boys, but as a rule he was wary of getting to close to them.

Nearing Louisville, a fleet of excursion steamers ran up to meet him, there was a very heavy fog as the folks on board were eager to see him, with the boats pushing close around him, before he could bear off to the city, he was carried over the falls, and picked up five miles below, the press boat following him over the falls and the occupants had to be rescued by the life saving crew.

Leaving Louisville next morning Paul intended making the run to Cloverport, over a hundred miles below, without leaving the water.

There was a strong head wind all day, washing the yellow

Ohio waves of his face, the night closed in with dark hanging clouds as an electric storm brewed up, flashing sheets of lightening ran over the surface of the water, cracking and spluttering as though angry at his presence. It was a great though fearful sight as tree after tree was shattered along the shore, splintered by the sharp peals of thunder adding to the grandeur of nature's display. Fearing the copper bugle would attract the lightening, Paul submerged it as far under the water as he could, all night he navigated through the fearful storm, arriving at Cloverport very tired and bruised.

He rested there for several hours and then made the run down to Owensboro, the mail boats, Idlewild and Morning Star steamed up from Evansville to meet him. Lashed together for the occasion, carrying a large crowd of people while flying Boyton's colors, the Geneva Cross, which are the colors of the International Life Savers.

Miss Maggie Morgan, one of Evansville's fair daughters, stepped off the Idlewild onto the press boat and presented Paul with his colors, as an amusing incident happened, as the young lady was finishing her speech and presentation of the flag to Paul.

The commander of the steamer Hotspur, taking the opportunity to make a few extra dollars, loaded the steamer with paying passengers assuring them a closer look than any other boat could offer ofBoyton's arrival, gambling on an exhibition before Paul left the water. As the young lady finished her presentation the Hotspur steamed up with masses of eager people on her deck.

Paul had been warned about the Hotspur by his agent, who was on board the other steamer. Despite the efforts of the captain and pilots of the Hotspur, Paul managed to stay closely between the Idlewild and Mayflower, keeping the Hotspur and its guest away from viewing the presentation for an hour or more. This amusing dance around the two steamers continued until the Hotspur's captain was heard swearing while he tramped up and down his deck's, in a rage and ordered the boat back to Evansville. To add to this insult, he could not collect a penny from the passengers on board his steamer, as they were unable to see Boyton.

Over ten thousand people were gathered along the wharfs, to see him land at Evansville, making it extremely difficult for Paul to get to his hotel. From Evansville the run to Paducah was on a swollen river, then down to Cairo, as a fleet of steamboats came out to escort him to the mouth of the Ohio river where he sent up rockets to mark the end of his one thousand mile journey. Remaining in Cairo for a couple of days to prepare to continue the voyage down the Mississippi.

His start again drew huge crowds, as Miss Fannie Pitcher, the Belle of Cairo, sailed out in a small boat and presented Paul with the cities flag. As he found himself riding on the swift muddy current of the Mississippi, he could not only see, but feel the difference between the European rivers and the Mississippi.

Comparing these rivers to the ones in Europe, Paul remarked, " how wide they were in comparison to the very small narrow winding rivers, he had navigated over in Europe." The main differences was how the wind from down stream turned the turbulent waters into a yellow foam, then having long lonely stretches of broad waves, with many lonely hours, much like being out at sea.

Loneliness had a peculiar effect on Paul, as he would reminisce about the stories from his childhood and many others, told to him during his many travels.

He was told it would be impossible to navigate this stretch of the river, as there were large furious alligators, that are really worse than sharks in many aspects, warning him to keep a sharp look out for their attacks. During the long hours of the night he would also think of the stories told to him, especially the one of a man that set out from Pittsburgh to New Orleans, rowing down this part of the river, whose body was supposedly later found, still in his boat, that had been washed out to sea. He had been dead a length of time, and to this day the cause of his death is still unknown. Such stories were Boyton's *bete noir as* they had been repeatedly told to him. It was not hard not to wonder about the stories, while hearing the strange unknown noises from the shore in the unearthly hours of the night.

Often turning over to put his ear to the water, with hopes of hearing beating of paddles coming down the river, instead the large fish would rise under him as if inspecting the strange object on the water.

The first miles down the Mississippi, were done in extraordinary time through a few nervous spurts and then he settled into steady paddling, the monotony of the surroundings, as both banks were dense timber from the rivers edge, for never ending miles, as he struggled through dead water and passed island number eight, which had slowed him down immensely. Arriving at Hickman, Kentucky at about six o'clock in the evening. After a welcome reception and good food Paul returned to the water, as nigh closed in a great feeling of nervousness came over him, at one time during the night he burned a red light in hopes of attracting a steam boat, that he thought he heard approaching in the distance, but she must have steered off to the opposite shore.

Day break the next morning he hauled himself up at Point Pleasant, where the captain of the Batavia gave him hot coffee and bread, that revived him so thoroughly that he moved on without resting. There he learned that the unexplained crashing noises in the night along the river, were the caving banks. An hour after leaving Point Pleasant, the Alice, a United States tender approached, and the Thomas Sherlock. Along this very wide river, before a long distance of nothing, but loneliness, no human being or trace of civilization, jusy yellow mud and foliage for miles adhead.

The sun adding it's hot rays to Paul's suffering, after loosing his sunshade the night before, his eyes were almost blinded by the glare, while the intense heat scorched his face.

Reaching Cottonwood at six o'clock that evening, after a continuos run of thirty two hours on the water Paul was totally exhausted, taking the opportunity to take a rest and get some food before back out. Returning to the tedious journey with the wind and high seas making it very hard, at two o'clock the head wind was almost taking him back up river as he struggled with the paddle. Keeping up a pretty good rate of speed, until a big storm off Hale's Point, the rain descended in torrents as it became so dark that he could scarcely tell whether he was going up, down or across. While trying to light the lamp he discovered that the matches were wet, so deciding to go ashore and search for shelter until the storm passed over, the woods were thick, and lightening fierce as Paul wondered if he wouldn't be better off in the water. While considering his options he noticed a little light flickering among the trees, tucking the little boat "Baby 'O Mine" under a log on the shore, heading in the direction of the light. It was a negro cabin, he unceremoniously pushed open the door and entered, scarring the owners half to death, a newly wedded couple huddled with fear in the corner, as Paul explained who he was. They took it with good humor, however, saying, "Yo' done scart de life mos' out o' us. I knows who yo' is now, do Boss."

"How about a little fire, my friend," asked Paul.

"Alright boss, alright, sah, yo' kin have a fiah quicker 'n yo' kin skin er cat," as the negro started tearing boards off the side off the cabin. It was too much trouble to go out and gather fuel in the woods or cut down a tree, besides, the boards burned quicker. Removing his suit and warming himself up, while the negro so tickled at having such a guest, disappeared into the forrest for quite awhile. Paul had dressed and about to return to the water, when he appeared in the doorway with a whole delegation of his relatives, including his elderly mother. The old woman was not convinced that he was of the earth as she looked at him with considerable suspicion, mingled with a great deal of fear. "Boss," she said from the corner as she peered over her son's shoulder, "yo' certny isn't got de looks ob de debbil, yo' face, but de say de debbil's got cow hoofs an I kaint see yo feet."

As he stepped out of the cabin, Paul could hear her sigh of relief, heading back to the water leaving the negro family to figure him out amongst themselves.

Another storm came up, as the rain and hail pounded him. The light on "Baby Mine went out, the waves had wet the matches he procured from the negro. In the darkness he was in danger being run over by the fleets of empty coal barges that are towed up from New Orleans, to Pittsburgh. The extremely large barges that cover acres of river space and it's very hard to tell in the dark, which way they are going to turn, the Government had lanterns placed along the river as beacons to guide the pilots of these barges. Seeing one of the lamp towers, Paul decided to head for it, taking his little lamp as he left the water and climbed the ladder to the lantern, suddenly a ferocious large dog rushed at him, preventing him from coming back down, eventually the light keeper was aroused by the dogs persistent growls and barking. Coming out with a gun to check on the commotion, he discovered Paul up the ladder. After quick and extensive explaining to the man, the keeper called off the dog, and gave Boyton a good supply of fresh matches, with the little lamp burning brightly, he forged his way down the river.

During the small hours of the night he passed the steamers, Osceola, James Howard and the Andy Baum, all of which spoke to him and offered fresh supplies, at daybreak the Osceola Belle stopped and gave him hot coffee as the City of Helena gave him a loud cheer.

Around Devil's Elbow he encountered another very heavy head wind, which required all his strength paddling against it, he was totally exhausted when he arrived at Bradley's, Arkansas.

Stopping for the night and getting an early start the next morning for Memphis, making good time after a nights rest and nourishing food.

Just above Memphis he was met by a fleet of excursion steamers, at the sight of his flashing paddle in the sunlight, from deck of the General Pierson started to fire off a ten pound parrot gun as a salute to Boyton. Heading to the gunwale of the gig, Paul was presented by the Belle of Memphis, Miss Jeannette Boswell, with an banner.

Holding onto the gunwale of the gig, in the politest manner, he thanked the young lady for the honor. The enthusiasm and reception in Memphis was very impressive.

Paul resumed his voyage Monday afternoon with the well wishes of the population seeing him off. That night another terrific storm almost sank him as large trees came crashing down, rain turned to hail as the river was whitened by the icy stones. The force of the storm was so great that Paul had to stand up in the water and shield his face with the broad blade of his paddle as the icy stones bruised his knuckles, at one time he thought the suit was damaged and leaking, fortunately it was only the extreme cold penetrating through the rubber, though terribly uncomfortable.

In the darkness he missed the cutoff at Walnut Bend, that would have saved him fifteen miles of paddling, as the day broke he saw a negro on the bank, inquiring where he was.

"Yo'se in de bend shoah 'nough Cap'en, but I'se pow'ful glad yo' missed the cut'ov, cause I wanted to see'yo awful bad." Paul did not sympathize with the man's joy as the unnecessary fifteen miles were the hardest paddling of the entire trip. That morning was very lonely along the river as he was still annoyed over missing the convient cutoff, way around the bend he could hear the distant beating sound of a steam boats paddles as it approached.

The sound animated Paul as he paddled with greater vigor, until he meet a boat that was loaded with tourists from Helena. He came along side as the passengers begged him to come ashore and visit their city. He was sore and tired, but declined their kind invitation. Other boats came up until he was surrounded, while they earnestly insisted he come ashore at Helena.

Finally agreeing to stop over and rest for a couple of hours, thinking he could get his lamp and watch repaired at the same time, that had been smashed by the hail the night before.

He was enthusiastically welcomed to the city, and a committee of citizens were appointed to get him anything he may need, the Mayor and several officials asked him to stay over that night and give a lecture, declining to do so, as his wardrobe had been shipped ahead to Vicksburg, he had nothing but the rubber suit and heavy underwear

That's alright," assured the Mayor, "we will fix you up with a dress suit and take care of all the details, We will get out bill's, hire a hall, get a band and just fix you up like a bug in a rug. Don't worry about anything, just stay here and rest while we make the arrangements." The people had been so kind, that Paul felt obliged to consent, the Mayor arrived with a swallow tailed coat, white vest, tie and a collar that fastened around his neck without shirt buttons. The upper half of him looked

ROUGHING IT IN RUBBER

alright and appropriately dressed for a public presentation, they waited for the man with the pantaloons, but he did not appear.

"Alright," said the mayor, "I reckon he's must have gone to the hall, there is a dressing room there, come on, just hop in my carriage and I will drive you there, no one will see you." They waited at the hall that was filling up fast, the man still did not appear. As the crowds became impatient. "That's alright," said the ever ready Mayor again, "we can fix that." He shoved a stand to the middle of the stage and taking a large table cover, arranged it so that it reached the floor, thus hiding everything behind it, from the eyes of the crowd.

The curtain went up, with the Mayor at his side, Paul looking as if he was attired in an irreproachable dress suit. The introduction was received by loud applause, as he began describing the rubber suit and his method of navigating the rivers, while recounting his adven
ture with the shark in the straits of Messina, becoming somewhat excited and without thinking, stepped from behind the protecting folds of the table cloth, in all the glory of a dress coat, white vest and violently red drawers, a gasp, then deathly silence followed with stares of disbelief, then the wild roar of laughter rose from the audience, Paul realizing what he had done, fled from the stage with an unfinished shark story still on his lips. The Mayor getting back the attention of the audience, explained what had happened, as they saw the humor in the evening, gave three rousing cheers for Paul.

To make up for the time he had lost with the hospitable citizens of Helena, Boyton was compelled to make an extra long run, he paddled to Arkansas City without leaving the water, a distance of one hundred and sixty miles in thirty one hours, which was the longest continuos run he ever made up to that time.

That night on the lonesome stretches of the river, he frequently startled a loon from it's resting place and it would fly off into the darkness with wild unearthly shriek, so ghostly were it's echo's that Paul would glance around for the dead man in his boat.

Early in the morning the voyager struck a big eddy and was

twisted around and around for quite a while before he could clear himself, as it threw him pretty close to shore. Through the thick groves of cottonwoods, a spiral of thin blue smoke rose, he was sure this would be a negro's cabin, blowing a merry blast on the bugle and before the clear notes had faded from the morning air. A venerably darkey with a whitened head and slightly bent, barely able to walk appeared on the bluff over looking the river, slowly and with some signs of fear the old man focused his attentions on the water, removing his old broad brimmed white hat, placing it on the stump beside him as he raised his eyes to the eastern horizon, then west as though scanning the river up and down.

He did not see Boyton at first, as another blast from the bugle caught his attention, raising his eyes reverently, and with out stretched hands he solemnly said, "He bloowed his trumpet on the watah. God, bless hum, God."

He remained in this position until Paul disappeared around the bend, no doubt expecting to be summoned home at any moment by the archangel Gabriel.

Directly after leaving the old negro gentleman, Paul though he saw something snagged a little down river, thinking it was probably just a tree branch, getting closer he discovered it was a large deer swimming across the river. Quickly loosening "Baby Mine", he removed the large hunting knife and started for the deer. He did not anticipated any trouble as he paddled alongside, as the buck discovered the pursuer it redoubled it's efforts to reach the shore, raising the knife to stab, the deer raised up and viciously struck out, Paul barely dodging the blows of it's front legs, which could have cut through the rubber like a knife. Again and again, he tried to get an opening for a thrust, however the deer with blazing eyes of a panther, beat him away with it's sharp hooves. Pul decided to follow it to the edge of the water, it would surely get stuck in the mud. Paul raised the knife, the animal sprang six feet above him with all four hooves together, galloping off and wavied a farewell with it's stumpy white tail.

That night he arrived in Arkansas City, very tired and cold, deciding to stay overnight at the hotel where he met an extraordinary character who appointed himself Boyton's body guard, without a word. He watched over him while he slept, stoking the fire all night, and was still at his bedside with a hot cup of tea when Paul woke up , without uttering a word. As Paul was leaving he stretched out his hand, the man wrung it as though parting with his dearest friend, yet he hadn't a word to say or would accept money for his services.

   A short distance below Arkansas City, a blast from Paul's bugle brought a troop of negroes to the bank, as they gazed in open mouthed wonder, he asked them the distance to the next town.

They were either so overcome with fright or astonishment, they could not answer, but one old auntie did however lean over the bank, and in a trembling voice ask, "Chile, does yo' belon to the chu'ch?"

She breathed a sigh of relief and seemed satisfied that he was a human being, when he answered, "yes."

The long lonely run of one hundred and forty miles brought him to Milligan's Bend where he stopped at a planter's house overnight. The next day was Sunday and as he only had a twenty mile run to Vicksburg, deciding to start later on in the morning to arrive on schedule in the afternoon. While taking it easy, chatting with the planter, and enjoying a fragrant cigar, the old minister of the parish arrived and introduced himself to Paul.

"God bless you my son," said the venerable gentleman, pressing Paul's hand, "I must say I have called especially to see you and ask you to do me a favor."

"I would be pleased to do anything in my power for you," Paul replied.

"I knew you would, God bless you," fervently spoke the old minister, " my congregation is waiting along the bank of the river to see you start, not a soul of them will enter the church until you go, even if it is not until dark, and I wanted to ask if you would start soon, so that I may begin services?" The old man spoke with such sincerity, his face brightened when Paul assured him he would start preparing to leave at once.

   He arrived at Vicksburg, four o'clock in the afternoon, and was met by the steamer Silverthorn towing a big barge loaded with tourists. It appeared as though the residents of the entire city and surroundings towns were assembled on the river banks, so dense were the crowds, that it caused an old negro to remark, "Ef dose yere people keep on crowding' on dis'ob town, de whole place are gwine fur tip ober in de ribber, suah 'nough."

With the aid of the city marshal and a few policemen, he got through to the carriage where the Mayor was waiting for him. As the carriage began to move off, a man jumped in and seated himself between Boyton and the Mayor. Paul did not think much of the incident, assuming the man was one of the Mayors friends.

As Paul told the story later, when we reached the hotel, " the man became obnoxiously officious as he pushed ahead of me, entering my room with an air of ownership, helping himself to drinks as though he was paying for it all. Eventually I became very impatient with this fellow, he was aggravating me, so I asked who he was. When I learned he was the most despicable character, who was known to have murdered at least one person and had the people so afraid of him that they feared objecting to his presence or behavior. I became outraged at this news, and as the fellow reappeared in the doorway, I gabbed him by the collar, threw him boldly over into the hallway, kicking him down the stairs."

As Paul said, "That cuffing did the fellow some good, it encouraged other men to cuff him, until he learned to behave himself." The desperado later admitted that he had never experienced such anger, as that of the navigator.

The next run was from Vicksburg to Nanchez, one hundred and nine miles. The start was made in a gale and Paul was not too far down when he felt the effects of fever, taking an enormous dose of quinine as the violent shivers racked his body, bracing himself, he kept pushing ahead. Arriving at Nanchez twenty six hours later, he was so ill on his arrival that he barely noticed the large reception waiting for him. Going directly to the hotel and to bed, immediately falling into a very deep sleep. A doctor was called and diagnosed swamp fever, by now Paul was in grave danger, but with the proper care he could be saved. Boyton felt better after the sleep assisted, by the doctors prescription.

ROUGHING IT IN RUBBER

One or two callers were admitted to his room. Among them was a gentleman, who stated that his wife was an invalid, as her window looked over the river, she had seen Paul passing on his way to Natchez, so composed a poem, which she begged the voyager to accept. The lady's name was Mrs. Francis Marschalk, the
verse read's:

> When All the waves of time are past,
> And earth's rude storms with thee are o'er,
> Oh, may'st thou sweetly rest at last,
> Upon the peaceful shinning shore,
> And may thy spirit's pastime be,
> Life's river and the Jasper sea.

Paul was deeply affected by such a delicate tribute from an accomplished stranger. Sending an apology with an autographed note of his grateful appreciation.

Eager to finish his journey, he did not stay long in Natchez, among the crowd that followed him to the wharf was the doctor.

That gentleman was very earnest in advising him not to go back on the water as he was still in great danger of being overcome with the fever.

"You have every indication of fever now, and if it attacks you on the water again, you will certainly die." said the concerned doctor.

"However if you persist on going, all I can do is to tell you that if the symptoms return, get out of the water and go directly to bed as soon as you can."

"What are the symptoms?" enquired Paul.

Paul waved goodbye to the multitude of people and headed out with the wind blowing, as the current quickly took him out of sight.

The night came on quickly, he was tired, and thought he felt the fever symptoms returning, as he was heading for shore, he heard a steamboat, he was burning the little red light so she slowed up with the passengers cheering him as the captain called out,

"How do you feel Paul?"

"All right, report me above," was the reply, the boat heading up river. The diversion gave him the courage to go on as he increased his paddling with renewed determination, moving at a steady pace he reached Baton Rouge at eight o'clock in the morning.

From Baton Rouge it was a home run of only one hundred and thirty four miles to New Orleans. He started early next morning, though feeling very stiff and sore. The weather was intensely hot and he suffered terribly from sun burn, his face almost black with blisters and peeling skin. About eleven o'clock in the morning, on the glassy surface of the water ahead he noticed something bobbing up and down in a very strange manner, pulling over to investigate, finding a dead mule all bloated, as he was looking at it, it's tail flipped out of the water as though it was alive, suddenly seeing a swarm of alligators feeding on it, he pulled away as fast as he can ever recall, moving over the water.

During the day he went through a thickly populated countryside, along the lower coast of Louisiana, the river was lined with rich sugar plantations and a majority of the negroes who rowed out to see him, spoke French Creole. Magnolia trees framed the beautiful valley, making a picturesque sight. While paddling a short distance from shore, Paul noticed the most unique and lazy style of fishing, up on the bank were two pairs of huge bare feet, from which fishing lines came, the corks bobbing on the surface a few yards away. The broad soles of their huge feet turned to the river, as the lines were passing between the large and second toes to the water, taking a nap while waiting for the fish to swallow the bait, the pull the line is felt on their toes they wake up and take care of business. Paul taking in the situation, quietly got close to one of the lines, gave it a jerk.

The negro rose to a sitting position instantly, when he saw the black shiny figure, on his line, he let out a shriek that would have been heard for miles, at the same time springing to his feet, sprinted away, yelling, as he ran, to his companion, "Hyah Bill, git away frum dar, git up an' cut, I'se done cotch de debbil on my hook."

The other fisherman sat up stiffly, and seeing Boyton, he went into an uncontrolled fit of laughter. He laughed so long,

ROUGHING IT IN RUBBER 219

Paul was became very concerned he would not be able to breathe, and choke.

Paul tried to stop him, but the laughter was uncontrollable, so returning to the water he paddled away still hearing the voice of that hilarious fisherman laughing for a distance down river.

As evening closed in he could hear the negroes, who had been paid, as it was Saturday night, singing and arguing along the shore. A dense fog soon enveloped everything, he could no longer see which way he was going, grabbing on to the roots of a drifting tree, knowing it would follow the current, he mounted it and sat there for hours floating down rive, as the mocking birds serenaded him all night. He would have remained on the tree until morning but heard the whistling of steamers below, he knew that a fleet left New Orleans every Saturday afternoon bound north and as each would be trying to gain the lead on the others, afraid of being run over so he quickly slid off the tree and headed for shore, that course was not without danger either, mingled with the beautiful songs of mocking birds were the hoarse barking of alligators. As he was not sure what might be waiting for him, as they are thick along the shore.

Sounding his bugle, it summoned a Frenchman who came down to the bank, Paul explained who he was and the man eagerly invited him ashore. "I am sitting up with my old master who is dead," said the man. "What was the matter?," inquired Paul, "Oh it wasn't the fever, you need not fear."

Paul decided to land and wait until the fleet had passed, then he lit his lamp and pushed off through the fog, preferring the solitude of the river to the grief stricken Frenchman. The fog lifted in the morning and he found that he was on time, only ten miles above New Orleans.

He was met by enthusiastic an crowd aboard the excursion steamers. Captain Leathers of the famous old boat, the Natchez, was determined to out do the other boats in welcoming the voyager, as Boyton was an old friend. He had a cannon placed on the deck of his boat, loaded to the muzzle, with a crowd of negroes, stretching their necks to catch a glimpse of Boyton, Captain Leathers fired right over their heads, you could hear the shrieks of panic from them.

Paul landed at New Orleans after the journey of two thousand and four hundred and thirty miles. He was honored and entertained in the Crescent City until he became bored with it all, he boarded a train for the north, weighing thirty pounds less than the day he left Oil City.

With thoughts of Elise still waiting for his return to France, Paul again sent off a letter to her, as follows.

On The Mississippi 11-2-82-79

My Dearest Elise,

Your welcome letter came to me. I was pleased to hear from you again. I often think of you as I voyage down the great rivers, my little flower of Garone is planted too deeply in my heart to be easily forgotten. You astonish and please me by writing English and I assure you, it is very well written indeed. Next letter must be all in English, you do much better than you think. I send you a photograph as you desired and I want you to send me one of yours.

I assume your (trust?) Elise I have. I have been engaged in making voyages down the Mississippi, Yellowstone, and Missouri rivers. The last voyage was the longest and most dangerous of them all. I was 64 days on the water and travelled a distance of 3500 miles. I just ended my voyage a week ago and since that time I have been resting.

I often think most ---- of the bright, handsome girl I met on the Garone. How I would enjoy taking a voyage with you in your little boat. I wonder if we will ever meet again I most ardently hope we may. I have always retained the warmest spot in my heart for my charming Elise, the fairest flower on the Garone. I cannot at present say when I will return to France. I only wish my business would permit me to return tomorrow, if it was only for the sake of seeing you. I must publish my book of travels now, it will take me all this winter to do it. After than I may go to Europe again. Write to me in Flushing. With love true and sincere dear Elise.

I remain ever yours Paul.

Returning to New York, once again to the delight of his family, especially his mother, who never knows if she will ever see him again.

The summer of 1879 was idly spent, Paul visited the most important water resorts of America and enjoyed a well earned good time with lots of rest and good food.

As the autumn leaves began to fall, his urge to return to the water started becoming an obsession, turning his attention to the rivers of the New England States. He spent many hours trying to find maps and information on the currents and channels, of these major rivers, with little or no success.

He went first to Boston making a careful study of all the maps he could find, decided to do the next voyage on the Merrimac, this river with it's numerous falls and rapids would create an exciting challenge. While in Boston Paul did have the promised photograph taken and sent off to Elise, following is a copy.

The start was made from Plymouth, New Hampshire, at six o'clock in the morning on October the seventh 1879. As the river was extremely rough that morning the decision to leave the little tender "Baby Mind." behind, a decision he later regretted. Paddling a short distance from the shore, the water became so shallow that he was forced to wade quite a distance before getting to deep enough waters to allow him to get under way, as he eventually left the cheering crowds in the distance.

About nine o'clock that evening as he was approaching a bridge, he noticed a figure of a man on horse back, outlined against the sky. The countryman seeing the queer looking

This is from the original of Michel Lopez's collection of Captain Paul Boyton. A Historian in France. Who has been kind enough to allow me to copy and publish them.

This photography was amongst the bundle of letters purchased by Michel Lopez in an antique store in Paris. Sadly there is no trace of her replies or the photograph that she sent Paul.

figure in the water. Jerking his arms up, slapped the reins on the horse's back and as it rose up they galloping off at a hasty pace, the countryman obviously did not read the newspaper. An hour later Paul saw a farmer in the fields, blew his bugle in front of the farm house that stood near the river, the people ran to the water's edge and began firing with such rapidity, as the bullets ricko-shayed off the water, he almost drowned dodging them from underwater.

Paul did not appreciate the rapid fire of the New Hampshire rustic's, pulled rapidly out of sight as the narrow river brought him closer to the banks, keeping a sharp eye open as he silently went by.

ROUGHING IT IN RUBBER

He was forging ahead when an old gentleman hailed, Paul stopped for a moment and was sorry he did as the man tried to chill his blood with doleful stories of the danger of the river below.

"Yeou air goin' straight ahead tew destruction," he bellowed, "that's a whirlpool jist ahead, where six lumberman t'was drowneded."

Paul had no fear of sharing the fate of the lumberman, so he left the man wringing his hands on the side of the river in disbelief that his warnings had gone unheeded. Reaching the junction of Squam River, he encountered the first whirlpool, as a crowd of men and boys had assembled on the bridge anxiously watching him dash over.

Emerging from the boiling foam on the other side of the falls, the surprised group cheered as he scrambled up on a rock as they thought he was lost. From here on down Paul found nothing but dead choppy waters until he reached New Hampton.

Many of the people in the towns down the river, offered him advice, and some comical. One man suggested that Paul, "should give up such an outlandish mode of travel," while another recommended to, "git on land like a human critter." While the advice sounded good to them, their form of travel was not without danger. He noticed on the grim rocks of the bluff above an upturned wagon and floating on the current, a seat and wheel.

"Where is the driver of that wagon?" inquired Paul, no one knew.

He paddled away hoping that he maybe able to find the poor unfortunate man who had evidently been hurled off the bluff, but no trace was ever found of him down the river.

Below, the sound of the rapids got Paul's attention. The smooth water began to break as if suddenly impelled to tear the rocks from the river and crushing every obstacle in it's path.

His efforts were in vain as he continued to be thrown against the rocks with considerable force, catching hold of a large rock that enabled him to briefly stand up and try to see which side was the deepest channel.

Seeing an older raw boned woman standing in the doorway of a little cottage on the hillside. Paul blew a calvary charge on his bugle as she dashed inside alarming all the residents. They crowded in to the doorway, giving Boyton a look of horror as he stood on that rock in
the midst of the rapids. Beckoning to them with his paddle was enough evidence that they took him for some Satanic majesty. "Lan' sakes, Zekiel!" one was heard to say,"go git gran'pap's old blunderbuster, an' shoot it."

Paul, feared the people that did not read the newspaper more than the rapids, he rapidly took to the water and flashed past as he was again drawn into another larger rapid as he was whirled into a place that he had to struggle over a bed of round slippery rocks in shallow water. When he tried to stand up to find a way out, his feet would slipfrom under him, this took over an hour to get out, by crawling, walking and paddling his way through as best he could. At five o'clock in the evening he reached Bristol, where he was advised to go no further in the dark, confirmed by a telegram from his agent.

The next morning the landlord's daughter drove him to the bank as large crowds watched him paddle away towards the whirlpool, knowing this one was going to be a tough ride. Negotiating the rocks and swilling waters that gave him a few too many submerging's. Paul got through it and headed for Franklin, arriving safely at one o'clock.

All the way he had kept a close look out for the doomed driver of the up turned wagon, with no signs of him. Before reaching Franklin he noticed bonfires were built along the banks, row boats had been waiting at the falls for the past two days. Learning later that the fires were in his honor as he had been expected two days earlier.

Resuming the voyage at eight o'clock the next morning and shooting over the informis Sewell's Falls. He was warned that this was a very rough tricky falls to negotiate, though an extremely invigorating ride. The river down toWest Concord was very long and lonely, until he was met by fleets of boats and deafening booming canons, as he stepped out of the water, again two days late.

Leaving after another short rest, Paul was warned about another rough ride ahead, Turkey Falls.

Asking one of the gentleman. "Which side of the falls should I take?" the answer came back without hesitation.

"Which ever side you take, you will wish you took the other." Both bank's of the falls were lined with people as he approached, Paul noticed that there were always larger crowds at the dangerous spots, where he was more likely to be killed. For a few seconds he was lost in the foam as the spectators stood in breathless silence. The seemly lifeless form appeared, then the paddle followed as he was swept rapidly along in to smoother water.

Their hero was not lost on that uneventful spot after all, there would be no legend to pass down the generations. One mile below the falls Paul encountered the first dam of this journey, a stretch of dead water for the next seven miles of tireless paddling until he arrived at Suncook in the dark and thoroughly worn out. Invitations to remain were plentiful, but he continued another two miles down river to Hookset where dry clothes and a hot meal were waiting for him with a good nights rest.

The next morning an early start was made, as he was now able to take "Baby Mine," for the balance of the journey, loaded with fresh supplies and his little red lamp.

The water from Hookset to Manchester was heavy and required a lot of hard paddling to keep up a steady pace. There were more signs of life as he headed down river. Children ran along the banks calling to him, and one little girl in particular called out.

"Come in here, Paul I want see you." demanding, as though he was a life long friend. Continuing on to Manchester, arriving at noon.

He had gone over two of the five water falls that intercepted the Merrimac River, as night fell with such intensity that he was forced to to rely on the sounds along the bank's to determine which direction he was going.

At eight o'clock he noticed lights in the distance, attracting some people with a blast of his bugle. He inquired, what the distance to the next falls was, as before he heard the diverse and wildly different opinions with the usual results.

By taking his own course he succeeded in reaching Nashua safely just before ten o'clock that night.

The next day dawned dull and rainy as Paul had a hard run on the sluggish water. He arrived very tired at Tyngsborough, as was nearing a crowed bridge where the people began to bombarded him with stupid questions. Dying of thirst and without looking up,as he asked,

"is there a hotel in town?"

"Naw," shouted a gruff voice, "ner yeou kaint git naw liker hure nowhere neether."

"I'll bet you never colored that nose with river water," quickly replied Paul as he went under the bridge.
The remark was followed by a roar of laughter by the towns people, as apparently his nose was a landmark and often joked about in the little town.

A number of small boat's met Paul as he approached Lowell, extending an invitation to stop at the Vesper Boat Club, now five o'clock, very thirsty and exhausted. He accepted the kind invitation to land at the club house, staying over until Sunday. Early Monday morning he resumed his journey, totally rested with lots of energy to face Hunt's Falls, as he shot over safely, coming back up through the foam onto the fast moving water. A steam launch was waiting for him with news reporters from Lawrence.

After Lawrence the river is effected by tides, forcing him to stay until four o'clock the next morning. Later that morning he landed at a frame house, with a sign that read Confectionery, over the door. Paul assumed he could get a hot breakfast,

ROUGHING IT IN RUBBER

as he was led into a room that quickly filled up with obtrusive question'ers.

A farmer seeing the pained look on Paul's face, volunteered to get him breakfast, as Paul was about to get into a plate of apples, mince pie and assorted pickles the man appeared with a genuine country breakfast of eggs, bacon, sausage and biscuits, more than his imagination could have dreamed up. It was fortunate for Boyton's digestion, that he needed to stay over five hours for the flood tide.

Directly after leaving, Paul was meet by a fleet of boat's that came up river to escort him down the last leg of his voyage. On board one of the boat's was Sir Edward Thornton, the British Minister of Washington DC. and his beautiful daughter, as they were old acquaintances, he enjoyed a pleasant chat with them and shortly after landed at Newburyport.

The two hundred mile voyage in seven days down the very rough Merrimac River, was completed, as he described it later.

"It had the most waterfalls, dead waters and hardest paddling that I have encountered on any of the rivers I have navigated to date."

Taking a couple of days rest, with lots of good hot food, Paul decided to do a run down the Connecticut River, the largest and most beautiful river in New England, starting as close to the headwaters, that he could get to, at Long Island Sound.

He arrived at Stratford, New Hampshire, where he had decided to start. The residents decided that Paul should have more than just a canon and people cheering when he took off. They wanted to show him just how honored they were to have him start from their town, requesting that he please begin at daylight.

Six forty five the next morning he was accompanied by great crowds of people to the rivers edge for a tremendous explosive send off. Created by putting a pair of anvils together, thus making an enormous explosion when combined with the canon.

After passing the railroad bridge at Coos, he had about six miles of rapid as the river was about one hundred and twenty miles wide and flowing fast, he averaged a good five miles an hour.

At eleven o'clock he passed through Stratford Hollow and inquired how far it was to Northumberland?.

"Seven mile b'road an twenty b'riber, b'gosh," was the native's reply. Though laconic, the answer was correct, for the river bowed and bent frequently, one time he was sure he passed the same farm house twice in an interval of less than two and a half hours, giving him the view of both the back and front of the old house.

About two o'clock in the afternoon a heavy storm blew in, with pelting rain blurring his vision while he tried to dodge the floating logs. Paul lost track of the distance he had gone, he should now be close to the next falls. Being warned constantly by people calling out from the banks, as he shot by, "Look out stranger, fur em,ere wuter fall."
Paul pulled over to question a man who looked like he was a waterman, as to how far down?, the fellow said he had gone over once on a raft when the water was much higher.

"They'll jus' squeeze d'life frum yeou, sure'n daylight."

Navigating the falls was not all that the locals had made of it, but still quite a ride, this one got his paddle, heading on down paddle less was another challenge in itself on the fast swollen river to Northumberland, he was forced to stay overnight, fortunately he found the paddle amongst the driftwood in the morning.

One of the drawbacks of the voyage was not being able to get fresh provisions at most places as they generally looked at him as if he was some uncanny creature.

When he did get food it was mainly pie, this seemed to be the staff of life with the people in this part of the country. Inquiring from a fellow, where he could get the best accommodation in Northumberland. "Oh, stop at th'hotel, b'all means. They'd feed yeou tip top, high up," said he, "I've been ter dinner there w'en they've hed all o'seven kinds er'pie on ther t'onct."

Jokingly Paul asked, "have they got apples and squash?"
"Yeou kin jus'bet on thet," was the enthusiastic answer.

Leaving just after nine o'clock the next morning, a few miles after leaving he found himself in a dam with very rough water, the weather became cold, snowy and squally. The cold cutting snow beat against his face, he plied the paddle vigorously and made remarkable progress. When he passed the farmers in the country, they would stare at him in disbelief and burst out laughing at the sight of a man paddling down a river in a driving snow storm.

Finally reaching Lanchester at one thirty in the afternoon, taking a break to warm up before he headed back down the river.

He felt the faster pace of the water as he got closer to Lunenburg, where the Fifteen Mile Falls begins, deciding to wait for early morning to go over this much feared falls. Staying over the night with a kindly farmer, Mr. Frank Bell who offered him accommodation and graciously entertained Paul.

He was prepared for the struggle when he started out early the next morning after a restful night and delicious breakfast Paul was rearing to go. The Fifteen Mile Falls proved to be as rough an experience as he had ever gone through.

Holbrook's Bar was the last pitch of the falls, M'Indoe's Dam and Barnet Pitch and the other sections of these falls were a constant run of swirling currents, foam, fast rough rapids and sharp jagged rocks. The amount of encounters were to many to describe in detail. Paul reached tremendous speed and he luckily only suffered a slight bruise and cut in his rubber suit during the descent. A local on the bank was heard during Paul's descent, to remark.

"Hure comes that pesky swimmer aroun' th' bow, an' he's a comin' like forty." The Vermonter's inability to understand what Boyton was going to get out of such a trip that appeared to be the main subject, as most of the people along the Connecticut. They would invariably ask, "how do you make it pay?"

Many of them would not give him any information when he asked, but would allow him to paddle along un-instructed, so they could enjoy the full benefit of the show.

After damaging the rubber suit Paul began getting really cold with water seeping in and the numbness taking over. A little stimulant would have been good at this stage, but the suspicious locals were not ready to oblige him, he could neither beg, buy or borrow anything from the spectators. He was now halfway through the Fifteen Mile Falls.

When he reached the Lower Waterford Bridge his agent was waiting with much needed fresh provisions, stopping there he was also fortunate to be able to repair the suit.

If any one the crowd that had watched him leave, been willing to answer his questions the damage could have been prevented.

Heading back out fully refreshed and rested he again challenged the unpredictable waters.

Fifteen Mile Falls. Scanned from the Paul Boyton Story.

Off Morris' place, Paul hailed a man in a turnip patch and as he cautiously approached the rivers edge. Boyton carefully removed the cover from an air tight jar suspended from his neck, took out a cigar and with a match lit the weed.

The rustic removed his hat, closing his eyes and scratched his head in great perplexity. "Wall, I sow," he exclaimed, "ef yeou hadn't spoke er I'd taken yeou fur th' devil an' swore yeou lit that er durned cigar wuth th' end o' yer tail, but ain't yer cold?"

Valley Hotel was where Paul and his party stayed the night at the Lower Waterford. How long it had been since the last guest booked in there, probably could not be remembered. The landlady was very accommodating, offering them her sitting room which Boyton and his party occupied, while reviewing the incidents of the voyage.

The local's came in and out looking at him as if it was some kind of free animal exhibit, they did not even knock, or remove their hats nor wait to be asked to be seated. Without as much as "good evening" they would just stare in the most ignorant manner, then return to the gathering at the store across the street relating their experiences to others. They could be excused, as Waterford is isolated from civilization. With no railroad or telegraph communication and few newspapers are ever seen to inform them of events such as this voyage.

Paul took the invasion good naturedly and joked pleasantly each time a group left the sitting room. Just before starting the next morning, an old gentleman approached Paul on the porch in front of the hotel, expressing great pleasure at meeting him, in fact, claimed they had meet before. Paul always glad to meet an old friend was inquisitive enough to ask where they had met each other before, the old fellow answered,

"yeou remember w'en yeou crossed th' English channel?"

"Yes," he replied Paul, as if he could ever forget it.

"An' thet ere rubber suit you wore?"

"Certainly."

"Wall," continued the old man, apparently tickled that Paul had not forgotten the event. "Wall, I saw that er suit at ther centennial in Philadelphy in '76, I wus thar." as he looked around catching the admiration of his town's people.

He was about to shoot Dodge's Falls as a lumberman, called out to him to hug the New Hampshire shore and he would go over safely.

That was the only sensible information he was given through the entire Fifteen Mile Falls. The worst of the run was now behind him, though there were still several falls and dams ahead with long stretches of dead water to paddle through, nearing Bellow's Falls the people were more enlightened and many offers of hospitality as the citizens showed more interest than fear in what he was doing as they rendered all the assistance he needed.

Shooting through the remaining falls safely, but narrowly missing disaster of being hit by a large log that came over directly behind him. From that point on Paul was treated with kindness and consideration as the people encouraged him, all along the river.

On the evening of November the seventh, he landed at Saybrook Light, completing the trip in just sixteen days from Stratford Hollow.

Paul decided to head to warmer waters for the winter of 1879 and 1880, as he had had more than his share of rough cold water for quite some time. Considering Florida as his next challenge, with a trip home to New York first.

His family was once again thrilled to see him, alive and intact after the months of his dangerous exploits. Paul had hoped to have, waiting for him the reply to his letter from the Mississippi to his beloved Elise.

The winter of 1879 was spent in Florida, hunting, fishing, alligator shooting. Paul started a new sport, canoeing, this became dear to his heart as it was more or less what he had been doing with his body as the vessel, for years along the rivers.

Paul's concerns grew as he still did not have the reply from his beloved Elise, so he wrote again from Florida.

A party of his friends and himself made a canoe trip far up the St. John's River and through Kissimme to Lake Okeechobee, where he had a great time of sport shooting, deer, bears and alligators, while at the same time the numerous moccasins and rattle snakes offered more amusement than enjoyed by many in the party. Returning north to Jacksonville, Paul made a run down the St. John's River to the ocean, crossing the shark infested bar at the mouth of the river.

On his way north during the spring, he made short trips on the Savannah, Cooper and Potomac rivers and Chesapeake Bay.

In June he paddled down the Delaware from Philadelphia to

Ship John's light.

That trip was a very strenuous one as the tide was sluggish, when the tide turned he would have to head to flatter water. Another quick reply to Elise was sent out in the midst of this whirl wind trip across the country.

Paul was becoming very restless while trying to decide what to do with his life, the heart longs to return to France, and yet he needs to still satisfy his lust for water exploits. He was really beginning to wonder if he would ever see her again, and decided he must at least appeal to her father in the hopes he will agree to their marriage.

That way he will be able to bring her to merica and continue with his adventures.

New York

25-8-82

My true dearest Elise,

The steamer that starts for France today carried a letter for your good Father from me, in which I have asked him for your dear hand. May God Grant that he will think kindly of my request and not refuse me the great love I ask of him. I ought to have written to him a long time ago but I never had the courage to do so.

How happy you and I would be dearest Elise and rest assured that the object of my whole life would be to make you as happy and wanted as you could wish to be. I have a handsome little steamer launch just large enough for you and I can make some voyages down the beautiful American rivers. And I hope by this time next year we will be making a voyage on the Hudson.

I have told my mother all about you and she told me to assure you would be welcome and would love your warmly for the sake of her son. No doubt your parents will object to your coming away to America but then just think it *only takes about twelve days from New York to Bordeaux and you and I could visit them every winter. When you are with me you will soon learn to speak English and you will teach me to speak French much better than I do now. I hope to be able to leave here after the New Year. That is providing your Father will grand me permission to visit you. If he will consent to me seeing you, think then no objection to our marriege. You must instruct me to what proper --- I will need to bring with me, for I have been informed that there is much formality in France.*

In regards to marriage and more particularly so with a stranger, I hope your father will be satisfied with my letter. I fear very much that my translations did not for my ideas into good French.

American Consul at Bordeaux in regard to the article that was published in the "La Gondone d'Bordeaux" and requested him to contest it. Doesn't say complaint and regrets the --------------.
And accept darling Elise my hearts warmest and most sincere love.
God bless and love you my dear girl and may he grant me the pleasure of one day calling you my wife.
With love dear Elise-
    Paul

   While undecided on what to do next, Paul made a few quick runs, one along the Jersey shore where masses of mosquitoes breed in the long grass , that almost eat him alive as he paddled through the area.
   Later he paddled the entire length of Lake Quinsigamund, in September he ran the Narragansett from Rocky Point to Providence.
   Paul once again home in New York, being pampered by his mother and sisters, while entertained by the cities nobles and authorities.
   He was never very comfortable in societies circles, so very

ROUGHING IT IN RUBBER

quickly bored of all the invitations to parties and banquets, with the same old stuffed shirts and their constant questions.

CHAPTER ELEVEN

One day in October, while Paul was walking down Broadway Street in New York, a gentleman tapped him on the shoulder saying.

"This is Captain Boyton, I believe?" when answered, he continued.

"I have just returned from Europe, where I have been looking for you. I have a message for you, from Don Nicholas de Pierola, but as I am an agent of the Peruvian government, it is not safe to talk here, there are many Chillian spies in New York as well as in Lima.

Meet me tonight at this address," Slipping a card in Paul's hand, the man hurriedly walked away.

That night Paul entered a house in thirty-fourth street where he met the stranger, who immediately got down to business, by stating that Don Nicholas de Pierola, wanted Boyton to leave for Peru at once, with his equipment and rubber suit, plus the torpedo cases, electrical appliances and everything necessary for the destruction of Chillian vessels of war. It did not take Paul long to get all the necessary equipment needed and arrange the preliminaries.

Before he left a contract was drawn up, by which he was to enter the Peruvian torpedo service, with a commission of Captain. He was to receive one-hundred-thousand dollars for the first Chillian vessel destroyed and one-hundred-and-twenty-five-thousand dollars for the second, one-hundred-and-fifty-thousand dollars for the third. Three vessels that were priority on the list, were the Huascar, Bianco Encalado and the Almirante Corcoran.

Next day as Paul was happily getting ready for this new adventure with the chance of making some good money out of it. He had agreed to go to Peru as Pablo Delaport a newspaper correspondent, receiving his passport and papers the following day.

Telling his family that he was just going to take a short trip to Panama. Not wanting to upset or worry his beloved mother with the details of the dangerous task he was undertaking in Peru.

On October the tenth 1882, accompanied by his assistant,

George Kiefer, he embarked on the steamer Crescent City for Aspinwall, arriving there on the nineteenth, from there they crossed to Panama and had to waite for two days for the Columbia to take them south to Peru.

> Ship Aroura
>
> On Sea 21-2-82
>
> My Dearest Elise,
>
> You must be surprised at my long silence. I will explain - soon after I write to you and your Great Father in Oct. I was ordered to South America on some private and important business. I left New York before I could hear from you. But before going I left instructions to forward all my letters to Panama. In Dec. I arrive at Piata Peru to the same address as I gave you before. Paul Delaport Callao Peru, my friend will get all your letters and forward them to me when he gets a chance.
>
> I am sorry to say that I must close Dear Elise the messanger is already in his house and about to ride away.
>
> With best love
>
> Paul

A Chilian man-o-war, the Amazons, was anchored at Panama on lookout for a torpedo launch that was expected from New York.

In his capacity as newspaper correspondent, Paul went on board the man-o-war to inspect her, with the idea that he might have an opportunity sometime to attach a one-hundred-and-fifty pound torpedo to her bottom. He was escorted through the vessel by the Captain and took copious notes of her construction and armament. As he was going-over the side into the boat to return to shore, an English engineer looked at him very carefully and remarked, "Your face seems familiar to me. Where have I seen you before?"

Paul replied that he could not possibly tell as his duties lead him to all parts of the world, and hurriedly entered the boat. The next day they set sail and soon saw Dead Man's Island at the mouth of Guayquil river. While on this second leg of his trip he was able to get another letter written to Elise. From a some points the island bears a startling resemblance to a gigantic man afloat on his back, hence its name, they steamed up the river about sixty miles to Guayquil.

The chattering of parrots and paroquettes along the shore was almost deafening. Flocks would hover over the vessel for several minutes at a time and then fly back to the forest.

Guayquil is one of the hottest towns on earth, though not one of the cleanest. The stench arising from the filthy streets is overpowering and, and fever flags fly from nearly every third or fourth house.

The steamer lay in the middle of the river while discharging her cargo into lighters, while the passengers took advantage of the waite, to take a trip across to the city. From the landing, crowds of boys followed them, offering to sell them monkeys and alligators.

After the cargo was unloaded, now the twenty sixth of October, the vessel went on it's way to Paita, the first Peruvian port, Paul took a long walk on the beach and for the first time saw the curious blood red crabs that are in myriads along the shore, from a distance they look like big red waves, but as you approach they disappear in to holes in the sand, their behavior is simular to theat of the hermit crab they are small, not edible, as quick as rats and as difficult to catch, there are countless thousands of them along the beach.

Chimbote was the main port in Peru, the steamer only anchored, long enough to take on mail as the port was then in the hands of the Chillians, they headed for Callao.

Callao was also now in the hands of the Chillian Fleet who had blockaded the port, steamers were not permitted to land there.

Just off the city the Columbia steamed through the blockaders, much to Paul's concern, while a little man on board had been asking Paul a lot of questions, especially what his inter-

ROUGHING IT IN RUBBER

est was in Peru. Trying as often as possible to avoid the man, as he was behaving suspiciously and could be a spy, fearing that he may try sending signal's to one of the blockading vessels, Paul was forced to keep up a running conversation with him.

Fortunately the Columbian made it through without any interception, in the port of Chilca where there were only a few miserable old houses. The passengers were sent ashore in little boats, it was late at night when they landed and accommodation was scarce and very poor quality. Making the best of the poor conditions Paul and Kiefer secured a room, they were nearly devoured by fleas, combined with having to guard their baggage as the locales scoured for anything they could steal. A train of mules was chartered to get them across the pampas to Lima.

All day long they rode those razor backed mules, much of it wild country, over bleak and desolate hills, and then across barren plains. Not even a spear of grass was visible as large condors and galanasas hovered overhead, waiting for a man or mule to fall when overcome with heat. As their water supply was getting very low, thirst was becoming a concern, towards evening with parched throats and weary bodies they reached an oasis. A very poor village where there was plenty of water, that was more precious to the weary group than the sight of great palaces. Once recuperated they headed for the town of Lurin, where they arrived late at night and found the place occupied by Peruvian troops.

An over ambitious officer, arrested Paul as a Chillian spy, the officer would not listen to explanations Paul tried to give him. Forcing his prisoner to travel through the night, though Paul was so exhausted that he could barely stay on the mules back.

There was no other way out, as Kiefer was left with the baggage and Paul, closely guarded rode off into the sultry night, during the early hours of the morning, the troop arrived at Chorrillos, at which place Boyton, now totally exhausted and hungry positively refused to go any further. The officer agreed to remain until daylight and go onto Lima by rail, as tired as he was, he could not sleep, the ravenous fleas devouring him, while he scratched himself like some wild man.

At daylight he was taken by train to Lima and arriving there was immediately marched to the palace, where he was to be presented as a spy to his friend, Don Nicholas de Pierola, the Dictator.

The impertinent officer arrived at the palace with his prisoner, under the impression that he would receive a handsome reward for making such a noble arrest. When Paul pulled out an envelope addressed to Don Nicholas, the fellow was rather surprised, but continued to treat the supposedly spy with the harshest treatment, until Boyton was taken before the Dictator, where he was cordially received and many references made to their prior meeting in Paris.

"But how did you get here so soon?" inquired Don Nicholas, "other passengers who were on board the Columbia have not yet arrived."

Paul telling the story of how he was arrested at Lurin, and the all night ride on the mule. The Dictator sent for the imperternet officer, strutting in like a peacock, expected a reward, but by the time Don Nicholas was finished reprimanding him, he slunk away like a whipped puppy. The impertinent officer will surely be more careful in interrogating any person, before arresting them as a spy in the future.

The Dictator sent Paul to the Hotel Americano, where fine quarters were prepared for him, taking the much needed rest, sleeping until the next day, when he was woken by Don NIcholas's messenger.

Don Nicholas wanted to accompany Paul to Ancon that day to try some torpedo experiments, Paul got up and got ready to make the trip. Ancon was a small seaside resort about fifteen miles from Lima.

At that time it was almost deserted on account of the frequent bombarding by the Chilian cruisers as they passed up and down the coast. The crews on the men-o-war would fire at the little resort for amusement as they turned their guns on Ancon and knocked over a few houses each time they passed by.

The party consisting of the Dictator, several high government officials, Boyton and Major Rabauld, who had been appointed as Paul's aide. They went down in a special car, driven by a little engine and known as the Favorita, supplied by the railroad company that was owned by Americans.

The experiments took place between several rocky islands, that were probably separated from the mainland and the shore by some volcanic action. The torpedoes were tried out on dummy vessels, while a troop of soldiers stood guard on all sides and approaches, preventing any persons or Chilian spies from seeing what was going on. Don Nicholas was in fine spirits and very pleased with the experiments. He was looking forward to getting rid of some of the powerful men-o-war that darkened his harbor with their frowning ports.

On the trip back to Lima, the Favorita had gone less than a mile when the little engine ran right into a pile of sand on the track, that was blown up by the wind. She came off the rails at an ancient burial site of the Incas. All efforts to put the engine and car back on the tracks proved fruitless, so a messenger was sent back to Ancon to telegraph to Lima for an extra engine to come to assist in righting the little train.

As the telegraph was slow, the party had to wait all day for the relief engine, it was almost dark when it arrived, taking barely any effort to put the little engine back on it's track's.

On the following day Paul went down to Callao, with a letter from the Dictator to General Astate, requesting he supply Paul with the best small boat available for torpedo work.

The General received Paul with the utmost respect and kindness, taking him out to Punta del Mar Bravo, where the armory was located, showing him some American parrot guns, as he patted one and smiled while remarking. "These are some of your compatriots."

With that the General gave orders to fire at the Chillian fleet which was then laying near San Lorenzo, an island several miles out from Callao, so high that it's cliffs disappear into the clouds.

Four or five shots were fired at the blockading vessels, but the fleet was too far off for the range of the guns, the iron balls could be seen splashing into the water, somewhat short of their target.

"That is a salute in your honor," remarked the General.

That evening after looking over all the available boats in the harbor, General Astate gave Paul a little sloop, the only one that could possibly be used in torpedo attacks, but far from being the powerful little steam launch that he had been promised.

The Peruvian steamers were alll corralled in the Callao harbor. They were not powerful enough for the men-o-war of the Chillians, that watched the Port, hence they remained inside under the protection of the guns on the point and where great piles of sand bags were erected on the seaward side of the docks, as a shield from the Chillian canon balls.

Before preparing for his onslaught of the torpedoes, Paul decided to write and tell Elise what he was doing, with the hopes of it being mailed from Lima. No one knew that he was in Peru, as he could not possibly write and tell his family or mother what he was doing, it would worry her to death, so he decided to confide in Elise.

In the Mountains with the army of ------

Peru, 13-5-1882

My Dearest Elise,

I have been informed that an officer will start for the sea coast in a few moments so I will send a short letter in hopes that he may be able to post it in Lima. Nothing has happened of misfortune since I wrote you that long letter that I sent on the 2nd.

I am enjoying good health and we are in hopes of making a successful assault on the Chilleans in a few days.

Write me soon, my dearest Elise.

Your ever beloved Paul

Paul got to work preparing the torpedo's for the coming

ROUGHING IT IN RUBBER

attack on the Chillians men-o-war, somewhat disillusioned by the very poor quality of equipment that was provided to him, but trying to make the best of it. The little sloop was called Alicran, she was quickly loaded down with provisions and crew, but before they could leave, Don Nicholas sent for Boyton, commissioning him, Captain of the Peruvian Navy, after all the pomp and ceremony. Paul eager to get started, excused himself and headed back to the eagerly awaiting crew on the Alicran.

As they sailed around the Chorillos, trying to find the best point to launch the operations against the Chilian Fleet, making his headquarters at a hacienda that a wealthy Peruvian businessman turned over to him for this operation. The hacienda was conviently situated out of sight and sheltered by the high cliffs, with a secure mooring for the little sloop directly below.

One thousand pounds of dynamite was sent down from Lima, by wagon, under Paul's direction. The crew began to manufacture the torpedo's, hurriedly stowing them away in the rubber cases. Once the torpedo's were ready, they cruised seaward in order to reconnoiter the movements of the blockading squadron, that at night would go out at sea, and out of reach of the torpedo's.

Paul drilled the officer's that were placed under him in the use of the rubber suit and handling the torpedo's, but none of the them seemed to be overly enthuastic about the operation, Paul's concerns grew as they were spending most of their time among the islands that were formed by great rocks from the many earthquakes.

Continuing to keep a close watch on the movements of the Chilian fleet, by day the blockading vessels remained in clear sight, at night they would move further out to sea and began cruising slowly up and down the coast until daybreak, returning to the harbors mouth again at daylight.

Paul and his crew closely watched for the opportunity to place one of their torpedo's under the dark hull of a Chilano, he wondered wether they were on an alert for such an attack as their movements were changed daily. Could they possible have found out that Paul had been hired by the Dictator, to implement such an attack.

The phosphorescence of the water at night was also against them, the least disturbance on the surface would cause a silver glow to flash, that could be seen for quite some distance. One night as they were watching from Chorrillos, a cruiser was spotted steaming slowly up the coast and Paul determined to test her alertness, deciding to take the risk, in his rubber suit and a one hundred pound torpedo in tow, paddled out as carefully as possible until he saw her head towards him.

Setting the fly torpedo across what he thought would be her course, then carefully paddled in to shore, as he reached a safe enough distance, he turned around to watch as the torpedo exploded, to his disappointment, the cruiser had turned a gatling gun on the torpedo.

The Chilians were more alert than Paul had given them credit for, had the cruiser picked the line up with her bow, it would have thrown the torpedo along her side, setting an automatic chain of events in action, resulting in a huge explosion destroying the steamer. After the Chilians discovered the torpedo the little sloop barely escaped by putting out her sweeps and drawing close up under the dark cliffs while heading for Chorrillos, under cover of the night.

At daylight a party of Chilians landed on the island close to where they found the torpedo, to search for those who had planted it, without success they gave up the search, fortunately for Paul and crew they had eluded the Chilians the night before. For the next two months the torpedo crew stayed under the shelter of the batteries on top of Moro, a high bluff. As they set up nightly watches, sadly discovering the Chilians were doing the same, as Paul remarked, "it's like playing the cat and mouse game, watching each other." while hoping the Chilians did not know their location.

As the sloop was so slow that it was almost useless and Paul's Purvian crew were afraid of the Chilians guns that can be turned with great rapidity in any direction. Daily they sailed to different desolate islands in hopes of blowing one of the Chilian vessels out of the water.

The Huascar cruised up and down the coast, often in range

of the Peruvian guns, as if deliberately tormenting, this was one of the men-o-war on the priority list. Paul just waiting and watching for his opportunity to blow her up. With these intentions, late one night Paul took the sloop as close as he could safely get it to the Huascar, sliding quietly overboard with a screw-torpedo, that would blow her as high as the topmost peaks of San Lorenzo.

It was a favorable night for this operation, dark, with choppy seas that automatically sent the phosphorescent glowing over the surface, distracting from his shape as he floated along hoping they would not see him or the torpedo he was towing. He could see the Huascar crawling slowly along the coast, without a single light on board, her fires were banked, giving Paul the indication that she was low on coal, she was being carried forward on her own momentum, when the danger of her loosing steerage, the engines would be started, and then shut down again as before.

Her bow glided by about twenty feet away, as he moved cautiously to her side, planning to catch hold of her rudder chain.

He saw the one hundred thousand dollars in his grasp, as he was about to get one of the most powerful enemies of Peru and would be prevented from doing any further damage.

As he was midship and reached out for her rudder chain, the steersman's bell rang a signal to the engineer, her wheel began to revolve and she slipped by him as those on board were totally unaware of what was about to happened.

Paul was sickened at the failed attempt, and wondered if he would ever get another opportunity to get that close again, he had only needed a couple more minutes.
Striking out rapidly to reach the shore before he was discovered, knowing that it would be impossible to catch up with the sloop, he left the torpedo floating out to sea.

Deciding to sail out to the outside islands, that are literally alive with seals and sea lions, in such large quantities that were becoming aggressive to anyone who approached. Often guns had to be used to scare them off. Making up his mind to tour these islands and see if his conclusion's were right, that due to the Chillians diminishing supply of coal, all the men-o-war don't sail out to sea at night, some remained anchored at the back of San Lorenzo. He decided to visit the island one night to see if his suspicions were correct.

One end of the island was broken away from the main part by volcanic action, know as Frouton, both San Lorenzo and Frouton are honey combed by an uncountable number of caves, carved out by the continual beating of the seas, forced by the trade winds.
The entire coast of Peru has a sieve like appearance, with caves that have never been explored.

Finally he realized the only way to find out is to go over and see if the Chilians were hiding out. If they could run the sloop to Frouton, he could paddle himself across to the main island, San Lorenzo, making his way as far as he could across this island, until he was able to see if the Chilian soldiers were guarding the approaches to the night anchorage. Paul realized he would have to wait until it was dark to put this plan into action.

His crew did not like the idea of this excursion and did not hesitate to make their feelings known to Paul. Undeterred he went ahead with the plans, placing two one hundred pound torpedoes on board the little sloop and sailed from Frouton. The crew were very nervous at the thought of going that close to the torpedo boats of the enemy, as Paul tried to keep them well occupied and focused on his plans. They glided along in heavy fog, but with his compass and allowing for the currents it did not bother him in the least, the crew were armed with carbines and ordered to make no noise as the sloop with a light wind nosed in through the fog.

Suddenly, as if coming through the thick mist, the sounds of approaching oars were heard, the crew was ordered to get ready to fire and hold their carbines at ease, but to Paul's astonishment he noticed they were ready to give up before they even saw an enemy, as they said, "the Chilians were bound to hang them for being in the torpedo service, even if they were not shot in the fight, it mattered very little if there was no chance to escape."

Realizing that prompt and harsh measures were needed to handle these quaking cowards, Boyton picked up a carbine and in his determined manner, told them that the first man that refused to fire when he gave the order, would receive a bullet through his head.

"Now stand by and await orders, no matter who or what is coming," he thundered.

A moment later, the strokes of the sweeps were almost under them.

"Que venga," hailed Boyton. The oars immediately stopped as a trembling voice answered in Spanish.

"Fisherman, fisherman, don't shoot."
Seeing nothing more formidable than a couple of poor fisherman who were willing to brave the vigilance of the Chilians for the sake of a catch. The crew at once became very brave and bustled about as if they were now willing to sail right into the fleet.

In a short time the breaker's were heard, booming in on the rocks of Frouton and the little sloop was run to a safe anchorage under the cliffs, in smooth water. Paul prepared for the trip to San Lorenzo and ordered the crew to remain by the sloop until three o'clock in the morning, as that would
give him ample time to reach the mainland before the Chilians could see him.

Attaching the torpedoes to a cord on his belt he then swam across the narrow but rough channel, intending to save the torpedoes for future use he remained under the protection of the tall dark cliffs as he made his way along until he could find a safe landing place.

At times finding great openings in the cliffs, that huge waves washed deep down inside, as the sound echoed from the the crashing waves in the bowels of the island, the heavy saline smell of seals mixed with sea lions escaped from deep within. Eventually finding a place to land without being smashed against the rocks. Hauling the torpedoes up the a sandy beach while looking around to find a rock ledge where he could safely store them.

Removing his pantaloons and boots, he attempted to climb the steep rocky face of the cliff, it was a tiresome climb in stocking feet and the thick rubber top of his suit.
Up over guano beds and steep jagered rocks, as the perspira-

tion poured down his face with an off shore wind. There was no breeze to cool the stifling atmosphere as he toiled on, determined to be able to see the bay where the Chilian ships moored. When he reached the top a cool land breeze fanned his perspiring face, with an exclamation of pleasure he sat down on a rock to cool off.

Within minutes a dark figure stood up, not thirty yards away and there was a sudden flash of fire as a bullet flew by Paul's head. Drawing his revolver and was about to fire at the retreating figure, deciding not to risk it as there could be more Chilian soldiers in the vicinity. With a lapse of only seconds Paul heard gunfire coming from every direction, he then realized there were sentries were placed all over the island. The general alarm had been sent out by the first shot.

Climbing back down the cliff as he was aware of the fatal consequences if they captured him, every moment during the decent he expected soldiers to pounce on him or capture him at the foot of the cliff. Not being as careful as he was going up, large amounts of rock and guano were loosed and the great masses showered down below. When he landed he was unable to find the other part of his suit, searching up and down the beach, then suddenly noticing a bit of black rubber sticking up from the debris, a foot of the pantaloons.

Paul quickly pulled it out and was soon paddling across the channel, as he ran under the cliffs where he left the sloop, there was no sign of her.

The cowardly crew had heard the firing, had raised anchor and fearing for their safety, sailed to Lima and reported that Captain Boyton was killed by the Chilian Sentry.

Realizing that he could not possibly paddle to the mainland in his rubber suit without being seen, considering waiting for dark before attempting it, but was not sure if he could make it before sunrise. Knowing San Lorenzo was heavily guarded and with no hope of shelter on Frouton, Paul was in quite a dilemma as to how he could get out of this situation, when deciding that the monsters of the deep maybe a better choice than the human foes.

Paddling back through the heavily rolling waves until he was once again sheltered by the high cliffs, looking back nervously watching for any enemy cruiser, while trying to find a safe landing, with a deep enough cave to hide out in. Seeing a blacker spot than the darkness that surrounded him, he knew it had to be the entrance to a large cave, as he entered the mysterious chamber, the mountain seemed to swallow him, hesitantly with straining eyes he moved forward further into the darkness, not knowing what creatures maybe waiting for him. As he heard the breathing and movements of what he presumed where seals, while dipping the paddle down into the water trying to judge it's depth, the paddle was not long enough to reach the bottom.

Reaching a rocky ledge that was very slimy from the seals constantly sliding over it, pulling himself up with the greatest of care as not to risk damaging the rubber suit on the many shells, reaching a place against the back wall that he felt he would be safely out of sight and hopefully not slide off into the water.

An omnibus growl echoed through the cave as Paul instantly shrunk back, then a deathly silence followed, then broken by a splashing below, Paul hoping it was only a sea creature as the rancid moist smells around him almost took his breath away. As the mournful sounds of the waves far back in the mysterious depths and heavy breathing of sea animals around him, he was not what they were, or if they would attack, he could not tell.

At sundown, the seals began pouring in and climbing to their respective ledges, uttering the weirdest cries as they snapped and snarled at each other, as though fighting over who's bed it was. The females continued snapping at the little fellows as if warning them of the stranger in their midst. Paul had not eaten or drank all day, as the cave was so damp he was not thirsty, but becoming hungry.

Twilight is very short at that latitude and dark follows the sunset quickly, he should start making a move, sliding quietly off the ledge. Trying not to disturb the seals as he quickly dipped his paddle gently into the phosphorescent water and headed for the opening and then paddled out of the gloomy jaws of the cave into a starlit night.

Making a wide sweep against the tide around Frouton, paddling rapidly while being very cautious not to be seen as he headed towards the shelter of the rocky cliffs of Callao.

Arriving too early in the morning forced him to waite for daylight before attempting to land, in the grey light of the morning as Paul landed, a sentry was standing above him with the weapon pointed at him. He shouted, "Peru, Peru," several times before the sentry lowered the weapon. Landing safely at last, he immediately headed for Lima and reported to the Dictator, then hurried back to command the sloop.

The reconnoiter of San Lorenzo had convinced Paul that the island was guarded from end to end and was useless to try and implement his previous plan. His next move was to cruise down south to the islands off Pachacamac and generally called by that name.

The little sloop wound it's way in and of the numerous rocky inlets off the coast, under the close shelter of the high cliffs and well hidden from the Chilian cruisers, that would shoot at anything that moved along the coast line.

The coast is extremely wild and utterly deserted, formed by lofty ledges of rocks, hollowed out by many caves that were created by the constant wave action. The chiseled doorways of these caves are rare specimens of nature's mysterious work, some large, some smaller with queer fantastic shapes while towering high above with a roof of land that supports the growth of scorching pampas grass, as uninviting as the waters below. The desolation of this unknown coast line has no reason to attract even the attention of the locals.

Don Nicholas and a group of Peruvian officer's were astonished when Paul told them about the caves, though they were born and brought up within twenty fives miles of these cliffs, none of them had ever seen or heard of any caves in the vicinity. The top of the cliffs are very desert like and has but a few trails that are seldom used, as even the fisherman give the caverns below a wide berth, being afraid and superstitious, as the strange cries echo from way down in the depths, that is mainly the reason so little is known about them, and have never been explored.

One day while a Chilian cruiser was patrolling the shore, and got a little to close for comfort as the little sloop with sails down and anchored, was tucked away under the lee of the island. Paul taking this opportunity to be out of sight and explore some of the caves, sometimes he paddled deep inside them encased in his rubber suit, but generally used a little gig. Carrying an ax, knife, carbine and a few biscuits, spending whole days in those lonely places, whenever the tide permitted. Once while sailing along the coast line he noticed a great table of rock, that had been washed down and rested on two natural rock pillars, forming the capstone entrance of a very large cave.

The sea was rolling heavily at the time, as Paul very cautiously backed the gig around, and he succeeded in getting it inside.

High above the rays of the sun penetrated through the crevices of the rocks, creating an amazing scene, one of nature's rare optical illusions, in the arched roof of the cavern that was illuminated with gorgeous colors the subterrainian vegetation hung like long snakes from the roof and walls. Here the curling vines and long tendrils glowed a deep purple as the reflections off the walls and greens of every shade of moss offset the shells, that were every conceivable color you could only imagine. Sea fans and sea plumes were there in endless varieties, the sides of the cavern was filled with mollusca, sea urchin's and innumerable specimens of marine life. Along the pale green rock ledges sea foxes, a furry little animals that are bright wicked little fellows, as they dart about uttering shrill cries at the intrusion of a stranger, as he drifted slowly back in the fairyland abode. Paul would have loved to capture one of the cute queer little fellows as a pet, but he did not want to disturb the grand serenity and beauty of the cavern. Thinking it was probably unsafe to penetrate further into the vast beautiful cavern, the gig was backed slowly through the brilliant stone arches until the light became dim and the dark recesses wore a grewsome look, Paul rowed out of the yawning mouth after picking up many shells of varying shape, size and color.

Next evening the anchor was raised and the sloop cautiously crept out from under the cliff and headed for Pachacamac, it was a beautiful moonlight night as they sailed close to shore along the white sandy beaches. One of the crew asked Paul if he liked turtle, he answering "yes," so they took the little gig and pulled ashore among swarms of them. Selecting two or three each of the smaller sizes, as most were too large to turn over by both men, the quickly turned them on their backs while the others ran into the sea with astonishing haste, considering their poor reputation for speed. Paul and the sailor returned with the catch to the sloop, transferring the ugly critters to the scientific ministrations of the cook.

About ten o'clock the next morning they pulled into a little bay, closed in with rocks and well hidden, on the shore side of the island of Pachacamac. Spending several days, with many fruitless attempts were made with floating torpedo's to destroy the steamer Pilcamo. They only worked at night, and laid low in the day under the friendly shelter of the rocks.

During the day, they would often explored the ruins of the ancient Inca buildings, as the island was originally the sight of their temple and used as a place of burials. There were many of their strange tombs all over this island. One of the crew was an expert in locating the Inca tombs, by sinking a pointed rod in the sand he could easily tell when a grave was below, and after some laborious digging the oven shaped top of the tomb was exposed. With a heavy pick an opening was made through the burnt bricks. Instantly a rush of foul air rose and assailed the nostrils, though the bodies had been buried there for perhaps a thousand years.

When the hole was made large enough, Paul and the expert sailor would drop through it into the oval spaced tomb below. There they invariably found several mummies seated in a circle, with their heads on their knees around which the arms were clasped.

Some of the bodies were incased in wicker work, others in cloth made of alpaca wool in brilliant colors and curious designs, the bodies were brilliantly preserved in the center of these weird circles were earthenware jars, containing petrified corn.

As the sun streamed in, lighting up the awe inspiring groups, whose history to this date is unknown, one can only wonder what secrets are hidden in these tombs.

Paul gathered many curious things of prehistoric workmanship and regretted that the limited space on the sloop prevented him from getting more of these beautiful objects. He was very interested in excavating the tombs, spending a lot of time trying to find objects that would throw more light on the habits, customs and ways of this strange race of people. Deciding that the laborious digging in the hot sand was not the best way to reach the mummies, to over-come the monotonous digging they decided to drop a charge of dynamite, which should have been sufficient force to give the dried up Inca's a headache had they still been alive. They found many stone idols, specimens of pottery, bracelets, anklet, chains and other ornaments made from gold and silver with strange designs engraved in them.

Several days were spent exploring the mysterious tombs, while at night they watched for the opportunity to place torpedo's on the men-o-war.

When they discovered that the cruiser they were after had hauled off, the necessity of them staying there was now gone. So they packed up the little sloop and headed back to Chorillos, and spent more time making short runs through the neighboring islands and watching for another chance to use the torpedo, while observing these islands they noticed a extremely large sea lion that frequented the same ledge on one of the islands, there were thousands of sea lions in this area, but none anywhere near the size of this monster.

One of the crew told Paul that the particular sea lion was well known by all the fisherman as incredibly cunning, hence it's size. That was all that was needed to challenge Paul, to make him want to capture the brute, with that purpose in sight he ran the sloop for several days to the point behind the island in sight of the big lion's resting place. For the first two or three days, when the sloop approached, the monster would rise on it's flippers, bellowing and then dive into the sea. As Paul was getting the lion used to seeing the sloop, he would sail in closer each time until the lion no longer bellowed or dove into the sea.

The huge sea lion would continue basking in the sun and occassionally roll over, the sloop was now moored just below as the sailors either slept or spent the lazy days fishing, often the huge sea lion would dive off and return after filling his belly, to bask back in the sun while the sloop was still there. Paul feeling that the huge beast was now comfortable with their presence, at the same time realized it was too large to consider capturing, giving orders one morning to the crew to stand by with carbines.

With sails lowered the sloop was allowed to drift in as close as it could safely get to the monster, as soon as it raised it's head showing signs of uneasiness, the anchor was raised and they drifted away only to return moments later as the crew pretended to busy themselves on board, without showing interest in the lion, as he moved his ponderous body from side to side settling down to sleep. Not disturbing him for an hour or more, then Paul ordered his men to get ready, raising his carbine he fired over the head of the huge sea lion, the shot had the desired effect, the brute sprang up on it's flippers exposing the great chest as the crew fired the fatal shots. The beast staggered, trying to reach the sea, then fell over while the frightened smaller sea lions dropped off the rocks into the water, convinced the monster was dead.

Paul ordered the boat lowered, none of the crew would willingly accompany him, they were so terrified, so taking a knife, axe and revolver, he persuaded one of them to back him along to the rock.

The sea surged heavily as he waited for the chance to jump to the ledge, he sprang over the waves that caught him clear up to the arm pits before he could reach it. With the next surge he managed to pull himself up on the ledge where the monster lay, plunging the knife into it's throat, making sure it was dead. He then realized his prize was fourteen feet long from snout to flukes, calling to the crew for assistance, but they were still too afraid to help him, though he assured them it was dead. The other sea lions were extremely excited and causing quite a rumpus around the sloop, Paul had to make a quick decision. Paul decided the only way he could deal with this huge sea lion carcus alone, was to firstly skin it on sight, the only way he could do this was to run the knife along the stomach, then removed the blubber, rolling the skin back as he did so. Taking out the entrails and throwing them into the

ROUGHING IT IN RUBBER

sea, as he finished carving out the flesh instead of just skinning the carcass.

All this time the other sea lions, were restlessly swarming around as he chopped of the flippers. Large numbers of sea lions leapt up on to the rocks forcing Paul to fire into them to scare them away. Once he had the skin minus the head and flippers clear, it was loaded into the sloop with the head, and taken to Chorrillos, where a couple of fisherman claimed they could do an excellent job of curing it for him. The monster sea lion's skin was the finest skin he had ever seen.

The next morning he was ordered to appear at the palace in Lima, where he remained for three days on business with the Dictator, about the new submarine boat.

Returning to the little sloop, Paul was surprised to see great flocks of galanasa (species of buzzard) and condors hovering over the beach, paying no attention to them, hastily ascertaining that everything was in order aboard the sloop. Going up on the roof to see how the curing of the lion's skin was doing, to his utter dismay there was nothing left but the polished skull of the great sea lion. The birds had torn it to fragments and eaten every bit, the artistic expression of his overpowered feelings would have frightened every galanasa and condor from every coast line, had they been familiar with English, French or Spanish languages.

Orders were received from Lima to sink torpedoes as far out in Chorillos Bay as they could reach without being shot by the Chilians, who would be keeping a close watch on them through their powerful glasses, from San Lorenzo. As there was only a lot of old Russian torpedo's available, and no more dynamite to spare, Paul decided to set dummies, knowing they would have the same effect on the Chilians. Procuring a lot of empty kegs and painting them bright red, with these aboard they sailed out as far as was safe, in an ostentatious manner, placed them across the entrance to the bay, so they would float within three feet of the surface and were plainly visible.

The approach of a steamer from the seaward, before the task was completed, forced them to hoist sail and head in to the shelter of the high cliffs once again. The steamer immediately opened fire on the retreating sloop, fortunately the shots fell short as her guns were answered by those on the El Punte. A few days later after completing the task, while under the shelter of the cliffs, they had the satisfaction of witnessing two Chilian men-o-war firing thousands of rounds of ammunition on one of the empty kegs that had come loose from it's anchor and floated to the surface.

The little sloop became a frequent target from this time on, one afternoon while Paul was relaxing under the awning, a whizzing got his attention, as a canon ball flew by, with the hazy afternoon conditions he was unable to see where it came from and thought it was just a stray shot from the fort. Another simular incident occurred a few days later, this time with clear skies and he was able to see the Huascar not twelve miles from where they were, that had some new powerful guns on board, as they were shrieking overhead and firing at the cliffs a few hundred yards away, the sloop was not as well hidden as it should have been, this prompted the crew to lower the sails and move her out of sight.

Next morning as Paul was about to go overboard for his morning swim he noticed a large dark shadow below the sloop, he hesitated. Fortunately for him, as, it turned out to be a very large octopus, known then as the devil fish, edging it's way slowly under the sloop towards shore. The great tentacles stretched out for nine or ten feet from the large round body and a more repulsive and dangerous creature is hard to find. One of the crew was an experienced fisherman, told them all to keep perfectly still as the fellow was going ashore among the rocks, which they normally do. The fisherman was correct as they watched it's powerful tentacle reach up and grasp a rock that was barely exposed. As it began to heave its large body, with assistance of the tentacles, twisting and contorting it's mass between the rocks.

A group of fisherman nearby were called to help capture the devil fish. Armed with spears, guns and boat hooks. They formed a circle a little way around the outside of the dangerous creature, and began splashing the water and yelling to prevent it going back out to sea. as it moved a few yards closer to the beach and submerged while discharging a black ink

ROUGHING IT IN RUBBER

like fluid that formed a camouflage around it. As the slimy tentacles started pulling it's self up the rocky beach, as the pudgy body was slowly coming out of the water on to the beach. A brave shirtless fisherman rushed in, striking it with a heavy blow on the head, as the tentacles slashed out barely missing him, he again thrust another fatal blow.

Rocks and pebbles flew of the suction cups that are attached to the long powerful tentacles, everyone was hit in some way or form as they tried to duck, the lashing tentacles of the huge angry creature. At last, it gave up the exciting battle by all against this massive devil fish, the fisherman made fast work of cutting it up and loaded it into the sloop, returning to Chorrillos to divide the much sought after meat, between all the men.

Paul assuring the fisherman that he did not want a share of the meat, as the hotel owner overhearing the conversation, offered a dinner that night in exchange for Paul's share.

The unexpected offer was quickly accepted and sure enough, a magnificat spread was put on with the main dish being the octopus.

It was some time before Paul could be persuaded to taste it, when finally agreeing, he was amazed to find it was one of the best tasting fish he had ever eaten, a delicate flavor and the flesh a little chewy. The native fisherman look on them as a rare luxury and always have a feast when one is caught.

Considering the very inferior quality equipment supplied to Paul for this task, he was finally successful in blowing up two of the Chilian men-o-war, by using some very sneaky maneuvers, they were the Loa and Covodonga. As previously describe the Chilian men-o-war would cruise slowly up and down the coast at night, avoiding being hit by torpedoes.

One foggy morning while the Loa was crawling back to her mooring after the night cruise, her watch noticed a small sloop with four crew aboard, who seemed to have problems, one up the mast repairing what looked like a peak halyard, looking as if it was disabled. The Chilians fired a shot over the sloop, the sailor hastily got down the mast, the four jumped into a light gig and paddled rapidly for the mainland, while the man-o-war lowered a boat and started the chase while shooting at the fugitives, as the Chilians realized they could not catch the Peruvians gig, they abandoned the chase, returning to the little sloop. Cheers went out when they discovered it was loaded with fruit, vegetables and much needed food. A line was quickly fastened to the the sloop and she was towed alongside the Loa, all hands helped hastily transfer the cargo aboard, as the excited crew willingly lifted baskets and crates of the much need food on board, with the largest heavy crate of vegetables being last and final prize.

The moment it was lifted clear of the deck, there was a terrific explosion, the mighty upheaval of the sea sent water spouts shooting skyward, mingled with fragments of the steamer and crew, as the spars and timbers dropped back into the water and floated where the once proud man-o-war had stood, the Loa was no more as she and her crew were swept into eternity.

Loud cheers rang out from the little gig, tucked far under the tall dark cliffs, as Paul and crew knew they had won that dangerous game they played against the Chilians.

The most emphatic orders were given by the Chilian officers to their crews, after the total destruction of the Loa, not to pick up anything without thoroughly examining it first.

One afternoon just days after the orders had been given, the Covodonga steamed slowly along on a bright calm afternoon on a southward cruise to Callao, one of the crew noticing a pleasure rowing boat. The Captain was about to order the guns turned on it when an officer approached him asking.

"Let us examine it? we may learn something."

The Captain agreeing, at the same time insisting they take a careful look before touching the row boat, repeating his orders as the officer went overboard. It was a beautifully built ladies pleasure boat that had broken free from it's mooring, with a piece of the frayed line still hanging from her. She was painted white and gilded, elegantly furnished with cushioned seats and handsomely ornamented. An open book was laying on the seat and a single oar rested on the bottom. The officer carefully examining the beautiful row boat as he passed a boat hook under her, while deciding she was harmless.

She was towed to the steamer and as the Captain was

ROUGHING IT IN RUBBER 259

assured that there was nothing suspicious about her.

"She will make a beautiful present for your wife," said the officer. The Captain responded, "If you are certain, hoist her aboard," lines were lowered and hooks fastened to the little row boat, as they fastened on to the polished brass rings in her bow and stern and started to raise her, a deafening explosion brought the fatal end to the Covodonga. The man-o-war was split in two and sank, supposedly sixty of the crew were saved, but Paul and the sloops crew never stayed around long enough to find out.

The little row boat was made with a thin false bottom, that was filled with nitro-glycerine, the friction pins were connected to the brass rings and the moment her weight was on them, the pins pulled out and the explosive was discharged, this was a brilliant idea of Paul's and sure proved to be successful. One would imagine after such costly experiences, the Chilians increased their watch and no longer approached anything seen floating on the water, at times they were even firing on seals in the distance, as Paul and his crew were now compelled to stay closely under cover.

As the Chilians began closing in on the City of Lima, Paul dispatched an officer to Don Nicholas, with a request to move his torpedo operation and crew down to Pisco where he suspected the Chilians would attempt to land troops. The answer received was,

"Impatience is a bad Counselor! waite for further orders."

If Paul had followed his own instincts, he could have knocked two or three more Chilian vessels out of the water, as they landed at Pisco a couple of days later, as they had very few guards on watch, he would have been able to put torpedo's under them.

The enemy had gradually closed in on both land and sea, so Paul was ordered to Callao to take charge of a new submarine boat that had been built by a Swiss engineer. The boat was run by compressed air under water and steam on the surface, it was a complicated affair, Paul had very little confidence in it's safety or reliability, this was further lessened when the Swiss engineer refused to go down in her. However he decided to give it a try by hanging it in a cradle of chains, then if it did not surface under it's own power, they would be able to hoist it back up. It was lowered into the water with Paul, the engineer and two crew members on board.

Paul gave strick orders to only let her sit for twenty minutes on the ocean floor, then to hoist her back up if she did not surface on her own, after fastening down the hatch, the valves were closed as an ominous hissing of air that sounded strange. As she was lowered to about twenty three feet below the surface, and settling on the bottom, he ordered the engineer to get her moving under the compressed air.

She wheezed and groaned barely moving along the bottom, as they tried to get her to rise up, groping about with his lantern claimed there was something wrong with a valve. He could not get any of them to work as he became agitated, Paul telling him to calm down as there was no danger, they would be hoisted back up. For the five to six minutes, that seemed more like hours to the trapped men as they tried every possible way to get the sub to function, it was useless, the sub would not rise. As oxygen became less and the lights grew dimmer, the oxygen valves beginning to fail the crew becoming lethargic and were not able to continue trying to get the vessel running. Paul was about to knock off the valve with the hammer, when the engineer pointed out that the water would come in with a risk of them all drowning, meanwhile the situation was becoming desperate with the oppressive high humidity and lack of air as the the men sat looking into one another's pale faces.

Looking at his watch Paul realized that they still had twelve more minutes before the crew above would even attempt to start raising the sub, he doubted they could last that long . for they were already beginning to gasp for air, with this thought, he clamored up the ladder with the hammer and started pounding on the hatch, hoping the sound would be heard on the surface, the excursion was too much and he fell helplessly to the floor, remaining there in a semi unconscious state. He vaguely remembers hearing the straining of chains, the hatch opening and a voice asking, "How is it?" With no response, the crew scrambled to drag the unconscious bodies out, once in the fresh air they all started to slowly come back to

ROUGHING IT IN RUBBER

life. After a close inspection of the sub, the engineer discovered the valves had been tampered with. A dispatch from the Dictator informed Paul that they believed a spy was amongst the crew and to be very careful, while the investigation was underway. At midnight two officers arrived from Lima and the crew were summoned before them, with an accurate description of the spy and close scrutiny, an officer placed his hand on the shoulder of one of the crew, saying, "this is the man." Followed by one of the quickest court marshal's on record, as the group of men walked a short distance out on the dock in the darkness, there was a click of a revolver and a dead Chilian.

The Peruvian troops were now gathering at Chorrillos to repel any further advances of the Chilian army that had landed at Pisco.

As the proud Peruvian army marched out of LIma in anticipation of battle, the brilliant ranks were composed of young men in gorgeous uniforms singing gaily as they marched through the streets to Chorrillos,with the native troops.

The Cholo Indians who had been driven from their homes at the back of Cordilleras, followed the army, as they volunteered to join in the battle, with the solidly marching through the streets, never turning their heads left or right, even though hundreds of them have never seen a town or city before.
As they were followed by a wild picturesque rabble of *rabona* women, carrying large bundles on their heads or strapped to their backs, shrieking and chattering in their native tongue like garibo monkeys, these women were the commissary for the native troops.

Whenever there was a break in the marching, the woman *rabonas* would quickly undo the bundles and hastily prepare some sort of soup like beverage that was sold to the Indian troops for just one cent a bowl. This was all done in minutes, we marveled at the speed and organizational skills of these fascinating woman.

The Chilian army had advanced beyond Pisco and the first battle near Lima, on the plains outside of Chorrillos, was imminent. Paul and his crew in the little sloop loaded with torpedoes headed down the coast to attempt to intercept some of the Chillian men-o-war. Sadly they were spotted and a Chillian cruiser opened fire, sinking the little sloop, while the Captain and his crew were able to swim to shore unnoticed. Joining the Peruvian army on the heights until other arrangements could be made, a dispatch was forwarded to Lima informing the Dictator of what happened, and waiting further orders.

Paul having time on his hands and realizing the clock was ticking on Peru, managed to get another letter out to Elise.

San Bartolome Peru.

14-11- --

My Dearest Elise.

It is a long time since I had a letter from you. I have written to you three times from Peru but I have never received a response. I will soon be leaving here as our chance is ruined and my chief, Montero has neither money nor men to carry on the fight. I intend to go to California and there do my utmost to repair my broken fortune. I am through with Peru forever. I am at present sad and it pains me to tell you that the chances of our meeting again are very slight indeed. And under the present circumstances it is not right for me to have you to continue to think of me and hope that one day our hopes might be realized. It is impossible Dearest Elise and it is not honorable for me to keep you bound to me and possibly prevent you from accepting the offer of marriage from some better man. I have more reason than one for this decision. In the first place my fortune and home in Flushing is broken up and it may be some years before I am again settled. I could not think of asking you to share such a life of wandering and uncertainty, even if there was no other obstacle in the way. But there is one and it is a little child who came into this world while I was in France last and his poor mother I must protect and if necessary marry.

You cannot imagine how much pain all this causes me Dear Elise. But it is better to say farewell forever than have you living in false hopes. Forgive me if you can and forget the past. Had my life's dream been realized and had you been my wife, I would have been happy, but alas, fate was against me, and it is ended.

God bless you my own dear friend and grant that you will forgive me. There is no use me writing again or in keeping the bonds of an unhappy friendship together. Frewell forever.

I can never forget you Dearest Elise.

Paul

From an original engraving fromthe A Veritable Merman. Pg.696: CAPTAIN BOYTON AFFIXING A TORPEDO TO THE MAN-O-WAR "GARNET."

Nobody has been able to verify if Paul did have a child born out of wedlock, as the dates don't match the record of his first child Paul. This maybe because he did not think he would get out alive and was trying to spare her feelings, as no one would have ever known had he been killed or executed.

On January the fourteenth, 188-, the Chilians began the attack on Chorrillos, the fashionable water resort about three leagues from Lima. Colonel Yglesi with but a handful of troops and the courage of a lion made a brave defense and had reinforcements been sent from Miraflores, where the main body of the Peruvian army was stationed, the tide of the battle would have been turned. As it was, he held out as long as he could and then retreated to the main body, after killing three-thousand of the enemy. On his retreat, the Chillians swarmed into Chorrillos, more intent on mass murder than honorable warfare. That night the Chillians broke into the liquor store and houses. Soon after the drunkeness increased their natural blood thirstiness. Prisoners were murdered in cold blood and woman and children were shot down.

Next morning the streets of Chorrillos was a sad and bloody scene, with the dead and dying every where. Many bodies littered the beach where they had fallen after being cruelly bayoneted off the cliffs.

After the retreat to Miraflores, a truce was declared and an effort was made to arrange some form of peace agreement, the foreign diplomat of the United States, Minister Christiancy and high military officers who were having a conference. The two armies were standing face to face while awaiting the results of this attempted peace agreement. A gun was fired, supposedly by a Peruvian officer at a cow, this triggered the Chilians to attack as an all out battle broke out, the rapid firing sounded like someone running their fingers over a pianos keyboard, it's believed that the delegation at the settlement table took off in all directions, admist the flying bullets.

It was said that the United States, Minister Christiancy was seen valiantly running across a field in his shirt sleeves, with some of the others following him behind in the direction of Lima. Not to speak flippantly, it was a genuine go-as-you-please hurdle race as they had to jump the low mud walls that formed the fences.

ROUGHING IT IN RUBBER

The Peruvians were outnumbered and hindered with inferior weapons, when Don Nicholas saw the battle going against him, he gallantly mounted his charge and rode to the front lines. It was too late, he turned in despair and fled to the mountains, followed by some of his officers and loyal troops.

It was reported later that one of the main causes for Peru losing this battle was due to a mix up of weapons and ammunition, there were two different calibre riffles issued and the troops were supplied with the wrong bullets, many were seen dropping the weapons when they discovered the ammunition did not fit, and fled in all directions unarmed.

Paul with hundreds of others fled to Lima, on arrival they discovered the city had been taken over by a mob of drunken rioting sailors and soldiers, who's large groups, were robbing and indiscriminately shooting people, the streets were strewn with the bodies.

Early the next morning the foreign residents banded together, appointed Boyton in charge of the Americans, took back the city by going through and shooting the unruly rioters. A small jewish community in a little row of houses, known as the money changer's had been the main target for the vandals, as they believed there were large amounts of money behind those doors, next morning the narrow little street was littered with dead rioters bodies as the desperate
Jews put up a successful defense from the holes they had made in their doors, to shoot through.

Many Chinamen were killed and robbed by a group of rioters that Paul and his American troop managed to track down and beat into submission, thus the goods, such as silks and gold were recovered and returned to the rightful owners or the families of them.

Meanwhile the remaining Peruvian army was setting fire to all the ships in the harbor at Callao, to prevent them falling into the hands of the enemy. As patrols by the foreigners were kept up in Lima, flags were flying of their countries, on their houses, to prevent the foreign residents from pillage or destruction. During this time, Paul and some friends had a chance to visit the battle-fields of Miraflores and Chorrillos, the sights they witnessed!

The gallant, young soldiers who had left Lima in brilliant uniforms, with the highest of hopes of success, and singing gay songs as they had marched. Lay in a confused mass of bloated corpses.

Four days of tropical sun burst the bodies, the stench was horrible. Fearing the spread of disease from the fields, the Chilians gathered Chinamen, forcing them to burn the remains with gallons of kerosene.

As night fell, the blue glow rising from these awful funeral pyres, lit up the sky and fields as bands of Chinamen leading mules carrying large containers of kerosene, were forced to patrol and reignite any body that was not totally burnt. At points on the roads, lay heaps of mangled dead as the roads and fields around were torn up by explosions from ground torpedoes, (land-mines) placed by some genius, who believed he could prevent the Chilians from advancing.

After two or three of these hidden explosives detonated, the Chilian army forced the captured Peruvians to march ahead, followed by herds of cattle, thus killing hundreds.

Paul stood on the cliff overlooking the once beautiful bay where his little sloop had been anchored so many times, sadly the destruction by the Chilian army was all that could be seen. As the injured were trying to assist each other, leaning on a kindly shoulder of another as they tried to reach help, many at the waters edge of the ocean, as the great flocks of hideous condors and galanasas circled above waiting on the ghastly feast below. This sight was enough to sicken one for ever, seeing the vaunted glories of the battle field.

Soon after the occupation, General Backadana issued a proclamation requiring all Peruvian officers and military personnel to surrender. The Chillians now knew that Boyton was in the country. but for what purpose, he was not sure, thus he was forced he surrender under his assumed name on entry of 'Delaport," an engineer.

A short court marshall and Paul was paroled to an isolated island off Ancon with another Peruvian officer, while there they spent most of their time trying to escape.

He procured a little boat, while his American friends in Lima smuggled food out to him, the first three weeks they amused

ROUGHING IT IN RUBBER

themselves fishing, hunting and exploring the caves, all the time hoping to attract the attention of the passing steamers, by rowing out under the cover of the high cliffs.

From almost any other country in the world escape would be easy, but Peru, both north and south was nothing but sun-parched pampa, while to the west lay the vast rolling Pacific ocean, patrolled by many of the enemy's ships, east was the Cordilleros soaring into the clouds, but they were occupied by the Chilians.

One morning while they were cruising amongst the outer islands, Paul noticed a cave in the cliff above the water high line, this he could not resist exploring. Pulling the little row boat in close he clambered up to the opening, while the Peruvian officers, kept rowing back and forth keeping the boat from the rocks. From the entrance he could see that it ran like a shaft sloping down through the island, picking his way down over the slippery rocks, as he was about half way down the incline when he heard a strange cry, turning he saw a creature that was not a bird, animal or fish, it was almost a combination of all three. Paul had heard stories from many fisherman of these strange creatures in the remote caverns, but never believed them, as they claimed that they were kind, gentle and affectionate in captivity, but extremely savage in their wild state. They are called Ninas del Maris, children of the sea.

He raised the gun to shoot, then deciding to rather try and capture one of them, moving further down the shaft he came on the most beautiful cavern, almost believing he had unconsciously stumbled into the playhouse of Neptune's rollicking subjects, as water formed a great pool surrounded by an ampitheatre of towering crags of fantastic shapes. Realizing this subterranean passage must have another entrance, the sight was so strange and unexpected that for awhile he almost forgot about the *nina*, recovering himself quickly he retraced his steps, being careful not to let the queer little creature escape ahead of him as he headed back to where he had last seen the little creature, after looking every where he could, and not finding it, decided it must have escaped through some hidden passage. Then he heard the cry again, and finding a little pocket in the rocks, instead of just one, two children of the sea were hiding in there.

Children of the sea are a species of the penguin, their bodies are covered with a downy type fur, neither hair nor feathers, they are about two feet high with very short strong legs and webbed feet.

While the bird shaped head has virtually no neck and a stumpy V shaped bill, there are two very small fins simular to those of a seal, with large round soft eyes that are circled by black rings against the soft grey body and white bib. They waddle around like an old fat man, and when sleeping, double over with the head only and inch off the ground, giving the impression of doing a great balancing act.

Without thinking of the consequences, Paul put his hand into the pocket in the rock, extracting one by it's neck. As he put his arms around the body hugging it close, a fierce blow from the feet tore his clothes from the waist up leaving a deep scratch below. Paul called for a rope from the row boat, by putting his felt hat over his hand and tieing up the snout's was able to capture both the sea children, loading his prizes in the row boat they cautiously headed back to Ancon. Placed them in a little room where he was staying, neither would take the fish that he tried to feed them for almost two days, eventually the little male started to eat and the female following suit and the *ninas* became very tame and affectionate pets.

Paul seeing no hope of escape from Ancon, arranged to go to Lima to consult with his American friends and wait for an appointment with General Patrico Lynch, who was in charge of Callo, just six miles away. From his name Paul assumed he would be a good natured soldier who would be happy to help a fellow military man.

With this intention he went to the military headquarters in Callo, requesting an appointment with the General. Paul believed that if he revealed who he really was, he would gain the confidence of the General, and was sure would get help to leave Peru, the aid-de-camp said he would have to wait a few hours, which he willingly did, while planning his interview intending to say, "General, my name is Paul Boyton, down here just like yourself from the States, etc."

He pictured that the General would receive him and give him his passport and maybe even invite him to dine with him that evening. Paul would except and regret that his clothes were dusty and torn.

Eventually the aid-de-camp said, "You may see the General now," Paul was ushered into a large room as the officer retired, looking around there was only a white haired, mahogany-faced old man who sat at a writing table. Advancing, he stood silently waiting to be noticed, at last a pair of cold steel gray eyes were turned up to him, this confused him as he stuttered in English, "Is this General Lynch?"

"Si," was the sharp reply.
In English, Paul continued, "General I am a paroled prisoner who came down to see if ----------,"
Paul was shocked as suddenly a heavy hand pounded on the desk as a stentorian voice rang out in Spanish, "Speak you spanish, speak you Spanish. Moerte Dios, I understand not much English." Paul mumbled a request in Spanish to have his parole transferred to Callao.

"No, no, Anda!" pointing to the door, Paul left disheartened and joined his companion back in Ancon. Three days later he received a message from his American friends in Lima, that worried him as it was to inform him that the Chilians were looking for him. There was no chance of him getting on a north bound vessel now as they were all being searched.

Late one night soon after receiving the message, he was woken with loud banging at his door, leaping out of bed to find the house surrounded by a squad of Chilian cavalry, the officer in command informed him he was wanted in Lima and to accompany the squad at once. He was taken to the capitol, and ushered in to see General Backadona. "What is your name?" thundered the General, striking the table with his fist.

"I surrendered to you General," replied Paul, "my name is Delaport."

"You were in the torpedo service?"

"Possibly, I held a commission from Don Nicholas de Pierola."

We believe your name is Boyton, and no one by that name was commissioned.

Paul never affirmed or denied the charge, as the General ordered him to be confined in the quartelle with the other prisoners. He was kept for some weeks while the victors were awaiting dispatches from Chili, that would decide his fate. He already knew what that would be, the firing squad, because of the men-o-war that he had destroyed.

Almost daily during his imprisonment he could hear the daily barbaric blare of the Chilian bugles outside the quartelle, the gates swing open and a party of Chilian soldiers enter. An officer would call the names of the prisoners wanted and surrounded by a firing squad, the unfortunates were marched out, followed by white robed priests walking at their sides offering them words of consolation.

With gay music playing they were escorted to a conveint place, strapped on boards with their feet on a step, lent against the wall, a sharp order, a bright flash with the crack of rifles.The planks with the bodies still on them were placed on the death wagon and then removed at the grave side.

Paul expected to hear his name called every time that fatal gate opened, but as the days and weeks passed he became more synical as his friends on the outside were desperately trying every possible thing to secure his release, with no avail. He had placed his belongings in safe keeping at the railroad company, with his two children of the sea that were also being takien care of for him.

For several days he noticed a particular guard watching him closely, to the point of making him very uncomfortable, this guy was giving him some strange looks, as if trying to ask or say something. One day the guard carelessly walked passed him and in a soft voice asked, "are you Delaport?." Paul said, "yes," as the guard walked away without any further response.

Next day four officers who looked like the bearers of the dispatches, rode in at the gate, the prisoners looking with concern at each other saying, "There's news from Chili." "Yes," replied Paul to one of them, "I guess my death warrant is here."

The officers dismounted, leaving the horses to stand unhitched, as Paul was stroking head of one of the foam flecked steads, an officer approached, touching him on the

ROUGHING IT IN RUBBER

shoulder, and whispered,

"*Venga,*" ------ come.

Without hesitation, he followed the officer, who opened the same door the others had entered, as his escort turned around with his finger on his lips they silently descended several steps into what appeared to be a basement. Groping around several pillars until finding a large heavy bolted door, through the crack a little sunshine could be seen. Boyton's escort drew the bolt and with a gentle push shoved him out whispering, "Anda," ------ go.

Finding himself in the street as a group of Chilian soldiers walked by, dropping his hat as he bent over to pick it up, and keeping his face hidden while they passed. Heading in the direction of the rail road company, hoping to see one of his friends, as he was crossing the bridge over the track, he noticed a train dispatcher waving at him, descending the embankment and entering the old warehouse. Mr Campbell of Allegheny PA, handed him a package saying, "Here is your safe passage through the lines, you are a submarine telegraph man going to the coast to repair cables."

"A mule is outside equipped and ready for you, in one side of the saddle bag your rubber suit and a jointed paddle, covered with coils of wire, the other side has more coils of wire and telegraphic tools and provisions. To all questions you must answer, *"Comision especial telegrafos del sue marina."*

"There's is an English steamer going north to-morrow, the Captain is aware of your passage and all your baggage will be aboard her. Go to Ancon and paddle out to the furthers island, and be sure they can see you, so the Captain of the steamer can pick you up.

Your biggest risk will be leaving the city and getting through the lines, you will have to do that part on your own."

Campbell then handed Paul a purse of money, shook his hand wishing him God speed for a safe journey and disappeared.

Unhitching the mule Paul headed for Pizzaro bridge over the Rimac, at the other end of the bridge he noticed a Chilian soldier eyeing him intently, fearing he was one of the guards and might recognize him, being careful not to make the soldier suspicious he leisurely rode up to a cigar stand, dismounted and purchased cigars. This seemed to satisfy the guard as he turned and walked away, lighting a cigar as he rode the mule through the outskirts of the city, it was almost dark as he reached the first line of sentinels and hearing that sound made is blood instantly surge.

"Hatlta, cavagna," shouted the sentry.

"Comision especial telegrafos del sue marina." he answered, displaying his forged pass, the officer examined the pass and waved him on. At the second outpost, which was quite a distance from the city, he went through the same procedure, but at the third or outer line of sentinels a young officer was in command who was far more thorough than the other posts. With sweat dripping from his forehead as the officer examined the pass, and then inspected the contents of the saddle bags as he arrogantly strutted around, Paul becoming extremely uncomfortable, as he saw his chance of escaping fading with every arrogant step of this officer.

Strutting haughtily over he said,

"This pass is not correct, you will have to go back to Lima."

UNDER THE CRAGS OF SAN LORENZO.

The Sea Lions.
Scanned from the Paul Boyton Story.

ROUGHING IT IN RUBBER

Keeping as cool as he possible could, offering the officer a cigar and talking about the weather and other interesting subjects while remarking. " I hope that you will honored to escort me back to the capitol, as I can assure you the officials would rather I am proceeding to do the wet and cold work that they have ordered me to do."

The officer was polite enough to regret that he could not accompany him to the capitol.

Paul trying again, "I would be sorry to see a brave young officer like yourself get into trouble over this," continued Paul.

"You know how anxious your superiors are to have the wires repaired in order to re-establish communications with Chilli, as I don't enjoy the work, I don't mind having my journey interrupted."

While Paul casually puffied at his cigar, the arrogant young officer was thinking the situation over, taking the pass back from Paul he began to examine it again.

"I think you are alright," said the officer at last, returning the paper to Paul said, "you can go on." With assumed reluctance he bade the officer goodbye as he casually rode off.

As soon as he was out of sight, he dug his heels into the mule and galloped across the fields, occasionally looking back to make sure he was not being pursued. About an hour later he heard the elating sound of waves crashing on the shore, riding up along the edge of the cliff, he hurriedly stripped everything off the mule and patting it's hind quarters, as he said, "good bye, old fellow, you served me well," as the mule turned it's head towards the fields, and scampered away. Quickly getting dressed in his rubber suit, with the paddle securely in his hand he climbed down the cliff and dove into the booming surf, swimming with all his might out in the direction of the islands.

Island after island was left behind as he aimed for the furthest seaward that looked like a huge rock looming up out of the water, at day break he saw the small sandy beach that was fully occupied by seals. Landing on the beach the seals began to fuss a little, ignoring them he climbed up on to a ledge that gave him a full view of Callao.

Removing his suit Paul began to relax and realized how

lucky he had been to escape, from this ledge he would be able to see the steamer as soon as it left the harbor, allowing him enough time to get back down and swim out to meet it.

The sun came up with a dull, red color promising a very hot day. By nine o'clock in the morning the heat was so intense that he began to suffer from thirst, realizing he had forgotten to get a good supply of fresh water, after having a small breakfast he began to tour the island in hopes of finding a cave that would shelter him from the extremely hot rays of the sun. There was no shelter or signs of fresh water so Paul resorted to quick frequent dips in the ocean to cool off, though this seemed to increase his thirst.

All day long he had been keeping an eye on the ocean towards Callao, watching for the black smoke of the steamer approaching. Hour after hour passed with no sign of it, he decided to get back up on the rocky ledge hoping for a bit of shade. As he sat watching for the steamer he was becoming intensely thirsty, the afternoon heat was no help. He became concerned when a huge black cloud began hovering above and as it circled around, he saw it was pelicans. They began landing in droves on the beach below, there seemed to be several thousand of them as he watched their richels. They would stand straight up in long rows, looking wise and solemn, while two very dignified birds marched up and down in front of the lines, just like military grandees reviewing a parade. This drill took almost two hours and the stench of these unclean birds was becoming unbearable, as they broke rank and flew back out to sea, diving in after fish.

Pauls thirst was became unbearable, with his tongue swelling and feeling as if his mind was wandering off, he thought he saw the steamer as the sun began to set. Thinking that what if the ship missed him in the dark, when would another one come and would they know to pick him up. Paul then decided that if the steamer did not pick him up he would return to Callao and give himself up. After all it would be better to be shot than die of thirst on this smelly island.

Once again his mind started to wander off again as he imagined seeing all sorts of sea animals, and almost thought that he heard and smelt running water. Snapping out of it, he started to put on the rubber suit and prepare to head out to sea in search of the steamer, the suit was hot after laying in the sun all day, struggling to get into it, finally he was dressed and with his paddle in his hand started climbing down from the rocky ledge.

Paddling out until he could see the steamer's mast as she was head on, laying still on the water, still wandering if this was just a game that his mind was playing on him. Closer and closer she approached until he could see the lookout, rising up in the water he began hysterically waving his paddle until they saw him.

To his intense relief, she slowed down, and a boat dropped from her side and he was soon on board, the crew hurried him below much to the amazement of the passengers. He was kindly received by the Captain and made very comfortable, his friends had taken great care in getting all his belongings on board including his pets, the two children of the sea.

The steamer only stopped at one more Peruvian port, that was Paita, and while they were there Paul went below and shoveled coal.

Due to the cables being destroyed the news of his escape had not got this far, so no search was done of the steamer.

Next morning they steamed up the river to Guayquil and Paul was able to relax as he was now free.

Panama was just a short run and the passage cost Paul twenty-five dollars in gold for the trip across the isthmus from there to Aspinwall, left him almost penniless. At Aspinwall he found the same steamer that he had sailed out on from New York, the Crescent City.

Transferring his baggage over he was able to make arrangements with the Captain for the trip north, once the Captain realized who Paul was and the situation he was in, he was received with open arms and extended his hospitality. While in Panama Paul was very surprised to find a letter there from Elise and the reply from her father. He really believed it was all over, so while on board he replied

23rd October 1883

Dear Sir,

   I should not hide you that the letter of which you honored me caused me as much surprise than of painful emotion. I believed for a long time disappeared from your spirit this first impression which was produced to you by the sight of my daughter.

   Indeed, how could I admit among the terrible concerns and the ceaseless dangers of your nautical peregrination the image of a child, hardly seen, had remained alive in your heart.

   But, Sir, did you think well of the consequences of the request that you make me? Do you think of the torments of a father and a mother seeing their daughter removed with their tender affection and missing for always out of their sight beyond the seas. I say for always, because I am certain, that left once, we would not see her again.

And what would be our existence!!

I do believe that I have the right to a certain extent to oppose the desires and wishes of my daughter but, and it is for that, Mister that I say to you... think seriously before going further!!

   Why you are keen to conquer all the thoughts of this poor child, do you believe by having my dear daughter Elise as a treasure of beauty of intelligence and rare morals and qualities? Her intelligence is perhaps above the average; her morals qualities her character leave, alas, to wish sometimes much too much. As for her beauty, you know probably already that it is disgraceful nature, you would be thus able to have any woman according all the reports.

   And then, America which you traversed in all directions, is it deprived of intelligent and pretty pleasant girls that you believe yourselve obliged to take woman beyond the ocean, a woman that you hardly know, seen and with whom you exchanged only some letters. Allow me my frankness to say to you that it is only a romantic imagination on your part. You speak to me about your situation in the business world. That worries me very little, because I know that a man of your value will always find a way to live within an honest ease, especially in America where the private initiative has more rise than in France. It is not the same for us here. All my vines are devastated by will phylloxéra. Consequently my revenues emanating of my property (vines) are null also I was obliged, in order to attenuate the deprivations of my family, to accept public office of the generosity of the French government.

I am a tax collector of the direct taxation to BAZAS (Gironde) for nearly three years, separated from my wife and my daughters with whom I will spend only one or two days per month. That will explain the delay in which I was able to answer your letter of last October, 23, of which I was only able to read some of the tardily text.

I stop here the short observations which I had to present to you. Now Sir, if you persist in maintaining your resolutions, if on her side my daughter absolutely wishes you for husband in spite of the disadvantages of all kinds and the future pains which can result for it and for us of, this union, I do request you to come and have your civilities with me when your business enables you to come on a journey to France. I will then see decide what it will take for me to consider the marriage.

Question seriously your conscience of honest man--------------
--- before you to present present yourself at my home, because I repeat to you the request that you addressed to me, is a major sadness ------------- thinking of the future of my daughter Please accept, Sir, the insurance of my distinguished consideration.

M. Sauteyron collector of the direct incomes to BAZAS

(Gironde)

This letter was translated from French.
From the original letter, Michel Lopez's collection of Captain Paul Boyton.

According to European traditions in this era, if you had to send bad news, the 'paper had a black border, hence Elise's fathers reply to Paul
was written on black bordered writing paper.

to her letter, that hopefully would be sent from London.
Paul released her father was right and at this time in his life he had nothing to offer any woman, let alone the delicate Elise.

London 13-83

My Poor Dear Elise.

I just received your letter of the 4th. I had been away from London or I would have gotten it sooner. My poor child I am sure you must feel just as much sorrow to receive my letter as it caused me to write it. From the bottom of my heart I regard the position fate has placed me in and the disappointment and sorrow I have caused you.

Believe me dearest Elise my intention was true and sincere. It was my greatest pleasure to think of the time I could call you my wife. But your fathers letter caused me to hesitate and ponder on what I was about to do and I assure you dearest Elise it was after long and deep thought I came to the conclusion I did. If you were my wife and anything happen to me I am sure it would break your fathers heart. I can see by his letter that he loves you very much and he fears my dangerous life would be the cause of having you left alone with strangers in case of my death.

I will be a prisoner or dead. It is hard to say what my fate will be and in consequence of this position I am convinced that it would be wrong and dishonorable of me to ask you to share that unknown fate. I would be very pleased to see and talk with you. It is possible that my business will call me to Paris this week, but I fear that it will be impossible for me to go to Bordeaux but I will do my utmost to do so. I do not wish to be seen at your home as it may cause much talk and if I am watched your name might become public.

Write to me when you get this and say what you think. If I can go, ehre do you think best for me to meet you. When you get this letter write to 14

Strand London and also write another letter in care of consul des Etats-Unis - Paris I will do all I can my poor dear Elise to see you before I start my next voyage.

With sincere and devoted love I remain dearest Elise Your ever true Paul

Eight days later Paul was standing on Broadway in New York, penniless but rich in experiences and the joy on his Mothers face as she welcomed him home, as if he were from the grave. The hundreds of thousands of dollars he should have earned, and anticipated earning, were never paid. Paul put it down the gamble he took at the chance to make his life's fortune.

Kiefer, who had gone south with him, succeeded in making his escape into the mountains where he remained for several years, collecting antiques and artifacts. Shipping them north for sale, he died soon after his return to the USA in 1889 of consumption.

CHAPTER TWELVE

In less than a month after his return from South America, Boyton was in St. Paul, Minnesota, ready to start on another one thousand and eighty miles down the Mississippi to Cairo, he was determined to navigate the river from it's source to mouth.

Over the past years Paul had figured out some improvements to his suit, and while he had some time on his hands his filed a new patent.

Though there were no unusual adventures on this trip down the Mississippi to write about, it was the stormiest one he ever had the pleasure of navigating through and he did encounter two extraordinary characters that accompanied him.

The fellow was a famous german artist, by the name of Dr. C., this was his first visit to the America, as a representative of the well known *Gaetenlaube,* newspaper. The doctor was a scholarly gentleman, but being unfamiliar with the American culture, that had been sadly misrepresented to him by some of his countrymen. They were probably joking with him, as they had exaggerated the form of dress he would need to wear on this trip. When he arrived at St. Paul, he thought he was not going to show his ignorance and acquired the clothing to suit this trip in the wild's with the Intrepid American.

He arrived dressed for the occasion to be presented to

UPPER MISSISSIPPI—DR. C. LOADING HIS GUN.
The Upper Missippi. Scanned from The Paul Boyton Story.

ROUGHING IT IN RUBBER

Paul, wearing a buckskin suit, with a revolver and bowie knife trimmings,looking somewhat out of place with the scholarly spectacles that bridged his nose. He really out-did the most fanciful cowboy of the far western ranches. Such an outfit, he must of believed it was just the thing for the trip among the wild characters on the Upper Mississippi.

The other member of the party was a broad nosed, herculean negro whom Paul hired to pull the row boat he had purchased for the Doctor's accommodation.

Boyton found the scenery on the Upper Mississippi far more beautiful than on any river in America that he had traversed, there was no startling grandeur, that is seen on the shores of other rivers.

With high butte's and pleasant shores, while the people were extremely hospitable all the way down the river, if the beauty of this river was better known, it would be a great restful vacation resort.

On the morning of May the nineteenth 1881. the official start was made as the crowds gathered lining the banks to see them off. Several of the Doctors friends had given him a keg of beer for the long journey, it was placed in his skiff. Unfortunately they forgot to give him the faucet, it was a long hot day and they all thought of the nice cold beer they could have had. Late that evening a steamer towing a raft, came slowly down the river, Paul told the negro oarsman to pull alongside and have them open the keg, they had no faucet, but they did have an auger, as they willingly started boring into the head.

Moments after a white fountain shot up and they all held out their hats to catch the descending beer. The trip went smoothly the following day and Paul was able to make good time. Reaching Lake Pipin on the third day they ran into a very heavy head wind and rough waters, that almost sunk the Doctor's boat, forcing them to land at Lake City and stay overnight. Next morning the wind had died down so they headed for La Crosse.

Arriving at La Crosse to blazing fireworks and booming canons going off, a great reception for the voyagers followed by a banquet.

Heading back on to the river between the willow laden banks, just below La Crosse the Doctor asked if they could stop awhile for him to go hunting, Paul was happy to oblige the scholarly gentleman who produced a shotgun that he had kept well hidden. Seeing that the Doc knew nothing of handling the weapon that had an improved breech loader, Paul instantly gave him some quick lessons, it looked so simple that the Doc assured him he could handle it with no trouble at all, the negro however was not as confident as he saw the Doc take up the shotgun.

"Ise not sayin' nuffin Cap'en" he remarked to Paul, "but dat man aint been raised aroun' whar da do much shootin' suah's yo' libe. Dar aint no tellin' whar he gwine fur to pint that weepin' an Ise running chances in hyah wid him. Dat's right, Cap'en."

He was assured there was no danger, but he was far from sattisfied and decided to keep a close watch on the Doc's every move. After further instructions to Doc regarding safety and to be very careful, Paul surged ahead of the boat, he had barely gone a mile when he heard a shot from the gun, looking around he saw both the Doc and the negro intently gazing up at the sky as a gull circled around, at a loss to why the bird did not fall down. As the boat pulled up closer to Paul he tried to explain to the Doc that the gun cannot shoot anything that far away, and it's very hard to shoot such a small moving target.

As the sun was sinking that evening, Boyton heard the negro yelling. 'Great Lawd, come hyah Cap'en! Oh my soul, come quick! quick! Dis hyah Dutchman gwine t' kill me suah!" Wheeling around, Paul witnessed the most ludicrous thing he had ever seen. The Doctor, with the muzzle of the gun pointed at the negro, was excitedly hammering a cartridge into the breech, while the negro was stretched on his back almost over the gunwale of the boat, his broad foot held up as a shield towards the muzzle, yelling at the top of his voice.

Doc had seen some blackbirds in the bushes and had forgotten how to put the cartridge in the gun, so was pounding it in with the handle of his bowie knife, of course it could have exploded at any moment and the poor negro knew the danger.

ROUGHING IT IN RUBBER

After some persuasion, Paul was able to convince the Doc to put the gun away and just enjoy the journey.

Below Dubuque the weather became very stormy with a lot of head winds and rough water, as they enjoyed the lightening effects as it's forked tongue lapped the water in the most eccentric way. Though dangerous, it was extremely fascinating and exciting from Paul's view on his back, as the poor negro cowered on the bottom of the boat with his hands over his face. Paul and the Doc were so evolved in the grandeur of mother natures display that they barely thought of it's danger.

After that evening whenever the dark clouds rolled in and the wind began to blow, the old negro would pull into shore and refuse to move until the storm was over, "Ole Mastah above kin hit me evah w'en he wants to, I knows dat, but den ise gwine to climb fur saoah foah dat lightnin' play tag aroun' dis niggah's head agin, dat's fur shoah as yo' libe." he explained to Paul after one of his hurried retreats into the bushes. Twelve days after the party started they arrived at Davenport, Paul's pace had be slowed down with all the false channels, sloughs and rough weather and the constant stops for lightening storms.

Early one morning emerging from one of those sloughs that he had wandered into during the night and wasted time and energy getting lost. As the sun was beginning to rise he heard the sound of music, the music seemed almost heavenly, it was so beautiful that he stopped and lay motionless on the water absorbing the sounds.

It turned out to be thousands of birds on one side of the river, bursting from the throats of feathered warbler's as the birds on the other shore added to the swelling chorus, it was a concert that Paul felt was worth paddling a thousand miles down the river for.

At Davenport and all the river towns they were treated with the warmest of welcomes, as all the members of the boat club at Burlington sailed out to meet them, causing a fascinating flotilla into the city. They frequently met rafts of logs, containing millions of feet of lumber, the raftsmen were always glad to meet Paul and converse with him while he paddled alongside. Below Davenport the Doc started talking about going hunting again, much to the disgust of his dusky oarsman.

He insisted on firing at some blackbirds and the promise of a quarter to the negro, persuaded him to row close into shore, as he took aim firing into a tree full of blackbirds.
Not one of them fell, but a cow that had been drinking among the willows, ran wildly up the bank with her tail in the air, bellowing mournfully. The darkey received the promise of another twenty-five cents to row away from the scene as fast as he could, it was Paul's constant complaint that the boat was too far behind, but after the cow incident, it was just the other way, they were now always so far ahead that he could barely see them.

The oarsman was rewarded for this unwanted speed with gifts of neck ties and other fancy articles sacrificed from the Doctors personal wardrobe, as he was led to believe that the owner of the cow would surely be in vengeful pursuit of him. While paddling along a couple of mornings later Paul heard a barrage of fire from the shot gun, while trying to catch up to the row he noticed it was surrounded in smoke, as he pulled along side the Doctor was holding a small object proudly, "see what I have killed," he enthusiastically cried in German. "Yaas," chimed the darkey, "day squi'l him swimmin' de ribber' an' de Doc, he shot' an shot' den I kill um wid de oar."

After leaving Quincy, the Doctor again believing he was an accomplished hunter fired into some ducks that he saw in the slough on the Missouri side. The negro was encouraging him to shoot, hoping to get rid of the rounds, but to their surprise he accidently killed one, as Doc had the negro row in and pick it up, a few moments later a gruff voice was heard on the bank, "Pull ashore man."

Looking up they saw a gigantic Missourian with his rifle pointed at them as the oarsman pulled in as though he was trying to escape another lightning storm.

"Mister, I want six bits for that pet duck of mine," the man remarked to the Doctor.

The price was promptly paid and the Doctor, was glad to get away from that wicked looking weapon which the Missourian handled as though familiar with it's use. After that adventure Doc lost all interest in hunting and stored away the shotgun to

ROUGHING IT IN RUBBER 285

the negro's great relief.

June the nineteenth, the party pulled in to St. Louis, where they were welcomed by a crowd of about thirty-thousand people.

The Mayor was on one of the steamboats and honored Paul with the freedom of the city, as the cheering of the people and whistles were deafening, he was treated with the greatest of hospitality fit for royalty. After a short visit he began the last leg of his journey, to hundred miles to Cairo, which he intended to do without stops, this would be longest run he ever made.

On this section he had problems with Doc and the oarsman, they kept falling asleep at the same time, on one stretch he lost sight of them for a couple of hours. Sometime later he noticed something limping down the river lopsided, that he could not believe was their boat, it was Doc rowing away as if his life depended on it.

As they got closer Paul saw the problem, one oar and a little staff that had a small German flag attached to it's end, apparently they had both fallen asleep and lost an oar, thus Doc had used the flag staff that had been placed on the boat's stern. They eventually all arrived safely at Cairo, forty one hours after they had left St. Louis, all parting good friends as Doc a little poorer and less clothing, while the negro oarsman a little richer and a new wardrobe.

While in Cairo Paul met a friend who was going up the Mississippi to St. Paul on his own private steamer, a great little boat with all the luxury's. He invited Paul to join him and knowing no better way to rest he accepted the invitation. He stopped often along the way, hunting and fishing, which Paul thoroughly enjoyed. The little steamer was quickly filled up with pets of all sorts they picked up along the way, coons, foxes, a possum, crows and squirrel's.

Above Burlington they ran across a snag, a pilot's union. They were compelled to hire a pilot to take them up the river, though they were perfectly capable of doing this themselves, or pay a fifty dollar fine.

They were moored at a wharf of an Iowa village when the heard this, and rather than have any trouble they agreed to hire the pilot. Enquiring where they would find a pilot, they were told there was no pilot in town, except the editor of the weekly paper, he had a license and would only do the work if he felt like it. Being in a rather awkward position, as they were reluctant to ask such a distinguished gentleman, such as the editor to pilot them, after many discussions were had, the decision was they had no option but to ask the editor.

Paul agreed to call on the editor and see what kind of man he was, if he seemed a jovial fellow, he could ask him to join them as their guest, which would be a politer way to put it, they were willing to pay the thirty five dollars but the same time were unsure how to offer him the money. After climbing a crazy flight of stairs on the rheumatic looking frame building, he found the editor seated on a stool at a case of type, setting up some pages for his next week's issue.

Boyton introduced himself.

"Well I'll be doggoned, Paul," exclaimed the editor, jumping up from the stool, "I'm mighty glad to see you," enthusiastically shaking his hand, "where in the thunder are you swimming to now?" "Oh I'm just going up river on a trip with a friend of mine, on a little steamer."

"Is that so, I'm glad to meet you anyway, I'll make a note of it in next weeks paper."

"Yes we are having a little pleasure trip, hunting, fishing and all that sort of thing, and we thought you may enjoy a short trip with us."

A cunning gleam shot through the editor's eagle eye, as he replied.

"Um, I guess you want me to pilot you up, don't you?"

"Well yes if you want to put it that way, you might assist our regular pilot if you wished. I can assure you a good time we have plenty of everything on board."

"I'll be doggoned if I wouldn't like to go up,, Paul, but don't see how I can do it. In fact it's impossible. You see I couldn't get out of my paper next week. Have to disappoint all my subscribers and you know that would hardly be right."

"We would have a good time persisted Boyton, "you could take a little vacation, you know, you can get someone to put out the paper for you."

ROUGHING IT IN RUBBER

'Couldn't do it, there aint a man between here and Chicago that could get out this paper. No sir, if I went I'd have to disappoint all my subscrib----."

"Well what would it take to pilot us up," interrupted Paul, willing to offer fifty dollars.

"You see I would have to disappoint my subscribers, the advertisers would fuss and want a refund, taking all those things into consideration, I don't see how I could go up for less than three dollars. Of course he was taken along and royally treated as well as paid the three dollars.

The week following the editor's return, his paper contained an article to the effect that, "owing to illness in his family, the editor was compelled to disappoint his subscribers last week."

At St. Paul, Boyton started on the preparations for the longest voyage he had ever undertaken, down the yellowstone and Missouri.

As this could be a very dangerous trip to make, Paul needed to do a lot more preparations for the undertaking. This part of America at that time really was still very wild, not just the animals, but people the to.

On September the fifteenth, 1881, Boyton arrived at the railroad terminus at Glendive, Montana, to start his three thousand five-hundred and eighty miles navigating the Yellowstone and Missouri rivers. Glendive then a little town made up of rough board houses and tents, it was the highest point on the Yellowstone that he could reach, he headed for the hotel to get a room, "I reckon you can," said the landlord, "there's only sixty in there now."

Paul was not interested in moving in a general sleeping room, the superintendent of the construction train offered him a place to stay in one of the cars.

General Terry sent out messages to all the military post and Indian agents along the river, informing them of Boyton's pending voyage, hoping this would help protect him, from being shot by the Indians or mistaken for some water creature.

He remained two days in Glendive, completing the his preparations, besides his usual equipment in "Baby O Mine," he added an axe, a doubled shotgun which could be taken apart to fit in the limited space, hoping he would only need it for hunting. This being a very unhabited area Paul would have problems acquiring fresh supplies, these with signal lights, rockets, compass and maps completed the Baby's cargo. He added two pounds of strong black tea to his provisions to be used as a stimulant, as his experience on many journeys, he had long maintained that, "hardship can be better endured without the use of alcoholic beverages."

General Merritt was in command of the post at Glendive and did everything in his power to assist Paul, during the last evening at the post, the General asked him what time he was starting in the morning. "Five o'clock," Paul answered.

"For goodness sake," facetiously replied the General "don't start so early. At that time our sentries are sleeping the soundest."

The river at Glendive is narrow and quite shallow, the channel was barely eighteen inches deep, the bottom is gravely but combined with the alkalis, it's almost become solid rock, the channel runs in all direction and is often diverted by large sand bars that are strewn with some of the most beautiful agates, Paul was sure that no human foot has ever stood on this area before him, in defense of General Merritt's wishes and a fellow sleepy sentry, Paul did not start until seven o'clock in the morning.

All the inhabitants of the town were at the river bank, among them the General's beautiful daughter, who presented him with a set of colors, that he flew on the Baby throughout the trip. As a canon salute was fired he began his long lonely and dangerous journey, in a very short time he was away from any signs of civilization.

The current was fast, so Paul was making good time on this fast and lonely river, he had been warned by the General to keep as close watch for the hostile bands of Crow Indians who were hunting in this vicinity, he kept a steady pace all day, now and again he would strike rapids that had to be negotiated very carefully as not to tear the rubber suit on the rocks. He saw a lot of game on his way down river, especially black tailed deer that frequently came to the water's edge, he often amused himself by blowing blast on the bugle and seeing the deer rise up and gallop off up the banks.

That evening he decided to camp on a sand bar opposite some cottonwood trees, that gave in some logs for a fire, both shores were heavily wooded. Taking off his suit, he went about gathering brush for a fire, while being careful not to create too much smoke, and thus attract the Indians attention. He cooked super and leaving a small fire smoldering, put his pantaloons on, using the tunic for a pillow he laid down, the hooting of the owls was so soothing that he quickly fell asleep. While concerned about the Indians, he slept very lightly, at about two o'clock he woke abruptly by the sound of what he thought was a canoe landing on the bank. He rose cautiously from behind the cottonwood trees. Instead of a canoe full of Indians, it was a magnificent elk, sharply outlined by the dark background of the shore, his sides glistened like silver from the water after his swim across the river. The huge animal was uneasy, throwing his splendidly antlered head back, sniffing the air and pawing the ground, Paul raised his revolver and fired. The great head swayed from side to side as the elk fell to it's knees, Paul thought the shot was fatal, throwing a handful of brush on the fire.

Paul seizing the hunting knife dashed forward to cut the elks throat, having first piled a load of brush on the smouldering fire. The fire blazed up behind him on brush he had just fed it. As the flames shot up the elk rose to it's feet and darted off. On returning to the camp totally disappointed, he saw his paddle on the fire almost burnt in two. Hastily snatching it out, he found one blade totally ruined, as he contemplated the rest of the journey in these wild's without the means of propelling himself, like a steamer without a wheel. He was not a man to be defeated, as with his hatchet he copped down a sapling and began carving out another with his hunting knife.

He worked steadily at it until ten o'clock in the morning before it was completed and he was able to continue his trip.

If anything the river was rougher and wilder than the day before, running between high butte's which formed the upper edge of the Bad Lands, late that afternoon, just as he noticed a break in the hills, he was startled by a tremendous roaring sound as the river seemed to quiver and dance, thinking it was just an earth quake, he paddled on. He barely got any further when a large commotion on the bank got his attention as a large herd of buffalo were approaching the edge of the river, coming down the slopes in a large dark shadow like form as they waded into the water and began swimming across. The water turned brown with them as it took almost forty five minutes for them all to cross over.

They paid no attention to him as he clung to the roots of a tree for safety as the last to cross were the calves and a few stragglers. Pushing ahead as soon as he felt it was safe into the churned up muddy water they left behind, it was the last great drove of buffalo to cross the river as they were all killed off a short time after. About sundown he decided to camp under some high butte, again building a fire and removing his rubber suit, in his stocking feet decided to climb the heights in hopes of seeing some habitation. For as far as the eyes could see there was no signs of habitation, only living things he saw was a herd of antelope in the distance crossing a hill, to the south he could see the butte's of Bad Lands. Returning to camp for supper, he then slept through the night and left at sun up the next morning, for two days he was utterly lonely, not a thing in sight except wild game.

Nearing the Missouri river, he suddenly realized there was something around as a bullet whizzed passed his ear and struck the water just below him, he stood up holding the Baby as a shield and sent out some blasts on the bugle. Noticing the Indian that fired the shot with the smoking gun in his hands, standing on the bank, Paul yelled lustily at him as he turned and ran for the cover of the woods.

Later that afternoon he saw a group of buildings with a pole out front, flying a flag at half mast, he had reached Fort Buford, sending a rocket whizzing in that direction, the bank was suddenly lined with soldiers. Paul was welcomed to the Fort, asking why the flag was at half mast?, he was told that they had just received the news of President Garfield's death.

He remained at Fort Buford for two days, one of the soldiers made him a new paddle, one of the finest he ever owned. While there he had the opportunity to visit the settlements of the Ree and Mandan Indians near by, it was by them that he was given the name of *"Minnewachatcha,"* meaning *"Spirit Of*

The Water." The Indians were
very curious and asked many questions about the suit and
his navigating. As he started again the entire garrison and the
two Indian tribes assembled on the banks of the Big Muddy,
shouting their good bye's as he was swept on down river.

The currents on the Missouri were far more dangerous and
faster, than those of the Yellowstone as he was whirled around
some undescribable bends, as he did every point of the compass in a couple of hours, if the Yellowstone was lonely the
Missouri was doubly so, especially after leaving Fort Buford.

With the wild beautiful scenery that could not be described
in words, as the butte's towered high up on both sides of the
shore as they were continuously being undermined by the
erratic currents, sending avalanches of yellow soil to slide
down into the water.

There was no sight or sounds of any human presence in this
wild territory through which this fast paced river winds, to see
a stump or wood that the crew on some boat had wandered
up on higher waters to cut, was a thrill in it's self to know
some human life had been here. A blast from the bugle was
echoed from butte to butte, as it was caught in the recesses of
one hill to be thrown back with double force into the solitude of
another, until from far below, the blast was returned with such
distinctness, that Paul would strain his ears to catch the sound
again.

He began to make thirty-six hour runs, camping every second night, his schedule was to make an early start, run all day
and night until sundown the next day. Just before leaving the
water the gun was assembled and ready to shoot a duck, that
were plentiful.

He removed the suit and built a fire, two stakes in the
ground with a pole across was erected for the suit to dry on,
then skinning the duck and frying the tender bits with strips of
bacon from his provision.

He always cooked enough for breakfast and supper. With
supper he would have a little beef tea, again put on the pantaloons, use the tunic for a pillow and have a restful nights sleep
and left at sunrise the next morning.

This routine was perfected so that no time was wasted,

often he would be woken with a honk, honk from the wild-geese, or the bell of the alarm clock. He was becoming obsessed with time and refused to waste any of it, when he was woken earlier he would put more brush on the fire, hurriedly eat the precooked breakfast and slip back into the water for an earlier start on another thirty-six hour run. This was beginning to worry Paul as he had never felt this way before about time. Knowing winter was following him, he wondered if it was the reason he was feeling this way.

Going along one afternoon, he thought he saw a man in a tree and speeded ahead in hopes of getting some information from him as to how far down the river he was. The man turned out to be a cinnamon colored bear standing up against the tree reaching for some kind of nuts or berries, the bear looked gravely at Paul as he passed and paid no more attention to him, even though he blew the bugle, splashed on the water, but a shot over his head from the revolver had the big fellow running.

When the wind blew up stream, which in the northern part of Dakota was very often, the current turned the water to a very choppy yellow sea that was hard to paddle through. While beating against one of those head winds one morning, half blinded, he saw a covered boat fastened to the shore, with a man emerging with a gun in his hand. Looking up river and seeing Paul as a blast from the bugle went out, raising the gun to his shoulder, the voyager frantically blew more blast on the bugle and waved his hand in the air. "Well, stranger," said the man as Paul drew up closer to the boat. "thet er's a lucky horn for you, I took yer fur a bar on er log." Paul was in and found out the man was a hunter and trapper. He offered Paul breakfast, that was beaver tail which is considered a great delicacy, though he found it too fatty, noticing his guest was not fond of the beaver tail, the hunter offered to go out and get a deer. Assuring Paul it would not take more than an hour, Paul declines as the hunter invited him to stay over a few day, happy to have company, as was Paul, but the necessity for haste was too pressing and Paul could not spare an hour, to the disappointment of the hunter, Paul said his good byes and slid back into the water.

According to the schedule, that was the regular camping night, heavy clouds began rolling in before sunset, the high caving banks on either side were too dangerous to approach as the least touch could start the treacherous soil to become an avalanche, that would definitely bury him.

Seeing no safe place to land he forged ahead singing songs to cheer himself, convincing himself he was not tired as the glow of a fire ahead got his attention as he stopped singing. He was trying to decide if it was friend or foe as a gruff voice called from the bank,

"Hello, there, who are you?"

"Hello, I'm Paul Boyton, who are you?

"Pull in, pull in."

"Can't see where you are."

"Come just around this point, you can get in alright."

Paul polled around as directed and saw the fire plainly, as three of four men approached the bank, heavily armed and carrying torches made of knots. He heard a whispered conversation, they were astonished at his appearance, but he was greeted kindly and invited to camp. Getting closer to the fire, he smelt something ghastly, one of the men explained that he had shot a skunk. There were eighteen in the party with two good sized tents and an abundance of buffalo robes, after removing his suit the cook prepared an excellent meal urging him to eat heartily, which he did. They also had a large supply of liquor, but he refused politely and they did not insist.

Refreshed by the good meal he lit his pipe and began to tell them about his travels, one man interrupted saying, "Great snakes! I know who you are, I read about you in the almanac."

He told the men his object in navigating the rivers and English channel. "Well." said another, "when I saw you coming down the river I thought you were a deserter from the fort." The same man told him they were traders, and pointed to all the cattle out there.

Seeing that he was very tired, they insisted he turn in under the buffalo robes, Paul insisted he could sleep next to the fire, not taking there bed. He was put to bed under the cozy robes and they toned their voices down to a whisper as he fell into a deep sleep.

Next morning they called him as promised, and after a very hearty breakfast and "Baby O Mine" was loaded down with fresh food, they all wished Paul, God speed with the warmest of handshakes.

About ten days later Paul learned that his hospitable friends were notorious "rustlers" the western name foe cattle thieves, and on that same day he left their camp, they had been rounded up by a party of rancher's and all of them were shot to death.

During the forenoon, after leaving the rustlers camp, Paul was hurled violently against a rock that tore his suit, though not more than twenty yards from shore, he was filled to the neck with icy water before he could land. Fortunately there was plenty of driftwood handy and he soon had a roaring fire going. He dried out and warmed himself while repairing the damaged suit, which he completed just in time to escape a violent rain storm that followed him all day into the early evening hours.

As he was entering a narrow passage between the butte's, he felt as if the suit was leaking again and landed on a bar to investigate.

The leak was not from the earlier damage, only an adjustment to the belt was needed. As his matches were now to damp to light a fire, he gathered up some brush and with a signal light placed in the barrel of the twelve calibre pistol, it fitted like a cartridge and threw quite a strong steady blaze, shoving the pistol into the pile of wood as he pulled the trigger. Instead of lighting the fire he was hurled several feet away, righted himself he realized his arm was numb and only the pistol stock in his hand. It was several minutes before he recovered from the shock and realized he was not injured, while finding the barrel that had exploded into many pieces. Paul realized how lucky he was not to have been blinded or have shrapnel embedded in his body on this lonely sand bar in the wildes.

Kneeling on the ground he earnestly thanked the Almighty for sparing him from a what could have been dreadful ending. He was so shaken by his own stupidity that he decided not

ROUGHING IT IN RUBBER

to try to light the fire, slipping into the water paddling away, to warm up at a good speed.

Between eleven and two o'clock in the morning, he found himself in a place with no current and realizing he had lost the channel, trying to stand upright and look around himself as his feet were in the slimy, working mud on the bottom as it was pulling on his legs. Suddenly Paul threw himself back onto his back, with his paddle and a lot of extra energy he thought he had extracted himself from the dangerous situation. He could make no headway as the mud seemed to be getting thicker all around him as he felt it touching the underside of his body, he realized he was in one of the "Mud Sucks," that are numerous on the Missouri.

The mud is simular to quick sand or quagmire and it's seldom that any thing escapes it's slimy embrace.

Seeing no way out he was becoming really nervous as he beat around with the paddle in every direction without any advancement.

Once in a while he would put his hand down into the water and could feel the deadly suction pulling at it, he had turned and twisted so much that he no longer had any idea where the channel was or from which direction he had come.

The shore seemed so close and yet impossible to reach, he began to panic and the sweat ran from every pore of his body, giving him the cold shivers, as he realized the frightful situation he was in. Beginning to think how he had got out of the quick sand on the Loire, it was worth a try, to inflate the suit, though the quick sand is not as powerful as this sucking mud.

With all his strength he began blowing, filling chamber after chamber to capacity until he was totally exhausted and could blow no more, though he had raised a little higher it was not enough to free him from the slimy mud.

Deciding to just lay perfectly still until daylight when he would be able to see around himself and which way was out. As Paul lay there he thought of how close his life was to ending in just one day, again laying helplessly on his back in the middle of nowhere he began asking for guidance from the Almighty.

He was startled by a bright light, it looked like a blaze of an enormous lamp, he could see it rising as if from the ground below him and moving slowly over to the Butte where he was laying.

The thought occurred to him that maybe God had sent the light to guide him to the channel, pointing his feet towards the spot where it was shining, he made an almost superhuman effort to break through the suction of the mud and move towards the light, to his intense surprise he was slowly slipping off the slimy mud and felt like he was at last getting to water, putting his hand back down to reassure himself, it was not as strong as before. It was to his intense joy and relief that Paul felt as if the current picked him up, and he began floating, he stood up gazing in awe at the light that was still glowing against the butte, as he uttered a heartfelt prayer of thanks!.

Boyton was never superstitious, but that incident had left a very strong impression on his mind as he told the story many times over the years. He understood that he only saw an *ignis fatuus*, a phenomenon easily explained, but he believed that it was sent that night by the great *"Pilot"* to guide a helpless human being out of danger.

Two days later he reached the Indian agency of Fort Berthold on a bluff over looking the river, he sounded the bugle to announce his arrival as soldiers and Indians swarmed down to the water's edge. They covered the banks like rows of statues watching for the water spirit - their name for Paul - who they had been told was coming down the river. Each one wearing a blanket of bright red or blue, forming a colorful picturesque foreground against the high bluff and sullen fort.

As Boyton came opposite he stood up in the water lighting a detonating rocket, not a breath of air was stirring as the thick white smoke bellowed from the rocket and hung over the water engulfing him. Indeed it looked to the Indians as if he had disappeared entirely, as the rocked exploded over their heads with the roar of a canon.

These superstitious people could take no more as they scrambled up the banks like a herd of frightened sheep, falling over each other to get as far away as they could get from him.

That night Paul met the Indian Agent, who told him that the tribe at one of their pow wow's, declared him as good medicine, meaning - "*lucky*." Paul could believed they were the only lucky ones, as these red men tremendously annoyed him as they stole every little thing from him, they could lay their hands on for their medicine bags.

Both the Ree and Mandan tribes have been peaceful for many years.

Next day, prior to Paul's leaving, all the Indian chiefs shook hands with him exclaiming, "how," which by the way is a most elastic word.

It means, good bye, how do you do, expresses anger, friendship,pleasure, sorrow, and all possible feelings from the heart, all depending on the vocal tone used and manner in which it is said. These Indian tribes are very stubborn and have never forgiven the Sious's for the battles and stealing they had done many years before, they are still considered a deadly enemy, each red man took a turn to watch around the clock for the Sious's approach. Not even the Agents or the army have been able to assure these tribes that the war is over, even though there have been no attacks in many years.

About twenty miles below the fort, Paul was again shot at, this time by an Indian boy whose aim, luckily, was bad.
He scampered away as Paul stood up shouting, "How, how, cola."

That night Boyton arrived at Fort Stevenson, where he was kindly treated with the greatest hospitality, and next morning started on another thirty-six hour run. Beating against head winds and heavy weather through another wild stretch of country, the next camping place was in a sort of circular basin that had been cut out of the prairie by the floods, while surrounded by high mud banks. Finding plenty of driftwood in the eddy, while picking out the driest it would still not really burn, just enough heat to warm his supper and not able to coax enough blaze to warm himself.

Night closed in as black as ink, he could hear the distant howl of the coyote that were being answered from all directions by others, in less than half an hour the top of the bank was covered with hordes of the dirty little beasts, snapping and snarling at one another, as their eyes shone like balls of fire in the dark night. They were frightened off by a couple of shots from Paul's revolver. but soon returned.

Looking up the bank he noticed the cowardly creatures creeping back as the blood curdling howls started all over again, Paul decided the river was better than their company.

It was hard keeping his eyes open, day broke cold and chilly with the same threatening sky as had darkened the heavens the night before, head winds were making it very hard to paddle as he was getting really cold and feeling totally miserable.

Towards evening he started looking for a camping place as he was desperately tired and worn out, below was a grove of trees that he decided would give him shelter and firewood, paddling over to it. Looking over to the right bank, Paul noticed a small log cabin on a small bit of prairie land. Immediately sounding the bugle, but there was no response, note after note and still no sign of life, so he headed for the cabin pulling vigorously crossing the channel. Reached the muddy shore, he decided to test it with his foot, it was not very firm, fearing it may be another mud suck, he moved a few more feet down river that seemed to have safer sand. He put the Baby down and headed quickly to the cabin.

Discovering the hut had been deserted for a long time, there were old deer antlers bleached white by the sun and bits of hide blackened with age lying all around and grass growing every where, pushing his way inside he found a large fireplace at one side and two rough bunk beds that were covered with old hay. Paul was delighted with his find, this would be a great shelter from the threatening storm. He felt like a king in a palace, as he headed out side collecting several bits of wood, placing them one after the other making several steps over risky sand to the waters edge to get the Baby, he soon had her safely in the cabin. Removing his suit as he went out and gathered a good supply of firewood. Closing and fastening the door just as the storm broke, over a blazing fire he cooked a delicious supper, filling his pipe as he settled down on the straw that covered the floor between the fire place and the bunks watching the smoke curling up to the rafter, while he marveled at his find. Dozing off he thought he felt a movement in the straw, deciding it was probably a field mouse, but again there was a stronger movement under him, leaping to his feet he was horrified to see a hissing shiny snake, as the reptile rose two feet or more from the floor swaying from side to side as though indignant at the intrusion. As it continued to uncoil it's ugly body, Paul picked up a piece of wood and swung at it's head, the creature slithered under a board as he heard the sound of it dropping. Moving some of the straw Paul found a pit covered with some boards, obviously some sort of storage area, covering up the pit and moving further across

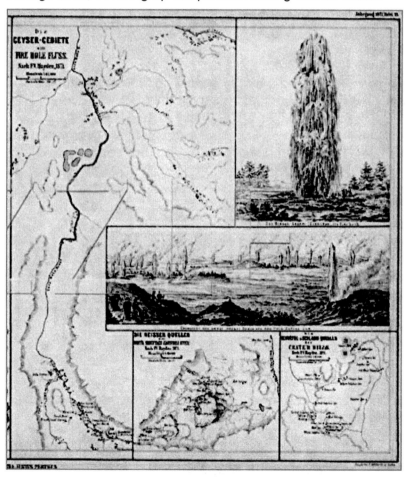

Map from 1885 of Yellowstone.

the room as he was determined not to be driven from this cabin by the reptile. Putting his suit back on and covering his face, he was soon sound asleep.

It was almost sunrise when he woke up, quickly replenishing the fire, he cooked a hearty breakfast. The storm had passed and the sky was cloudless, promising a nice day. After breakfast as he was ready to make a early start, Paul decided to remove a couple of the boards under the hay and look down into the pit where the snake had fallen into, the night before. Holding a burning log down in the pit, the sight sent chills through every vain, the pit was alive with a squirming mass of hideous reptiles, hissing and squirming around as they were being disturbed, they were obviously settling into hibernation for the winter.

Had he looked down there the night before, he said, "I would have risked the mercy of river and the storm, before sleeping amidst with these deadly reptiles."

Dropping the burning log amongst them, while pushing the planks over the opening as he made a hasty retreat to the river, he had not gone far down the river when he saw a column of smoke rising, and realized that was the cabin of snakes burning. He had not intended to burn the cabin, but was not sorry that the pit of ghastly reptiles were being destroyed. During the afternoon a flat bottomed boat drifting in the current just a little way ahead of him, got his attention, as he headed towards it. A few blast on the bugle woke the occupant, he gazed curiously at Paul for a few moments and then exclaimed,

"Well, drat my buttons, I never thought I would see a human critter goin' down the Missouri in such a rig as thet."

He leaned back and waited for the critter to come along side.

He was a tall raw boned man with reddish gray hair and a matted beard, as a pair of keen grey eyes peered from under the heavy overhanging brows. Though he had the looks of a farmer, he could have been anything from a deacon to rustler or even a judge. The boat he was rowing down river was loaded with an assortment of household goods and a couple of sad eyed hounds that were his only companions. Paul quickly

ROUGHING IT IN RUBBER

noticed all this as he pulled up overhearing the boatman's remark, as he asked, "How far are you going down stranger?"

"Ain't pertic'lar how fur so as I git outen this country. I had a farm once, but she's gone now, stranger, gone slick an clean."

The constantly changing currents of the Missouri, frequently cuts in and swallows up acres upon acres of land on one side only to leave as much exposed on the other side. The man on one side gains more land as the other can loose his entire farm. Thus the expression is common in the Upper Missouri that, "a man go to bed owning a fine farm on one bank and wake up in the morning to find it owned by the fellow on the opposite side."

"Well where do you intend going now," asked Paul.

"I don't intend goin' anywhere, I only want to git outen this country. She's a holy terror an' I stood it jest as long as I could, dis'ere cantankerous river has done me up. I think God Almighty built her all right, but I don't think he's made up his mind whar to locate her yit. She's runnin' wild, stranger, she's runnin' wild, I'll tell ya."

He leaned back against a worn mattress with a melancholy sigh as his boat floated off down river.

About the middle of the afternoon he was startled by a peculiar noise above him, black heavy clouds hung low over the prairie lands as the atmosphere became oppressive, an ominous roar made him turn around and look up stream. Alarmed, as he saw a funnel shaped cloud heading to the east across the river, in less than a half an hour another one bore down from the butte's and sped across with a deafening roar, about one mile down river.

Thankful for the moment that he had only been sandwiched between the two whirlwinds, he was horrified to see another coming down the river directly at him from the west, as he frantically paddled towards some willow trees for shelter. Before he could get to one the outer circle of the cyclone caught him. Grasping "Baby O Mine," as he was swept around and lifted up in a great spout of water, as though he was no more than a feather, swirled around several times and then dropped. When he recovered from the shock, he found himself stuck in the mud on the opposite shore, it was some time before he was able to return to the water, fortunately uninjured.

It was nice the next couple of days and he made up some of the lost time as he headed towards Bismarck, arriving there to a great welcome and entertained on board the Northern Pacific transfer boat, by Captain Wolfolk and Mr. James Creelman of the New York Herald.

After a good nights rest on board, Boyton and Creelman the correspondent, who had been sent to Bismarck by the paper to accompany him for the rest of the journey, and write an article on the Indian country.

Getting under way early the next morning with Creelman following in a canvas canoe down the muddy river. Setting up camp that night on a sand bar with his usual camping routine they were able to get under way again at sunrise the next morning, ranges of butte's stretched for miles ahead covered with blushing autumn foliage as every gully and stream poured it's clear water into the muddy yellow river. Game was fearless until frighten by a blast from the bugle or a couple of shots A bank was used for camp again the next night and at ten o'clock the next morning, the white tepees of the Indian village came into view, the piles of wood along the river indicated they were getting close to some settlement. As they swept around a large bend, Fort Yates and the Standing Rock Agency loomed up ahead. They were both warmly received by the officers of the Fort and treated to a good meal. Among the notorious Indians Chiefs they met at Standing Rock, were Rain-in-the-Face, Gaul, Low Dog, Long Soldier and the young chief Flying-By, plus several others.

On the morning of October the fifth, they continued down the river as the banks were lined with soldiers and Indians cheering them on their way, after passing an Indian village a few miles below Fort Yates, the country that the Missouri twisted and turned through was very lonely with no signs of human existence. Mile after lonely mile was passed as the sand bars divided into five or six different channels that took very careful paddling to avoid many obstacles that stuck up out of the water. The shores were strewn with driftwood and floating logs that had been knawed from their roots by beavers. Many

ROUGHING IT IN RUBBER

horns and bones of wild animals were mixed in amongst the piles of driftwood heaped along the sides and on the multitude of sand bars. Amid all this desolation the Big Muddy flowed, making fresh ruins at every turn. That night camp was pitched on the bank and a wild goose was the main course for dinner, capped off with a cigar.

The next day proved another lonely one, not a single habitation could be seen on the rusty hills that rose on either side. Towards evening they noticed a ranch and landed hoping to find friendly inhabitants. The farmer was a squaw man and his family. A name is given to a white man that marries an Indian woman.

The travellers were cautiously invited in and later kindly invited to spend the night. Several homely half breed children sat around the room while supper was being prepared by a good looking Indian squaw, noticing the inquiring looks from Boyton and his companion.

"Yes them's my children and that's my wife. She cost me a tidy bit, too, I gave up a durned good horse fur that squaw."

"How long have you been married to her?" inquired Paul

"Wall I ain't been married very long to this 'un, I had another mighty good lookin' one, that I lived with for some years, but she got tired of workin' an' run away to the tribe. This un' a good cook an a hard worker." Supper was announced by the woman, who spoke to her husband in her Indian tongue. The travellers and the master of the house sat at a small table, while the woman and children, retreated to a dark corner near the fire to eat.

"Will your wife not join us?" politely inquired Paul.

"Eat with us!" exclaimed the rancher in total astonishment, "I shud say not, do you think I would eat with a durned Indian?"

After breakfast the next morning the headed back down the river, the squaw man extending an invitation to drop in again if they were up that way.

As they passed the mouth of the Grand river, the scenery began to change, instead of grassy butte's, the prairies were crowned with clay hills, that looked as if some volcanic action had formed them. The river ran under the slate colored cliffs. About four miles below Grand River, on the bluish cliffs that jutted out in the water, at almost right angles. Landing there they found many beautiful specimens of petrified fish that had retained their prismatic beauty. The mother of pearl shells were the extinct anomite type that lay around as though they had been in an ocean bed. The shore was covered with agates that were gray and a pleasant change from the brown mud sucks, there were pebbly beaches for some distance, with banks that were eaten away by the river, exposing layers of clay and soil.

The storms had carved some of the massive cliffs in to forms of castles, arches and columns sculptured by the rain as they stretched for miles on either side, at night the scene was ghostly and your imagination could easily see images prowling deep within, around midnight it looked as if it was going to rain.

Paul blew the bugle again and again in hopes of attracting some attention, but only the musical notes echoed back from the airy cliffs. As they were about to land and set up camp a voice called out, another kindly squaw man offering them shelter on the floor of his house. He had several half breed sons that could not speak a word of English, one of them had just returned from hunting and had slaughtered two hundred buffalo retrieving all the hides and leaving the carcasses to rot on the plains.

Starting the next morning on a long tiresome run to Fort Bennett, during the afternoon they managed to shoot a goose and a duck, there was a lot of game down this stretch of the river.

When sun finally went down the country side lit up with beautiful hues that faded away as the moon rose clear and bright. Some of the bends in the river gave them the impression that they were landlocked and then the channel would carry them safely through the quagmires and sand bars, many times floating amongst flocks of white swans that would fly up with shrill cries startling the cranes that set the geese cackling then ducks followed creating quite a site between the stark cliffs. Towards the early morning a heavy head wind sprang up as they battled their way through the turbulents, then into another vast bend that was about twenty-five miles long. Yet the distance across land was only about four miles.

At four o'clock in the afternoon they reached Fort Bennett, where they were the guests of Major Love, who transported them to his home in an Indian ambulance.

Paul was exhausted after paddling for twenty eight straight hours and much of it against heavy head winds. The following day they were shown the local sights and everything of interest at the Indian agency. As Creelman needed information on the tribes, so they stayed over for another day to visit some of the chiefs. There were over two thousand Cheyenne's under this agency, the main chief was Little-no-Heart and among the others were Rattling-Rib, White Swan, The Charger and Four Bears, they were a peaceful tribe and farmed crops and live stock on this reservation.

After being driven about two miles to a tree that according to the tribe a number of Indians had been buried, it was an elm that had grown straight up to a height of about twenty-five feet and the trunk was spread out into a dozen gnarled and twisted limbs. The peculiar black bark gave it a very airy unnatural appearance. Among the yellow leaves hung decaying garments and bones, in some cases the storms had torn away the funeral paraphernalia and whole skeletons were exposed. All the implements that the dead are supposed to need in the Happy Hunting Grounds are placed at the corpses side. So many Indians have been placed in these branches that it's said to have grown faster than in other in the area, surely due to the extraordinary fertilization.

The Indians have been stopped from doing this disgusting form of burial since the agency took over managing the reservation.

There was an Indian school on the reservation that Paul and Creelman also visited. The officials are having hard time trying to get the children to attend school. The elder's are opposed to educating the younger generation and do not want them to learn to speak English. Some of the children that are able to speak English are too ashamed to do so around their peers. Though they are smart people and able to comprehend with great accuracy, the Government hopes that with time the prejudices will be over come and these people will become more civilized.

Noon the next day Paul and Creelman set off down river with another head wind, the couple of days rest had restored their strength so with the storm passing over they were again able to make good time. Some of the butte's below Fort Sully are shaped like pyramids with walls that loom up into the sky. Paul said, "he imagined himself floating down the Nile and gazing at the sphinxes among the temples in Egypt." Occasionally the voyager would be startled by a splash of a giant catfish as it leaped out of the water, and the loons driven southward by the approaching winter, filled the air with their melancholly cries.

Shortly after midnight a gale blew in, churning the water into heavy waves and by daylight a regular hurricane was blowing. Acre's of fine sand swirled about in the air making it very hard to see more than a yard or two ahead and almost suffocating them. By day light the fury of the storm was so great they had to pull over and lay down on the bank. When they set off again they discovered the town of Pierre was only one mile below where they had camped.

A brief rest was taken at Pierre in a comfortable little hotel, Paul settled down with his pipe to relax, when he was disturbed by the editor.

This bustling little man that was overly enthusiastic came into the room in a breezy manner introducing himself, while offeringinformation on the resources around Pierre. His astonishment when Paul refused to have a swig from his hip flask left him speechless for a moment, but he soon started right back into the resources of the country, putting down lumps of what Paul assumed to be mud, though the editor said it was samples of gumbo that the divers had found.

After a good nights sleep Paul and Creelman visited some of the sights in the town, including the grave of "Arkansaw." He was the desperado that was believed to have be able to put to shame the worst of the Rocky Mountain ruffians. A year before his death he crossed from his home in Fort Pierre over to Pierrie with the intentions of cleaning out the town. Crossing the bitterly cold icy river he decided to have a quick drink for courage at the local bar.

ROUGHING IT IN RUBBER

The bar owner called him to the door as the party of gentlemen known as the vigilantes were waiting for him. After a brief encounter Arkansaw was shot to death. The following speech was made at his burial, indorsed by the citizens of the town.

"*Arkansaw, was a good feller, boys, and no mistake. He on'y got of his bearin's w'en ther idee struck him thet he cud clean out this ere town. But he were clear game. Three Cheers for the corpse!*"

Three cheers were given as another vigilant cried out.

"*A tiger fur Arkansaw.*"

With that the hero was lowered into the grave, that remains one of the tourist sights of the town still today.

It was freezing cold the following day when Boyton and Creelman got back into the water, and Paul knew the rest of the journey would be a race against the winter which was now following very closely behind him.

He paddled between the gumbo hills all afternoon, these black masses are composed of a sticky substance that becomes very slippery when wet. Nothing will grow in gumbo though occasionally you can see a couple of blades of grass where the soil has not yet been covered or managed to push through, while ducks and fowls cower in the niches to escape the howling wind.

The sky was overcast, without a ray of sunshine, except a momentary gleam during the brief rain storm which occured late in the day. Shortly after starting the river narrowed considerably and they were forced to paddle through a natural obstacle course close to the west shore, with numerous beaver slides going down the slimy banks.

The banks were hived with hundreds of their holes and nawed roots, proving that these industrious little animals are far from becoming extinct as commonly reported. Several traps were set by the trappers that deal with the sale of the much sought after fur for the favorite beaver coat.

Night came on cold and cheerless as they paddled on, around midnight they went into the longest bend on the Missouri where two steamboats were already grounded on a sand bar.

Paul blew the bugle several times without any response so

continued on down the river when they noticed, a dull glow that soon brightened into a blaze, they able to see the line of flames and smoke spreading over acres of prairie land.

At the mouth of the medicine river the air was clouded with feathered game, migrating to warmer climates from the frosty air and cold winters of Montana and the Dakota's.

Nine o'clock in the morning the voyagers stopped on the banks and cooked breakfast, after a short rest they resumed the journey, about noon they went into another long curve of the river that was walled in on one side with rock that resembled a large causeway of an arched cathedral. The rain water had worn a fretwork down the sides as the ribs of blue clay brought out the tremendous effects against the rock.

At midnight a fierce gale blew in forcing them to land and seek shelter on the east shore under the towering cliffs. With a warm driftwood fire burning and supper cooked. After two nights on the river without stopping, not even a gale could keep either one awake for long. Next morning as the sun was melting the frost it exposed bunches of wild grapes above them, that hung like clusters of pearls in the suns rays.

But the beauty of the scene faded in to nothingness when they found they had camped out in the bitterly cold night while the Crow Creek Agency was opposite them on the other side of the river, the journey was resumed in silence as just a few miles below a glimpse of the Stars and Stripes flying in the opening between two the hills. Approaching Fort Hale where they were welcomed heartily by the officers and were soon resting in snug quarters.

They remained at Fort Hale until Sunday.

Monday morning was so clear that there was not even a ripple on the Big Mud. At last John Creelman had got his camp appetite and was no longer being so finicky about the food. At the beginning of Creelman's trip with Paul, he would not drink coffee made from the river water nor eat the blue bacon fried in pan that was open, time had hardened him as now he would eat a piece of duck that was washed in the muddy river, even picking up a piece that fell on the ground and eat it without a thought.

Early in the afternoon they reached the little town of

ROUGHING IT IN RUBBER

Chamberlain, it looked as if the entire town was out on the bank to see them pass by. An hour later they reached the Lower Brule Agency.

Doctor Bergen of Fort Hale and one of the officials had travelled with them relieving the monotony. With their pleasant conversation, at the same time giving the voyagers a lot of valuable information about many of the dangerous places further down the river.

Before reaching White river Paul decided to have a bit of his usual fun with an Indian fisherman, almost scaring him out of his wits.

The Indian fisherman took off leaving his catch behind so they had fresh fish for breakfast that morning.

Later that morning a couple of Indians rowed out to the party, and in very good English, asked if they had any whiskey for sale?, Paul ran them off by threatening to sink their boat, liquor trafficking was becoming a big problem in these remote areas. A short distance below they heard loud lamentations coming from a clump of trees near the bank, getting a little closer they discovered a group of Indians having a wake for a deceased friend.

The mourners were trying to sing, but It turned out to be no more than a series of howls and weird chanting whoop's, that were enough to make your blood run cold. The night passed without any further incidents, after breakfast Paul had to spend some time repairing a couple of weak spots in his suit before doing the next run.

Large flocks of gulls were heading down to the South ahead of the winter for St. Louis. These birds are found near the head of the Missouri River. They start from the sea coast in the spring and follow up the stream for over five thousand miles, retracting their course as winter approaches, never changing this same course.

Around midnight it was getting really cold and the mud sucks becoming more evident, the two men decided to make camp and waite for daylight.

That night while relaxing around the campfire, both Paul and Creelman were puzzled by what seemed to be the sunset in both the east and west at the same time, watching this very carefully until the sun sank low enough revealing number of prairie fires raging in east and the reflection of the flames on the sky, caused the double looking sunset. They both had a good restful night sleep, awakening to the chattering voices of a group of Indian women at the edge of the river.

"Sitting Bulls Tepee."
Sitting Bull, Captain Paul Boyton and Mr. John Creelman.
Scanned "The Paul Boyton Story."

These woman were doing their morning rituals in the river, as one of them was closely examining "Baby Mine," in bewilderment, and when Paul approached them, they scrambled up the bank, Paul was curious to know where they were going, hastened after them.

Suddenly he heard a stern, "Halt."

Just ahead on the path stood a large army sentinel, the soldier said they were near Fort Randall, and he was one of the guards from the camp of Sitting Bull, and other prisoners of war who had surrendered to the United States authorities after a disastrous outbreak that had drove them over the border on to British Land. - Canada.

Word was sent to the fort of Paul's arrival, and a transport was dispatched to take him and his companion to the garrison, where they were warmly received and enjoyed a steaming hot breakfast, after which they were escorted by an officer around the hostile camp.

The camp was on a level piece of land about one mile from the garrison, there were thirty-two tepees housing one hundred and sixty- eight people, forty of whom were males over sixteen years of age, and the rest women and children. One solitary white man was standing guard in the front of each tepee. He was wearing a dark pair of pantaloons with a brown duck overcoat and a large broad brimmed drab brown felt hat on his head, that had big dings in each side of it. Known as an Allison, the government scout and interpreter. The Allison's entered the hostile camp the year before and brought in the main body of Sioux warriors, led by Crow King, their main duty was to protect Sitting Bull, the famous Uncapapa chief, after greeting the visitors he led them into the dreaded Sioux leader.

Whatever has been said of Sitting Bull, he certainly had the appearance of a man born to lead men, he was five feet ten inches tall and weighed about one hundred and eighty pounds.

His expression was unusually intelligent with a large forehead, a dignified man though modest, as he invited the travellers into his tepee. His spirit was good considering he was a prisoner. A number of Indians also entered at the request of Sitting Bull, among them his nephew Kill-While-Standing. The two wives of the chief shook our hands, while several of their half naked dirty children, heir's to the Sitting Bull family, starred at us, among them were twins who the ladies of the garrison had named Kate and Duplicate.

The respect that Sitting Bull still has over his people is described in the next instance. Paul, Creelman and a couple of army officers were seated in the tepee with Sitting Bull, when a group of his people asked to see him, interpreters translation. "They are arguing amongst themselves as to how the *Minnewachatcha* floated upon the water without effort, although he appeared to be constituted the same as other men." Not being able to solve this problem themselves, they were bringing it to the wisdom of Sitting Bull to resolve. Sitting Bull had probably being trying to figure this out for himself, but dared not show any form of ignorance. He never hesitated to share his knowledge, even if not correct with his people.

His dignified manner would have given credit to any statesman. While standing up facing the deputation with Paul standing at his right, began a harangue in his Sioux tongue, interpreted as such.

"I am a the great chief, that the Great Spirit has made known all thing, the *Minnewachatcha* has good medicine. Tapping Paul's shoulder, though Paul appeared to be like other men, he has no internal arrangements, hence he can float on the water like an empty food can."

The Government issues canned foods to the Indians, once they remove the contents, when they throw the empty can in the water, it floats. Sitting Bull used that as the example to how Paul floats. Satisfied with the great chiefs answer the delegation left completely convinced that Boyton had no lungs, stomach, etc.

A great friendship developed between Paul and Sitting Bull, as the later's daughter was presented to Paul, Minnestema was a very beautiful young women and much sought after by eligible young braves, through out the valley. Paul tried to flatter Minnestema through the interpreter, by saying he had heard of her great beauty, that had even spread to the big cities.

She had just one question for him, dispelling any chance of romance.

"Do you have a plug of chewing tobacco?."

She looked on Paul as second to her distinguished father in his greatness. Their friendship lasted for years, and when the old chief was on tour of the east in 1885, his face lit up when he again met Paul. Soon after Sitting Bull was killed in the excitement during the famous Ghost Dance in the winter of 1889.

Paul and Creelman left Fort Randall, October the twentieth, after he was dressed in his rubber suit, the Indians refused to shake hands with him, only a little girl put her hand into his as all the the chiefs marvelled at her bravery, exclaiming, "how." Keeping a respectful distance from Paul, White Dog, Scarlet-Thunder, Kill-While-Standing and One Bull were all there to witness the *"Water Spirit"* float on the water, as he stood on the slope before slipping into the water and floated away. The afternoon was pleasant as they glided down on the fast current, followed by the wandering eyes of the soldiers as well as the Indians. Paul and Creelman were refreshed and vigorous and made good time. Just after dark they passed the Yankton Indian Agency and were cheered by the many Indians gathered along the bank.

That night was dark, even the stars were obscured by the clouds, a number of prairie fires threw a bit of light on the water, but barely enough to safely navigated between the obstacles. At daybreak they reached the village of Niobrara and Running Water, as they passed it was very early in the morning, they kept going for a couple of hours until reaching a sand bank, the weary voyagers hauled up on the bank and cooked breakfast.

Barely under way, a boat with a rough looking stranger approached, carrying a shotgun and rode along side without uttering a word, though silent he seemed to get a lot of satisfaction just floating along with Boyton. "Where are you going to with that gun?" Paul asked at last.

"Kill a goose," was the laconic reply.

"Oh, I see, you going to commit suicide," said Creelman.

Not a muscle on the strangers face moved as he suddenly rowed away and disappeared between the sand bars, with a peal of laughter following behind him from Boyton and Creelman.

Springfield was passed at noon as the residents rushed to the banks at the first sound of the bugle, cheering the pair on. From Springfield to Bonhommie, the river was smooth and straight.At Bonhommie the river narrowed and the current picked up to six miles an hour as they were swept under the high cliffs that the town stands in a roaring sea of whirlpools and rapids. Cheer after cheer came from the banks as they shot passed, the voyagers did not have a chance to respond to the people as it took all they had to navigate through this exceedingly difficult fast moving obstacle course safely.

Eight miles below they managed to land on a sand bar piled with driftwood, they built a nice warm fire and cooked supper. They had no sooner settled in when the rain started, huddling over the fire to stay warm, at three o'clock in the morning the fire went out as the fog rolled in and hung over the Missouri. Paul thought they would be warmer paddling, than sitting in the mud shivering, so they resumed the voyage down the river, while the rain beat at their faces, barely being able to see ahead of them, it was more by chance than skill that they were able to continue. At day break another stop was made and breakfast cooked, as the fog cleared they could see Yankton, where they landed an hour later for a warm welcome and a brief rest.

Leaving Yankton, they arrived a couple of hours later at Sioux City without any more incidents and began to think they had at last reached civilization as the shouting multitudes followed them to the hotel and scarcely permitted the two voyagers to get any rest.

Next morning the same enthusiasm was shown when they left, but there was still two hundred miles of the snaggy river to paddle before they could enjoy the luxury of a bed at every stage. Less than seven miles below Sioux City the weather turned stormy again, Paul was hoping it would clear up as the sun went down but the wind kept blowing, he decided to push on to Omaha.

The faster paced current just kept eating away at the already soggy banks, as the small trees started falling into the river with sheets of mud sliding down. While trying to find a place to land, the channel was shifting and the river becoming deadly especially in the dark.

By midnight they had still not found a suitable place to land, and became worried as the rain was definitely intensifying.

One o'clock in the morning they were swept into "Hell's Bend," with the deafening roar of the water as it tore at the banks and swept debris down, filling the river with obstructions. Suddenly Boyton and Creelman in the little canvas canoe were flung over onto a huge pile of drifting wood. Not thinking of his own safety, Paul struggled to free Creelman, as a large swell picked them both up, and releasing the canoe as they were then able to get upright. Creelmans paddle was lost in the struggle. There was no way they could continue in the dark and decided to get over to the shore where they built a fire and waited for daylight.

The little village of Tieville was just below, and when the villagers heard that Boyton was in the river, they flocked to the camp where the weary paddler lay stretched out asleep in the mud, looking more like an alligator than a man.

Resuming the journey at eight o'clock in the morning, soon after they replaced the oar at Decatur.

A disheartening struggle against adverse winds followed until noon, letting up as they passed the Omaha and Winnebago Indian reservations, during the night they were hoping to see the lights of Blair.

A smokey smell got their attentions, there was a camp fire on the water's edge as they came around the bend, with two men sitting around it, one was drunk and trying to sing. Boyton blew a blast on the bugle as they waved him over to join them, offering to share a roasted wild goose with the navigators. The night was clear and they wanted to paddle on, so declined the kind offer. The drunk man raised his gun, yelling. "You won't come in, won't you," as he fired a shot barely missing Paul's head.

At day break they reached Florence and found out they were only sixteen miles from Omaha. At they next bend they labded to cook breakfast and rest, they met a man that turned out to be yet another boring loud mouth who persisted on telling them about the great flood of last spring, this fellow was aggravating Paul to the extent that he finally said. "Hop into that boat and get out of here, or I'll pitch you into the river, where you can tell your miserable flood stories to the fishes."

Every town they stopped at, they heard the same flood stories, just the word was enough to nauseate Paul as his patience wore thin with the locals stories. A little further down river a man came alongside in a row boat, trying to tell his side of the great flood.

"Strangers, you couldn't land on that er' bank so comfortable --------."

"Get out of here," yelled Paul impatiently.
As the startled man, could not believe the anger of the navigator, he started to row away, then turning and resting on his oars he yelled back, "It was high enough at er' bank -----------." A club was thrown at him, while he disappeared around the bend.

Rounding the next bend to Omaha, they saw the Union Pacific bridge that spans the river, "Ah," yelled Creelman, "We're out of the wilderness. There's the first bridge."

They were met by a large party of friends and pressmen, who escorted them to a hotel in the city, where thousands of people were patiently waiting to welcome them. A man on the bridge, who probably was intending to commit suicide, threw off he coat while shouting, "I can swim as well as that fellow," jumped off the bridge. His body was found some days later. That evening after washing up and getting into clean clothes, that were shipped ahead of them, Paul and Creelman met a party of friends and newspaper men in their room, entertaining them with stories of the adventures on the trip.

Leaving Omaha after a pleasant rest and relaxing day, realizing the winter was sweeping down from the northwest faster than the estimated, they would have to make better time to avoid the ice and snow reaching St. Louis before they do.

While there were still many wild stretches, the scenery was changing from high butte's and buffalo grass, these hills were heavily timbered and well kept fences with farmlands and cattle stretched for miles on each side of the river.

The first night out of Omaha, they passed the mouth of the Platte river and next morning reached Nebraska City. Many towns and villages were passed with large crowds gathered on the banks to cheer the navigators, many dissapointed that they would not stop.

As they were enjoying their pipes one evening while relaxing around the camp fire, they were startled by a gruff voice calling out.

"Hello there," as two heavily armed men walked up to the camp fire,. One was a tall muscular fellow, and the other shorter and slighter built, both giving the impression of men not to be messed with. They were very friendly, and chatted pleasantly for some time with the navigators, while asking about the trip down the river, both held good intelligent conversations. Two hours later shaking hands with Paul and Creelman while wishing them a safe journey, they left. Later Paul found out that their midnight visitors were none other than the notorious Jessie James and his pal Bob Ford, who later assassinated Jessie James.

At sunset the next evening they reached St. Joseph and as they were going in, got stuck in the mud, while crowds gathered along the shore watching them struggled through the mud to the bank.

It was already dark by the time they landed, during their stay they were honored by a continual round of receptions and serenades. They were joined by Mr. Blake a corespondent from the Kansas City paper, who was to accompany them down to Kansas City, with his unwieldy skiff.

The party set out early the next morning to the cheers and well wishes lining the banks, towards night fall the weather grew very cold, every drop of water that splashed into the boats was quickly frozen as was Paul's head covering and hands.

"Boys, he said this is going to be a rough night, the best way to get through it will be to alternate by rowing for an hour and sleep for an hour, I will keep the time and wake you." They were happy with the plan, as Blake rolled himself up in the buffalo robes instantly falling asleep on the bottom of the boat, while Creelman rowed. Fifteen minutes later Creelman softly called Paul alongside. "Say Captain, Baker hasn't rowed all the way down from Bismark say we wake him, tell him it's twelve o'clock." he suggested.

Paul saw the joke, and moved away from the canoe, blowing the bugle to tell Blake it was his turn. The Kansas City man took the oars as Creelman rolled up for a good warm nap. After about twenty or so minutes, Baker called to Paul, "Say Captain, Creelman has rowed all the way down the river and is used to this sort of thing, I'm not and it's about knocking me out. Suppose you call him and tell him his hours up."

"Alright," said Paul," and in a moment Creelman was rubbing his eye's.

"Confound it, Captain." It seemed to me that was a mighty short hour." he said.

"It's one o'clock," assured Paul, "times up." Creelman took the oars without any suspicions that Boyton would play the same on him.

Paul repeated this procedure again without either man suspecting what was going on, as Paul was determined neither one got the better of the other, while he chuckled at the prank, as both men rowed through the bitterly cold morning hours.

Leavenworth and other towns were saluted as crowds gathered along the shoreline to see the navigators go by. The following afternoon they pulled into Kansas City, almost frozen to death as the last two miles of the banks were a solid mass of humanity, yelling and screaming, at least their hearts were warmed by all this attention as they landed.

Among those who greeted them was Paul's uncle, his mothers brother. Mr.Peter Behan, who Paul had never met, he was a famous guide and one of the first men to take a wagon train across the plains to California, and believed to be one of the sheriffs at the OK Corral. The voyagers were bestowed with the freedom of the city followed by a large lavish banquet in their honor. The next morning they continued with the same multitude of humans cheering from the banks as they set off on the next leg.

Speed was now the main thing if they were to stay ahead of the winter, as he did not fancy finishing the journey on skates,

ROUGHING IT IN RUBBER

if they did not reach St. Louis ahead of the cold wave that was coming down the river. They passed the United States snag boat, Wright, soon after leaving Kansas City and in the evening paddled to Berlin.

Wild geese and ducks were still seen in great numbers flying ------- for migration, occasionally several mud hens where amongst them.

At Camden and a few other towns large bonfires were built by enthusiastic citizens who were determined to catch sight of the hardy navigator, as he passed by day or night. There was now only four hundred miles left and the winter was closing in with severity, the ice formed rapidly on the river as they went through snow storms, at the same time the river was getting higher and faster allowing them to travel up to twelve miles an hour on some stretches.

Below Wellington they made camp on what they thought was a sand bar covered with driftwood. Building a nice big warm fire. They were soon soundly asleep, but towards daylight they were startled to find that they and the camp were floating down river, making them start off a lot earlier than planned. After passing Lexington and Booneville the banks of the river were more fertile with miles of rich grape growing country, populated by Germans who have established wineries and are known for their excellent table wines.

At Jefferson city they were again met by the Mayor and honored with the freedom of the city, staying over night. Early next morning they toured the wine vaults, and were told the soil in this area is equivalent to the best on the Rhine in Germany. Wagon teams were now crossing on the ice along the upper river.

During this voyage Paul had lost a fair amount of weight and acquired a bronzed tan much like the Indians.
At last one Sunday morning, sixty-four days after the trip began, they camped for the last time at the mouth of the great Mississippi, St. Louis was just twenty miles away.

Entering St. Louis on the Sunday afternoon, after completing three thousand five hundred and eighty miles in his rubber suit. This was the longest and roughest journey Paul Boyton ever made.

The long trying voyage of Yellowstone and the Missouri was so exhausting that Paul returned home to rest and enjoy being around his family again.

He recuperated so quickly, that when he received an invitation from friends to go hunting on a private steamboat, he could not refuse.

The steamer was already on the Mississippi, so he joined the group in Memphis, her nose was turned for the south western
waters. They steamed up the Arkansas to Bayou Meta, and were soon far in the depths of the woods. Though the water in the bayou was very deep, it was so narrow in places that trees and vines had to be cut away so the boat could push her way through.

Several weeks were spent shooting deer and bears, catching coon, possum and other game, at their homemade salt licks they succeed in taking all deer they wanted. Paul's love of pets soon got the better of him and every little nook in the steamer had an occupant, among these was a bear cub, captured after killing the old one, by throwing a coat over it. It was a vicious little brute at first, spitting and clawing at every one that got close to it, it seemed almost impossible to train. After about every thing had been tried without any luck. A stick dipped in honey was pushed between the bars, ar first it fought with the stick, then discovering the honey on it's paws, soon went for the source. In a short time the little bear was eating out of Boyton's hand and in a short time was as tame and playful as a kitten.

Paul very quickly got tired of hunting and longed to return to the water. While packing the rubber suit, he could no longer resist the current of the Arkansas. The steamer was heading to Ft. Smith. He started above that city at the mouth of the Poteau river in the Choctaw Nation's, Indian Territory.

Starting on January the twelfth, 1882. For a four hundred mile run to Pine Bluff, the weather was cold with the chill of the Rocky Mountain snow in the river. The course was rather lonely, winding between bleak hills for long stretches, the first night stopped at a farm house, asking for shelter for the night, the women informed him that the men were not in yet, but she, "reckoned he could stay, though there was no bed." Paul assured her he did not need a bed.

The men welcomed him, after supper they sat around the spacious fireplace where Paul would sleep, smoking their pipes. A very pretty little girl of about four years old, though shy at first, finally got enough courage to go up to his side and asked. "Please sah, gimme a chew tobacco?" "Why my dear you do not chew tobacco at your age, do you?" exclaimed Paul.

Leaving the hospitable farmhouse with the tobacco question still un settled, an early start was made to the Ozark, on approaching he was in a highly wooded area as he heard the the rhythmic melodies of the plantation worker singing, noticing an old negro rowing across the river ahead of him. Paul decided to have a little fun with old fellow, standing up and shouting,

"Aha, I've got you now." the dark faced man swung around, seeing the curious figure, the shocked look on his dark face, as he took off for the shore yelling, "Tain't mine, tain't mine, sah, it's de kunnel's, 'taint mine." the old man jumped out of boat and took off. Paul not wanting to see the poor soul lose his boat, took off after him, as he noticed she had a cargo of several stone jugs filled with "Arkansaw lightning," with corn cobb stoppers. The old negro was smuggling liquor to the Indians on the reservation. That night he stayed over at the Ozarks, the next two days the weather was miserable, camping another night on the sand bar, not even the blazing fire was enough to keep him warm.

The following night he knocked on a cabin door, and was invited to enter, as he went in a line of black kinky heads rose from the beds on the floor, several pairs of eyes gazed inquiringly at him as others shrieked and covered their heads, as a powerful negro rose, snatching up an ax went for Boyton.

"What's the matter with you?, said Paul, stepping back a few paces," put down that ax. I am on a trip down the river and need shelter for the night." After some persuasion the man put the ax down and gave his queer guest permission to sleep in front of the fireplace, while the children peeped at him curiously through the bed clothes.

At daylight they all came out, he was surprised to see how many were in that little cabin as they followed him to the river.

As Boyton approached Dardenelle, a party of reporters met him in skiffs, informing him that a steaming hot breakfast was prepared for him at the hotel, as Mr. James K Perry was so insistent, Paul willingly accepted the kind hospitality. A huge mass of humanity was gathered at the wharf as he got into the carriage provided to take him to the hotel. Mr. Perry invited Paul to dine at his home that evening, due to having no suitable clothing he declined, but the hospitable citizen would not allow a little thing like that to stand in the way. A complete suit was delivered to the hotel. As Paul dressed, the pantaloons were too large, which forced him to walk down the street holding them up, much to the amazement of the locales.

Next morning was dark and threatening as he slid into the water, hoping to make Lewisburg by dark, late afternoon he again ran into rain, as the rain and sleet almost blinded him, as numerous islands made it difficult for him to stay in the channel. Seeing smoke pouring from a cabin that was dangerously near the brink, he sounded the bugle in hopes of attracting attention. A frowsy individual sauntered out glancing over the river, without any interest started arranging some crocks and pans at the door.

"Hello my friend," shouted Paul, "how far is it to Lewisburg?" The man slowly turned, ramming both hands into his breeches,

"It's putting good distance," slowly answered the man.

"How far do you call that?"

"O don't never call ut as I knows on."

'Well is Lewisburg one mile, five miles or a thousand miles." asked Paul impatiently. "I reckon it's one o' them numbers," replied the man.

Beginning to get very very frustrated with this old fellow, he realized that he was conversing with a lineal descendant of the "Arkansaw Traveler," determined to get some information he pointed to an island just below, he tried asking again. "Which side of that island shall I take?"

"Which side you's con's best, I aint tendin' t' other people's business." Paul tried again, " how long does it take you to

ROUGHING IT IN RUBBER

go?.

"I don't never go." Now out of patience, Paul sharply said, " I think you are the damdest fool in Arkansaw."

"Yo're the devil come up too cool himself off," blurted out the old fellow as he entered the cabin and closed the door behind himself.

Paul luckily struck the channel around the island, and paddled away.

Four days later he arrived at Little Rock, the State capitol, where he was pleasantly greeted by many of the residents, when he continued he was accompanied by Opie Read, the famous humorist, who really enjoyed the river experience. They amused themselves with the negroes, who many thought Boyton was a drowning man as he floated by, with Read rowing a little skiff behind him. They would call to Read, "Hyah, man. Doan yo' see dat ar man drownen"
"G'on an pick him up."

"No I won't pick him up," Opie shouted, I'm going to let him drown."

Hearing one old auntie say as they swept by, "Dere's de onliest man ebber I see dat'll let a fellah human drown afore he's eyes. Him de wickedest man in de worl." As it got darker just below Little Rock, they saw a small steamer, they were invited to spend the night aboard, while relaxing with their pipes, Opie offered Paul some of his tobacco to refill his pipe, as the aroma of the tobacco was enjoyed by all with pleasant conversations. Paul eyes gradually became yellow and his skin turned pale green, his words tumbled over one another and got all mixed up. "Look here," he said struggling to keep his eyes open, "where did you get that tobacco?" "In Little Rock," replied Opie. "Wow! its stronger than the falls of Arno," and turning over, he slept, to dream of red oak tobacco sticks, bare legged boys with green hands, killing worms. He had apparently smoked what is commonly known as "Arkansaw natural leaf."

Next morning they headed out for Pine Bluff, the last run of the voyage. Just above the city the steamer Woodson met them with a party of tourists on board, Captain F.G. Smart of Jefferson was to give a welcoming speech to Boyton and

Opi. The Captain was a great admirer of Boyton's and had taken numerous doses of "Arkansaw lightning," to calm his nerves. As Boyton swung into sight the Captain hopped up on a sack of salt at the railing of the steamer, throwing his hands up as if a highway man had him covered with a Winchester, he began his speech. "Standing here on this sack of salt," he roared, I say standing here on -------" "Git off me," yelled a colored roustabout, who was taking a nap when the Captain had stood up on him. "Get out of my way then," replied the unsteady Captain, don't give yourself the authority of a rostrum unless you have credentials," continuing "I say "ladies and gentleman, we have assembled on this boat to meet a man coming down," the roar of laughter drowned him out. The Captains voice was again drowned out in around of cheers and the sound of the steamboats whistles, as Boyton was spotted and escorted down river to Pine Bluff.
This compled the four-hundred miles in six days.

Again joining his friends on the little steamboat, they cruised down the Mississippi to the mouth of the Red River.

CHAPTER THIRTEEN

For the next two years Paul, with the exception of a run down the James River at Richmond, spent his time in business, including the sale of rubber suits for the purpose of life saving devices.

During this time he also became an agent of the Haytien Insurgents, as a purchaser of supplie. Barely escaping going out on the ship Lapatrie, that was captured and all on board executed, by the orders of Hippolyte.

In 1884 Paul decided to give up his adventurous life, and settle down, he married Margaret Connolly on February 14, 1884, in Chicago. Their first child P Boyton, then Neil, who later became a Jesuit Priest and wrote many adventure books for children. Neil was always involved in the Boy Scouts movement from a very young age.

Paul devoted himself to business until 1886, when his health began to decline. He was advised to get some outdoor life for awhile so he decided to make just one more voyage to get back in shape.

Looking through his maps he realized he had navigated all the major rivers in America, except those in the far west. Deciding to go out to San Francisco to do a run down the Sacramento, from Red Bluff, that would be a four-hundred and fifty mile run. March the twenty-eighth, 1886, he entered the water on a beautiful morning, as hundreds from the town gathered to see him start. A boat load of reporters accompanied him, intending to only go as far as Tehama.

As Paul felt the beloved water under him, he threw his paddle up with a "Whoop." as the canons and cheers rung out from the banks.

Directly after he got started he discovered "Baby Mine," was leaking, she had had a lot of wear over the years and rust had eaten little holes in her bottom, with no solder available, they tried tar off the bottom of the press mens row boat. With no luck in repairing the little boat Paul was open to any suggestions, when a young man stopped by and offered a big lump of bubble gum, it did the trick and the journey was continued. Techama was reached around noon, where they were saluted by volleys fired from shot guns, rifles and revolvers, Paul landed as people showered him with questions, while all he wanted was some glycerine and oil to treat his sun burn.

While he rested on the dock answering many questions about his name, age, fighting weight, etc, etc, an old gentleman stepped up front and said, "Captain, why don't you come out? Techama is famous for it's widows, they are beautiful and there are more here than any other town of her size in the world, if you ain't married. I guarantee you will be in an hour after you come up."

He spread the oil and glycerine on his face and slipped back into the water, leaving the newspaper men behind. Doing an all nighter, he passed Chico bridge just before sunrise. As the sun rose he noticed an unusual tree, that seemed to be covered with white feathery like blooms. This tree was so magnificat that Paul quit paddling and floated around gazing at it's unusual look, when opposite he noticed it was a roost for some type of white water fouls. He blew the bugle, sending the flock of heron rising up and hurriedly flying off.

Going down a stretch of very lonely river where the ranches were very far from the banks and the sand bars were full of geese, ducks and heron, with many buzzards circling up above. He had started the run on Friday and thought of the old sailors superstitions that worried him, he did not like the way the ill-omened birds kept him compan, they were too far out of range of his pistol. He grew very nervous watching the buzzards above, that he barely noticed the river as he was trying to think of a way to get rid of them. Taking one of his powerful detonating rockets from Baby O Mine, he fired it into their midst, they scattered in all directions towards the Sierras. There was one companion he could not get rid off, the snow capped Mt. Shasta. It was always there, never getting any closer. He often thought he had left the mountain behind, then around the next bend she would loom up in front of him again, he saw it at sunrise and sunset for days, gloriously colored as the variations of light bathed it's towering sides. He would often pass by family and Sunday school picnics on the river banks, waving to the cheerful people.

One day there was an arch amidst a large group of chil-

ROUGHING IT IN RUBBER

dren. "Baby Mine" was spelled out in roses, this intrigued him, so he went ashore and shook hands with the little ones in their pretty Sunday dresses.

The next evening he was met by a gentleman in a boat with a servant, inviting Paul to spend the night. The magnificent home on the bank was owned by Hon. John Boggs, it was an eleven thousand acre ranch, with herds of cattle and droves of sheep, that required employing hundreds of men to run it. Ocean going vessels were docked at his warehouses and loaded with beef and mutton for foreign ports. Paul always remembers the night spent in the magnificat home and ranch in California was one of the best evenings in his life.

Next day he headed down to Colusa and for some distance below, people lined the banks and school children ran along side for a mile or more waving him on. At one place a tall, raw boned woman, who had a mind of her own, gathered up her skirts and trotted along the bank for quite a while, talking to Boyton. She wanted to know if he gave lectures.

"No, I am taking notes to write a book." replied Paul.

"Well you are just the fellow I'm looking for, I want you to take notes about the slickens that are filling up this river, and

The Salt Sea Lake.
From The Paul Boyton Story.

go for the miners who make them." With that she dropped her skirts and pointing her index finger directly at Paul, saying, "now don't you forget that, young fellow," then turning around she retraced her steps.

The slickens that the strong minded lady was going on about, are sludge from the mines filled the channels of the river.

It's produced by hydraulic mining and the powerful streams of water that wash the dirt down from the hills into the river. Paul also found the slickens annoying and unsightly along the once beautiful banks.

At the mouth of the Feather river he met a boat load of Sandwich Islanders, who were up river fishing. They stayed alongside him for several miles and proved to be very intelligent people.

That night Paul noticed a ranch, so blew his bugle as he approached to attract attention, then leaving the water he climbed the bank, as a group of Chinamen were approaching. Seeing Boyton they immediately retracted into the house. Realizing that he was not going to be able to ask for accommodation here, he returned to the water and headed on until another ranch came into sight. Again blowing the bugle, this time a man instantly responded. Boyton requested lodging for the night. "Certainly Captain, glad to have you come in, "I've heard all about you."

The host explained, that he was a bachelor and lived alone as he bustled about the kitchen baking bread, biscuits and boiling eggs. The next morning there was the same liberal meal as the night before, Paul devoured his serving, while the bachelor remarked.

"You needn't think Captain, that because we had eggs last night and this mornin' too, they're cheap. No, sir. Why 'pon honor, Cap, them eggs is worth fifteen cents a dozen in Sacramento."

Paul assuring him that they were very nutritious and he heartily enjoyed them. Before leaving that morning Paul noticed that at the back of the ranch there were thousands of acres of splendid land that was being flooded by the slickens and now becoming useless as it flowed into the Sacramento.

ROUGHING IT IN RUBBER

From the egg producing ranch the river changed dramatically, more like the southern bayous. Trees and vines hung over into the water, that was clear and beautiful as numbers of water snakes chris crossed the river. Paul noticed one really good looking yellow snake, that he decided to try and catch, taking off after it. Catching the three foot long snake without it even attempting to bite him, it just curled around his wrist and up his arm, so he placed it in the Baby as his companion for the rest of the journey.

Groups of Chinamen were often seen along the banks and on the trees fishing, many offered to share their catch with Paul, while others ran away at the sight of him. One afternoon he saw two celestials in a tree, he quietly floated under them and gave out a high pitched yell. One Chinaman was so startled he fell into the water, while his companion remained in the tree with his teeth chattering like castanets. Further down river the head winds kicked up as the sun burnt blisters on his face and the slickens flowed over him.

On April the first he reached Sacramento to the usual hearty Californians that put on a grand show in his honor. For five days after leaving that city the going was hard and tiresome having struck tide waters below. The run through Suesun and San Pablo bays were very tiring. Saturday the April the sixth he landed at John's Lighthouse at he head of San Francisco bay, and remained there until four o'clock in the morning. Intending to start on the last run to San Francisco on the ebb tide. He reached Angle Island at seven that morning, where he had to stop to prevent the tide taking him through the Golden Gate into the Pacific ocean.

When the tide turned he headed back out across the bay where he was met by a fleet of boats that escorted him in, foremost among these was the yacht owned by Mr. Matt O'Donnell.

Calling to him Paul said, "hello Matt, I have a present for you," as he passed the curled up yellow snake into his friend Matt's hands, before he had a chance to see what it was. The reptile coiled up around his wrist, the shock made Matt shake it off on to the deck and that caused a lot of screaming and jumping around by the other guests aboard. As Boyton paddled off, O'Donnell assumed a oratorical attitude, calling out. "Thanks for the snake!"

Before Paul could reach shore the wind kicked in and the tide swept him in the direction of the Pacific, he frantically paddled into Sauscillito where he became an over night guest at the yacht club. Next morning he made his way back across the bay and safely to San Francisco, after a laborious journey of twelve days.

Paul later said, "I will always remember the great hospitality and kindness of the Californians." After a few days rest in San Francisco, during which it's believed that he was contacted about a purchase of rubber suits, to be used during the construction of the Golden Gate Bridge.

He then decided to go on to Salt Lake City and try the waters of it's wonderful inland sea. It's believed to be so dense that he thought he may almost be able to walk on it in the rubber suit.

When lightly inflated, the attempt was not successful. He actually found very little difference between a lake and the inland sea.

Paul hoped to maybe float on top of the water, that did not happen either, the water was as clear as a crystal and lacked any form of marine life other than some little worms on the bottom around piles of dead wood, hence he believed that was why it was named the Dead Sea. Determined to prove that it was devoid of life, Paul purchased some young trout, they died instantly on contact with this briny water, as if by some electric current got them.

On the second evening he entered the water to paddle out to Antelope Island about fifteen miles from shore, though he was warned about the dangerous winds he thought nothing of it. After slipping over the glassy surface of the lake, he paddled towards the island. About ten miles out he noticed the dark clouds rolling over the surrounding mountains. In a short time he was in a choppy sea with squalls blowing thirty to forty mile an hour, with the nasty brine foam almost suffocating him. As he struggled to reach the island, knowing there was no other life there other than sheep that had been transported there to graze, soon after he was thrown against the rocks,

ROUGHING IT IN RUBBER

fortunately with no serious injuries. There was something he needed really badly, fresh water to wash down the nasty foam, soon after groping around he found a stream of fresh water.

The gale continued all night, making it impossible for him to return, early the next morning a little steamer was sent out to look for him. They transported him back to shore as he was pretty badly used up. He remained at the lake for several more days without any further attempts in that water.

During the month of March, 1887, Paul returned home from his short visit to the south feeling feverish, almost malarious, regardless of the test and remedies prescribed freely by his friends and doctor, who warned him about going out in the ocean. He also felt the need to get back in shape before he attempted going down the Hudson.

On Wednesday he boarded a pilot boat named Fannie, Saturday he got back into his rubber suit and slipped over her side, with the intention of paddling down to the Jersey Coast. The weather was not very cold when he went over board, and the water was smooth. As the time went by the wind got stronger, the harder he tried to go west, he had to fight against the elements all day and night.

Many vessels passed as he signaled to be picked up, assuming they just did not see him out there, the wind seemed to be shifting to the east though he continued to battle the stiff wind of the land. His compass was not working so he tried to determine his direction by the stars. The shifting wind, though more favorable did not help as he was too stiff and sore to now take full advantage of it.

All day Sunday he paddled with all he had in a westward direction and about four o'clock in the afternoon he spotted the smoke stack of a steamer and paddled in to her course, sending off three rockets to attract her attention as he waved his flag that was fastened to his paddle. His heart sank as she glided by, obviously never saw him either, then suddenly she stopped and a boat was lowered.

Paul was taken aboard and he discovered that he was on the William Lawrence of the Norfolk and Baltimore Lines, with Captain M.W, Snow. When picked up he was seventy miles off Sandy Hook. The Captain and all on board treated him very kindly, once in the cabin Paul slept for twelve hours straight. He landed at Providence on Monday and immediately wired his friends in New York to let them know he was alright.

The voyage down the Hudson river had to be delayed due to ice, but on the fifth of April, a freshet broke it up and Paul started from Hudson with a group of representatives from the New York papers. They followed in a boat with the famous oarsman, Wallace Ross who was assisted by George Whistler. The voyage was not over exciting other than having to forge ahead through the ice floes and the was extremely cold. Due to having to constantly go by the tides, the journey was slower than it could have been, they were enthusiastically greeted at each town and village. Several physicians along the way strongly advised him not to continue, as the current temperatures could prove fatal. Making very little of their advice, Paul pressed on regardless.

One of the most interesting things happened in the middle of the Tappin Zee. An enormous tow of one hundred canal boats and five schooners, was passed, deawn by four powerful tugs. Six hundred people lived on this floating village and they all stood waving from the decks of their migratory houses, going north for the spring like the ducks and geese. Each tug gave a salute as the oyster dredger's cheered Paul on.

Less than seven days from the time he started, Paul landed in New York, after being escorted down the North river by a large party of friends aboard a gaily decorated tug. Twenty thousand people had turned out to see the finish, much of the success of the trip was due to Wallace Ross and George Whistler who rowed the reporter's boat.

They watched Paul like trained nurses, ignoring their own exhaustion. while they kept a close eye on the tides, and were always exerting their own muscular power to make this trip a success.

In March, 1888, the Captain had a thrilling experience on Lake Michigan, in hopes of staying fit and keeping his weight down, Paul would often do short runs through the icy water. Getting caught up in an iceberg and the tides, his quick short morning dip landed him in South Chicago seventeen hours later.

During the spring of 1888, he made another long run of eight-hundred miles down the Ohio, from Wheeling to Evansville, just for fun and then followed it with, as he refers to it, a quick run of two-hundred miles down the Missouri, from St. Joseph to Kansas City.

CHAPTER FOURTEEN

Late in the winter of 1889, he again visited the Pacific coast, his object was to capture sea lions. He was assured they were plentiful along the Oregon and Washington coast lines.

Travelling on a steamer to Astoria, Oregon, from there in his rubber suit he navigated the coast line looking for the best place to start trapping, sea lions. Discovering a large rookery below Tillamook Head, that could only be accessed from a very difficult and dangerous trail. It took until the twelfth of March 1890, to have all the preparations done and nets ready to go. Paul decided this was worth the risk although it was not how he originally planned to capture and transport the sea lions.

Leaving Astoria on the morning of the twelfth, accompanied by an assistant, they headed to Seaside. Arriving there they first secured pack horses and then embarked on the trail to Tillamook.

This route proved to be all that had been described, and a great deal more that had not been mentioned. The rough terrain and insurmountable difficulties, took them eight very long weary hours in traversing the most difficult conditions over the seven mile trip to a ranch on the coast, that was to be their base camp.

To add to the already exhausting day they were tartly received by the owner of the ranch, when they arrived there late at night, worn out and hungry.

The owner was a very ill natured man and did not try to conceal his aversion to entertaining them, Boyton made several polite attempts at conversation, but was answered with frowns and monosylables. There was no where else to stay, so they would just have to put up with this ill mannered landlord. At supper the man served a great roast. Paul again attempted to reach the rancher's heart by complimenting him on the excellent meal.

"Is that elk, meat sir?."

The man became aggravated at the question, then angrily answered,

"No, sir. Do you suppose, I would kill elk out of season, it is

ROUGHING IT IN RUBBER

illegal at this time of the year."

Paul apologized for unconsciously insinuating such a thing, and deciding to just ignore the ill manners of the landlord in the future.

Next morning while Boyton was checking out the area where the seals gather on the rocks, his assistant told the rancher who Paul was. Returning to the ranch Paul noticed a change in the mans attitude towards him, why Captain," he said, "I thought I knew you. I helped you take off your suit once at Rock Ferry, in Liverpool."

The sullen host became bright and cheerful and wanted Paul to go elk hunting with him the next morning, explaining that he was under the impression that his visitors were in search of violators of the game laws.

The nets were finally unpacked and Boyton, with his assistant and three men from the ranch, started for the rocks. As they went through the forrest they could hear the lion's bellowing above the sound of the breaker's. Reached the cliff that towered several hundred feet above the beach, from where

Report: The Boyton Electric Torpedo.
Successful experiments were made at sea with Boytons electric torpedo.
We have never witnessed a more extraordinary sight than what we saw today when Boyton fired off on his big torpedo.
You would not have known that there was a propeller useless you were able to see below Mr. Boyton as he sped along the surface of the water at an amazing speed.
This device certainly warrants consideration by the Navy as it could have many valuable uses.

The Penny Illustrated Paper. Saturday. Oct. 6th 1877.

they had a fantastic view of the rocks and rookeries below that were literally alive with sea lions. Finding a path, they made their way down, Paul stopping to put on his rubber suit.

Taking one of the nets he succeeded in getting it through the first line of breaker's without much trouble, but reaching the island proved to be a lot more difficult than he had thought. His appearance did not seem to alarm the large mammals, even when he got close to them.

Going around the island looking for a safe place to land, while being carful not to loose the net, as he cautiously approached a promising young lion that was basking in the sun, unaware of Paul's presence. Throwing the net snare over the beautiful young lion, it instantly beat around for a couple of minutes and then slowly calmed down to Paul's soft reassuring words. Pulling the line to tighten the mess. He returning quickly to the mainland where he joined a rope to the snare, while the others pulled, Paul gently pushed the lion off the rocks, as it snapped viciously at him, but did not bellow or make any other noises as he gently guided it over to the land without disturbing the others. An hour later another was captured and landed with the same process, then two others

Three of Captain Paul's four sons.
Paul died in his teens in California at College.
It's believed that he was a football player.
Neil became a Jesuit Priest and author.
Joseph joined the circus and married Adela Evans a high wire trapeze artist.
Claude, either not yet around or in the photo, later changed his name to Paul Claude in memory of his brother.
Claude was a business man and remained in the New York area.

The Childrenwas picture was kindly loaned by the Dudley family.

followed soon after. Just before capturing the last one Paul crawled into a large ravine where there was a number of lions, one was a five or six year old fully developed specimen.

Paul would have loved to capture this particular one, but doubted his strength and the nets, that they would be able hold on to it. Rising from the recumbent position as the beautiful sea lion turned, it rolled off the rock snapping at him, and Paul said later.

"I will never forget the malevolent look of those green eyes." The fourth net was followed ashore as they began to get these mammals up the face of the cliff, trying to pack them up proved to be futile as the earth gave way under their feet, finally the three men went to the top of the cliff and let down a half inch cotton rope.

Joining the rope to the leading cord of the net, then the men pulled it half way up the cliff face, until it caught on a stunned bush that was jutting out of the rocks. Trying hard to free it, as the fraying rope slid over a sharp rock and sheared through, that sent the sea lion crashing down onto the rocks one hundred feet below. Paul was devastated and decide to leave the others safely in the nets below until morning, when they could take the mules down and pack them up.

Paul's Mother
From Authors Collection

Paul's Brother Michael
From Authors Collection

Schutes The Shoot at Coney Island.
A card of unknown origin from my own collection

That night a terrible gale came in, that wrecked ships along the coast and left their trail impassable. Late in the afternoon they managed to reach the beach and realized it would be impossible to get the catch up the cliffs, Paul released the beautiful mammals back into the ocean.

At daylight the following morning they packed the mules and started on the trail back to Seaside, on route to Astoria.. The trail was in a lot worse condition after the gale, than when they went in. Each time they missed stepping on a stone or root, they would find themselves knee deep in mud until they became so tired, that they seriously considered discarding all the trapping supplies.

The fishermen at the mouth of the Columbia River, considered the sea lions more dangerous and brutal than sharks, they claimed they would mutilate anything in their way, especially drowned bodies.

During Boyton's stay in Astoria a sea lion attached an old Indian man that had startled it while hunting, its teeth tore the flesh clear down to the bone from the mans shoulder to his finger tips, though he was rescued, he died within hours.

While in Astoria Paul and his companion missed the regular steamer. Paul was very impatient, so decided to risk the trip across the bar and along the Washington coast in a small boat. The trip to Ilwaco went smooth, so the next day they went on towards Sand Island and captured several seals along the way. Sunday a storm came in, delaying them until

ROUGHING IT IN RUBBER

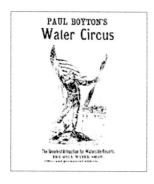

Posters from the collection of Stan Barker a freelance writer.

Monday, when they continued up the coast. Although they had been advised not to attempt the journey by the local fisherman and the guards at the Life Saving station, in that small of a boat. Heavy seas were a challenge as they continued until they passed Sand Island, when the waves were so high that they were in danger of being swamped. Throwing her bow up and drifting nose on, while being tossed about on the turbulent water. Adding to this discomfort they had no food or water on board and were drenched to the skin. That night they got under Scarborough Head where the calmer water let them land, a blazing fire and fish that they had caught put them in better spirits.

The following morning they returned to Astoria, despite a story that had been published in the local papers along the coast, to the effect that they were lost at sea and gone to "Davy Jones' Locker."

A Recap From Captain Paul Boyton Himself.

"Well, thank goodness, we are through, and I can get out for a little aire once more."

Such was the remark made by Boyton when the preceding chapter was completed, that completed the history of his adventures.

He did not enjoy the confinement to which he was subjected to, while putting together a mass on notes and memos. Several times he was at the point of abandoning this project altogether.

"One thing that gratifies me," he added, *"I'll never have to talk about myself or my voyages again. The book tells the story."*

Though Paul Boyton was for many years in the public eye, at the time of his book he was still in the prime of his life. It is possible that he will not attempt any more long dangerous voyages, though his passion for the water is still evident. He was frequently seen going over maps and charts and talking of the possibilities of navigating more rivers, during the summer he can be seen daily in the water.

While through the winter he spent most of his time inventing water and new devices for amusements. In the basement of his home he had fitted up one of the most curious workshops, water shoes, marine bicycles, torpedo and submarine boats, paddles etc, lie around in bewildering confusion to a person unaccustomed to aquatic sports. Boyton knew where each belonged, and insists on it's being kept there, his early sailor training in the USA Navy, making him a martinet of order.

He never lost his love of animals, adjourning the workshop, is a large tank of marine life, also a favorite of his three little boys who enjoyed a plunge. Sometimes he is forced to clean it all out, when the marine life multiplies and the boys bathe in it to frequently.

One thing that continually annoyed Paul, was that in the United States they could never spell his name right, spelling it "Boynton," while in Europe or other countries it was always correct. "BOYTON."

One thing he always also regretted was his inability to remember names, as he remarked that:

"People always stopped and talked to me all over the world, I have always been embarrassed that many of them I had met before, and often recognized them, but could never remember their names."

While keeping himself busy in his workshop running through charts, frequent hunting expeditions and always found time to

ROUGHING IT IN RUBBER

make runs in his suit on Lake Michigan, near his home.

"Just to keep my hand in," he said.

Like most men who have led a roving life, he was passionately fond of his home and a pleasant smile always lit up his face when his little children climbed all over him asking for a story.

On July the fourth 1894, Paul Boyton opened the first known Amusement park in Chicago. It's believed that there was a sea lion exhibit first and admission was charged, then he added "Shooting the Chutes." After a fatal accident in the park and things changed.

He later sold it and moved his family to Sheepshead Bay in Brooklyn New York, then started up again in Coney Island.

Chicago.

It was 8:18 p.m. with several thousand people watching from the main park stands, when McGee began his climb up the Lagoon tower. A strong, muscular young man, McGee had dived professionally for more than four years. He was under contract with the Boyton water carnival to jump 103 feet, 6 inches, but had never tried that height. As McGee stepped from the ladder onto the small diving platform at the 60- foot level, much of the crowd's attention was elsewhere as a mock battle between miniature warships was waging in the lake. Adding to the confusion, one of the miniature gunboats accidentally exploded in a violent roar. The battle, complete with fireworks, was a popular nightly attraction at the park.

With everything going on few who actually witnessed what happened McGee could be found after the tragic accident. Those who did view the tragedy said McGee tumbled through the air, frantically trying to regain his diving form. He was not successful. He struck the water with a tremendous splash, which threw a spray of water in the air and obscured any view of McGee in the lake.

Coroner W. W. Tarvin was called. He pronounced the cause of death as "shock from a fall."

With McGee's death the Boyton troupe ended its stay at the Lagoon.

James Creelman.
Photo from John Creelman

He also built "Shooting the Chutes," in Boston, England and Europe for various World Fares. In 1895 he added "Shooting the Chutes to Coney Island and again was the first person to enclose the area and charge admission, in the very fashionable Coney Island beach area.

Acknowledgements

With many thanks for all your help!
I could not have done it without you.

<u>Firstly Michel</u> Lopez who responded to my bulletin board posting in 2000, and that started this amazing story.
<u>Stan Barker</u> for the phone number of the family and sharing his research on the Amusement Parks.
<u>The 1800's Group</u> that share all their research.
<u>My daughter Tamsin</u>, who I drive crazy with Boyton talk, but always finds a way to help me, even when I find a "Boyton" on ebay.
Love you for your unending support.
<u>My son Grant</u>, that put up with it all while I was in New York. I've totally bored him, with it all.
<u>Craig Dudley</u>, Paul's Great Grandson, who had his mom, Geraldine go through all the old family photos. Sending me tons of info, thank you - love you for believing in me.
<u>Sue</u> for all the help with proofing. And all the others that have motivated me and supported my efforts - Thank You.
<u>The Support from France:</u> Many thanks to Odile Girardin-thibeaud, Thérèse QUEYRAUD and the GRHESAC, (historical Society of Castillon the Battle (Gironde) who was kind enough to carry out the research as a favor and thus allowed Michel Lopez to get the answers to his questions and thus complete the research that would have other wise taken many years.
<u>A note from Michele Lopez in France:</u>

I donot believe in random meetings, but in the emotional meetings that are played out through time. I have been a passionate amateur collector of old books and documents for more than twenty year, and that is how I became involved in researching Paul Boyton.
Elise:
Mr. Joseph Sauteyron, Elise's father was a notable, landowner, wine producer, and mayor of Paillet, a small city of the Gironde.

The recent research, allowed us to trace Elise Sauteyron and discovered that the wounds of love did Indeed take time to heal.